This fine piece of writing explores the rubberband personal faithfulness to God and group-think. I fell in love with Saul and Anna Mary, and the last scenes moved me to tears!

—**Dr. Carl Rutt**
Psychiatrist, Oaklawn Psychiatric Center

Ken Reed has the rare ability of getting inside the head of Mennonite characters. For more than 20 years I required my students to read his book *Mennonite Soldier* in the course I taught every semester on Amish Society. It is absolutely the best descriptive analysis of Mennonite response to war and the manner in which Mennonites were treated by the military during World War I. My students always voted Reed's book as their favorite reading during the semester—because it was most believable and most captivating.

—**Professor Emeritus Joel Hartman**
Rural Sociology Department, University of Missouri

In his remarkable book, Ken Reed engages us in a search for integrity and meaning in one's faith claims. His novel lays bare the tensions that build when people confuse application with dogma. Dogma—the core of our faith. Applications—which vary, but when elevated to become dogma become idolatrous and divisive. I recommend this book for its exposé of the human elements that have confronted the church from Ananias and Sapphira and Diotrephes and Demas of the Early Church to individualistic revivalists and controlling bishops in our own day. Our faith is not based on human leaders or even systems of thought but on Jesus Christ as Redeemer and Lord of the Church.

—**Dr. Myron S. Augsburger**
Church Planter,
Author of *Pilgrim Aflame,* on which the 1990
CINE Golden Eagle Award winning film *The Radicals* was based.

He Flew Too High explores a universal theme—the vision for change and the power to resist. Suspense will keep you glued to this story, even though the tragic intersection of the families representing these two forces is clear from the start.

—Omar Eby

Author of *A House in Hue* and *Fifty Years, Fifty Stories*

He Flew Too High is a cautionary tale and illustrates the Mennonite penchant for schism instead of dealing directly with disagreements. We learn too that the voice of the prophet is not necessarily the voice of God.

—Daniel Hertzler

Editor Emeritus, *Christian Living* and *Gospel Herald* Magazines

Part love story, part apocalyptic narrative, part suspense tale! The message of *He Flew Too High* for Christians is clear: weigh any prophetic word against the proof of Scripture or risk disaster. I recommend it for your reading!

—Mark Weising

Sr. Managing Editor, Regal Books

He Flew Too High

He Flew
Too High

Best Wishes, Connie

 Um Reed

July 15, 2009

I can Bill

To Patricia, who loves deeply

Also by Ken Yoder Reed:

Mennonite Soldier

He Flew Too High

a novel

Ken Yoder Reed

WinePress Publishing (PO Box 428, Enumclaw, WA 98022) functions only as book publisher. As such, the ultimate design, content, editorial accuracy, and views expressed or implied in this work are those of the author.

Over the almost five hundred years of their existence, Mennonites have argued over their beliefs. In an effort to establish the spotless Kingdom of God, they have scattered to almost every corner of the globe. However, this particular story is a work of fiction and the product of this writer's imagination. All people and events are fictitious, and any effort to find resemblances to living or once living persons or actual historical events should be resisted.

ISBN 13: 978-1-60615-006-1
ISBN 10: 1-60615-006-5
Library of Congress Catalog Card Number: 2008909662

And if I had the gift of faith so that
I could speak to a mountain and make it move,
without love I would be no good to anybody.
—1 Corinthians 13:2, NLT

"O Icarus," he said, "I warn you: fly a middle course.
If you're too low, sea spray may damp your wings;
and if you fly too high, the heat is scorching.
Keep to the middle then."
—Ovid's *Metamorphoses,*
Book Eight, "Daedalus and Icarus."

Contents

Part One

Visions

October–December 1955

One

WAS IT A man? Was it a woman?—that shadow scorched onto the granite step of the Mitsubishi National Bank.

"Brothers and Sisters, we'll never know, but I picture a woman. Mother of three, perhaps, in a kimono with London blue chrysanthemums, come to take out cash to open the till at the noodle shop. And in one second—in the time it takes to swat a mosquito—the Bomb! The *pika*, as they say in Japanese. So brilliant it melted eyeballs like ice creams on those misfortunates three miles away who chanced to glance up as it fell without a sound. The 70-some thousand at the epicenter were incinerated in that millisecond, like the woman at the bank. A hurricane of fire 400 miles an hour just blasted them. She was lucky, so much luckier than the 75,000 who got the radioactive seeds of death planted deep within their bones forever!"

He didn't know what these people knew about that bomb. None of the men had served in uniform in the last world war. Conscientious objectors. Smokejumpers, he'd heard, mental asylum caretakers, farm deferees. Could they relate to a bombing strategist? Of course, they'd read their newspapers, but had they even experienced that war?

He had seen the placards with his military-uniformed picture on them stapled to the telephone pole outside Weaver's Country Mart when he pulled into town that afternoon:

REVIVAL MEETINGS
Saul MacNamara Testimony (Sunday only)
—Former Army Intelligence—
Kittochtinny Chorale
With Wolf Landis Conducting
and
God's Message—Bro. Jake Krehbiel
KMC Chapel
October 7 to 9, 1955
7:00 Sharp

The placards always brought the crowds in.

"Brothers!" he said, plunging ahead with his story anyway, addressing the crowd of 547, according to the Head Usher's whisper. He pushed pulpy, uncallused fingertips through his black and sprawling hair. "Brothers! I was on my bed in our barracks that afternoon, on my back watching the ceiling fan cycle. Bmmmmp. Bmmmmp. Bmmmmp. Propeller blades of the Enola Gay on her fateful trip from the North Marianas to Hiroshima. *I'm planning the next generation*, I kept thinking. Not Little Big Boy, but Harry Truman's hydrogen bomb, a hundred times Hiroshima, for some little shopkeeper in Kiev.

"And every bmmmmp, bmmmmp, bmmmmp was another second closer to eternity for that little woman. Ohh God! I remember sliding off the cot to my knees. Ohhhhh!" He wanted the people to hear the chaos and tears clogging his throat because they had risen there, as they always did at this point in the testimony. "I'm guilty. I'm guilty as hell."

The already dark Indian summer night snuggled around the chapel, windless and silent. It was muggy for October. The ushers had cranked wide the eight-foot, vertical windows to let in the night.

4

He reviewed the front row, her spot directly below on the right side, from which he always received the encouragement to finish his story. Tonight, he'd have to do it alone. Four weeks on the road, giving this testimony thirty-one times, touring solo across this big country in a little '52 Ford coupe, gave a man too much time to think about things, especially in the silent miles between radio coverage. He'd thought about how fierce his desire was to turn his story into a philippic on the choice between the broad road to the fires of hell and the narrow path to the fields and villages of paradise. He'd thought about how much he missed her and the boy. But mostly, he'd thought about his desire to preach.

Two

SHE WAS LYING on the deep purple, velveteen, overstuffed davenport in the family room. He tiptoed in the back door, carrying the black dress shoes desperately in need of a polishing in one hand and the old suitcase in the other. He stopped in the doorframe. The fringed lampshade glowed purple above her head. She lay curled, asleep, in the white silk nightie with the periwinkle blue lace hem, sleeves, and collar that he'd given her, shopped for expressly for him last Christmas at a Hong Kong boutique by the Colonel. Her hand propped on one arm of the sofa as if she hadn't wanted to sleep, only rest her head.

The house lay quite silent and dark, except for this one colored pool of light with her in the center; she, the Guardian Spirit of the house. Prrruppp! Prrruppp! Peeper frogs wooed their mates in the wet meadow below the house. The aroma of something sweet in the air—doughnuts maybe? He turned back to the kitchen table he'd passed in the dark on his way, and he could see them, now that his eyes had adjusted to the dark: two shadowy rows of chubby circles, still warm, smooth, and flaky to the touch. Rolled in confectioners' sugar—his favorite.

He bit a mouthful. Home! It hit him like a Caterpillar dozer demolishing a coal bank. He dropped the suitcase and bit again. Bones loosened. For the first time this day, a great drowsiness fogged over him; especially his eyes, which itched. He could hardly push them open.

$$=\!\!=\!\!=\!\!=$$

"I waited up for you. I waited till 10 o'clock, but I just couldn't wait—" He whirled around, and through the door frame, saw her swing upright, dip bare, white toes to the floor, and brush hair out of her eyes. Unbound hair. Her prayer veiling lay on the end table atop the battered black Bible. Never been cut, she'd said. Just like all the girls around here. Was it possible? Here it was the 1950s, and this incredible fact about Mennonite women still remained. *Mom, now,* he thought, *her hair was like Lucille Ball. Red, with perfectly sprayed curls in a row on top.* But Anna Mary's had never been cut. It rippled in a black stream over both white shoulders and brushed her hips as she sat up.

He dropped the doughnut on the table and strode across the room to the couch. He fell on it, both arms encircling her back, and pulled her into himself. Sleep brought the blood to the surface of the skin, he'd heard, warming it—like the doughnut, delectable and warm, smooth and aromatic. She'd taken a bath, and the scent of mysterious tropical fruits lingered in the bundles of hair. He thrust his nose from lock to lock.

"I missed you."

"You been eating my doughnuts." Two scented fingers brushed his lips. He grabbed the fingers and held them against his mouth, biting them, his free hand tracing the river of hair to the hips.

"I missed you." He maneuvered the warm hips onto his lap. He was completely awake now. The drowsiness had burnt off like mist, and now all his senses were open wide and drinking, like flowers in sunlight, just as he'd felt when they first kissed on the Creek Walk.

"Ummmah." He tugged her mouth sideways and kissed.

"I didn't know what to do when you weren't here." Her eyes hung only inches away, so close that they seemed to be two identical wood-green creatures on top of each other, like Picasso's distorted and reassembled faces. "Some days, after I did the milking in the morning, I went back to bed for awhile. Just seemed I didn't know what to do, not needing to wash your clothes or cook for you. Was the doughnut good?"

"Mmm." His mouth rooted among the dark hair bundles again as his hand slipped smoothly under the lacy hem of the nightgown.

"I don't know." Fingers trapped his, just above the knee. "I have to get up and do the feeding at six."

"Isn't Aaron here?" They had hired her 18-year-old brother to run both daily milkings in return for his board and keep while he went to State College during the daylight hours.

"Yeeessss." The teasing upturn of her lips was heating him up for the next move. "But I do all the feeding, wash the milkers, and let the cows out to pasture after he's done with the milking."

"He puts the cans into the cooler?"

"Of course. Lifts them straight up over the edge and down into the water without stopping on the rim. Not like some skinny guy I know." Her fingertips dug between his ribs.

"Hey! I'll do the chores tomorrow morning. Nobody will care when you get up. I'm home. Come on . . ." His right hand broke loose. The hungry fingers raced all the way up this time.

"Look." Her body flipped in his grasp, out and away. She tugged the vagabond arm back down and straightened the nightie over her knees again. "Look!"

The little face between the door drapes to the upstairs was disembodied, poked through and hanging there. It gazed shyly, as if uncertain whether entry was permitted.

"Daddy!" A canary-yellow sleeper attached to the face appeared, a Mickey Mouse character on his chest. "Daddy!" The yellow legs motored across the plain, cold linoleum. Saul scooped the boy with his free right arm, levered him up, and toppled backward with the two of them on the outsides and Anna Mary between.

"I got a fractor!" Schnoogie's arm jerked away and brought up a homemade wooden tractor, painted a deep and glossy green, with wheels that rotated and a hitch behind for pulling things. It hung suspended a few inches over Saul's nose. "See, it even says 'John Deere.'" His fingertip traced the letters he himself couldn't read. "Grampa made it. Not, Mommy?"

Even at three, the Kittochtinny Dutch-flavored English, Saul noted wryly.

"What are you doing up?" Anna Mary was on her back, facing the boy on her chest. It was a mock reproach. She wasn't upset, and the boy knew it.

"I heard you'uns talking. I couldn't sleep."

"How would you hear us? Your door was shut."

"I was in you-guys' room." A guilty look crossed his eyes.

"You were!" The parents chuckled simultaneously. *How much he is talking,* Saul thought. *He was a slow starter, but consider him tonight. Adorable.*

"The tree was making noises. I was scared."

"It rubs his window, Saul. You need to cut the branches back. He thinks it's—"

"Bad men with guns." The boy stiffened his body.

"Why don't you take him up and tuck him in?" Anna Mary's torso lifted free of his grasp and she stood.

"No! No! I'm not going to bed!"

"You see. He's developed a temper like his dad."

She stood between him and the purple lamp, her gown transparent in the purple glow, painting the familiar bodylines. *Lord! It's gasoline on my fire . . . recalling my sins . . . but now mine, my Love.* Warm blood coursed to the top of his head. Forgetting the boy was still on his lap, he strained, reaching out his hand for hers. But both hands were gone before he could snag one, entwined across her breasts in the move he knew as "wife business agenda."

"Are you hungry? Did you have supper?"

"Not really. Polish dog and sauerkraut at Weaver's on the way in. At three."

"Three? You're hungry! I'll do up a hamburger, and it'll be ready when . . . you know when." Her eyes reviewed Schnoogie knowingly.

"I want a burger," the boy said.

"Schnoogie, listen, you're supposed to be in bed. Now look—" Saul gestured to the yard beyond the black window panes where a small, tinny bark was sounding. "We've got Zwingli awake too."

"Wing-lee!" The boy grinned. "I like you home, Daddy." The boy's long, blond curls fell back against Saul's chest. Small fingers explored his chin. "You're scratchy."

"How 'bout I tell a story?"

"A story!"

"But upstairs in bed."

The boy eyeballed him, weighing whether or not this was an offer worthy of giving up his time out of bed. *Like his mother, he calculates*, Saul thought.

"Okay." He slid off Saul's knee, tugging his dad's large hand at the same time with his small one. "Gramps and the Indian chief."

"And a piggyback." Saul hoisted the yellow flannel bundle onto his back. Like a crab coming to life, two hands and two flannel feet immediately spread out and pinched onto him.

"That gets him so excited."

"He needs to know his heritage. Ready?" Saul shrugged to seat the boy securely on the shoulders.

"He's nodding 'yes,'" Anna Mary said.

Saul took off, bouncing his shoulders and neighing like a mare, headfirst through the drapes, up the stairs, down the hall, and into the dark room, which he skied across in stocking feet, ricocheting off the iron bed frame. He then shook the happily screaming boy headfirst onto the dimly seen mattress.

It was a great story—Gramps MacNamara's visit to Buffalo Bill's traveling road show in Cheyenne and the show opener, when two silver stallions cantered out. Buffalo Bill, in full Western cowboy regalia, and alongside, in matching Apache regalia, the famous outlaw Indian, now a roadshow attraction, Geronimo (the Apache chief)! The Colonel, only 10 at the time, got to ride on the saddle with Geronimo, touch his scars, and stare at his sunburned eyes. The Colonel, long before he became one, made up his mind right there to become a cavalry officer himself. Saul had loved that story once, but now it troubled him. This boy should grow up admiring peacemakers, not a cavalry officer. On the other hand, it endeared the old man to his grandson—and that was good, wasn't it? After all, did he want his son loving cows and farms instead, like his Grampa Krehbiel? Not hardly.

"And so Gramps made up his mind right then. 'I'm gonna ride horse in a blue uniform someday.' What do you think of that, Schnoog?" The boy, however, was already sound asleep, one arm around Bear-Bear, the oversized teddy from the carnival last summer who'd already been loved to the point that he'd dropped an eye and needed arm reattachment work.

Saul descended to the kitchen. *What to expect?* he thought. *Can we start over again?* The naked ceiling bulb glowed and all was visible, including the rows of doughnuts on the table and his own half-eaten one. "What happened to the toy soldiers Dad gave to Schnoogie?" he said when he saw Anna Mary.

"I put them away. I didn't want him playing with soldiers." The hamburger noisily spat up hot fat in the pan behind her. "It's better he plays with a tractor, don't you think?"

"But they're a gift from the Colonel."

"Still, I thought you . . . you of all people, wouldn't want your son playing Army games."

He mulled over the thought. It was true. War games made boys want to be soldiers. *Look at me.* He took the usual spot at the table head and revolved the chair one turn south to watch the back of her as she worked. She'd looped her hair up and knotted it—she was definitely on wife business agenda. He worked on the half-eaten doughnut.

"What's this?" A blue ledger book lay shut on the table's edge by the chair where she always sat.

"The cow book. I'll bring you up to date on how it's looking." She slapped the hamburger onto the bread. The plate came down in front of his face, vapors trailing upward through the bread.

"Come on! Not tonight. Me just home after four weeks, and I just wanna take you to bed—"

Pixie-like, the warm body flitted out of reach. "You need to know what's been going on." She pulled condiments out of the refrigerator, set them by his elbow, and cracked the ledger as she sat down. "Sooo . . ." Neatly penciled rows of names descended the page, followed by similar neat rows of numbers and headed by columns labeled by the month. "This tracks by the cow." Her pencil tapped their names.

"Tiffany—80 pounds a day average since she came fresh in September. Fantastic, huh? Even Dad's got only a cow or two can beat her. *Eighty pounds of milk.*" Her large smile lifted, warmed him for a second, and then dropped again to the ledger.

"Mae—71 pounds. That's good, and it's over a month since she calved. Something we need to work on, Saul. Getting groups of cows to freshen at the same time so we can steady up the output. It takes planning." The pencil tapped down the list of Holsteins, the heavy producers. "Now the Guernseys." The page turned.

He bit the burger savagely.

"Sue—53 pounds. But check the butterfat." The pencil tip paused over a small figure sandwiched below a slash on the milk poundage. "Three point eight percent. She helps us keep the whole herd above that three-point-zero Hernleys says you gotta have for Grade A.

"And Goldie. Twenty-seven. Disgusting! Calved in August, and look! I don't care if she's purebred. Let's butcher her. She don't produce. Just points out our need to up the quality of the herd."

The more she went on, the more animated she became, warming to the task. Too bad—he'd warmed to his task 30 minutes ago, and now he was freezing. The ice water of cow facts had doused his fire completely. He hadn't spent 15 minutes thinking about this farm since he had left four weeks ago today. *Her? Yes. How I missed her. Schnoogie? Yes. Yes! The cows and the farm? Arrrrrarrrghhh!* He wanted to rend his white shirt with both hands and shoot the buttons across the room. Nothing but dumb beasts. Love *them*? How could she, lingering tenderly over their production charts?

"Twenty-four thousand pounds!" She discovered the summary statistic, underlining it with the pencil. "And it happened in a month you weren't even here. Remember how I predicted? I said we'd go over 20,000 pounds in a month, and we did it! You know what it means, Saul?" Her hand fell on his. Not a pudgy teacher's hands, like his, but firm and muscled. "Six dollars and a quarter a hundred right now. So that's what?" The pencil scribbled a quick multiplication on a blank page at the back of the ledger. "Fifteen hundred for the month. We sent out 10 cans yesterday."

Drowsiness began to slink across his mental landscape. This conversation needed to end now and move on to . . . what? He could think of no way to go back, short of seizing her by force. And that, as he'd learned months ago, brought only an unhappy ending.

"I've paid all the bills, as usual." She drew the checkbook out of the leather valise that he now saw propped open on the chair beyond her.

He swallowed the last wedge of the hamburger.

"Some milk?" she asked. When the refrigerator door opened, he saw the two gallon jugs looming there, cooling.

Not milk. I'll get sick and pitch my supper.

"You have any iced tea?"

"Sure." She filled a glass with the chartreuse, spearmint liquid. "All I need yet is your checkbook so I can reconcile the two. Yours with mine."

Warning bells! You don't want this now. There must be a better time. Open this now and all's lost for tonight. No falling asleep fat with love and affection with our arms about each other. No. Maybe even ramifications beyond tonight . . . more warning bells. Maybe she'll see a rat . . .

In the weeks that followed, he pinpointed this moment as the jumping off place for everything bad that followed. He retrieved the battered suitcase and opened it on the tabletop, pawing through the dirty underwear. He pulled out a paper sack that contained his checkbook, the bank receipts, numerous other receipts for tax purposes, and his traveling bank—about $75 in various note denominations in a plastic bag along with an assortment of change.

"Here."

"What's this?" She upended the sack, and everything clattered out. A few bills floated down. He picked them off the floor.

"Look here." The little stack of bank deposit receipts was stapled together, right in the middle. "There's $3,830 in that—the love offerings from the last four weeks, Anna Mary!" He took her muscled and chapped hands between his pudgy ones. "Three thousand, eight hundred and thirty dollars. Think about it. That's more than twice what we made on the farm in our best month ever!"

"Wow!" He hadn't imagined how she'd respond to this figure, but one thing was evident: she liked what she'd just heard. "That's . . ." her eyes rolled upward, calculating, "five thousand, three hundred and thirty for the month. Saul!" Her hands clasped and unclasped in front of the lovely blue lace of the nightie that only a short time ago he'd thought he'd be pulling off by now. "Saul! We can buy half-a-dozen Holsteins. This is just wonderful."

She returned to the contents of the bag, picking up his checkbook. The whirr of her mind tapped out in the pencil as it traced down the entries in the checkbook. Was there any chance to stop this? He surveyed the kitchen. Any emergency he might declare to stop this?

"You can be a preacher and a farmer. Lots of men combine them. Pop, for one." Suddenly she found something and scowled. "Five thousand . . . what's this? Tamaqua equipment?"

"It's a Caterpillar dozer."

"A Caterpillar dozer?"

His chair scraped backward. He'd had it all worked out—how he would tell her. They'd truck Schnoogie to the grandparents, and then over to Harp-in-the-Willows. Over pie, he'd lay out the plan he'd hatched during the 1,500-mile trip across the plains. But it wasn't going to happen that way. Suddenly, the teachable moment had thrust itself upon them. *That's it,* he thought. *Carpe diem. Seize the day.*

"Anna Mary, I'm not going to farm anymore. Honey, listen . . ." He had his agenda now. "I'm not a farmer. Never have been. God called me to preach, but we need to finance ourselves, right? We need bigger money than these cows will make. Much bigger money. I told you about coal. Back in August you and I, we drove out to the Chilly Creek coal banks. Remember? Okay . . . well, it's come through, Anna Mary. Susquehanna Electric signed Monday while I was still in Virginia, and they want coal dirt. A contract for all the coal we can haul, me and Bennie! The U.S.A.'s on a boom here with Eisenhower, and there's a hue and cry for energy. Yesterday morning, Bennie picked up the contract in Paxtang—"

"Bennie?" Her eyes flared. "I don't trust him." There was an awkward pause. "He flits around. Always changing jobs." She paused again and delivered the coup de grace, both eyes perfectly round and blue. Yes, they did that. Green to blue, and blue meant beware—China-doll eyes looking resolutely into him. "He don't know what he wants."

"He's your brother-in-law. Married to Edith."

"As if I didn't know? I don't trust him."

"Well, you don't need to like him, so long as he does his job. I'm running the dozer; he'll use his dump truck and haul the coal to Rohrer's Ford. This is real money, Anna Mary."

"Do you think it'll work?"

"Get me a clean sheet of paper."

She rummaged in her valise without looking—she was focused on the figure she was scrawling in the back of the ledger. "Look!" she said, stabbing her pencil at the figure she had scrawled in the back of the ledger. "It's a $1,470 gap between the $3,530 in contributions you received and the $5,000 you spent. Fourteen-seventy out of our October budget."

"Listen, Honey."

"Ouch." A frown sharply creased her mouth.

"SORRY. Sorry." He released her hand and patted it. "Anna Mary, you need to see the scope of this. Okay . . ." He turned upright the clean sheet she had given him.

$100

"One hundred dollars," he wrote in one-inch numbers at the top of the paper. "That's what we get a truckload, Anna Mary. You saw the coal banks, right? How many truckloads would you guess? Literally 10,000. Or more. How many do they want? Many as we can bring . . ." *She must grasp this*, he thought, *so slow it down and make it stick.*

X 6

"Times six." He lettered it out precisely. "A pretty good estimate of how many truckloads we do in a nine-hour day. One roundtrip every hour and a half. Twenty miles to the power plant in Rohrer's Ford. (Twenty over, twenty back, loading time, et cetera.)"

$600

"Six hundred dollars." He underlined the figure and wrote the extension. "Times what? Times the number of working days in a year. Two hundred sixty, Monday to Friday. Times 600 is what? One hundred fifty-six thousand bucks."

"That so?"

He wouldn't write that figure down yet. Every figure he put down had to be unshakeable. She'd catch missing pieces.

"But 260 is unrealistic," he continued. "Bad weather days. Truck repair days. Holidays. Let's say more like 220 workable days. Those 40 days I don't work, plus maybe, let's say 20 days a year—60 days total—I preach, travel to preach, and take care of the equipment. So we get—" He was ready to write it down now.

200 X 600 = $120,000

"One hundred twenty thousand bucks—versus $1,500 a month on the farm, times 12 months equals $18,000." He set the $18,000 off against the 120 in one-inch numerals on opposite sides of the page so she could clearly see the enormous difference.

$120,000   **$18,000**

"Maybe we could double the farm figure if we doubled the herd, Anna Mary, and added a full-time hired man.

$120,000   **$24,000**

"Subtracting 12 grand a year for the hired man, you can still see the difference."

"I don't want to quit farming." Her body twisted sideways in her chair as she turned away. "I've always wanted my own farm." It was the bugaboo that he knew he'd eventually encounter, and he was prepared.

"Okay," he replied. "We do both. You and Aaron run the farm. You're good at it. I do the coal business, and together, with two income-streams, we're going to pay off this farm double clip. I'm fine with that."

"You are?" She swung partway back, picking up his paper. It was going better than he'd thought when he'd walked through this conversation in his mind. All those miles through the cornfields and soybeans and hick towns of Indiana and Ohio he had thought about it. He didn't expect that the conversation would happen the first night home. Tonight was love time; tomorrow moneymaking time. *That's how I planned it. But up it came, and I dealt decisively with it. She's going to buy it.*

The pencil doodled over his paper, scratching figures. "Divided by two, right? You and Bennie."

"Of course. One hundred twenty divided by two, or 60. Sixty thousand a year!"

"Less your rent of the property on the creek. How much does he charge?"

"Ten percent. Okay." He wrote it down.

$120,000

-$12,000

$108,000/2 = $54,000

"Fifty-four thousand net. But the trees alone, which we can log— there's 50-foot high maple and poplar—Bennie figures we can get $10,000 worth of lumber alone, which would pay Beamesderfer—that's the property guy—his share. Bennie brings his chain saw over and we drag them out with our Cat. But okay, leave that aside for now."

"Fifty-four thousand a year? But if we double our herd, we go from eighteen to thirty-six per year. And we do it together, *man and wife.*" She said the phrase carefully, her eyes round, blue pennies now, as she appealed to him.

"Less a hired man."

Her eyes rolled back and forth. Saul's stole away to the clock. It was practically midnight.

"It's a dream." Her eyes advanced like cat's claws. "You don't know if you can do this."

"What?"

"The variables."

Variables? He didn't know she knew the word. Was economic sense one of the traits fixed in the Krehbiel genes?

"Lots of variables. What if the price of coal drops?"

"What if the price of milk drops?"

"How 'bout competition? Might be a good business for someone, but if it's that great, you'll get competition. How about when Benny tires out and wants the next big project—he always does! What if—what's his name? Beamesderfer—what if he gets greedy watching you pull in good money. He'll want more for rent. Do you's have a written contract with him?"

"Not yet." *Darn*. It was a clear oversight, and she'd caught it right off. "But we've talked several times. He's ready to sign."

Silence. Not even peeper frogs anymore. Her eyes went to the clock.

"I'm gonna see your dad next week," he continued. "I'm gonna ask him to make up his mind and let me preach."

"You going to tell him your dreams, too?"

Why say "dreams" when it's "plans"?

"He paid the down payment," Anna Mary said. "So he really owns this place." Her forefinger thumped several times on the tabletop. "And . . . I do want to trust you, Saul." She flipped the checkbook open again and paused the eraser tip of her pencil on the $5,000 Caterpillar figure.

"How we gonna pay it off? Five thousand dollars. We *know* the farm makes money." Her eyes drilled now—mosquitoes going for blood. "You don't know if this will work out, Saul."

There was more than doubt coming from Anna Mary. It was hostility. He'd never seen that in her before.

"Trust me," he said. He tugged the pencil from her and massaged her hand on the tabletop. Both hands yanked away.

"Why should I?" He had seen that mouth and eyes before. When she said that she was pregnant—that Schnoogie was coming. The eyes beady and sideways, the mouth set in a hard downturn, as if he'd double-crossed her somehow. As if he were more responsible than she for the pickle they were in, and that from here out, she'd be watching him. "Your dad," she said, "he thought he'd get rich quick building houses in Washington, D.C., like that guy Levitt did in Allentown, and look—he bankrupted. They sheriff-saled that big house in Washington, and he's put your mom in a trailer park."

UHH . . . a kick in the you-know-where. Military guy or not, he was proud of his dad. He'd gone down bravely as a housing contractor. Who could know a Levittown wouldn't work in Washington?

"I'm not my dad!" He leaped vertical, crashing back against the refrigerator. "I'm not! And I've been successful in business. Look at college. Number One World Book guy for metropolitan D.C., and it paid my entire tuition. I'll do it again! A dozen times over!"

"This is much bigger. Five thousand borrowed to start with—"

"Anna Mary, stop!"

"You won't succeed."

"Stop!"

I hate naysayers. Those 10 spies who came out of Canaanland, the country of honey and milk, and said, "We can't do it. Big fortresses. Eight-foot giants. Us—grasshoppers." Grasshoppers nothing. I hate a cowardly spirit. What does it take to drive out that cowardly spirit?

"You're not responsible with our money."

"Stop!" Blood buzzed in the ears. The Shiva god was whirling inside him now, and he could hardly block it from coming out. "Stop!"

"I don't trust you." Her mouth clenched abruptly, just like her mother's did. "I see the check is dated yesterday. I'm gonna put a stop on it."

"What's wrong with you?" He pincered her wrist, reeled her up against his chest, and flung her with both hands outward backward up against the refrigerator door. Her flailing right arm snagged the chair she'd been sitting in and tilted it backward. The cow ledger skittered across the floor and under the sink. The chair went over, thumping loudly. He vice-gripped both shoulders. *Shake sense into her like the Colonel used to do to me.* He yanked her shoulders back and forth. Her body flopped, Gumby-like—thudd, thudd, thudd against the refrigerator as her face went very dark red.

"Suh . . . suh . . . suh . . . stop!" Her chin quivered uncontrollably.

From overhead, he heard a loud cry and a banging. Schnoogie was descending the stairs, wailing. He clawed through the drapes.

"I'm scared! I'm scared!"

He unlocked his grip, and her frame slumped against the refrigerator. He sprinted through the family room doorway. The boy stood in the center of the room clutching Bear-Bear. Terror filled his eyes. "Bad men fighting, Daddy! Hhh . . . hhh!" He gulped air with his cries. Saul was on his knees now, his arms encircling the trembling yellow figure. "Hhh! Hhh!" He hoisted the boy preciously and carried him through the drapes into the darkness.

"You were scared, huh? A bad dream, wasn't it?"

"Uh-huh."

"Daddy's here now." He went up the stairs, with only the faint light of the upstairs bathroom sink to guide his steps.

"Uh-huh." The boy's words were more languid and slumberous now.

"I'll tuck you under the cowboy quilt, and you can listen to the peeper frogs talk to each other."

Schnoogie was hard asleep and didn't respond.

On his knees in the dark by the boy's bed, his face scraped back and forth on the hard quilt. *Oooooh, remorse.* The monstrosity of throwing one's most valued possession, shaking her until she cried in hysteria. "I'm sorry" seemed too feeble and unconvincing to carry the blood sacrifice necessary to right the wrong. And after the apology, then what? They couldn't go back in time, for sure. Nor forward as if nothing had changed. Some declaration of new realities—some new direction—had to be stated and agreed upon, God willing. But first he needed her eyes on him with trust and affection once more. Like a puppy's—he knew the look. Her eyes, trusting and affectionate . . . the need ran as palpably in his veins and arteries as the fire for her body had an hour ago.

He stood slowly, his prayers finished. His hands fumbled the wall and into the darkened, big bedroom. No lights; everything was still—even the peeper frogs. He dropped his trousers and shirt over the unseen chair back and felt for the bed. Rolling onto it, he stretched out his fingers and arm in penance, the words welling sorrowfully off his tongue. "Anna Mary . . ."

The bed was empty.

He tumbled out the far side and punched the bedside lamp to light his way to the stairway. He jumped downward, three to four stairs at a time, and tossed aside the drapes. Yes—a small light glittered up ahead in the kitchen, the small bulb on the range top. She stood by the table, backlit, a doughnut in hand.

"Anna Mary." He slumped into her chair, seized the empty hand in his and pulled it against his forehead and down to his lips. "I was wrong. How could I—shaking you like that? Anna Mary—" His lips rubbed across her hand repeatedly, with a kissing sound. "I'm sorry . . . sorry . . . sorry . . . ."

She stopped, like a Freeze-Tag player, the doughnut suspended in her left hand, the right hand lifeless in his. "Are you going to quit the farm? Are you going to buy this machine?" Her voice was emotionless, robotic.

"We need to talk. Anna Mary, I need you to understand something really important."

She tugged her right hand loose and, as the doughnut in her left hand dropped away, swung back to the tabletop for another. Her arm moved cross-body, relayed the doughnut to her left hand, which mechanically dropped the second doughnut over the edge of the table. He leaned across the table to see where they had fallen. A tin trash box was there.

"What was wrong with that one?" He lifted the box and searched it. Dozens of doughnuts lay mounded up. He dropped the can. "What are you doing?"

Her right hand selected another doughnut and swung across the table to connect with the left. "It's all spoiled."

"What is? The doughnut?"

"Our life." The doughnut dropped into the can. "Pop's the only one who understands." Her right hand mechanically returned for another doughnut. Her head shook rhythmically, side to side.

"Anna Mary!" He caught her arm mid-air before she could relay the doughnut to the dropping hand.

"Don't touch me. I'm afraid of you." Her voice wasn't fearful. It was an emotionless mouthing out of the mask-like face. Her hand lay wilted in his.

Saul sprang up and threw an arm around her shoulders. "Let's go to bed." He pried the doughnut from her. He went for the range light, turned it off, and felt his way back to the doorway. "Anna Mary?" He could hear deep, even breathing by the table where he'd left her. Like the sound of her asleep. He felt for her hand and took it. The hand didn't resist, or respond. When he stepped ahead toward the doorway, she towed behind, like Bear-Bear trailing limply when Schnoogie crossed the house at bedtime. Silent. No direction on its own. Mindless. They went up the stairs that way.

Three

IBOUGHT A little spiral notebook, and every evening back in the barracks I'd scribble in verses as I read this book—" He lofted the tattered black Bible, the one he'd bought at the time, to show them. It was only an artifact for him now: too simple, too unannotated, too narrow in the margins for the notes he needed to make.

"Plan the hydrogen bomb during the day; read Jesus' words on the way of nonresistance at night. In my frustration, I formed a plan: I'd write the C.O. and tell him why I could no longer strategize these terrible bombs. And I'd see if there were someone, anyone, somewhere—some other human being in the pages of history who believed he could not plan the destruction of other human beings at the price of his immortal soul."

The Anabaptists! He loved them. Their meaty Swiss-German names. Hostetler. Krehbiel. Souder. Stoltzfus. Defying the magistrates and priests, the burgermeisters and executioners. With their bell-clear words of witness: *We won't carry your swords or fight your wars. We won't baptize our babies into your pax europa.*

Ferreted out of their homes and roped to poles in the public squares of Geneva and Amsterdam and burned alive. Yes, incinerated. Not in an instant like the woman on the Mitsubishi Bank steps, but slowly, methodically, with lots of time to change their minds. That's what his research had dug up. Etchings in musty books of women and men lashed to posts, faggots stacked and accessorized with straw bundles, a smoky brand thrust into the straw or onto the hem of the dress and lighting up the night in Amsterdam or Zurich with flaming wood, flaming clothes, flaming hair, flaming flesh, until the cries of "Ohhhhhhhhhh Jesus!" died away in the ears of the curious crowd.

"*Are there any of these Anabaptists left on earth*, I kept wondering as I read. And that's where the miracle happened. As clearly as I heard Jesus say, 'I forgive you,' as I read those texts, I heard this man's voice—"

Saul canted sideways at the pulpit, pointing back. The man was there, beneath one of the fat overhead chandeliers that hung like pale, glowing German sausages over the row of elders and deacons. The Bishop, with only his pink head and muscled hands protruding from the stuffed black skin of the notch-collared coat, somewhat resembled a knockwurst himself. He winked at him.

"I found him in the *Yellow Pages* under 'Mennonite Churches.' Correction—I found his name. They had to track him down, as he was out at Paxtang Auction that day selling his calves and, I'm very sure, fetching a handsome price for them."

The men laughed. The Bishop's notoriety for business savvy was as secure as his reputation for order in the hundred-some Conference churches he presided over as moderator.

"Maybe if he'd known I was going to go after his daughter, he wouldn't have—"

The women laughed.

And perhaps we could have become soul mates, he and I, if I hadn't gotten his daughter pregnant.

He pushed on. "Brothers, I sent copies of that resignation letter—12 typewritten pages—to the Commanding Officer of our division, to the Adjutant General of the U.S. Army, to the Commander-in-Chief—to Harry Truman himself—and to my father, Retired Army Colonel Owen

R. MacNamara. I could no longer personally participate, personally commit to warfare in the flesh or any military institution conducting such warfare, at the price of my immortal soul!

"He sprinkled me with the waters of baptism on September 5, 1952, and I mean to go on telling this story—" he angled back toward the Bishop again "—preaching in our Conference churches, Lord and the Bishop Board willing, as long as God—" He paused and saw them look up. He slammed both fists on the pulpit top and saw them startle. "People of the living God, I have found you!"

He began to sing, the way he always did to end his public testimony. Not a carefully modulated voice like their voices, but rough and unpolished.

> People of the living God, I have sought the world around . . .

He knew the notes weren't marshaled correctly and that they were perhaps off-key. He wasn't quite sure.

> Now to you my spirit turns—turns a fugitive unblest;
> Brethren, where your altar burns, oh receive me into rest.

The faint sweetness of silage, masked in Old Spice, reached him before the hand that fumbled onto his shoulders.

"God bless you, brother," the Bishop said, squeezing his shoulder. The arm rested there as the Bishop walked him offstage. No one applauded, because they never did.

Should he love that hand or hate it? The Bishop had come up with a solution to the early pregnancy that spring three years ago. He bought a fourth farm and gave it to Saul and Anna Mary as a wedding present. Not the title, of course—just the down payment and financing. They would get the title when they paid off the bank loan, 140 months from now. But they had the right to farm it.

Saul's large, dark secret wanted to swallow up the vision of this people of God. Yes, he had a large, dark secret, just like Anna Mary had one. He'd promised her the day of the Creek Walk that he wouldn't tell anyone hers. But his secret was darker.

I hate the farm. Like 24 iron weights the shape and weight of baseballs, each welded to an iron chain with links the size of hands, the 24 cows hang around my neck and prevent me from God's work. Even though he also loaned us the $20,000 to buy that herd of prize Holstein milkers, I am not now, nor ever will be, a farmer. I'm called to preach, and only one man can make it happen.

He and the Bishop sat down on the front row as the chorale filed on stage.

I'll speak to him next week.

Four

THE BISHOP'S FARM lay at the bottom of a long hill just east of Paradise Valley. From the top of the hill overlooking the farm, Saul could see a third of the valley below, with Deer Lick Run looping through the bottom. On all sides, ripe, dried cornfields and meadowlands spread out with farm clusters. Amish windmills plopped here and there, like stones to anchor this pretty picture and keep the winds of the incoming winter from rolling it up and blowing it out into the Atlantic. On both sides a worn-out, gentle Appalachian foothill sloped up.

Everything about the valley said peace. Centuries of peace.

The Bishop's farm was an enterprise zone. Five generations of Krehbiels had farmed it, each adding its own contribution. But the Bishop's father had been a slouch, and things had deteriorated until the Bishop came back from sowing his wild oats in his mid-twenties. He had started a beef-cow side-business to the dairy and opened up a stall at New Cumbria's central market to sell fresh beef cuts and the jams and jellies his wife had canned. In the heart of the Depression, he took over the entire management of the farm and began a modernization that had continued to the present.

The farmhouse, built of limestone in 1790, was the only thing old about the place. In the drizzle of the November morning, with the maples on the far hill strutting their ochres and scarlets more brilliantly than usual under the gray skies, the farm appeared to be a Grandma Moses painting. A large, rounded steel-roof structure housed the four-stall milking parlor, cycling 20 cows per hour through the milk cycle. The bulk milk cooler held a ton of chilled Grade A milk. These were innovations few farmers in the valley had, as the tanks alone cost $5,000. The herd of 50-some dairy cows was even now milling in the feedlot, the morning milking finished.

A large, open-sided building with a peaked roof lay east of the milking parlor, and a hundred or hundred-and-twenty-five red beef cows besieged the hay and silage troughs there. Below that were several storage sheds with out-of-sight green tractors and planting and harvesting equipment. Twin royal blue, steel silos stood over the complex like medieval watchtowers. Across the road from the Bishop's farm, his son Norman (whom the Bishop had groomed to take over the business) ran a smaller complex that focused on chickens and tomatoes—cash crops he could manage while running the family's dairy business.

Even now, Norman was waving a gloved hand at Saul from one of the already harvested cornfields where his tractor and spreader tossed up big globs of straw and cow manure to nourish the cornfield for next year's crop. Beyond the creek and near the top of the hill road above the Krehbiel farm complex, the third member of the Krehbiel father-son trio, Noah, lived in a smaller cottage, its roof a soggy palette of red and yellow now, where the road disappeared into the woods. He was farm-less but possessed a large, gray cinder-block building behind his recently built brick house where beef sides and slaughtered pigs hung in cold storage in preparation for their turn under the spotless glass-fronted counters of the Krehbiel's Red Steer market stall.

Everything about the valley said prosperity—*centuries of prosperity.* The tiniest details of this farm and its neighbors were exquisitely cared for, such as the fruit trees in front of the Bishop's house, which had trunks painted white up to a height of exactly three feet. "For looks," was the only answer Saul had ever been given when he had asked about this. The Bishop's birdhouse on the front lawn had four stories, with a vertical line of four entry holes on each of four sides—16 little "high-rise apartments," in effect—with a small rod for perching outside each hole. A colony of purple martins came every spring to occupy them. The birdhouse was painted green and white and was shingled. A cable had been attached through an eye ring on the roof to lower it to ground level for cleaning the house when the birds went south for the winter. The stone walls of the farmhouse had been painted eggshell, although ivy, luxuriant forest green throughout the winter, covered the entire south wall. The corncribs were already full up out of sight with robust ears of golden corn.

I'm coming to tell him I'm ready to preach, Saul said to himself. The word "preach" jangled in his brain like the little steel ball that zoomed around the barracks pinball machine, hitting the fixed deflecting targets. Bang! Up against the milk parlor. Bang! Caroming off the silos. Nrurrrump! Settling back down the long groove of his mind. Ding! Ding! Ding! It collided with the red bodies of all those milling beef cows. *Preach. Preach. Preach! PREACH!*

He carried his agenda in his hip pocket, scrawled on the back of the empty envelope that was supposed to carry the mortgage check for the Bishop. *Now it's me explaining*, Saul thought. *God, I hate excuses . . .* He'd memorized his opener: "I don't have a mortgage check because we needed to buy that dozer, and can I pay you in two weeks when I get the first check from Susquehanna Electric for coal?" *So we need to start right there.* "I'm not a farmer. I'm an entrepreneur, and check out this business opportunity—ten thousand truckloads of Chilly Creek coal. One hundred dollars a truck load." *And then we move on to preaching.*

He parked the old Ford under the leafless catalpa tree next to the Bishop's truck. As he stepped out, he saw the truck rocking side to side and heard the calves inside bawling, their pink noses and desperate eyes jammed between the sideboards of the truck. They were on their way to today's auction, of course. From the feedlot, he heard the responding lows of their mothers.

He pushed through the gate in the ornamental wire fence that separated the outer yard from the inner yard. Into the inner yard, a small grassy orchard with an English walnut tree, plum trees, cherry trees (one sweet, one sour, he'd been told, although he didn't know the difference), gooseberry bushes, an arbor with twin loveseats where waxy roses bloomed all summer long but now stood forlorn and faded-paint ivory, with the roses already pruned back to ground level. He passed flowerless lily-of-the-valley and petunia beds on the north side of the house and the adjoining woodshed, where the Bishop's daughters split wood for the living room stove. He crossed the summer porch, with its table clustered with flowering plants in bloom, and shouldered open the heavy wooden door of the house proper. The kitchen on the other side was the command center for all the Krehbiel businesses.

"I say . . . Saul!" The elderly woman, Mrs. Krehbiel, stood over the kitchen table, her arms plunged into a large, galvanized tub of ground pink meat, with lots of oily silver flecks, which continued to fall out of a meat grinder being hand-cranked by Edie, Anna Mary's older sister. They wore their farm clothes—dresses, of course, but old ones, covered in front by non-frilly, practical, small-flowered aprons that tied around their necks.

"Whatcha making?" he asked.

"Sausages." Edie felt in the large enamel dishpan beside her and dangled up a yard of stuffed sausages. "We go to market Fridays, you know." Actually, he had forgotten that fact. "And you? I hear the place was packed last Sunday night." Edie was the jolly sort, self-confident like most of the Bishop's kids, and highly practical. She produced a stream of canned fruits and vegetables every summer, and she and Anna Mary competed each July to see who could get their peaches jarred first.

"Was the trip worthwhile?" Her mother eyeballed Saul.

Never felt any real kinship with the Bishop's wife, Saul thought. *Too nuts and bolts for me. No smiles.*

Before he could answer the question, he heard the Bishop behind him on the telephone. He'd apparently been listening to a long explanation, but now he was scuffling his feet. He sat in front of a large, oak roll-top desk with numerous slots in the upper overhang storing neatly stuffed envelopes and upright files. Other slots contained opened letters or bunches of keys.

Reminds me of his birdhouse. A little home for everything.

The Bishop rocked back on the old, wooden swivel chair and crossed his legs. His rubber galoshes flapped open, unbuckled, and his coat—an old, gray, Mennonite coat that was worn out and featured denim replacement elbow patches—hung lopsided over the back of his chair. The Bishop liked hats—today it was a worn-out straw one with a little green-and-red feather stuck into the band, riding down to his ears. It appeared he'd been interrupted on his way to take the calves to auction.

"Well, we can't allow that." His voice was barely audible. He swiveled and raised one hand and a finger in acknowledgment of Saul's presence. A few more moments of silence. "The church is very clear about divorce."

"Why don't you sit down?" Edie said. "Sometimes it's a while. Or do you need to keep moving?" The Bishop stared back at them and shook his head no, meaning he'd be done in a moment.

"All right." The Bishop swung back into the desk, dropped both feet to the floor, and hunched over the phone. "You need to tell Ressler he's suspended from preaching until further notice. Give Cyrus Brubaker a call this afternoon and tell him he needs to get his body over there Sunday morning and handle the service. All right? All right." The phone clicked.

"Same old thing at Slippery Run," he said. "Amos Beiler's been allowing communion to a divorcee who's been coming to services and still living with the second husband."

"Wha'd you do?" Mrs. Krehbiel asked.

"I pulled the plug on him."

"Shoulda happened a long time ago."

"Saul!" The Bishop rose. It was less of a lunge, as he probably once did, and more of a vertical uncoiling of his body. He squeezed Saul's hand and then fell back into the chair again, his legs and galoshes splayed in front of him. "Not moving as fast as I once did. Decide to pay us a little social visit?" He made his eyes twinkle. "Or is there some business?"

Saul propped his arm on the back of the chair. "I know the mortgage check's due today." The Bishop's eyes didn't change.

"I don't have it, and I apologize. There's been a development."

"Okay. Tell me."

"Jake, I bought a Caterpillar dozer." It was a stretch. He and Bennie had both put in $5,000, but he wasn't sure how much Edie knew or didn't know.

"Is this about that coal up on Chilliswalungo Creek?"

"Exactly. Jake, I had a lot of time to think on my trip West. I'm not a farmer. That may be hard for you to understand, seeing's how you and your entire family—"

"No. Not everyone's cut out for it."

"So I bought a dozer. Benny and I start hauling coal this afternoon."

"You never told me," Mrs. Krehbiel said, turning on her daughter.

Edie shrugged her shoulders. "I just can the peaches and raise the kids. He puts the potatoes on the table."

The Bishop chuckled.

"And I'll get that check to you soon as we get the first paycheck from the Electric Company."

"Which is when?"

"Two weeks."

Silence ticked on the old mantel clock above the table. Tick. Tick. "What does Anna Mary think about this?" the Bishop asked.

"She's not for it," Mrs. Krehbiel said. She lifted her chin as she started, then dropped it on the last word.

But the Bishop held up his hand. "Just a minute, Mommy."

"She's thinking about it. She doesn't like it much. But I told her she can continue the farm—with Aaron's help."

"Anna Mary always wanted her own farm. From when she was a little squirt. You remember?" The Bishop turned to his wife, who had resumed the stuffing of the sausage skins. "She was two and a half, I think, and we were playing 'Whaddya Wanna Be When You Grow Up?' with the older ones. 'I wanna be a tractor!' she says."

The gate outside screeched and interrupted their shared laugh. A capped head appeared shortly, framed in the curtained front door, as it swung open. A beefy man in jeans came through, chap-faced from driving a tractor in the fields for an hour already, though it was only 9 A.M. He pitched a set of paper-clipped and carefully penciled graphs behind Saul's back onto the kitchen table, landing them next to the ground sausage pan.

"Take a gander when you get a chance, Dad." It was Norman, oldest son and heir-apparent. "We did 51,000 pounds last month. Hey, Saullie." He clapped Saul's back with one of his large, gloved paws, the fingertips missing on the glove to allow for small motor tasks.

"Think it over," the Bishop said to Saul, rocking back in the chair again. "Think it over before you commit to this."

"Commit to what?" Without waiting for an answer, Norman crossed the room and approached the Bishop. "I'm gonna inspect Myers' herd this after and see what we can cherry-pick. He's going to auction next week. Dumb Bunny, getting out of the dairy business at a great time like this. If I can pick up four or five of his Guernsey heifers, whaddya say I bid for them?"

"You said they're Bismarck daughters?" the Bishop asked, referring to the prize bull whose semen was populating Valley Guernsey herds with record producers.

"All of them."

"At least 225 to beat out the low-ballers. Two-fifty max."

"He'll never go that low. He's asking 300."

"He'll go. He'd do better at a private auction, but at Paxtang? Never. And he needs to feed another week and then haul them back again next week if he doesn't go with us. Two-fifty max."

"Got it, Pop." Norman wheeled away. "You want me to pick you up a couple for your herd, Saullie?" He rubbed Saul's shoulder familiarly, squeezing it and grinning broadly, showing his gold tooth.

"No thanks."

"Bye, Mom." Norman tugged open the door. He yelled ahead but intended it for the family he'd just left—"Two new calves this morning." He pulled the door behind him and then flung it open again, inserting just his capped head from the sun porch. "Don't forget those charts, Pop." He pointed at the clipped papers with one gloved hand. "I want to cull a couple cows. Tell me who should go."

It was now or never. Saul couldn't wait to think up a lead-in. He had to get it out before another business interruption hit.

"Can we talk?"

"Thought that's what we were doing." The Bishop snorted a laugh. He collated several papers, closed a manila folder, and pushed it into a slot. He swiveled back to face Saul. "Your coal business dream? Or something new?"

Just like his daughter, the same phrase. Coal business dream. But the Bishop had opened the door, and Saul intended to walk through. "I'm ready to preach. Jake, you advised 'a cooling-off period,' and it's now been two years. I confessed my wrongdoings. Not that anyone forgets, but we were wrong—" *With passion now,* Saul thought, *for I feel it every bit as urgently as I felt the desperate drive to get out of the Army.* "There's a revolution going on, Jake. And the antidote is revival."

"Sit down, why don't you. Mommy, any coffee still?"

"Think so. What d'you want me to do about it?" Her hands were in the ground pig. She itched her cheek sideways against her aproned shoulder, the usually tied prayer veil strings dangling on her neck.

Saul finally sat down.

The Bishop poured two coffees at the range. Saul watched him pass the kitchen window without glancing out to check on his calves. *Such focus! I do love him. I do trust him. I have submitted to his rule.*

"Jake. I've been on the road four weeks. Ohio, Kansas, Michigan. Back to Virginia, Pee-Ay. What's going on? Incredible money is washing around everywhere. People are gobbling up television shows, radio 'Top 40,' new cars from Detroit, new houses. It's a mighty tidal wave of stuff."

"Your solution?" The Bishop was back in the desk chair. His hand covered his mouth, with one finger extended upward to stroke the cheek under his eye. *Is he masking his reactions?* Saul wondered. *I don't want to think so. Take a sip, just black, and give him my conviction, piping hot and black.*

"Someone needs to stand in the gap. Someone needs to hold himself up like a big flashlight in the night sky and say, 'Look out! A powerful wave is coming that you can't outrun. Go thattaway!'"

"I agree. Call it a revolution. America's not what you or I grew up with. This next generation is the richest . . . the most privileged . . . no comprehension of the Depression and the War. My Norman," the Bishop's jaw jutted toward the door that Norman had just exited, "he's rip-roaring with this farm, and he won't stop with a 50-cow herd and our three farms. Four, counting yours. He wants a 100-cow herd and 1,000 acres under till. In K County, where an acre goes for 1,000 bucks!" He shook his head. "Can't believe him. *No* more plain coats. And he wears neckties at the dairy council. Takes his wife and the little ones to the Shore where they do mixed bathing with everyone there. But you know what? He's past his rebellious streak. He's coming to church again.

"Now, Gloria—" he rubbernecked his wife and Edie, perhaps weighing his words. "Gloria, she wears her hair down, like one of these hula dancers, with her prayer cap propped on top—and cuts the ends, because she says it's strubbli otherwise. But so earnest for the Lord." He came back with a waving, advancing index finger. "She's singing in the chorale; she's a youth group leader. Let's review the good stuff. We got the college going, the chorale, the church is grow, grow, grow. We got new programs popping up all over the place. The new old folks' home. Our own mental hospital. Youth teams every month out to New York or Philly."

"Activity, yes," Saul said. "But where's *the fire*? I used the example of a locomotive the other night with someone. A steam locomotive up there at Penn Station, all polished up, all the bearings greased, the boiler full of water. Fancy equipment, like all these fancy church institutions, if you will, with an engineer at the controls. A guy is shoveling coal. *But there's no fire in the box.* No fire for the Lord." *Fire? Yeah, fire! That's how committed the Anabaptists were. They didn't let the bonfires of Europe stop their mouths.*

The Bishop smiled benevolently, his legs still sprawled in front of him. "We need your enthusiasm, Saul! But there's a process, see. You know me; I was 13. Year 1906. Just came out of the outside privies—no indoor plumbing in 1906, you know, and Bishop A.K. Mast was coming the other way, in. He sees me and says he's been watching me. Said he heard me talk to people and such. 'I think the Lord's got his hand on you for a preacher,' he says."

"That's how it was," Edie said from the kitchen table.

"But I waited till the church called."

"He left school at 15, Pop did," Edie said. "Worked for his dad five years on the farm." She paused the meat grinder. "And then took the railroad west for seven years, and when he got back—"

"I got serious." The Bishop was warming as he told the story of his life, his shoulders squaring up in the chair with enthusiasm, his eyes shining. "This was before I met Susannah. I went to camp meetings in Philadelphia and heard the gospel and got straightened out. But—" He paused, considering Saul. "I didn't preach until the lot fell on me."

"He was 38." Mrs. Krehbiel thrust another wad of meat down the sausage skin.

And there it was. *The lot*. That stupid, medieval tradition based on a few peripheral Bible verses, such as the one about replacing the dead man Judas with another disciple. "They cast lots and the lot fell on Matthias." Saul had watched the mechanics of it for four years. The Bishop would call together a congregation on a Sunday afternoon and encourage them to nominate three or four men. Mostly the popular men, it seemed. They had no particular training for the job, and maybe no public speaking skills, but between them they'd led a couple winter Bible School classes.

The following Sunday afternoon, with 200 or 300 absolutely hushed people waiting, the men would file somberly into the church and sit on the front bench. The drama of it! The Bishop would distribute hymnbooks with a white slip in only one of them. Then it would be, "Open your books, brothers," and one man would thrust up his book as his wife, waiting with the other wives in the women's side of the house, fell apart publicly. While those around comforted her, the unchosen men hung their heads a bit and then embraced and kissed the winner. The next Sunday, the new preacher would begin to drone all the thoughts he'd ever had about clothes—plain clothes—and the terrible effect of pride, expressing himself in plain-spoken Kittochtinny talk mixed with phrases from the King James Bible, like "whosoever," "in the fullness of time," and "woman—the weaker vessel." The kind of pastor it produced was as predictable as the groundhog's shadow every February second.

"And I began to preach," the Bishop continued, "and it was hard slogging from '31 to '39. A wife—"

"Seven kids," Edie said.

"Thirty cows and a church. But God gives grace when He calls." The Bishop hit his fist emphatically on the desktop.

Could God do that? Sure, He could do anything. But was this how He did it every time? Didn't He also call men to preach and tell them so directly? Mention Isaiah, the great prophet of Israel.

Saul appraised the man opposite him. He didn't see a Mennonite bishop. He saw the Colonel, his earthly father, slashing his cigar in hand like an officer's sword straight-armed at him as if he could physically burn his stubborn son with it and block him from proceeding. Cussing him he said, "You're doing what? You're resigning your commission? Disgracing our family? No! I won't have it. No! I'll go to your C.O. myself and tell him 'no'!"

On that thought, the final interruption walked in. It was Noah Krehbiel, the second son, his white butcher's apron covering his work clothes. The apron was blotted up and down the front with cow's blood, and he had some red smears on his ear.

"I just picked up the beeves at the Amishman's." He pointed out the window at his white refrigerator truck for transporting meat. "How many steaks you think I should saw off?"

"How's it trending this month?" the Bishop said.

"Thirty/thirty-five T-bones and ribeyes, twenty/twenty-five roasts a week."

"Boost it 25 percent from here to Thanksgiving."

"How many's that?"

"Come on!" Edie said. "You passed math."

It was only a tweak, but apparently the kind Noah was used to getting. "I was just asking," Noah mumbled when challenged. His blue eyes were popped and cow-like as he gaped at them, a contrast to his brother's exuberance. And he went out. The door closed behind Noah, and the Bishop studied the clock and took off his glasses. It was 9:45.

The little interruption was all Saul needed. *I need to appeal to the Bible. He's a Bible guy. He'll buy that.* "The day you baptized me," Saul said, "I've told no one else to date, but . . . I went back to my seat, wiping the water out of my ears. Like the heavens opened—I felt that overflowing with the anointing of God's oil and warmth and light, and I flipped open my Bible and just like that—" he snapped his fingers. "—Isaiah 6. 'I saw the Lord. Sitting upon a throne, high and lifted up.' That's the verse, and I was seeing it as I read it. 'Whom shall I send and who will go for us?' 'Here am I. Send me!' I heard it, Jake."

He felt the Bishop's eyes, like an old turtle's eyeballs hooded and moving slowly, watching him like a beetle he intended to swallow. Impenetrable, maybe even hostile.

"'Go and say to this people,'" Saul had memorized the verses from thinking on them so often. "'Hear and hear, but do not understand; see and see but do not perceive. Make the ears of this people fat and their ears heavy and shut their eyes. Lest they see with their eyes and hear with their ears and understand with their hearts.' I'm to preach to the deaf and blind church, Jake."

The Bishop got up. "I gotta get these calves to market," he said. It was as if he hadn't heard a word Saul said—as if he were still calculating how many ribeyes to cut. Then he stopped, his feet wide spread, doffed the corny straw hat with one backswiping hand, and gripped Saul's shoulder with the other. Saul didn't know the Bishop was praying over him until he said, "And Lord, show him how to wait for the call of the church."

Then he squeezed Saul's shoulder again and passed through the doorway. Saul watched him cross the first set of windows and then the second set until he came to the gate. The Bishop's face was turned away, his galoshes open and splashing in the mist puddles. The squared-off body in the old Mennonite coat with elbow patches. Saul remembered a history-book picture of Napoleon.

Five

SAUL THOUGHT ABOUT the honkers that filled the skyways over the Susquehanna this time of year when the first frosts were hitting.

The chorale members coasted across stage like migratory birds. Sequenced steps and regulation dress. Dark suits with white necks, like the chinstraps of Canadian geese. Some in the Mennonite jacket, some in layback lapels with somber bowties. The men crossed the risers in the back while a column of young women in white, moving the opposite direction and from the opposite side, passed on the riser below. Their heads were all capped with white organdy prayer caps that let you see through to the prescribed hair buns beneath. If the men were Canadian geese, were the women trumpeter swans? Weren't they white? Of course, he'd never seen any in the skyways here.

Like geese V-ing up behind the lead bird. Or lead girl.

The lead young woman stopped at the end of the riser and glanced confidently at him with a flash of silver, smiling as she waggled her fingertips tucked close to her waist. *Gloria. Anna Mary's kid sister.*

The director lifted both hands, a thin wand in the right one.

"They've been on tour," the Bishop said. "You missed the announcement. All college kids." They had found places in the front row of the audience after Saul gave his testimony. The Bishop slouched sideways against Saul, whispering over his shoulder. "All of August in the Midwest and Ontario, and he's good." He pointed his chin at the conductor.

"I don't think I know—"

"Brother Landis. Wolfgang."

The arms snapped downward. Fifty-three voices, unaccompanied, broke into their trained parts, lifting up the mighty anthem:

> Praise God from whom all blessings flow . . .
> Praise Him all creatures here below . . .
> Praise Him all creatures here below . . .

It was not the usual doxology, but Joseph Funk's Southern Harmonia Sacra version of it. Massed bass voices sallied forth, then paused to let the massed tenors carry it, then the massed altos joined in and finally the sopranos joined in before the full-voice choir chorused: "Praise Father, Son, and Holy Ghost; Praise Father . . . ."

"Wolfgang?" Saul said, watching the brick-colored thatch of hair between the rising and falling hands, the moving brown shoulders that matched the hair. "As in Mozart?"

"Some famous musician," the Bishop said. "His mother taught piano. I guess that's how . . ."

Saul thought again about Wolfgang, the name, as he stood after the performance at the head of the stone steps on the portico outside the auditorium and greeted the well-wishers who always queued up with their questions.

The steps descended to a circular driveway, with one-half of the circle looping below the chapel and the other in front of the silent, shadowy four-story bulk of the women's dormitory, where cars were unloading students for the coming week. Chorale women clustered in ovals of light under the four globe lamps in front of the dormitory, fluttering from one knot to the other like a gathering of white cabbage butterflies on a summer day, their pale dresses luminous under the globe lamps.

It was nagging him, this thought that the whole thing was a beautiful play-set, a Potemkin Village, if you will. Handsome young men and beautiful young women. Voices like the heavenly hosts. A perfect October evening decrescendoing now, the last purple light fading over the Amishman's corn shocks out beyond the end of the driveway. He knew—and maybe only *he* knew—that forces were on the move just offstage; moving in to sweep away everything in their path.

"I say . . . can I get an autograph?" The choir director came from across the portico with several of his musicians trailing behind. Saul got his first good look at the man. Up close, the director was even more handsome than on stage, his natty beige suit and brick-colored waves offsetting the huge smile, following the outstretched hand.

"Excuse me," Saul said as he turned from the queue, which had pretty much already tapered off. They grasped hands. The choir director's were like his—not hard and callused like a farmer's hands, but soft, like a teacher's. The choir director kept coming, moving right up, his coat brushing against Saul's.

"Wolfgang Landis."

"Yes, I know, Brother Landis."

"You know . . ."

"The Bishop."

"Ah! The good Bishop!" Wolfgang pumped his hand up and down. "Your father." He gazed past Saul at Gloria and her chorale friend, who had seated themselves on the large, limestone blocks that capped the top of the wall on both sides of the stairway. "What a story, huh? You should write it up. 'Army Spy in Amish-Land,' or some such. Hnh! Hnh!

You know the bestseller list needs sensational titles to sell, but hey!" His hand made a fresh grip on Saul's.

Gloria approached and stepped alongside Wolfgang. "I wanted you two to meet. Wolf's got so many ideas!"

"We're cutting a record. The chorale. I guess that's what she—"

"Wonderful music." Saul studied the man's limpid blue eyes and concluded that they were both the same age. He was certainly less than 30. "What a tribute to God."

"Thank you! Thank you." The Director's free hand patted their gripped hands.

"Truthfully. I've heard plenty of pipe organs and swing bands. But your music communicates God—"

"We have a good base of choral in this community. People actually sing. Blame it on whatever. Tradition, maybe. The rest of the world moved on to instruments, but we stayed simple. Plan to take them to Europe next summer—the whole chorale. Show them the cathedrals. Visit the Opera House in Paris."

"Really!"

"Wolf sings opera." Gloria had parked just off the director's elbow, her cheeks thrust forward and grazing his beige shoulder.

"Not much. I did Marcello in *La Bohème*. Giacomo Puccini. Mmmwah!" He did the Italian hand kiss-off. "Love those Italians."

"He calls me '*Musetta*.'" Gloria slipped her arm through Wolf's.

This is him, Saul thought. Anna Mary had written that Gloria had a new boyfriend. *A very good catch! she said. But no name. It's him. The choir director!*

Wolf pinched her cheek. "*Musetta!* 'Quando men' vo soletta per la via . . .*'"

"They're doing it here in New Cumbria," Gloria said. "Maybe you'll get a chance."

"Keep it mum. Not everyone appreciates opera around here." Wolf turned to Saul. "You like opera?"

"No."

"Just like that: *no.* You ever heard one or you're making a prejudiced judgment like a lot of people—"

"I've gone. The Colonel—he gets tickets to all kinds of social events, being in D.C., and he's taken me a couple times. Opera? You know—kidnappings, murder intrigues, adulteries . . . I like your music much more. It's more truthful."

Wolfgang paused, his mouth open in a small *O.*

"Feels to me like we're reversing directions," Saul said. "I'm coming into the Mennonites and you're looking for a way out!"

The director's mouth closed, clamshell-like, just as the globe lights snapped off on the portico and on the driveway below. They continued to glare at each other.

A large, chubby, golden moon, swollen and flattened on top and bottom by the atmospheric smoke, had risen like a great jack o' lantern over the Amishman's corn shocks in the last 10 minutes. Below them, in front of the women's dormitory, the crowd of chorale men and women were tinted silver by the moonlight. They surrounded a two-tone '56 Chevy convertible, right off the floor window, no doubt, as the new cars had just come out. The second color was not readable in the moonlight—it was a contrast to the white, whatever it was.

Moving like a monochrome hero on a drive-in screen, a chorale man put his arm around the girl in white who stood by the hood of the car. He escorted her to the far side, popped open the door, and watched her slip in. They were clearly visible now in the open-topped car as she snuggled against him on the driver's side, waggling her fingers goodbye to friends on both sides.

Almost immediately, rollicking, driving notes of the new music sensation blew out of the Chevy. It cut the stillness, drowning the sound of the whippoorwills, crickets, and distant traffic on the Pittsburgh Pike.

You ain't nothin' but a hound dog,
Cryin' all the time.

"Hey, I like Elvis. Turn that up!" It was the girl's voice. The Chevy owner turned it up.

YOU AIN'T NOTHIN' BUT A HOUND DOG,
CRYIN' ALL THE TIME . . .

By this time, everyone on the portico was facing the Chevy as it roared to life. The glass mufflers vibrated. The tree leaves, the globe lamps, even the bodies of those standing around the car seemed to vibrate in sympathy with it. The crowd parted, as if the sound was carving a hole. The Chevy accelerated suddenly through the gap, and the couple thrust back in their seats. The white and dark rear-end fishtailed, its tires yelping as it exited toward the main highway, carrying Presley's song along in a fade away:

YOU AIN'T NEVER CAUGHT A RABBIT
AND YOU AIN'T NO FRIEND OF MINE.

A small cloud of dust and smoke settled limply back toward the driveway, and the students standing around the spot where the car had been, sensing the dwindle of the muffler rhythm and the voice of Elvis, began to applaud.

The group on the portico turned back to each other and all seemed to exhale at the same time. Saul broke the stillness. "Lost." He looked at the silvered faces of the director and Gloria, whose dress glowed as if lit by blacklight. "Lost."

"Is this about Clair Martin and his '56 Chevy?" the director asked. "He's a 1-W boy just back from Denver. So he likes hot cars."

"I agree with you." Gloria disconnected her arm from the director's and turned her illuminated body toward Saul. "A lot of them, really. It's just about cars and music."

Saul felt the conviction stir in him again. It had been growing in him for four weeks on the road, although he'd never articulated it this clearly before. He felt as if he were giving birth simultaneously to the conviction and the phrase to describe it.

"There's a tidal wave coming," he said. "Fifties prosperity. Houses. Hot cars. Money. High times. Rock n' roll. It's a tidal wave of apostasy."

"That's one way to look at change," Wolfgang said.

"And someone's got to stand in the gap. Someone to point which way to go. Like that trooper out there on the Pittsburgh Pike an hour ago."

Wolfgang shifted and crossed his arms. The moon silvered one side of his face, casting the other in complete darkness. "And that someone is you?"

Saul suddenly wanted to go home. It had been a very long road trip.

The director pulled Gloria away and started down the stone steps.

Six

"TWO . . . BIG . . . *white horses!*" Schnoogie gestured as high as he could. He was jammed into the front seat of the car and unable to stand up to show the height of these creatures. "'N Buffalo Bill had a white hat. I'm Buffalo Bill." He doffed the straw cowboy hat, squinting at his mother to his right, then jammed it back on as she reached over to adjust the throat string so it would stay on. "'N 'Ronimo had a black hat. Didn't he, Dad?"

"He was Apache. He wouldn't wear hats. He wore feathers."

"Feathers? 'N 'Ronimo with 15 goose feathers." It was the largest number he knew and the only large bird he knew. "Did he glue them on?" Without waiting for an answer, he plied the pistols from the holsters on his belt. "Pow! Pow! I'm killing 'Ronimo."

Anna Mary pulled the guns down. "We don't shoot people. I'm taking the guns away now, Jakie." She began to pry his grip, but the boy immediately appealed.

"Daddy said I could bring 'em."

"But only if you don't shoot people," Anna Mary replied. "And they're not going into Grampa's house. He does not allow 'Cowboys and Indians' in his house." She regarded Saul over the boy's head.

"I like Gramps 'Namara better. He plays 'Indians' with me."

"You see," Anna Mary said to Saul. "You shouldna got 'im guns."

But Saul was pumping the brakes to avoid rear-ending the car that was dawdling in front of him. They were driving through bare, leafless trees, the weekend snow already melting under the clear winter sun, although it still covered the fields. There, before them, lay the broad Kittochtinny Valley.

"Schnoogie, you heard your mother."

"Pow! Pow! I'm shooting tigers!"

The Pow! Pow! of God. It was right on this road, overlooking the valley, that he had experienced it one morning two weeks ago. On this same spot, emerging from the trees. He was mulling over Isaiah 6 and the Lord's "Who will go for us?" and yes, Isaiah's answer was his answer: "send me." Preach to a people, Scripture said, whose hearts were anthracite—beautiful, sooty, and stony lumps that refused to light on fire—and thus wouldn't see, wouldn't hear, and wouldn't get healed. Isaiah's next question, the very letters of it, burned in tangerine and blood-red flames at the front of his brain: "How long, O Lord? Until their cities are destroyed."

Pow! Pow! Pah pah pah pah pah pah . . . he could hear it coming. Pah pah pah pah pah pah . . . he couldn't make the aircraft out through the low clouds, so low-flying that morning, but he recognized all the bomber engine sounds. Pah pah pah pah pah pah . . . out of a large fortress of clouds a silver-tipped nose appeared with a great green set of teeth, jokingly painted on it by the crewmen, bearing what insignia under the wings? The hammer and sickle. Saul's feet went wobbly on the gas petal, and he yanked the steering wheel hard right, the Ford scraping bushes as he went off the macadam to avoid crashing as he fixed eyes on that bomber. He knew it wasn't real, yet it seemed so.

My brakes jammed to the floor right here, overlooking this Valley, and ooooo my God!

He seemed to see a little, falling bomb out of the curiously clearing skies. *Minuscule in comparison with the winter sun now visible, but as I count, it grows.* **Four.** *Glowing already, meaning it has ignited, like a garish, bloody moon, dropping from the sun.* **Three.** *Rivaling the sun now, like the sci-fi mag paintings of sunrises elsewhere in the galaxy—twin suns coming up over an alien landscape, one yellow, one red.* **Two.** *Dwarfing our mother, the friendly sun, hugely swollen now, impossible to watch, lighting everything with a scorching and brilliant whiteness like an arc welder, crackling sharply, already the air dry like one's head stuck into an oven.* **One.** *Blotting a third of the sky for that last breath before the nuclear moment . . .*

He had no recollection of the explosion. Only the sense that God had judged this valley. And now what?

He had painfully opened a fearful eye. The valley was burned to the ground. A rolling movie trailer in color abruptly switched to shades of black, white, and gray as all color—all life—incinerated. Only the ashes and the skeletal remains of the unburnables—stone, steel, and concrete—lay scattered across the valley as if the mouth of a great monster dwarfing any Godzillas or King Kongs had licked up all of the trees, houses, and roads; chewed them to a gray paste; and spat them back out.

The Bishop's enterprise lay blasted. He saw two ruined, whitewashed, stone walls, standing 30 feet long, connected by a corner facing him. The guts of the former farmhouse had been burned out completely. The former roof of the milking parlor was now a blackened, curled tube of sheet metal. A single silo, roofless, stood peeled upward as if with a can opener and charred with soot down one side, the formerly blue steel melted into large, sagging teardrops. Blasted trees held up ghost fingers.

Then Saul saw color. Pink bodies, dozens of them, by the stream on both banks. They lay on the edge of the bridge and stretched hands out past its iron edge, as if grasping for the water but unable to move to get it. All of them were nude, with shreds of shirts or blouses burned fast to the flesh, and all were spotted and blotchy, as with hundreds of giant chicken pox. The bodies that did move hardly crawled—more like slithering—more like earthworms left bereft on the roadway after a rainstorm, dying by degrees.

$$\equiv\!\equiv\!\equiv$$

"Are you sick?" Anna Mary asked. "You look awful. I asked you twice, and he's asked you too."

"About what?" The landscape snapped back to the riverbank greens of winter, the brown creek running high from melted snow. It was devoid of any bodies, except for the hundred red Herefords that were milling beyond the bank and very much alive.

"'*Edie*', I said. She was supposed to tell you if we were to bring ice cream for the apple pie. Why aren't you listening?"

"I'm sorry." He rubbed Schnoogie's shoulders with his free hand. *Hwoooh . . . like reliving that nightmare again. Stuff it back down like a demon Jack-in-the-Box and pin the lid with the hooky.*

"My Christmas present!" Schnoogie whined. "How will I get my present from Grampa 'Namara, Dad?"

"He'll mail it, buddy." He felt Anna Mary boring holes through him. "I don't remember Edie saying anything about ice cream." This mistrust had been going on for a month now. They were established in the new routine: he hauled coal dirt, and they were making some money. She and Aaron did the milking. She spent her days with Schnoogie, and at night she curled off to the side of the bed. Would they get this worked out?

"We're here, buddy!" Saul throttled down and stopped beside the cars under the overhang of the catalpa tree.

"Edie's here. And Normans, Noahs, Gloria, and Wolf—" Anna Mary pointed at the robin-egg blue Volkswagen that had never come to one of these gatherings. "Aaron's pickup." She waved at the truck parked down by one of the corncribs. "We're the last ones."

"We come the furthest. Daniels?"

"Still in Cuba. You know that. They don't have furlough till next year. Give me the trunk key." She was already out of the car. Schnoogie stood up on the front seat and waited for his dad to lift him out.

"You want to carry Grampa's present?" Saul lifted the boy, planted his feet on the dirt, and then bent to take off the holster and pistols. Schnoogie peered up in protest, but he squelched it. "Mommy said 'no.'"

"But my hat!"

"Of course!"

Schnoogie smiled broadly, and both hands felt for the rims of the hat.

Saul hoisted the box with the six homemade pies and the jars of spiced cantaloupe. Anna Mary carried the presents for her mother in one hand and led Schnoogie by the other, while he clutched the rope tie holding the box with his Grampa's new straw hat. They passed through the gate on their way to the house.

Christmas was modestly celebrated by the Krehbiels, in keeping with Conference recommendations, except for the food, the one item of extravagance. Unlike so many American families, there were no Christmas trees, no lit-up Santas or reindeer on the front lawn, no enormous pile of Christmas presents—the Conference discouraged all such symbols of the pagan side of Christmas. The only decorations included a wire strung behind the potbelly stove in the living room with

50 or 60 Christmas cards hung over it and a leather strip with sleigh bells hanging down from the front doorknob, a gift from one of the Amish neighbors who used sleigh bells on the traces of his workhorses this time of year.

But the food!

Saul sat with his back against the wall at the big table, the far-end away from the Bishop. From here he could keep an eye on Schnoogie, who was sitting for the first time with seven other grandchildren at the kids' table. Saul was snitching green olives, his favorite, while Mom Krehbiel finished the final details.

Dishes stretched away for 12 feet, the length of the table: Two sets of mashed potatoes, in identical yellow-green clay bowls with pierced lids, emitting thin vapor trails and hot lima beans in milk—Norman's Bertha's contribution. The lime Jell-O salad with embedded baby marshmallows and whipped cream on top and the creamed and baked sweet potatoes—Noah's Velma. Home-canned sweet pickles, the olives, and four loaves of home-baked bread with apricot and elderberry jellies canned last summer—Edie, Bennie's wife. Two jars of spiced cantaloupe, now distributed in little glass condiment dishes, and the six pies for dessert—two mincemeat, two shoofly, and two snitz apple—that was Anna Mary's work, although the pies were out of sight, still in the box in which they'd been transported. And the *pièce de ré-sis-tance*—Mom Krehbiel's roasted duck.

"I wanted to do duck once," she said. "I just didn't figure enough time." She pierced it and watched the pinkish liquid well up.

"Let me try." Anna Mary scraped back her chair and jumped up from the table, her arm extended, and stuck her fork into the duck breast. "Mom! That's done!" Her sisters at the table chuckled.

"No, it's not."

The Bishop rapped his knuckles on the table. "Would you girls stop arguing and get to the table?" Another outburst of laughter from everyone. Anna Mary stood beside her mother, still tasting the duck as she darted her eyes toward her father at the head of the table.

"I love that green dress," Edie said to her.

"It's a pattern." Anna Mary straightened the blouse front and then brushed off invisible pieces of lint.

"Yes, but you always do such nice sleeves. Mine . . ." Edie examined her own sleeves. "I don't get my gathers even."

"Well then." Mom Krehbiel brought over the tray of the sliced duck, her hands clasping the tray with two potholders crocheted by Norman's oldest, the 13-year-old who'd distributed seven sets of handmade potholders last Christmas. Anna Mary came behind her with the Chinese Willow platter, her hands protected by tea towels. She set the brown meat parallel to the first dish. It was steaming. They pulled their chairs, sat down, and turned towards the Bishop.

"Are we doing a song first?" The Bishop peered over his reading glasses at his wife.

"That would be Wolf," she said. The music teacher sat next to Gloria, across the table from Saul. He smiled effusively at his task and led out in that tremendous baritone he'd been using to deliver the arias in the *Messiah* in downtown New Cumbria's Lutheran cathedral.

"Praise to God, immortal praise . . ."

The rest of the family jumped in.

"For the love that crowns our days . . ."

Saul could never tell them what he'd come to tell them. This was all too beautiful: the Bishop, his wife, his seven children, and 17 grandchildren—like a happy South Pacific island tribe unspoiled by the white man. Tables full of sumptuous food, barns full of hay and corn and record-breaking cows, market stall windows chockablock with red meat cuts and sausages, pies and jams and jellies on the countertop.

The prophecy was too horrendous, too shocking. What was wrong with them just as they were? *Wait for the church, he told me. So I'm going to wait.*

The Bishop dropped his chin into the white collar and Mennonite coat he always wore on occasions like this. "Our heavenly Father . . ."

The clock on the mantel measured the passage of time, competing with the Bishop. TICK, tick, TICK, tick, TICK, tick.

"Whom shall I send as a messenger for my people? Who will go for us?" I don't know, Lord. I'm not sure anymore.

TICK, tick, TICK, tick, TICK, tick.

"Amen."

"God bless the cook," Wolf said.

"Is that what they say?" Mom Krehbiel scanned the duck with an embarrassed smile. "Here then, Pop." She gave the Bishop the plate of dark meat. "Everyone else just grab what's in front of you."

"Clockwise? Counter clockwise?" asked Wolf.

"Which way is it?" Temporarily confused, Mom Krehbiel ran her finger through the air like a passing dish.

"Counter clockwise," Edie said, passing a dish. "Oh, and your spiced cantaloupe." She speared several. "You just can't get these anywhere else like Anna Mary makes them."

"Ock. You always say such nice things about me." Anna Mary regarded the cantaloupe with the same embarrassed glance her mother had used on the duck. The food circulated.

"Tell me," Wolf tossed his head of beautiful waves. "What relation are you to Walter Krehbiels?"

"The preacher in Franconia?" asked Mom Krehbiel.

"Yeah. Big strapping guy. Kind of red-complected. Has a junior at KMC, and she's in chorale. Nancy."

"He'd be Jake's second cousin. Right, Jake?"

"Once removed, I think." Norman sat just left of the Bishop, where he always sat at these gatherings. "Isn't that what you say when it's your cousin's son? His pop and our pop were first cousins. His great-grandfather, Pop's grandfather, were the same."

"Ezra Krehbiel," the Bishop said. "And Ezra was third generation on the farm, which was actually purchased 1815 by Ezra's grandfather, my great-great, in 1815. Jacob Krehbiel also. We go back to 1750 in

Pennsylvania. Before that, Alsace Lorraine. And before that, a farm in Switzerland."

"'Iron Jacob' they called him," Edie said. "Because once a thief broke into the house, this house, through the egg cellar door, shortly after Jacob bought it, and he knocked out the thief somehow, hog-tied him, and slung him over the shoulder like a sack of feed. He took him up the hill to his neighbor man's, who just turned out to be the sheriff of Paradise Valley. Bet you never heard that story before." Edie turned to Gloria and Aaron.

"I think it's neat everyone's related around here," Wolf said.

"If we check it out, we're probably related to you," Edie said. "Maybe not Landis, but what's your mother's name?"

"Baumgartner. Lucretia Baumgartner."

"Lucretia Baumgartner!" Norman hee-hawed. "Ain't that Aaron Baumgartner's daughter, over on the Old Cumbria Pike?"

"Exactly."

"Dated her younger sister for a while. Phyllis. What you squirming about?" Norman stared at his wife across the table, and everyone laughed. "Baumgartners are what to you?" he asked his mother. "My mother's mother was a Baumgartner."

Saul's task got easier when they went on like this. Weren't these all the big yawning pits that people fell into when they slipped off the highway to heaven—the prosperity, the food, the genealogies?

"Sure enjoyed your music program Saturday night at the school," Norman said, talking downtable to Wolf. "Beethoven's *Messiah,* wasn't it?"

"'Hallelujah Chorus' and 'For Unto Us a Child is Born.' Handel."

"We missed that," Saul said to Anna Mary, uptable.

"You were giving your testimony in Paxtang County," she said.

"Right."

"Menno Time," Wolf said. "Love it. Love it. I missed all this at Julliard. The food," he gestured the tables. "Family get-togethers. In the city everyone's so isolated, and you're lucky if you have one person in the whole city that's a blood relation. The who's-related-to-who stuff."

"I was thinking we'd do dessert in the living room." Mom Krehbiel dropped her fork on the plate with a little clatter after her last bite and stood up. As always, she moved on her own efficient agenda, regardless of what else was happening.

"How about the presents?" Norman's oldest yelled from the kids' table. "'Cuz we want to go out and sled too." General laughter erupted, but Norman's wife, Bertha, went over to instruct the children that it wasn't their prerogative to ask about the timing of the presents.

"Well, why not?" The Bishop stood, stripped his coat, draped it over the chair back, and rubbed his belly, which paunched gently between white and leather suspenders. "Why not look at a few now, a few later?" He started for the family room, the jubilant grandchildren hopping up to follow. They were only restrained from leaping and skipping by their parents, who had turned in their chairs like a line of wasp guards, vigilant for improprieties.

The Bishop unlatched the closet in the living room and towed out a rather large bundle of presents wrapped in plain brown paper, easily recognizable as butcher paper from the market stall, all tied together with baling twine for easy retrieval.

"I made them. And it's one per family."

"When did you find time?" Saul asked, astonished. His father, the Colonel, hardly had time to mow his own lawn as he dashed about on his business deals, a driven man, even at 61 years.

"One representative from each family." The Bishop separated the first brown-papered present.

Saul nodded to Schnoogie, who ran forward, took the package and wobbled back toward Saul, who was on his haunches next to the stove.

"Heavy!" The boy dropped it on the floor, and the cousins turned to watch him undress the present—a two-foot high, wooden track zigzagging back and forth, with an entry hole drilled on top to insert marbles.

"And here's the marbles." Aaron, Anna Mary's brother, produced a little net bag of cat-eyes. He crouched to help Schnoogie pry open the drawstring and then directed the boy to pluck a blue cat-eye to drop through the hole. The marble zipped back and forth down the track while Schnoogie clapped, and then it ceased in the wooden bowl at the bottom.

"Did you say 'thank you'?" Saul whispered.

"Thank you!"

"No. Give your Grampop a hug and say it."

Schnoogie, never shy with his feelings, ran and flung himself on his grandfather's back. The Bishop laughed and bent an arm backward to tickle the boy's ribs. *He's a good man.* Saul thought. *I could never hurt him.*

"That was thoughtful," Saul said.

"Aaron helped a lot," the Bishop said. "He cut the wood lengths and ran them through a jointer. I just mitered the ends and glued them together."

"And designed it," Aaron said, one arm around Schnoogie, his other hand fetching two more cat-eyes out of the bag. "You can race them." He dropped both a maroon marble and an amber one into the hole.

"You can race 'em!" Schnoogie shouted to his father.

Ten minutes later, the children had all scattered, leaving their racetracks and torn wrapping papers around the room while they bundled into coats to go out into the snow. Aaron took Schnoogie. The women brought plates of pie without ice cream, as that had been forgotten in the day's preparation. The adult Krehbiel children all just asked for theirs with milk, in bowls.

The men distributed themselves around the room in the Krehbiel's maple chairs that had been hand-tooled and painted with tulips, distelfink birds, and scrolled leaves in the popular Pennsylvania Dutch style by a local Amish shop and varnished for easy upkeep. The Bishop got up from his kneel on the floor, limping heavily with arthritis. He turned the backs of his legs almost against the hot cast-iron stove for a few minutes before he settled down between his two sons, Norm and Noah, their backs to the coal stove. Bennie sat to his far left, by the east windows, his back to the china cupboard. Wolf sat further around the room, in front of the closet that had held the marble-runners. Saul, after bringing in extra chairs for the women to sit (each next to her man), sat down himself at a right angle to the Bishop, with his back to the kitchen door.

"You putting out a garden next spring?" The Bishop asked, opening the conversation in the new set-up by addressing Saul, who was positioning Anna Mary's chair next to himself, although she was still finishing dishes with her mother in the kitchen.

"I expect. Anna Mary always likes fresh tomatoes. And her spiced cantaloupes, you know."

"Potatoes?"

"Maybe."

"You know you can't plant 'em nexta onions, don't you?"

"Really?" Wolf said. "That's something I didn't know." He said it to Gloria, next to him, his hand on her far shoulder.

"Makes their eyes water." The Bishop turned his spoon with a piece of pie on the end upside down in his mouth and closed down solemnly on it. The men howled.

"Lands, I've heard that so often," Edith said, slapping her cheeks. "You too, Mom, huh?" she turned to her mother, who was entering the room with Anna Mary. Wolf hadn't heard it before, however, and he snorted and fumbled for a pocket hanky to capture the eruption from his nose.

"His eyes are watering, maybe." Norman couldn't hide his glee.

"I'll remember that," Wolf said. His nose was back in order, and he cut his pie into neat pieces.

"Who's in the lot at Hernley's Corners?" Anna Mary asked her father, breaking the short silence.

"They ordained Eli Junior."

"Eli Junior?" A chorus of surprise went up around the room.

"They ordained already?" Norman said.

The Bishop wiped his mouth with a napkin, opened the front of the potbellied stove he sat next to, and tossed the napkin onto the burning bed of coals. He turned back. "Two were nominated, Senior and Junior, and Senior backed out."

"That's going to make a difference," Edith said.

"Senior's for black stockings, no radios, and the cape dress," Gloria said, speaking up for the first time.

"You mean there's still churches where they don't allow—" Wolf's voice carried a cold undertone of outrage.

"Yes, Wolf," said the Bishop. "There's a whole conservative constituency in the Conference, and two of my congregations—"

"The young folks don' wanna dress modest no more," Mom Krehbiel said.

"Susannah," the Bishop interrupted, without even a sideways glance at her.

"I'm glad Eli Junior got it," Anna Mary said.

"For awhile I didn't know. People have no idea how emotional the issues are among our people still. The whole thing at Hernley's Corners, like you said, Gloria, was plain clothes and the radio. That's why Stanley resigned. That's what they wanted a new minister for, to tell them what to do, and as soon as everyone knew who it was going to be, the losing side planned to walk out."

"You were there?" Anna Mary asked.

"In the anteroom, taking nominations with Weaver Hess."

"And Eli Senior and Eli Junior were both nominated? Hochochoo!" Norman slapped his leg.

"The worst was this: it was rigged."

He casts a spell, Saul thought. *See them listen. They lean back in their chairs; they watch. They laugh because he makes them.*

"Eli Senior couldn't get three nominations in that congregation. People really wanted Eli Junior, But Eli's people—that's Senior—sent in a retarded girl to nominate him."

"A retarded girl!" they all said.

"Honestly." The Bishop unfolded upward from his chair, lolling his tongue, mouth, hands, and eyes in a mime. "Her hands were hanging down."

"You're joking," Edith said.

The Bishop sat down. "No, I'm not. She wasn't really bad; she could talk." He did the imitation again: "Eli Stoltzfus, Senior." They laughed. "Really, it wasn't funny at all. We're ordaining a preacher. For life, maybe. At Hernley's Corners, anyway, if he stays. So I called them both in, Senior and Junior. See, we'd anticipated Eli Junior was going to be nominated unanimously."

"Why did you anticipate that?"

"Because Eli Senior said the day before he didn't want it. Well, we called them both in, separately. Eli Senior comes in first. You know Eli, Wolf?" Wolf didn't; he had been out of the community for too long. "He's a business success, would you say, Mommy? But no preacher." The Bishop chuckled. "I don't think he ever even gave a Sunday evening topic—not that God couldn't use such a man, but . . ." He shrugged his shoulders.

He does control God with this ministerial selection stuff. Speaking for God. That's his secret. How do the Holy Spirit and the fire He puts in a man fit in?

The Bishop finished his pie. "Eli, that's Senior, says to Weaver and me: 'I feel the Lord calling me to perfect the saints here.' And I said, 'I thought you weren't in the running, so to speak.' And he said, 'I felt the call again this morning.' Well, I sent him away, and I told Weaver, 'We're not going to tempt God with the lot when it's very clear who should be pastor.' Weaver says, 'Let's call Leah in'—that's Eli Senior's wife. So we do. Weaver says, 'How do you feel, Leah?' And she says, 'I want my son to be the preacher.' Okay, that's it for me. We get Eli Senior back and confront him with what his helpmeet and son just said, and he sort of dilly-dallies. Pretty soon, real small voice he says: 'I'm not sure what that voice was I heard this morning.' Upshot is, he wants to back out. But he wants to talk to the congregation first.

"So, back we go to the congregation. Eli Senior says—now remember, he got supporters all over that congregation—he says, 'When Junior was born, Leah and me dedicated him to be preacher. Today—I just don't know.' Well, Junior stands up, and Pop and Junior throw their arms around each other and . . . and," the story was upsetting the Bishop, ". . . and weep." He fished out his handkerchief, reached under the steamed glasses, and wiped both eyes. Edith also fingered behind her cape for a Kleenex. "'I didn't know if I was going to stay with Hernley's Corners or not,' Senior said. 'But I just now decided to stay and work with my boy.'"

"That's neat." Anna Mary smiled approvingly to her father. Everyone else was still facing the Bishop, who now picked up his saucer and coffee.

"That's how we decided," he added. "We didn't have no lot."

Gotcha! "We're not going to tempt God with the lot," the Bishop says, and then he works it all out. Now, should we call that God's Spirit moving? Or diplomacy? Or manipulation?

No one spoke as they finished up their desserts.

"Guess you defused a ticking bomb and got 'em all out safe," Norman finally said, working up a summary statement.

"Question is: is the preacher filled with the Holy Ghost or not?" Edie's husband, Bennie, blurted, his eyes bulging. It was his first full sentence the whole afternoon.

"No, it's handling people, that's what it is," Norman said. "Pop's good at it, that's all."

The wives circled, collecting the dessert plates, and took them to the kitchen.

"How about you, Saul?" Norman unbuttoned his shirt cuffs and rolled them up. "Heard something about you giving up on farming?"

"Not really. Anna Mary and Aaron do the milking. Myself—yes. We're hauling coal dirt to Susquehanna Electric. Me and Bennie." He gestured to Bennie at the end of the room, who had slipped back into an inscrutable mask of silence. "We did 80 loads since November 15. Ninety bucks a load, so we grossed $7,200."

"Not bad. Not bad. At that rate, you'll do $65,000 a year, huh? Not what I heard you were gonna to do, though. Wasn't it more like a $120,000 annual run-rate you predicted? Didn't I hear that somewhere?"

"We have some issues. A lot of wet weather when we couldn't get the truck in and out. Only ninety bucks a load, when we'd been promised it would be a hundred . . . ." He shrugged. "It's soup on the table." He paused. "I'm really hoping to expand the preaching ministry."

"Preaching?"

"I'm waiting on the church." Saul rocked back on his chair and turned toward the Bishop, who was working his teeth with a toothpick.

"Not good for the Amishman's chair." Norman said to Saul, pointing a thick, callused finger at it.

"Oh, sorry."

"Which church? You've been nominated? Isn't that how it goes, Pop?"

The Bishop nodded, his face scrunched and unreadable.

"I've been called," Saul continued. "But I don't know the answer to your question."

"Who called? One of the bishops?" Norman turned to his father. "Did you call?"

"No." Saul chuckled. "God. I heard that, clearly."

"Like those voices in the Army?" Wolf stirred, sat up, and ran his hands through his waves. "What do you think, guys? Does God do that? Isn't that just Old Testament?"

"He calls," the Bishop said, "and confirms it through his people. That's why we wait for the lot."

"What's your message? What is it you feel . . ." Wolf's hands fluttered like birds at his chest. "What do you want so badly to tell us?"

The Bishop stood, cracked the stove door, and, concluding that the stove needed coal, took the tin bucket and went out.

"The Bible message: return to the Father and He'll forgive your mistakes, your failures in relationships, and put in you a new heart, as it says in Jeremiah 31." Saul leaned forward, both hands on his knees. "And save you from the destruction that's coming."

"There's destruction coming?" Wolf said. "What's that?"

Saul noted Wolf's easy smile and sensed that he was the tomcat playing with the cornered mouse before it pounced and crushed the head. *Only I'm not cornered.*

"It is biblical. Look it up in Isaiah 6."

"What's it say? I don't have a lot of passages memorized. Now music, okay, hum me a Verdi aria, and I should know it." He refocused on Saul. "Sorry. You were saying?"

"The people won't hear that message. The church has gone deaf and blind to its problems, and they will not turn, call on the Lord, and be healed. 'Until'—Isaiah 6, the Lord speaking—'their cities lie waste.'"

"Which cities?" Wolf took on an edgy, prosecutorial tone.

"The ones where God's people have gone deaf and blind. Kittochtinny Valley, for one."

"Destroyed? Am I the only one that finds this fantastic?" Wolf turned to Norman, then to Noah, and then back. "When?"

"Soon."

"Incredible! How?"

"I don't know. But I saw something." There was no way out but to tell it. Wasn't it a discernment call? Did Wolf have a believer's heart or just the heart of a cultural Mennonite? No way to ease into it. The diamond tip of truth would etch a line in whatever it came up against.

"I heard God call me to preach the day I was baptized, and he used that Isaiah passage as I sat there on the bench. But lately He's said there's more to the passage: 'Preach until cities are destroyed!' I saw a vision of this valley blasted by a nuclear bomb—a Soviet nuclear bomb—and all this beautiful land, these beautiful farms, this wonderful family . . ."

He couldn't finish. The horror washed over him again, as debilitating as it had been on the drive over. He slapped both hands over his face.

"Cockamamie!" Wolf glared.

"Get Dad." Norman poked his younger brother. "He needs to hear this."

"Here. Hold her." Noah passed off little Cecily, who'd been playing on the floor between his legs.

Only Bennie sat impassively, his face not even twitching as he watched Saul intensely.

The Bishop returned with the coal. "What's up?" He set down the full coal bucket without checking the fire again.

"God's sending Russian nuclear bombs to hit this valley, he says. Because the church isn't behaving. Who are you?" Wolf's face flushed red with disgust. "Nostradamus?"

"Is this true?" the Bishop asked.

"You agreed with me that the church is going through a social revolution. God's calling some of us to stand in the gap. Tell Laodicea, the pondwater church: repent! Or what I saw—and I have no way of knowing God's *when*—this vision will come true."

"Ben's been meaning to call you," Edie said. All of the women had returned, prompted by the men's rising voices. Edie stood behind Bennie. Anna Mary stood by herself in the doorway. Saul knew that she was watching him. He'd gestured her to come to the empty seat beside him, but she'd given him a negative headshake. "Tauferville's in charge of Snow Camp this year, and he and Cyrus want you to lead the Bible study," Edie said. The comment was not relevant to the conversation, but it triggered Bennie.

"Loodaseah." Bennie looked as if he'd just grabbed an electrified fence without knowing it. "The lukewarm church!"

"Spit out!" Saul fished for his handkerchief, cleared his throat, and spit into it.

Norman lurched up. "I don't know about the rest of you, but I won't sit here and listen to our church get run down. Get the kids, Bertha." His hand bumped loudly, accidentally, on the hot stove door. "Ahh!"

"Wait a minute." The Bishop held both hands palms upward and moved to block the doorway. "Let's not have anyone go away mad."

"You heard him, Pop!" Norman grabbed his daughter's new marble runner, tucked it under his arm, and pushed past the Bishop.

"I wanna hear more." Noah dangled a blue, rubber rattle in front of Cecily, who lay on her back clawing at the rattle with hands and feet. "This is the first we discussed church in years."

At that, Bennie leaped to his feet, his fists clenched tightly as he looked over all of them with a complexion of wonderment. "I . . . I just can't believe . . . Loodaseah! The lukewarm church. Lots of activities, but no Jesus." He shook his fists pugnaciously. "And me thinking—God! When will you judge this? When will you act? And now you, you—" He broke off, his eyes fixed with admiration on Saul. "I just—" He clapped and clasped his hands, his eyes closed now. "Praise the Lord!"

Two tears rolled down Bennie's fat, whisker-dark cheeks. The children, playing on the floor, stopped and watched. His voice rose. "It's the Word of the Lord!" His mouth contorted as if the musical nonsense syllables pouring forth were scalding hot mush that he couldn't spit out fast enough. The voice rose and fell, slowing gradually to a murmur, his lips still mumbling and eyes wide open again, his hands overhead waving back and forth, back and forth.

Wolf canted sideways to watch the man only three feet away off his left elbow. "Crap!" He twisted his mouth with disgust. And then, "sorry," viewing Gloria. "I—I can't believe—"

Norman and Bertha were noisily collecting their coats and children in the kitchen. The Bishop and his wife had gone out, first to dissuade Norman, and then to see them off. The sleigh bells on the front door clanged loudly.

Saul looked for Anna Mary. She had disappeared. He wondered if she'd stayed long enough to hear Edie's words. *Speak at Snow Camp? Even if the invitation comes through a cracked vessel like Bennie, isn't it the church calling?*

Part Two

The Thrill
of Flying

February 1956

Seven

SNOW SWARMED AROUND Saul's face like a cloud of summer mosquitoes. It went into his ears, down his collar, even backdrafted up his nose. Miniature, dry flakes so close and, with the sun down 15 minutes already (though it was invisible in this whiteout), it was darkening here in the woods. He felt lucky to have made it, even with tire chains. The weatherman was calling for six inches more by midnight.

The lodge looked wonderful, like a welcoming jack-o-lantern aglow in the growing dusk with windows in place of carved eyes. He popped the door and hwooh! Sharp oak smoke mixed with the sweetness of hot chocolate assailed him. That and a stentorian voice.

"Hold it right there! Gotta broom off. Someone take him the broom. Oh, sorry, it's you, Brother MacNamara. They all look the same when they're snowmen." Longenecker, the assistant camp director, was seated at one of the lunch tables next to the kitchen bar in the spacious lodge, registering latecomers and making cabin assignments. He smiled congenially. "We got 63 kids and 12 adults. If every one of them drops a blob of snow this big on our floor . . ." He gestured the size of a softball.

A teenager swooped the broom over Saul's shoulders, down his coat, and across his back and front, while Saul swiped off his hat and simultaneously stomped up and down. He moved forward, and the spring on the door banged it shut after him.

"Thanks!" he said to the teenager. "I need one of those," he said to Edith Fisher, Bennie's wife, who was ladling a steaming brown liquid into a row of cups on the kitchen bar. He shucked his gloves and cupped both hands around the chocolate. "Heater's not working right in my car," he explained to Edie, and then he surveyed the lodge.

Above the limestone fireplace, a large bull moose, its antlers like great gesturing hands and a massive Roman nose, thrust, as it were, completely through the wall from the other side and paused midway down a destructive charge over frozen tundra to kill them all but forever hesitated there, was leering out over the Lodge with eyes like glass golf balls. The teenagers below seemed unconcerned about the threatening moose. They lounged and squatted on the rock ledge between empty pairs of trousers drying by the heat thrown up by the leaping flames of a recently restoked log fire. On the right, a steady blip-blop blip-blop sounded each time the ping-pong little white balls hit the table top, only in a double rhythm, as there were two games going. To the left, teenagers occupied a collection of sofas and stuffed chairs. Two more were seated on folding chairs, working on their guitars.

In between, a little game of aerial football progressed. The passer was a good-looking, lanky, twenty-something, whom Saul didn't recognize. The receiver, barefoot like the passer, was Bennie. He snatched a wildly tossed ball one-handed, ending off-balance on one leg just short of the lunch tables, which were already laid out with condiments for a sandwich supper.

"Got it!" Bennie jogged the ball back to several guys who had been running interference and trying to knock down the passes. "Here!" He handed it off, puffing in the center of the floor. His shirt underarms were wet, and perspiration beaded on his balding head.

"Bennie, you need to do something about this." The passer patted Bennie's stomach, which hung over his belt.

"Hey!" Bennie threw an arm around the young man's shoulder. "*Wie bischt mit der Pepp?* Been meaning to ask you. *What?*" He scowled at the interference boys, who were laughing. "You don't know what it means? How is he, Rolly? Your Dad?"

Rolly eased down on the arm of a sofa, unrolling pant legs that were wet nearly to the knees from snow play.

"Same old, same old." Rolly slanted away toward the fire.

"Yeah?" Bennie play-punched Rolly and let his fist stick against the boy's shoulder. "How about next Sunday? How about we do some Dkkudkkudkku?" His tongue clucked as his arms mimed the action of a hockey player's stick moving down the ice ahead of the skater and carrying the puck with little back and forth taps on the inside and outside. He regarded Rolly and repeated it. "Dkkudkkudkku—how about it?"

"What's that?" Rolly laughed. "Dkkudkkudkku . . . anybody know what that is?" He gawked around for an answer.

"I'd say he's talking hockey," Saul answered from his spot next to the kitchen counter. He drew the terribly hot liquid past the marshmallow with a loud slurp.

"Hey, it's Saul!" Bennie immediately crossed the lodge with his farmer's gait, a long, springy step with his head always forward, a definite impression that he was moving with a goal in mind. He rounded the table, grabbed Saul's shoulder from behind, and with his free hand seized Saul's hand and mashed it. It was less of a shake than a vibrating squeeze. "GLO-ry!" The first syllable rhymed with "glow." "Thank You, Jesus." This last not a normal "thank you" either, but all together like one, multi-syllabled word, dropping his voice on "Jesus."

Makes me feel good, Saul thought. *As he always has.* Bennie's large, open hand—beefy and puffy-fingered as an over-fed farmer's hand—extended and crushed Saul's. His face was stretched in a wide grin.

"How 'bout we haul some coal today?"

Oh yeah, coal. It was one of three bonds that tied the two of them together. That and the Krehbiel sisters, and now the Tuesday morning group at Harp-in-the-Willows Restaurant.

≡≡≡

The sisters had stood side by side in the MacNamara kitchen that Sunday afternoon nine months ago, cleaning up after Anna Mary's fried chicken, sugar peas, mashed potatoes, and gravy dinner. The kids played HideyGoSeek in the front yard green and lilac bushes, and Saul and Bennie lounged on the velveteen couch. Edie and Anna Mary would talk children and canning and who's-related-to-who the whole afternoon. Saul was wondering how long he could hold out before descending into his Sunday nap when Bennie interrupted.

"You ever think about not farming?"

"All the time. If it weren't for her, I wouldn't—" He cast an eye at the kitchen. He'd been farming close to two years by then, two of the most godforsaken years of his life and enough to convince him: *I need an alternative, and quick.*

"You got an hour or so?" Bennie asked. "I wanna show you something."

Saul didn't ask what. It might have been rude. This was the first time Bennies had come over for Sunday dinner, although Edie and Anna Mary were close, like all the Krehbiel children. He felt he had nothing in common with the man.

"Where you going?" the women said in unison.

"A little drive. I got something I want to show him. Personal. You got any gunny sacks, Saul?"

Bennie started the pickup, his family's main transportation, a gray 1950-or-so Ford, with the bed fairly dented up. The aged Sheltie that went everywhere with the family woke when it heard the engine and began running from side to side inside the bed. Bennie took a shovel from behind the front seat, binder-twined the sacks to the shovel, and threw them in the back. The Sheltie ran up to him, waggling its entire rear-end. Bennie seized its ears and kissed its nose. They drove upcountry about thirty minutes. The Blue Mountains were looming when Bennie cut off the main road and rattled the iron bridge across a sizeable creek.

"Chilliswalungo." He pointed out of the open window at the broad and shallow creek below the bridge.

"Must be an Iroquois name."

"I don't know. We just say the Chilly." He nosed the pickup off the macadam onto a dirty trail that led through a canopy of tulip trees, their large, waxy blossoms overhead like oversized tulips, and then he abruptly stopped. Bennie got the shovel but left the sacks behind. He dropped the tailgate and whistled to the Sheltie, and she bounded out the rear obediently.

Saul noticed the honeysuckle. The vines made a solid wall to their right, seven or eight feet high, and he guessed there was an old fence or something beneath, supporting them. Long yellow and tan trumpet blossoms hung thickly, and the air, too warm and still for late May, seemed stiff with the smell. He plucked a twig of blossoms and sucked the juices as he ambled behind Bennie and the Sheltie.

"Get a look-see at this," Bennie yelled.

Beyond the man's burly shoulders he saw the Chilly, murky and deep and bending toward them. Bennie's shovel socked the ground. "Know what this is, Saul?"

"Can't say I do. You see nightcrawlers or something?"

"Nah." He punched his foot down on the back of the shovel and spaded it over. "Whaddya see?"

"I don't know. Dirt?"

Bennie picked up a handful and spread it on his palm. It shone in the light.

"Huh? What is it?"

Bennie's fingertips searched out one fragment that was bigger, maybe the size of a small fingernail, and Saul watched in the irregular, shiny edges the colors of the rainbow reflect in the smooth obsidian surface.

"What? Coal?"

"Exactly."

"You brought me all the way up here to check out some coal?" He was joshing. He had nothing else to do that afternoon. But what was the big deal, anyway?

Bennie seemed a little hurt by the jibe. "You size it up. These banks, everything we're walking over, is coal dirt." He commenced walking toward the river, waving Saul along. "Four to five foot thick here, because the creek bends. Dumps everything over here. It's even in the water." He indicated flecks wheeling in the current just off the edge of the bank. "Comes down from the coal breakers and washeries upriver in Tremont and Pine Grove." He pointed his shovel at the hollow where the Blue Mountain gapped down to their level to let the river pass through, although they couldn't actually see the river much beyond the bend because of the thick tree cover. "It's endless. Keeps renewing as long as they wash coal up there."

"What's it good for?" Saul kicked a clump of grass and watched the black coal sand drop off the roots as it cartwheeled.

"You tell me. Susquehanna Electric makes their electric on what? Coal. I know the guys over at Rohrer's Ford, where the power plant is. I haul nut coal for people's stoves every September to April. More fun than milking cows all the time." He smiled wryly. "Good cash on the side, too. Anyhow, the plant guy, Winerich, says they wish they could get their mitts on this stuff. Says they could run their plant a lot cheaper than present. Says they'd buy as much as they could get."

"Wait a minute once. What's your hauling coal to make pocket money have to do with Susquehanna Electric?"

"Nothing." Suddenly, Bennie's face lit, his hands came alive, and his short, round body began tromping back and forth on the little patch of exposed coal between the marsh grass clumps. The little Sheltie nipped

78

at his heels. "No! Everything! I could haul coal dirt for them if I had a scoop. Scope out this—" His hand swung from the honeysuckle wall to the grassy, open spaces to the tulip trees and the river itself. "There's 10,000 truckloads in here."

Saul mulled it over. Was this worth getting excited about, or just a bust? *Coal. Heat. Coal burning, heating boilers, blowing up steam, generating electricity . . . electricity lighting streets and cities, powering up radios, vacuum cleaners, TVs. Think Levittown, with its 17,440 spanking new cookie-cutter houses a mere hundred miles from here. All lit by electric. And just like that I GET IT. Eureka! The Greek Archimedes, sloshing in his bathtub, finding the answer to the puzzle! I GET IT. My freedom road from farming. Haul coal for the furnaces at Rohrer's Ford.*

"Bennie! I could buy a Caterpillar dozer. I dig, you haul."

"'A hundred smackeroos a load,' Winerich said. Times what? Ten thousand truckloads? What's that make?"

"Well, a million dollars."

"We'll be," Bennie's mouth flapped wide open, "*millionaires.*"

Saul ran to the pickup and fetched the feed sacks. In less than 45 seconds, he was spading samples into a burlap sack while Bennie held the sack mouth open.

"I always thought swimming in the Chilly as a kid that there oughta be some use for it. What if we turned out millionaires? Hallelujah! The Lord sent you to me." Bennie's chubby, callused hands closed around Saul's. "You know that? You know He sent you to me?" The Sheltie teetered on its hind legs, dancing, barking.

"I had a feeling first time I met you. How you look out of your eyes, I think." Bennie's finger moved back and forth between Saul's eyes. "Deep. They just go through me." Bennie shivered and wrapped his arms around himself. "Brrrr." Then, leaning forward against the pickup bed, he scrutinized the bag of samples that Saul was tying shut. "I never thought much about it after that, but this after, there on the couch at you guys' house, this coal thing rared its head up, and I thought to myself maybe you—well, I don't know what I thought. Ain't that funny?" He slapped his thigh, and Saul verified Anna Mary's observation: the man's white shirt cuffs and collar were ragged and worn out. "And we end up taking samples to the Electric Company. Huh?" He brought up his hand and stuck a finger between Saul's ribs.

He's a passionate guy! Like that about him!

From that Sunday, they were business partners and friends. But Saul didn't know the spiritual side of Bennie. That was to come.

The door of the lodge flew open, and Saul saw something, bundled from top to bottom, stumble in. It was followed by Wolf, a stocking cap pulled down over his ears, holding a snowball over the bundle. Hands and a head came up out of the bundle—it was Gloria. "Don't!" She fought off the snowball with one hand and her pursuer with the other. "Don't!" She swatted the snowball, trying to break it.

Wolf leaped back, and in that quick interlude she turned and ran toward the fireplace. "Protect me!" She ran up, her static-electric-charged hair flying up behind her head like tail feathers, and darted around the armchair to the front of the fireplace, where she crouched, trying to hide. "You quit?" She gave a heave of relief. "You're terrible, Wolf."

Gloria unzipped her winter coat and hood and took them off. "Ooooooh . . ." She strained forward, pulling up the back of her blouse at the same time. "Don't look!" She extended a melting, dripping snowball. "Oh, you nasty—he stuck it down, and then he chased me so I couldn't pull it out."

Saul's eyes crossed with the music teacher's, and he saw it again. Wolf's eyes were more frigid than the ice ball. He nodded recognition. The eyes skittered away as his face turned.

"Wish I could take your class this week," Saul said to the back of Wolf's head. "Maybe I'd learn to sing."

"Some never do." Wolf addressed it to the lodge door, which he pulled and slammed behind his disappearing back.

"Brrrrrr . . ." Bennie said. "He spiting you or something?"

Gloria finished adjusting the wet clothes around herself. "We were really hoping you'd make it before supper, Saul. We wanted to dedicate the time."

"And lay on hands," Bennie said. "Where's Brother Brubaker?"

"And Yoder." Gloria inspected the fireplace collection of youth. "Is he out still with the tobagganers? It's half dark already. Oh, Yoder!" She spied him.

The skinny, horse-faced, but intellectual looking college boy joined them. Bennie returned with Brubaker.

"To the library," Brubaker said, leading the way.

Cyrus Brubaker, his face boyish and jubilant, even at 70-something, had spent six years as principal of the church college and high school in Paradise Valley before resigning the year before Saul joined the faculty. The man seemed too gentle and too thoughtful to deal with perverse teenagers—too willing to trust his feelings. He'd also suffered through thyroid cancer, and a New Cumbria doctor had taken half his voice box two years ago. His voice was only now becoming understandable. But Saul trusted the man. Because Brubaker was directing the Snow Camp, he'd said "yes" to the assignment.

"Yes," Brubaker said when they were all assembled in the library and had shut the door. He stretched hands both ways to initiate a circle. "I wanted to get everyone together before the session starts, to pray."

"Especially for you." Bennie's fist bumped Saul's shoulder.

"And the kids!" Gloria said. "We have 63."

"But the key point." Yoder pursed his lips and bobbed his long, distorted face. "We have at least 12 unsaved."

"There's the eight from Ruby Street. The mission." Gloria turned to Saul. "A couple of them first came as fresh-air kids out of Philly, but for most of them, Snow Camp's like a big outing from the city."

"Actually, one of their girls knows the Lord. So it's seven unsaved."

"Oh, okay. Well then, 11 total?"

"Still 12. There's five from Paradise Valley District." Yoder counted them off on his fingers. "Glennie Fahnestock, Arnie, Phil, Ike Zeiset, and Rolly."

"All boys?"

"That's it." Yoder's body nodded back and forth. "Our young people are jealous of the Amish young folks and their *rumspringa*—'sowing the wild oats,' they call it. Lots of our guys have to quit school at 15 to help on their dad's farm—they don't get *rumspringa,* and they hate they have to go to church and stuff."

"So, they didn't want to come to camp?" Saul was trying to understand the issue with the young men.

"Camp's different. Camp's fun!" Yoder said, and they all laughed politely.

"Okay." Brubaker played his role as emcee with a soft touch. "We have these 12 especially, and we have Saul—"

Yoder was squirming, glancing back and forth at Gloria.

"Go ahead," she said. "Say it."

"I don't know—"

"What is it?" Brubaker asked.

"Just a thought," Yoder said. "That's all. *To fast.* To fast till they give their hearts. I mean, Jesus said we should 'fast.'"

"Well?" Brubaker croaked. "What do we think?" No one responded. "I do keep asking myself, *What will light revival?* Especially my last years at KMC. I looked over the students some days and thought, *What does it take?* We have some cockleburs, and Jesus did say that the tough ones need extra extra." His smile seemed incongruous with what he was saying. "Fasting and prayer, hmm . . . I'll cast my vote."

"Me too," Saul said.

"You mean fast till everyone decides?" Bennie asked. "How long's that? The wife's in charge of meals. What are the cooks supposed to do? And it's supper right now and some of us been chasing around in the snow all afternoon—"

"It'll be voluntary," Brubaker said. Bennie mulled that wordlessly. "Okay, then we're decided. Saul—" Brubaker hobbled up, because of his arthritis, and seized a folding chair that he unfolded in the middle of them. "To the hot seat, Saul."

The group circled him, and he felt their hands touch his shoulders and his neck. Then, Bennie—he knew it was him by the size of the fingers—pinched the crown of Saul's head, and the words began to tumble, just as they'd tumbled every Tuesday morning since Christmas at 6:30 A.M. in the restaurant.

≡≡—

I had no idea. Thought I was the only one carrying this curse around my neck like some folks wear a cross. The curse of "standing in the gap." The curse of knowing someone needs to do something and I'm called.

But here, at Bennie Fisher's invitation, Saul had met six more men who each felt that he, too, was called to stand in the gap.

"I know the group for you," Bennie said after that Christmas dinner, when the strange gibberish finally stopped falling from his lips.

That was how he first met Cyrus Brubaker and discovered the man's heart.

With the coffee, eggs, and home fries now finished—the group was together in one of the little conference rooms off the main dining at Harp-in-the-Willows—Cyrus got up with his old, tattered-cover Bible and started rasping. (It took Saul several meetings to fully understand what seemed like a foreign accent.) "We're here in Acts 7:55. 'Then Stephen, full of the Holy Ghost'—we keep running across this, don't we. Peter, filled with the Holy Ghost, challenging the Sanhedrin Council. Paul, full of the Holy Ghost, defying that sorcerer. Barnabas, full of the Holy Ghost—men, it's throwing up a pattern here." Cyrus laughed his habitual wheezing laugh.

"Have you got the Holy Ghost? For myself, I don't want to preach without Him. I don't want our Sunday School teachers to teach without Him. I don't want to fall out of bed in the morning . . . without the Holy Ghost! There's the fire this Conference needs! So, have you got Him? If you don't know, you don't have Him!"

The aged prophet seemed so withered that a summer thunderstorm might have blown him over. But when he opened his mouth, his words singed the air like live coals.

They made a standing circle, arms around each other's shoulders. The waitresses were too busy with customers in the big room to bother them. Then, with their hands stretched toward the rafters, they began to sing in unison:

> Melt me, mold me,
> Fill me, use meeeeee . . .
> Spirit of the Living God,
> Fall afresh on me.

Nothing seemed to happen. What was supposed to happen, anyway? It had only been three weeks for Saul, but the rest of them had been doing these meetings some years already. Would it be tongues of fire jiggling on their scalps, like at Pentecost?

He felt Bennie's fingers on his scalp right now. Only it was more than touch. Those fingers gripped.

"Touch our brother. Anoint his mouth and tongue." Bennie's singsong voice surged and waned, peaked and died. "Anoint the words. Fill him with the Holy Ghost. Jeeeeeesus!" Bennie's fingertips vibrated irregularly with his words. "Give him that little bitty voice . . ."

He's doing it! Filling me. Doesn't feel like anything special, but He said, "Ask and you will receive," and we asked.

"Thank you, brothers and sisters," Saul said when the prayer had ended.

Just then, a huge draft of cold air tunneled under the library door. They heard a chorus of young voices, saw through the glass panes of the Library door the colorful scarves and caps, and heard them stomping shoes in the Lodge entryway. A dozen teenagers, cheeks and ears bright red from the cold—except for the Ruby Street kids, whose black faces didn't show the cold, although the upward, milky plumes of breath did. The tobogganers were back for supper.

Eight

"NOT MAH SISTAH, not mah bruddah, but it's me, Oooo Lahwd . . ."

Felipe McCullers' black eyelids were sealed and he smiled hugely around each word and they swallowed each word eagerly. The twenty-five white Snow Campers—they were all still in their outside clothes because the leaders had let the log fire die during the day, and it took the boilers in the furnace room some time to respond to the command to send hot water charging through the pipes and into the cast-iron radiators.

Yoder and Gloria were busy towing back the sofas and directing four or five high school and post-high-school boys, all in ubiquitous plaid shirts and pegged Levi's with turned-up leg cuffs. Each had a good German name, like Ressler, Erb, Kauffman, or Lehman. The boys dragged in folding chairs and set rows between the sofas, within six feet of the fireplace, where Bennie was just now hunkered down on the hearth about a foot above the Lodge floor. He was shaving off snivels of pine to drop on the still-glowing coals that Ike Zeiset was turning up out of the ashes with a large soup spoon. A curl of smoke rose over the first shavings, and then a yellow tongue of flame.

"Standin' in dah needa prayer!"

The youth group all chorused now, swaying in the overstuffed lounge sofas and armchairs.

Saul had one leg propped up on the hearth, his talking points all prepared in a folder on the lectern off to the side, as he watched the youth with amazement. Incoming youth, brushing off the snow that had again started falling outside the lodge, headed immediately to the singing crowd around the lodge chairs. They circled the chairs like yellow jackets circle an open soda bottle, eager to find a friend to sit next to.

═══ ═══

"Not dah preachah, not dah deacon, but it's me, Oooo Lahwd!"

Felipe had first sung the tune earlier that afternoon on the balcony of Pomeroy's in downtown Reading. He had leaned forward over the curved and ornate railing, his articulate black fingers resting spread and relaxed on the polished brass, while the customers on the first floor below gathered, interrupting their post-sales Christmas shopping, to gaze up at the students. Thirty muffled and bundled students formed a backdrop to Felipe.

Saul shut his eyes. It might be a Negro song with its roots in Central Africa, preserved through a hundred years of slavery in the cotton fields of the South—a hundred years of Jim Crow legal oppression in sharecropper shacks and city ghettos—and revitalized Sunday after Sunday by the gowned choirs in those D.C. churches he knew existed but had never visited because of the social wall. *Solo voce—a man crying out to his God,* Saul thought. *Not like a Mennonite song, marinated 400 years by people and endlessly rising and falling in my part, your part, four parts. Working together, wife-and-man, horses-and-man, church-and-man, brother-and-man, like chords on a musical bar, sometimes compromising, sometimes together, sometimes point-and-counterpoint, but always a group effort. Harmony.*

No sooner had Felipe finished than Rolly Kurtz poked him. "Can I say something to 'em? What the Lord's doing?"

"Sure!" Saul gave his blessing.

"Hi, Rolly Kurtz here."

Saul noted that the clerks had also stepped away from their cash registers to listen. *This store's not making any money right now.*

"Everybody knows my case. Back at Camp, I mean." He smiled slyly. "I came just to check out . . . the girls." The Snow Camp girls giggled like a school of minnows, moving together in the current of his words. "And stir things up. Saul here told us last night: 'The End is coming.' It'll be fire and destruction of all this." Rolly's hands waved overhead to embrace the entire, fantastic store, the crown jewel of downtown Reading, its ochre-and-ivory-granite columns soaring two stories and anchoring the layered balconies and the new marvel, the escalator. The elegance of the store spoke of another, more genteel era than this utilitarian post-War one. "Who knows when? But Jesus said it, and he—that's Brother Saul—says to us, 'What about you? Are you ready?'"

Two unbelievable things had happened since the leadership team prayed that Sunday in the Library and began the fast. The first was that Rolly Kurtz had found salvation. Rolly's overly long, dark hair was shiny with Vitalis and brushed back on both sides. It formed a point in the back—popularly called the "D.A." or "Duck's Ass"—over the upturned, black leather collar of the iron-studded motorcycle jacket that he wore as his signature.

Anna Mary had pointed out the defiant young man and Old Man Kurtz one afternoon at the Red Steer Market. They made an odd couple. Rolly, with his steel cleats, jacket with studs, epaulets, and zippers, clicked along 15 feet ahead of the white-headed man who hobbled with arthritis, his slate-colored Mennonite coat as defiant as his son's jacket. It was hard to say who seemed more the rebel—the son or the old groundhog hunter and furniture maker with his obstreperous opinions. Their inability to talk when facing each other was legendary. The son's drinking bouts were also legendary.

"For the first time, I 'fessed up to myself," Rolly said. "I'm not ready. I'm gonna burn. I don't wanna burn! Next thing we're all—me and about 10 of these guys"—he broke his story to wave over the students behind him—"we're down on our knees saying, 'God! I don't wanna burn!'"

The second unbelievable thing had occurred a morning in the Lodge Hall. Seventy hours out from their arrival at Snow Camp, Saul had held a pitcher of mountain water and poured it handful by handful into Cyrus Brubaker's cupped, parchment hands, stretched over the white and black heads of the eleven little pagans who had all been saved and wanted water baptism. Handful by handful, they baptized all 11, and then broke the fast together with Edie's scrambled eggs and bacon.

The campers were euphoric. "People need to get saved! People can't go to hell like a bunch of torched marshmallows without *someone* warning them! We could do it! We could go store to store downtown, giving out tracts! We could pray with those wanting to get right with God, on the spot!"

Edie, the practical one, had said, "But it's free time Wednesday afternoon. Don't you'uns wanna toboggan and ride the inner tubes?"

Not one of them did. So they loaded the campers into the 14-foot bobtail and the old school bus, now painted the color of a green pie apple and bearing two-foot high block letters that read "Mt. Sinai Mennonite Camp" on the sides, and drove down into Reading with all 63 campers aboard, singing their throats raw on Christmas carols, to Pomeroy's.

"I even called my dad," Rolly said. "And me and him—" he scowled around—"we go way back, and it's all bad news. I apologized last night. That's what only God can do with a cold fish heart like mine." He thumped his chest loudly.

"Can I go next?" another teen asked. "Can I go next?"

Saul cut them off after Rolly to keep his promise to Mr. Southworth, the store manager. They did one more hymn and then massed onto the polished silver and elegant down escalator. To Saul's astonishment, as they descended the shoppers and clerks gathered around the bottom, chirping, "Thank you! God bless you!" Then the campers all filed out into the 20-something-degree afternoon under iron skies that were threatening to snow again.

One store wasn't enough. The campers spread out with pocketfuls of gospel tracts into the butcher shop, the shoe shop, a couple of bars, a couple of restaurants, and the funeral home, all passing out those little Chickies cartoon booklets depicting a man waking up "The Day After," his body six feet down in his coffin, while his soul wiggled wraith-like out of the body to address the Judgment Day Angel on the grass overhead. It was a cartoon with the riveting horror of an Alfred Hitchcock movie.

⸘⸘⸘

"Itsa me! Itsa me! Itsa me, Oooo Lahwd! Standin' in the needa prayer!"

The student band, swollen now to include most of the 63 teens, chorused loudly. They lined the sofas and rows of chairs, arms circling each other's shoulders, swaying right, now left, with the chorus.

"Cyrus!" Saul solicited the attention of the old Bishop, who stood painfully, watching the flames jump briskly upward through five or six oak chunks. "Cyrus!"

"Yes?"

"Whaddya think? I'm thinking a testimony meeting. Forget our program. At least my part."

"Isn't this what we've prayed for?"

Saul turned to address the youth. "Folks!"

"Needa prayer . . ." The song diminished to a whimper.

"Really hate to interrupt your fun. But we're here to learn more tonight." The youth, in touch with their general euphoria, applauded this. "Brother Cyrus and I just discussed a time of testimony. What you saw and learned today—anybody have something like that you'd like to tell?"

Nearly every hand went up.

"Wow! We could be here all night, Brother Cyrus!"

Cyrus' head tilted side to side, and he chuckled. "Why not?"

"Let's limit it, though. There's class after general session, and your teachers have prepared. So . . ." Saul reviewed the teachers who were scattered around the lodge hall: Bennie, Cyrus, Wolf. "If you had a good experience today, fine. Keep that to yourself. Share it with your best friend. But a second category here: You have something valuable for the whole group to hear. Those individuals, you stand."

The response was slower. Rolly, Felipe, and Ruth Ann, the college girl who planned to be a writer, instantly bounded out of their seats. Soon, there were others. *In fact, practically everyone,* Saul thought. *And gawking about, laughing, enjoying this little game.*

"What do we do here?" He conferred with Cyrus *sotto voce*.

"Most fear public speaking," Cyrus said. "Make it hard. Make them come down front and stand alone."

Saul turned back. The youth had begun to shed their bulky coats and mufflers as the room warmed, talking all the while in whispers to each other.

"I guess I play Gideon. Got to winnow this down. Okay, you'll come down front and address us from here. Everyone who doesn't want that"—Saul flapped his arms up down and up several times—"needs to sit down."

Something is moving here! We only lost five or six on that move!

"I don't mind," Bennie spoke from the radiator, where he was adjusting the valves. "Hey! It's more important than what I had to say anyhow."

Wolf, standing by the kitchen bar with Edie, seemed less enthusiastic about the change of schedule. He shrugged his shoulders. "The people have spoken."

"So, who's first? Remember, down front, address the group."

Why shouldn't they take time for stories? Wasn't it significant that they even volunteered? Would their parents do that? Saul couldn't imagine it. Or was it the old trick of group-ness? Wasn't it all the camaraderie and contagious mood of America's paratroopers, side by side in the dark belly of a troop transport, destined momentarily to leap through the little, open door downward onto occupied Korea? Of course, as pacifists, these folks would hate that comparison.

Here's Felipe McCullers, and he gets a chuckle. They like him.

Felipe did not turn around when he got to center spot below the moose head, as instructed. Instead, he faced the crackling, smoking logs, his shoulders buckling forward. He wrapped both arms around himself, all 10 fingertips clutching his lower back. Then: "Daaaaaaaaaaaaaaaaad!"—like a massive oak door rusted fast to the frame of a dilapidated cellar, its long-neglected hinges yielding slowly, protesting. His shoulders rocked slowly, and the second time the cry went much higher in pitch. "Daaaaaaaaaaaaaaaaad!" He dropped to his knees.

Saul hustled for the front, eyes scanning for Cyrus, who had disappeared. Felipe spoke again, his whole body rocking rhythmically. "Jeeeesus!" It was no louder than a hoarse whisper.

Saul crouched and peered into the boy's face. Contorted, just as he had expected. The boy's throat and face muscles were popped, his eyes squeezed shut. *It's how they do it in Negro Church, no doubt. Holy Rollers. Never heard of any teenage boy wailing over his own father, unless it was a funeral. But here comes Rolly! Rolly will know what's wrong—they're buddies.* Rolly didn't come alongside, however. He folded several feet away onto his knees, facing the fire. His voice sounded more human, the yowl of a man in distress, weeping without controlling it.

"I want Andy . . . to meet . . ." Saul thought it pitiful to hear a full-sized man bawl like this—and more disturbing than Felipe, frankly. "Jesus!" *And he isn't Negro!* Rolly pitched face downward onto the wooden floor, lay still a moment, and then twitched. A series of twitches followed.

"Convulsions!" someone said.

"Put him on the sofa," Saul said, pointing to the sofa just outside the library door. Several high school boys reached for the boy, while Saul took a shoulder. "On three. One . . . two . . ."

When they touched Felipe's shoulder, it convulsed. Saul said, "Wait, don't touch him."

A boy gestured toward the public phone hanging in view inside the library door. "If I call the doctor—?"

"A blanket!" said another student.

"Let's try again," Saul said. This time he barely brushed the boy with his fingers. The slight twitching now became violent twists and jerks. *Need to give myself a few beats to think what next,* Saul said to himself. "Okay, sit down. Everybody. Felipe and Rolly just said who they want us to pray for and—let's pray!"

Saul's eyes had hardly pinched shut when a sharp in-sucking from the front row forced them open again. A girl's mouth had flapped wide, goggling past him and Rolly, toward . . .

Felipe! The boy's long, black arms straightened in jerks, and he began to turn slowly, falling backward. Saul stretched out but failed to catch the boy, who hit one elbow with a sharp crack on the floor and continued to tumble, arms twisting. Spasms followed, similar to Rolly's, only more terrifying because Felipe ended on his back and his eyeballs could be seen traveling under the lids.

Jesus and the epileptic boy—and what did the epileptic boy do? Tossed to the ground. Convulsed, it says. By the demon. Can it be? That the Evil One would enter a little group praising God?

"The devil at work!" Saul leaped to his feet, addressing the student group. *I'm guessing fear is painted all over my own face, for it's mirrored in theirs. Where is Cyrus?* "Say it with me: 'In the name of Jesus!'"

They murmured in response, their voices timid.

"Louder. Believe as you say with me: 'In the name of Jesus!'"

He faced the two on the floor, both of whom appeared to be unconscious and occasionally convulsive. ". . . Complete power over you. In the name of His Blood, I command you—come out!" He fully expected that the teens would cease abruptly and sit up weak and pale, perhaps smiling with embarrassment.

They jerked on.

Saul did a rightabout, motioning the youth to their feet. "Call on the blood with me!" He began to sing, hoping it would summon a higher, controlling power:

> There is power! Power!
> Wonder-working power,
> In the blood . . . of the Lamb!

Bennie fumbled and banged behind his back, tossing more wood onto the fire to heat up the room.

Saul's eye caught the sliding face in the audience, pale and colorless, falling through the girls beside her. "Louder! Louder!"

> There is power! Power!
> Wonder-working power,
> In the precious blood . . .

Ruth Ann, the college girl, bumped on the floor.

"She's not moving, like them!"

"Is she dead?"

"Hey!" Bennie said, coming alongside Saul. As always, his face was round and almost cherubic, but his look was not one of fear. "You sure? The devil? Are you sure?"

"If not the devil, then who?"

"What if it's what we prayed? For Him to touch us like Pentecost?"

He regarded Bennie, doubting, and shook his head negatively. "It's the devil, no doubt, confusing our meeting." As he spoke, several high school students gathered around the boys to sing. They linked hands and pinched their eyes shut. Gloria also now arrived, just off his elbow, and waited.

"How can we tell?" Saul asked. "And where's Cyrus?"

Gloria shook his elbow. "I need to talk."

"Maybe gone to bed. He gets terribly tired," Bennie said.

"Yes?" Saul lowered his ear sideways, keeping his eyes fixed on Rolly on the floor.

"Privately."

"What is it?"

"I don't want nobody else hearing—" The usual vitality in her face seemed washed away. "It'll hit me next," she whispered. "I'm sure."

"Keep the singing going," Saul said to Bennie. The group was now singing in huddles around the three on the floor and among the chairs. "And it's too hot in here," he stage-whispered. The radiator valves hopped and whistled, and all of Bennie's wood seemed to have simultaneously caught fire. Sweat beaded on Saul's forehead, and his back felt scorched. "The library." He pointed the way.

The air in the library was 15 degrees cooler. Saul stopped just inside, holding the door ajar so he could monitor the noises of the main hall. The library was dark, but to avoid calling attention to themselves, he didn't hit the wall switch.

Gloria sat by the window, and light from the pole outside fell on her. *Like a face under moonlight,* Saul thought. He remembered Schnoogie's fairy tale book, falling apart now from overuse. *Like the comatose Snow White, waiting for the Prince's kiss.*

96

"I'm afraid. What if they die?"

"I actually thought of that." Saul knew she couldn't see his face, because it was backlit. He tromped on a floor lamp switch.

"What about hell?"

"What about it?"

Gloria's face dropped forward into cupped hands. Her long, straight hair fell forward over her shoulders and hung there, concealing her face.

"What's wrong, Gloria?"

"It's Mom. What I told you before."

"Go on." He couldn't get his mind off the sounds in the lodge hall.

"It's Wolf—she detests him. She sorts through my trash for letters."

Once Gloria had said that much, the rest seemed to flow without effort. "I don't want to hurt her, but things come out. Then I think how it must have sounded, and I come looking for her to say I'm sorry. 'Mom,' I say, and she glad-eyes me—as if nothing ever happened—and says, 'What?' Oh, what that does to me! If only she'd be mad, I'd say, 'I'm sorry you're mad,' or put my arm around her shoulder. But she says 'what?' all business-like, and smiles. *For no good reason,* she smiles at me. . . . So I walk off and—and I hate her. No, not hate her." Gloria stopped, and her mouth dropped in discovery. She nodded vigorously. "Mmhmm. Hate her."

"All right. That's enough."

"I didn't tell you yet the things I do."

"We don't need to know. If you're sorry for them—"

"You have to know everything. Days we go to market, she comes in the car to get me at 9 o'clock, and I often pretend she's a stranger. Like I don't know her when she comes in, so the other girls won't know she's my—. I just grab my pocketbook and walk out past her on my way to the car."

"Gloria."

"And pretend I don't know her. I run away from her."

"Gloria!"

"It's not the worst."

"Wrap up all that bitterness." He symbolically swept the air and rolled it up like a dirty tablecloth. "And wash it away. We can pray." Nodding, she slipped off the bench and onto her knees. He covered her head with his hand, arching his fingers so that all the pressure came right into his fingertips. "There's power in the blood!" He felt keenly that he was in the arena with his lion. "He can't resist it." *Hear it, Old Nick.* His fingers encircled her skull alternately. With a jumping move, they gripped, then relaxed, and then jumped to grip the scalp again. "In the name of Jesus!"

"Yes . . ." she murmured, her mouth open against his shirt sleeve. "Yessssss . . ." Her fingers bumped his wrist, and then she clutched it.

"You're clean. Believe it." His hands fell away. His fingers tingled and still held the gripping sensation.

Gloria slowly stood. In the dim light next to the window, Saul saw her face turn toward him. "I feel . . ." She slanted away. "I didn't tell you. I also have menstrual—I don't . . . doesn't come like it's supposed to, and when you prayed I prayed it would heal—"

"Yes!"

Her arms encircled him. "Thank you!" she blurted, snuggling her face against his belly for a moment before backing off. "I feel sooooo . . ."

"Yes?"

"I'm so tired, but should I go to bed? Or back out there?"

"It's up to you." Saul opened the library door and went out ahead.

Bennie broke away and rubbed his palms against his pant legs. "I shouldna made the fire so big. But—I thought first it's happening 'cuz they're cold. What do you think?" Bennie scouted his face. "What d'you think it is?"

Saul noticed that no one was singing. The little knots were all praying.

"Her!" Bennie pointed past him. "Her!"

Saul turned 180 degrees to see the figure in the doorway of the library. Still half in darkness, the figure swayed back and forth as the hands lifted slowly, and then smooth, sensuous syllables poured from the uplifted plane of Gloria's face. "*Umda shakem umdalia ma umda . . .*" The figure chilled him, as if a wraith or spirit was materializing there in the dark empty space.

"The Gift!" Bennie pointed.

The students gaped. "She's gone mad!"

"Gloria!" Her eyes lowered and peered his direction. They were glazed and not focused at all. She was seeing some point back on the wall, through him, as if he were a window. "Gloria!" He clapped in her sight line.

"It's the Gift," Bennie said. "Don't stop her."

Saul watched in disbelief, waiting to see if she would drop to her knees and convulse like the boys. "It's the devil." When he said it, he felt the hairs on his arms and legs stand up.

"Listen, Brother!" Bennie grabbed a handful of the flesh on his neck and gave it a painful squeeze.

"Owwwch!"

"The Holy Ghost! Come upon her, oh glory, see her smile. Behold that smile." Bennie himself smiled luxuriously and swayed. "It's the Sign." He put one hand on Saul's shoulder and with the other motioned toward Gloria, still stalled in the doorway. "First you burn all over. Like sunburn, itchy. Then chills, and you know it's coming. Glory! Then the Holy Ghost pours in, and it's got to show itself." Bennie began to clap, erratically, arrhythmically. "Behold her." He clapped and bobbed like a hot air balloon about to lift off, barely restrained by the anchoring ropes.

For no clear reason, Saul felt his own insides begin to burn. *Is whatever that's in this room that powerful? Against my will and invisibly leaping on me like a mugger in a dark lane? Or is it like that night in the barracks? Didn't I break out laughing? Didn't I sense a wonderful*

Being with me? Not physically, yet so palpable that it might have been my own tonsils? Could He be here tonight? Could she be smiling and singing because she sees Him? *Could it be*—the hypothesis struck him with the ferocity and shock of a hard snowball to the face—*that the ones on the floor right now see Him, and*—He couldn't admit it. Mentally, he granted the possibility, but other cells inside of him argued against it vehemently.

"Turn. . ."

Saul turned from Gloria to look at the group around Rolly. Some of the students were kneeling and others were on chairs, their faces propped on their hands, leaning forward and praying. He peered around, assuming Bennie had addressed him. "What?"

"In . . . your . . . Bible . . ."

"He's speaking," Bennie said. "It's English."

Rolly lay belly-down, with his damp face sideways on a pillow that someone had stuffed under his head, his body uncovered, as the lodge was still overheated. The spasms had gradually diminished, and for the last five minutes he'd been still—so still that one high-schooler had knelt down fearfully to listen for breath. When Rolly began to speak, his head was in that same position, his eyes closed. The words wrenched loose, a combination of a stammer and a 78 record player losing power.

"To. Acts. Two."

"Turn in your Bible, turn in your Bible!" Bennie waved for attention. "Who has one?" In the hubbub, he missed Rolly's next words. "And what? I missed it."

"Seventeen and eighteen."

"Two: seventeen and eighteen."

"You . . ." Rolly said.

"I'm getting it." Bennie tore open the proffered Bible, licking his callused thumb and forefinger to peel pages faster.

"Shall understand."

"Let's hope," Saul said, eyeballing the boy. Rolly's damp, jelled hair fell forward over his ears and eyes. His face, still and colorless, sunk into the pillow.

"Seventeen and eighteen? Listen! 'And it shall come to pass in the last days, saith God . . .'" Bennie lined the words as he read. "'Saith God, I will pour out of my Spirit upon all flesh: and your sons and your daughters shall prophesy, and your young men shall see visions, and your old men shall dream dreams . . .'"

Is it that? My Spirit upon all flesh; your sons and daughters shall prophesy?

"This is it!" He shook Bennie's shoulder with both hands. Bennie was reading the next verse and glowered, annoyed. "This is *that*!" Saul appealed to everyone in the lodge. "All of this." The youth sat unmoving, bug-eyed. "God's Spirit, pouring into them, and this is the sign. Language." He clarified. "Prophecy."

"In . . . the . . . year . . . King Uzziah . . . died . . ." Rolly moved in a slow, mechanical motion to a sitting position, both eyes still sealed. He exhaled a loud puff and began again, his voice more certain, less robotic. "I see seraphim. And seraphim. And seraphims. And each. With six wings."

One of the girls near Ruth Ann waved a handkerchief and shouted. "She sees an angel! She says she sees an angel!"

Gloria, still swaying in the library doorway, was singing a sort of nonsense song in a strong alto: "*Oh shakem salamaria allelu—*"

Saul contemplated Bennie. The man's face was empty, his mouth expressionless. He gazed back, eyes flicking first left, then right over Saul's face. "Hufuuu . . ." Bennie sucked air sharply.

"Bennie!" It was the first Saul had laughed all evening. He laughed a tired laugh, his chest shaking helplessly, with no effort.

Bennie's mouth opened wide. "Hey!" He grabbed Saul's lapels with both hands and pulled him. Their bodies collided and embraced. They stood with their arms clutching each other's damp shirt backs, swaying, laughing into each other's ears.

Part Three

Warnings

February–March 1956

Nine

I WANT HER to feel it! The Spirit's on the move. It's big—it's the Glory Train, thundering at the station platform, steam pluming from the boiler, great iron wheels straining forward against the brakes. Get on board with us!

Saul fully intended to dash into the house with that message, but two things derailed him.

The farm lay dreaming in the frigid full moon, a three-dimensional Christmas card. The lane off the macadam road had been plowed to the width of two cars, right up to the spot on the hillock where they always parked the car. (Neighbor Boeshore, of course. They had a standing agreement. Boeshore plowed their lane after snowstorms with his scoop-fitted tractor, and in return, his wife got all the pears she wanted from their front lawn for pear butter.)

To the right, as Saul stepped from the car, the light on the barn first floor glowed butter yellow. Aaron was finishing the milking. To the left, a light in the kitchen suddenly blinked as Anna Mary's body came between the gridded, frosted window panes and the solitary overhead bulb. He saw a hand fly up and waggle. It was a good sign.

He clutched the suitcase and picked his way down the shoveled, flagstone path between two knee-high snow banks—stepping carefully because the light-reflecting surface of the stones indicated ice—and entered the darkened washhouse.

The washhouse was the family workroom. On 100-some year old houses like this one, the previous owners often tacked outlying rooms onto the main house. The washhouse was added to accommodate the wash machine, wringer, and shelves of canned fruits and vegetables. Like the rest of the house, except for the kitchen and the living room, it was unheated in the winter.

Bouncing moonlight from the snows that surrounded the house dim-lit the washhouse, but it was the smells that temporarily caused him to forget his mission.

Sauerkraut! And something baking!

Saul toed the rubbers off his oxfords, squatting on an upside-down wash pail in the dark. He knew her rule: no outside shoes in the main house. With the suitcase still clutched under his left elbow and the overcoat wedged on top of it, he pushed the inside door wide with his right elbow and stepped up into the kitchen.

She turned under the light, hearing the doorlatch. Several dark locks had escaped the bun and prayer veil and had fallen forward across her flushed face. A dry, orange smear of pumpkin pie filling, perhaps, scarred the apron that matched and form-fit over her green flowered dress. Would anyone but he have known that she'd sewn it herself from cotton feed sacks to save on the cost of fabric?

The billow of warm sauerkraut-scented air reached him seconds before her body and sturdy thighs and breasts pressed against him. With that, his mission completely flushed away in a coursing of hot blood.

"I missed you."

"Me too." Her uncosmetized lips, only inches away, lured him forward, but only for a single kiss. At that moment, a shrill, jiggling whistle broke from the stovetop behind her. She lifted his hands from her waist and spun. "The potatoes." The pressure cooker whistle drooped

106

quickly to a gentle soughing, and then she popped it, wincing back as the scalding cloud rose.

"Mashed potatoes, too," Saul said. "Honey, you didn't need to after such a big week. You never cook Sunday nights."

"But you were coming home." Her smile was big and spendthrift. She held the open pressure cooker with both hands, steam plumes rising.

Because she kept moving, assembling the meal, he took care of his own business. He hung the overcoat and hat, stored his suitcase by the closet wall, checked the coal in the living room stove, and shoveled on two more scoops. *She didn't push away,* he thought. *She's glad to see me, too. After four months of absence from the farm work, scooping and selling the river coal, she's accepted it. She's forgiven me. Or maybe just accepted it.*

"Where's Schnoog?" He returned to the kitchen. He rolled the sleeves of his dress shirt and loosened the collar button and then, self-consciously, combed his hair with his fingers. "Where's my boy?"

"You remember." She brought the plate to his chair at the table head. It held a great pile of sauerkraut, shredded pork, and cratered mashed potatoes, into which she now poured a gravy that sent up curls of vapor. "He's at Pop's. I thought we could go get him together after—"

Which was better? he thought. *The creamed potato forkfuls or her sweet face kitty-cornered from him at the table?* He held her left hand with his left and ate with his right.

"So much to tell you!" Saul said, remembering his mission. It was just like those evenings long ago when he'd stop at her dad's after a weekend speaking trip and they would linger at the Bishop's kitchen table eating cookies. He would lean forward, gesturing with the cookie, dipping it again and again into his coffee while he told a story.

Suddenly, she'd laugh. "You lost the cookie," she would say. Sure enough, it had fallen apart into the cup.

"Did your talks go okay? Did they like them?" She asked now.

"Anna Mary! Something big happened. The Holy Spirit showed up!" He paused between bites on the slab of her mother's sourdough, which she'd smeared with apple butter for him.

"Did you's do lots of tobogganing? That's what I always loved about Snow Camp."

"They didn't want to. We did a hymn sing Wednesday afternoon at Pomeroy's in Reading instead."

She gawked. "A hymn sing instead of toboggans?"

"Like I said. The Holy Spirit just took over. Twelve kids saved."

She abruptly looked down at the plate. "Is the pork still good?"

"It's wonderful, honey. Everything!" He talked through the mouthful of sauerkraut, massaging the back of her hand. "I can't believe you did all this. I just wish . . . if you could have been with us."

Her sense of duty hardened her jaw. "No. Someone had to take care of the farm. And Schnoogie. So you could be free to do it."

"Thank you. But you'll see. You'll get a little taste. They're coming over."

"Who?"

"The leadership team."

"This week?"

"Tonight, actually."

"NO!"

"Something wrong?"

"What about us? And Schnoogie—we need to pick him up. And the house—" She sprang from the chair. "Saul, you didn't—"

"Invite them? Sure, I did. They're friends. We've been together all week. We can go at nine for Schnoogie. They won't be here that long."

"Nine-thirty till we get to Pop's. Way past Schnoogie's bedtime. And Pop's too." She examined her dress, which was spattered on the stomach with several drops of the pork juice. "And my dress." Her voice rose. "You can't do this to me, Saul. Every time you're home from a trip it's some surprise. Every time, Saul! Every time!" She ran out through the living room. "No consideration. No consideration at all!" Her footsteps retreated up the stairs to the bedroom.

He slapped his leg savagely with the table knife. He'd intended to call, to warn her, but the line at the camp payphone was too long.

He'd wash the pots and do penance that way. He peeled down to his tank-top to save his dress shirt and worked on the pots, cracking the washroom door to chase out the cooking smells. But that brought a new smell. When the pots were finished, he walked around the kitchen and discovered the source.

The wooden dry sink was an antique piece from the days before running water and indoor plumbing. It was lined in her grandfather's day—she'd bought it at his estate sale—with zinc to contain water spills from the basins of dishwater. Her enterprising brother, Noah, had ripped out the zinc and sanded, stained, and shellacked it a rich red oak. The sink was lined with tea towels and covered with three rows of cookies, still warm to the fingertips. Red and green sprinkled sand tarts, fat sugar cookies, pinwheels of variegated doughs, and cookie men with M&Ms arranged strategically over their rounded bodies, like snowmen, marched the entire length of the sink.

Saul was eating his second sand tart when he saw the photo album. She'd been working on it during his absence, pasting down triangular corners to hold the Brownie snapshots, labeling the black felt-paper page below each photo with a white ink. He looked at the clock and mentally gave himself 15 minutes.

September 21, 1952. Saul and Pop.

His baptismal day. In the photo, he stood bony and Lincolnesque in his first plain suit, a navy blue Mennonite coat that Esbenshades Clothiers had altered, cutting back the lapels and steam pressing the notch-collar until it looked like a Nehru Jacket. The Bishop stood at least a foot shorter and clutched a large Bible across his waist. The pale limestone face of Paradise Valley Church filled the width of the photo behind them. They were both smiling broadly.

Me, Annette, and Rachel R. The day he took me to the Singing.

Three young women, side-by-side, holding hands, their Conference dresses hanging without padded shoulders or flaring to a midpoint below the kneecap. Matching capes over the dresses, attached at the beltline front and back to modestly conceal the precise womanly figure, which they did well. The regulation prayer veil, immaculate white organdy, neatly stitched together from several pieces, straight-pinned into place over the waves on top and covering the twisted knot on the neck behind. The monochrome snap failed to capture the color of the day or the importance of it.

It was that same Baptismal Sunday, and the Bishop had stationed Saul at the back door of the church after services to greet well-wishers and answer questions about his testimony. It was the first time Saul had experienced people asking him questions because it was his first public testimony, but the questions usually followed a pattern.

"Did you actually see that stone from the bank, the one with the woman's shadow burnt on it?"

"Weren't you afraid they'd jail you—what with all the information you knew from spying?"

He was answering the second question, clarifying that strategic intelligence didn't mean spying, when he saw *them* over the shoulder of the questioner. One in blue, one in yellow, one in green. "Excuse me, there's something—" Saul realized he'd left the last questioner with his question dangling several feet off the ground, but he was determined not to let them slip away.

"Hi, Ladies." He knew they weren't locating there by the queue line by accident.

"Oh, hi," the Blue Dress said, the one who seemed to be the leader. "That was *quite interesting*." She seemed articulate and self-confident; perhaps she was a schoolteacher. "We took an outing to D.C. last fall and climbed the Washington Monument. Is that close to your folks' place?"

The Yellow Dress seemed to be the cheerleader. "Yes, we found Washington fascinating."

The Green Dress stood just behind the Blue's shoulders, and her eyes met his. "I liked the part about you lying in bed, looking up at the fan, and how it made you think." Her eyes that day seemed deep green, like small leaves on a woods shrub, but in the afternoon, closer up, they were doll's eyes, china-blue. Was it the light or her moods that changed them?

"Are you going to the Singing?" the Blue Dress asked.

"What Singing?" Saul asked.

"Ressler's Quarry this afternoon."

"Are you all going?"

"Of course." They giggled together, in a line, watching him.

"Well then . . ." he turned, still clutching the testimony notes against his chest, crossed his arms in a gesture of self-control, and jutted out one index finger. "Can I take you?"

The Green Dress stiffened, and he saw the coloring spread up from her throat and across the cheeks. "Me?" She felt it, too, and quick-slapped both cheeks.

The Singing was a wonderful introduction to Kittochtinny social life, as he was still only six weeks old in the community. The Green Dress pointed out the different varieties of Mennonites. The Black Bumper girls wore their hair combed straight back without waves, parted precisely in the middle, their large, angular prayer veils covering most of it. The covering strings were tied under their chins, and they had no collars on their dresses. The Ohio Conference girls were "worldly," Green Dress said. They wore small organdy caps that clung precariously to the backs of their heads, with the bobs escaping below them, and cape-less dresses that showed their figures. The Kittochtinny girls were somewhere in between.

"Like the geese," he said. "You can tell them apart by their plumage."

She laughed at the comparison.

The wooded hillside in front of the quarry was thick with couples and groups on blankets, most of them participating in the singing. Saul hummed along on the songs—all hymns and gospel songs that he didn't know—trying to figure out what part he was. Everyone else seemed to know theirs. Between one of the songs, she asked if he "had a girl." Somewhat later, she asked if he'd like to come to the Creek Walk.

The Creek Walk, October 5, 1952. He kissed me.

The physical borders of the photo hardly seemed able to contain the Paradise Youth Group. There were 30 or 40 of them, all still in their Sunday clothes, but looking playful. The guys were barefoot and wore their shirtsleeves and pant legs rolled up. Some had straw hats. The girls wore bandannas in place of prayer coverings and went barefoot as well. Saul stood in the back row, with several people between Anna Mary and her girlfriends and himself. The Walk would change all that.

After the picnic lunch, everyone herded for the creek, which ran about 25 feet wide and 12 to 18 inches deep at the entry point. The boys plunged ahead, splashing noisily, yelling back how good the water felt.

Saul noted that the group had different cliques. There were the "steadies," who held hands and traveled together; the "unattached," who walked en masse with either the boys or girls; and those in between, like he and Anna Mary, who walked side-by-side but didn't touch. He had his car, a brand-new Ford he'd bought with Army money, and he had brought her and her girlfriends along from church. The girlfriends walked on the far side of Anna Mary as they headed for the creek.

"Would you care . . ." He tugged her elbow and she turned, inquisitive. "If you and I hung back, didn't walk with the big group?"

"I . . ." she hesitated and checked with Annette and Rachel, who immediately began to talk together, their eyes focused on the creek ahead. "I guess . . . ." She glanced at the retreating backs of Annette and Rachel. Then, "Sure, why not?" Her serious eyes crossed his, and then dropped.

The creek ran evenly upstream, almost imperceptibly rising in elevation, for perhaps a mile through tree-thick meadows and then into dense broadleaf woods. The group soon vanished into the canopy of foliage that overhung the creek, although Saul could still hear their voices for a while. The two of them walked silently except for the splash and burble of their feet going in and out of the water.

Anna Mary kept a three-foot gap between them, and Saul suddenly realized that he didn't know what she was interested in. He couldn't think of anything to talk about. So they walked on silently, except for the sounds of their feet. After some minutes, she began to point out things. "You know what it is?" she asked, pulling down a branch with mitten-shaped leaves from the overhead canopy and breaking off a leaf. "Bite it." He did. The taste was green and spicy. "Sassafras," she said. "The root bark's good for tea. Mom likes it to treat boils and such."

A little farther along, she reached overhead into the massed foliage that hung in vines across the creek, which was narrower and deeper here. She shucked off a handful of marble-sized berries that stained her open fingers purple. "Wild grapes," she said. "Mom sends Aaron out every year about this time to pick them for jelly. Try one." Saul bit through the very pungent peel into a tart, jelly-like blob.

Then she pointed out the broad, plowshare-sized leaves that grew abundantly in the wet inlets of the creek. "Arrowroot. The root numbs your tongue."

"What good is that?"

"Playing tricks on someone." She laughed at his wry response.

"How do you know all this? About plants and stuff?"

"Ock. I've always lived here. Here's something else . . ." They'd come to a bend in the creek, where the water rattled swiftly over large, round stones. It was only inches deep on their side, but looked to be four or five feet deep on the far side as it moved darkly under oak roots that hung out nakedly from a deeply eroded bank. She stooped, moved one of the larger stones, and lifted a two-inch, twisting creature with downward snapping jaws. In the same movement, she tossed it toward the roots. The surface of the water seemed to open and immediately shut as a large, sable nose surfaced and sank away.

"Hellgramites," she said. "Trout love 'em."

Saul was fascinated and wanted to know more. "Tell me about yourself."

"Whaddya want to know?" Her face seemed washed clean of any motives except to answer his questions and respond to the changing scenery of the creek. Without waiting for his answer, she said, "Bishop Krehbiel's my dad. Did you know that?"

"No."

She studied him carefully from where she stood, four feet ahead of him.

"D'you like me less, now that you know?"

"*No.*" He said it indignantly. "More, I would think. I admire the man."

"I'm his bookkeeper."

"He's got a couple farms."

"Three," she said. "And a hundred head of milk cows." She folded her arms. "Eighty beef cows. Plus the market stall proceeds. I wanted to go to college, like Gloria, but . . . on the farm, everyone helps out. He sent me to KMC for two years, and I got my AA in accounting and bookkeeping."

"Interesting work?"

They had almost reached the woods. It lay just on the other side of two barbed wire strands that strung across the water—part of an extended fence to keep cattle on this side of the woods, it appeared. He held the strands up while she ducked under, and then went under himself.

She turned on the far side, both hands on her hips.

"Frankly, you're the most interesting thing this year."

He took it as an invitation. She had to be 24, and in this community, most girls were married by that age. Maybe she was too strong for the guys. It couldn't be said that she was unattractive. In fact, just now, she seemed very attractive, like a summer peach that lay ripe and soft to the touch . . .

Directly ahead of them, the creek swung in a long, slow curve. Floods had deposited a large sandbar on the north side, and beyond that the water gradually deepened, the decaying leaves of an overhanging sycamore mottling the bottom until it edged off darkly and the bottom couldn't be seen.

She stepped off the sandbar, hiked her skirt aside with one hand, and bent away from him, the gray water lapping against the white insides of her knees. She came up with a dripping, coal-colored shell that shot a fine squirt of water from between its bivalves as it tried to retract the pinched pink and soot-spotted flesh.

"Mussels. Some folks actually gather and eat them. See if you can find one." Her mouth teased.

"How?"

"See that little black line?" She pointed with her toe. "That's it." The line disappeared into the mottled sand. "You have to move fast. There!" She pointed to another one.

He stepped off the sandbar, and immediately the water surged to his belt, soaking his trousers. He stumbled straight ahead, catching himself on the branch of the sycamore that flung thick as a man's torso across the creek. He gasped and stepped sideways into shallower water.

She pointed her face away, her shoulders shaking. She waded along the shore to the sycamore and stopped a few feet from him. "I'm sorry . . . making shputt . . . . ."

"*Shputt?*"

"Making fun of you. You looked right at that dip in the water. I can't believe you looked right at it and then fell in."

"Okay!" He laughed now too. He gawked at the trousers. "They'll all think I peed my pants."

Their backs rested against the sycamore while they laughed. The tree had a down-thrust, smaller branch jammed into the creek bottom that held it motionless against their weight. Saul's arms were flung both ways along the trunk.

"Tell me about your family."

"Well, there's seven kids. Eight," she corrected. "Actually, seven."

"You're not sure?"

"Seven living. One died. Our sister, Mattie Mae."

"I'm sorry." After a respectful pause, he asked, "How and when?"

"A farm accident. She was three—and a half."

"Oh." Another silence. "What happened?"

"We were playing. She fell down a grain chute . . . and smothered."

"How old were you?"

"Five. I was supposed to be watching her."

"How horrible."

"Mom brought tea to the men in the barn. Us girls tagged along. The men were haying and unloading the wagon on the second floor. I wandered off into the granary, and she followed. On the farm, accidents happen."

"Yeah, but still—"

"Mom always said, 'She's better off now. In heaven.' She was too good for Earth, my aunts said afterward. Not sassy like me." She made a painful smile. "But sweet and light."

"But still, how did you feel?" He found the story unbelievable. No, not the story. The matter-of-fact telling of it.

"Everyone said—" she paused, and he waited. *She'll give her real feelings now,* he thought. He repositioned his body on the sycamore to face her profile. Then he noticed it—no cosmetics. He didn't know one woman in D.C., old or young, who didn't wear at least lipstick or eye shadow. But the skin was so healthy, the blood pinking it right beneath the surface of her throat and glowing against the white blouse.

"They said, 'God lets terrible things like that happen in this world.' But Pop and I cried. After the burial, when we came home. We shared a bed, Mattie Mae and me. He came up to the room. We sat on the covers, and I seen he was crying. Not out loud. But tears. They sang 'Safe in the Arms of Jesus' at the graveside. So whenever I hear that song—"

Her face turned away. "Ock!" Her shoulders twitched. "I don't know why. I still get this feeling sometimes." She balled her fist between her breasts. Of course, he noticed.

"It's all right," Saul said, covering the other hand with his. She had gripped the branch next to him with one hand, and he was noticing her strong fingers, unlike his own puffy, blanched, and nail-bitten ones. He didn't imagine anyone in the secretarial pool at the Pentagon with fingers like hers.

In her profile face, a large tear escaped and coursed down. He slanted his body toward her, one arm still wrapped around the sycamore branch for balance, and clutched her hand. He pressed his lips against the cheek where the tear was running.

"Oh." Her eyes immediately dropped sideways toward the water flowing over the mussel bed. He didn't have time to say anything further, because a distinct splash ruptured the silence. He dropped her hand, and they turned simultaneously to watch a large, white bird, its neck in an elegant S, lift off through the sycamores along the creek. "A crane!" She squinted after it, and a smile transformed her face. "They like the mussels."

She took his hand when they walked down the stream.

Our Honeymoon, Niagara Falls, April 2, 1953.

He'd snapped these prints himself as she posed on the bank overlooking Niagara River. Plum blossoms hung into the picture from an offstage tree that early spring afternoon. She was wearing an ivory dress and a vibrant smile that was completely fixed on the photographer.

≡≡◄

Exactly as she stood before him now, the white blouse precisely defining the rounded breasts, except there was worry in her eyes.

"Do I look all right?" she asked.

"Wonderful." The Creek Walk photo was still under his left thumb. It seemed like yesterday. He propped the photo album back at the head of the cookies and caressed her hand. "Such good memories! Oh . . ." He looked at the clock. "I need to run and change too."

He hadn't been watching the time. Now, he heard Bennie's pickup in the lane before he even had time to button the denim shirt and comb his hair. He wanted to be back downstairs to guide her impressions, but the first two guests had already entered the kitchen by the back door by the time he bounded down the stairs. He came through the drapes into the warm living room and saw Ruth Ann, the college girl, addressing Anna Mary out in the kitchen.

"Isn't it wonderful, Sister Anna Mary? Isn't God good?" Her arms rose sweetly as she said it and folded around Anna Mary's neck. Anna Mary saw him over Ruth Ann's shoulder and her look signaled alarm.

Rolly pushed past Ruth Ann. He reached for Saul and embraced him, his padded winter jacket bulking him up like an oversized chickadee fluffing itself on the overhead wires in winter. "Like hugging a panda," Saul said, and they guffawed together, feeling again the camaraderie of the week just gone by.

"I'm about as hungry as one," Rolly said, anticipating the cookies in the dry sink.

"Sure," Saul nodded. Rolly took one. He greeted the campers as if he hadn't seen them for years, when it had only been two hours since their cars had parted on the main highway. They stood around the kitchen and out in the washhouse by the doorway, each eating a cookie.

Bennie came through the kitchen door from the washhouse and struck a pose by the kitchen table. He clapped his hands and lifted one leg, bending his head downward in a pose reminiscent of a Hopi dancer, and threw the other arm around Saul's waist. "Hal-le-LU-jah!"

"We're meeting in the living room," Saul said. "Since the stove's there." He nudged Bennie. "Get something started, okay?"

But Bennie had already sniffed the cookies. He drifted across the room and reached down into the dry sink.

"Hey, a cookie man!" He spoke in a falsetto. "Can I . . ." He held up a cookie man.

"Sure."

Bennie bit the head off as he passed into the living room. "Mmmm. Mmmmm."

Anna Mary spoke first when the Snow Campers had all left the kitchen. "They just walked in without knocking," she said to Saul, turning her back to the living room door so she wouldn't be audible. "They just helped themselves to the cookies . . ."

He pulled her toward him, completely out of sight of the living room. "They're family. We've all been together a week. They feel at home with me. Are they for something special?" He gestured to the cookies.

"What do you think?"

She got the small stepstool from above the refrigerator and stood on top of it to reach the empty canisters in the cupboard. Without stopping her steady motion, she moved to the dry sink and made a long hand swoop beneath the cookies, piling them along her arm and funneling them into the canister. "For sewing circle tomorrow."

Strike two. He wanted to slap himself again.

She set the canisters in the cupboard, latched it, and replaced the stepstool on the refrigerator top.

"Come." He tugged her hand and led into the living room, where the Snow Campers had gathered in a large circle, their winter wraps hanging unzipped and unbuttoned. They stood with their eyes closed and hands raised toward the blonde Celotex ceiling tiles while Bennie led out in a sort of tuneless song.

"Oh, glory, glory, Jesus, Holy Ghost, and Father." Bennie mouthed the entire phrase in a high, minor note that didn't change pitch, his face canting toward the ceiling, the light glinting on his baldness. It wasn't loud; it was more like he was singing to himself. Before he reached the end of the phrase, the group all began chanting the same note, or one below or one note above, always returning to it and then repeating the phrase again.

Saul closed his eyes. His doubts vanished, and their praise fell directly onto his heart like ether on a frosty diesel engine, thawing it until it roared to life, the words pouring from it just as they poured now from these people's lips. With his eyes open, he saw their faces and was distracted by thoughts about what each was doing, but with his eyes closed he couldn't distinguish one voice from another. Which voices were theirs? Which might actually be the saints of heaven choraling in his ears?

"Oh, glory, glory." He canted his head backward and sang. *I am singing to Him.* Faintly, he began to hear the cabalistic musical polysyllables: "*O anoramo anayano Jesu . . . abadaba abadaba rahmanama Jesu.*" *I'm glad I don't have my eyes,* Saul thought, *because I'd want to know who.* His voice streamed together with the strange tongue, like the Japanese temples he'd seen, a single pillar of smoke curling skyward from a hundred exhaling incense sticks thrust side by side into the same sand pot. "Glory, glory, Jesus . . ."

No one gave a signal, but the voices began to die off, fading like the peeper frogs in the meadow when he invaded just one patch of it. *How did they all know? At the same time? How do we all know? Isn't there a feeling of One? That we're all One here?*

The voices stopped.

"Oh, wow!" He shook his bones to loosen them and popped both eyes to see friendly mouths and smiling eyes.

Bennie opened his mouth in a giant *O.* "OnnhHoHo! . . . Fantastic!"

"Ohhhhhhh . . ." Rolly's head was thrown back and his eyes were fixed on the overhead light. He was moaning, an incongruous grin on his face.

"Is it a church song?"

Saul's eyes dropped to Anna Mary's face, realizing with a start that she was beside him. For a few minutes he had completely forgotten that. He'd let go of her hand. Simultaneously, he heard Rolly moan again.

"No, it's worship,"

"I never heard *that* before." Her eyes darted across the room, then back, and then across again. He saw them blink shut once and open wide. They were blue, but neither angry nor happy—just blue and wide. Her lower jaw sank open. The eyes remained fixed, unmoving.

"Are you okay?"

"He got the Gift!" Bennie said.

Saul's eyes followed Bennie's glance to see Rolly twitch and go motionless against their outstretched hands. He seemed quite unconscious as they lowered him to the linoleum floor. Except for his eyes. They rolled, and it seemed that the long moan that escaped from his mouth was the cry of his eyes, roving about frantically for a place to hide themselves.

"Convulsions," Anna Mary said. "It's convulsions."

She's taking the same route my mind took Wednesday night. She's probably afraid.

"No, it's not. It's—"

"It's convulsions."

"Anna Mary." Her eyes didn't leave the boy. He had no way of knowing whether she was listening or not, but he went ahead anyway. "It happened at camp, and we were scared. *The devil,* I thought, but the further we went that night, I realized: It's God's Spirit touching him. That's the Sign." She twisted to peer at Rolly, rolling an embroidered silk handkerchief that she had brought out of her cape over and over between her fingers.

"Sends shivers up and down my spine, don't it you?" Bennie said, bobbing and moving continuously as if he were a wind-up top. "Shivers!" He looked up to the ceiling and began to address the group. "Alleluia. Just say 'yes' . . . say it out loud or in your heart. 'Yes! I want the Gift, too.' Yes! Yes!" He bobbed away from Saul and crossed the room to Rolly again, his hands held open upwards at shoulder-height, the fingers widespread. "He's here." Panting, panting. "I can feel Him." All the while he bobbed.

Saul heard Bennie's sharp cry and saw arms extend as he bounced higher. Dancing. Chortling. He saw Anna Mary visibly recoil, and it was through her reaction that he first realized what Bennie had done. Disdain colored her face, and he heard the pattering on the linoleum floor as the singing died abruptly. Bennie examined his fat hand, his skinned knuckles whitish and abraded red in streaks.

"I—" Bennie said.

Saul remembered the four-foot-tall Christmas angels they kept in the cellar in his grade school, where he stumbled upon them once when he was sent down there for punishment. Blackened spider webs and rat dirt sat on their white heads and the top edges of their wings. Only on Bennie, the dirt covered his thick shoulders and bald head.

He stared at the hole in the Celotex ceiling tile where the fist had gone through. "What are you doing? Destroying our house or something?" Everyone quieted and gaped at Bennie.

"I didn't intend to. I—"

Saul grinned. "I'm sure we have some extra tiles in the attic, so . . ."

"Well, King David, he danced too," Ruth Ann said. "Before the Ark, I think it was. His wife despised him for it."

"What do you think, Saul? About the hole?" Saul realized it was Rolly speaking. The boy still stretched stiffly on the floor, his eyes resting shut and no longer convulsive, but rather appearing to sleep-talk. "How about a ceiling full of holes, what would you think of that?"

"Tell him 'no,'" Anna Mary responded. "No, we don't want it, Saul." She put one hand on each of his wrists and pulled him toward her, out of the circle. "This is not God's Spirit. I know what Pop would say. It's mumbo-jumbo."

"We don't want to quench the Spirit," Bennie said. He stood a few feet from them and had been listening to her conversation. "We learned that at Snow Camp. Right, Saul?"

"I think—" Anna Mary looked at the hole in the ceiling. "It's of the devil, I think."

"I wouldn't say that, Sister. Could be the unpardoning . . . not pardonable . . . *What?*" Bennie shook his head in frustration. "The worst sin?"

"The unpardonable sin." Ruth Ann rolled the mellifluous phrase off her tongue.

"Un-pardon-able sin. Saying it's Satan when it's the Holy Spirit. I wouldn't, Sister." He squared off with Anna Mary in the middle of the family room.

"You can't be sure. How do you know?"

"The Spirit told us, in Snow Camp."

"Well, He didn't tell me."

"Maybe you're out of touch with that Spirit. Maybe He's not on talking terms with you."

Anna Mary jerked sharply away from the circle as if she'd touched a hot stove. She wheeled toward Saul, shock written large in her eyes. "Saul, did you hear? He said I'm not a Christian."

"In the last days," Bennie said, "men will turn lukewarm."

"He gets excited and oversteps," Saul said, addressing Anna Mary's back as she marched toward the kitchen. "He didn't say you're not a Christian. He said that some don't hear the Spirit speak in the way we have—"

"Listen!" She spun around. "He did say it! Why do you believe him instead of me? You're defending him. You're not protecting me. I can't deal with it, Saul. In my own home."

Strike three he thought to himself. She began to move in an agitated manner around the kitchen, and he only realized what she wanted when she succeeded in pulling the car keys from his overcoat. "I won't stay," she said, bolting toward the kitchen door. "You don't believe me." She eluded his surprised grab. "I'll get Jakie myself." It was the boy's formal name, the name she used when she wanted to separate herself and the boy from him. She ran through the back door of the house and out on to the shoveled path between the snowdrifts. She had no winter coat.

Saul fumbled right and left for his shoes in the dark washhouse. He stumbled out into the freezing, clear night and saw her ahead of him, not running but fast-walking. He made the mistake of running. His smooth-bottomed oxfords skidded sideways on the iced flagstones, and he pitched face forward into the snow bank.

The snow had a crust, thanks to daytime melting temperatures and freezing temperatures again late each afternoon. The crust slashed the bridge of his nose and his upper lip, and he tasted blood as he rolled himself out, hardened snow chunks falling off his chest. He'd gotten one knee up when the brake lights came on.

"Anna Mary!"

The car engine raced as it backed around. He caught up to it the moment she reached the end of her reverse. "Anna Mary!" He slid into the front of the car, catching the hood ornament and doubling over the hood. "Listen to me!" He waved his free hand and lunged around the car to her window. She was focused straight ahead, not acknowledging him. "It's a huge mistake." He was addressing a closed window. Her darkened face didn't shift gaze to him but continued to scrutinize the lane ahead. He tugged the door handle. She'd locked it.

"Wait'll I get your coat. I'll come along."

The car ground into gear and shot forward. She was either skilled or lucky—she maneuvered by the parked cars in the lane, their shapes clearly visible in the frigid moonlight, only flipping on the headlights as the car squeaked across snow riffles and onto the macadam.

When Saul came back, the Snow Campers had gathered in the kitchen, watching him step up from the washhouse. Bennie was sober. "I made her mad."

"She doesn't understand," Saul said.

"Like we didn't," said Gloria. "What's wrong with your lip?"

"She went to pick up Schnoogie," he said.

"You said you have more tiles. Come look." Bennie led the way back into the family room and pointed at Ruth Ann, who was standing room center on a chair and stretched up to letter around the ragged hole in the Celotex tile with one of Schnoogie's red crayons. Yoder stood below her, a paper with scribbled words in his hands. He'd been reading out the words she was copying.

Ruth Ann's head rested sideways, cramped against the ceiling. "Shall I read it?"

Bennie took the paper from Yoder. "Listen." He read: "'I am very well pleased with this. I am about to bring revival on the earth, such as never was seen.' He's the one said all this." He pointed to Rolly, who was lying still and apparently unconscious on the braided rug.

"Like the prophecy at camp from Acts," Yoder said.

"'Greater than Pentecost,'" Bennie continued. "'I could use—'"

"Not so fast, not so fast," Ruth Ann said as she lettered on the tile.

"Let me read the whole thing to him. 'Greater than Pentecost. I could use a mule to do it.' A mule!" Bennie's head shook with disbelief. "Can you believe? A smelly old mule like us Amish used to use. 'But I've chosen humans. And what you have seen thus far—'"

Where's proof, though? Saul thought. *Where's the scriptural backing? How do we know it's from Him? Wasn't it what we prayed for—the Tuesday Breakfast group? For God to speak to us?*

"'A drop and a half in a 10-quart pail compared to what will come.' He said it," Bennie pointed at Rolly, "while passed out."

The campers clapped wildly.

Ten

THE THREE LEADERS of "the Revival," as they initially referred to it, had been praying in the church anteroom for the upcoming meeting, and Bennie stepped out now to size up the audience. How many could one expect after another week of heavy snows?

"Cyrus." Saul threw an arm around the frail man's shoulders and felt the bone structure beneath his hand. "Cyrus, you understand women."

The old man's eyes skewered him. He wheezed a dry, high-pitched laugh. "I don't know . . . ."

"She's completely shut me out since last Saturday night. Doesn't speak to me. She walks by me. Like I'm a piece of the furniture."

"Understandable." The old man's head bobbled as he rasped out each word with great effort. "Those holes in the ceiling. The Holy Spirit talk. And tongues. Let's hope—let's hope for a better reception tonight."

"No, it was Bennie's comments that upset her—that she's not on talking terms with God. As if she were a pagan."

"Keep a hand on Bennie, you know. He's unstable. Fervent, yes, but unstable." The overhead light shot through the one silver, sparse backcomb of hair and gleamed on the old man's mostly hairless scalp.

"She's not communicating, you say? You want to say more about that?"

"She sets meals out and goes to bed, like I'm the family dog. But here's the worst—" It embarrassed him to admit it. He felt naked from the waist down, a flashback to the shower stalls in his basketball days. Unable to conceal anything. "She won't sleep with me. She's gone to the guest room since Saturday and locks herself in, although it's near freezing in there. At least we have the stove pipe coming up through in our bedroom."

"Calls for great patience, Saul. I've experienced the same—"

"Edith? Edith locked you out?"

"Several times."

He didn't push further. The old man's loss and grief were still too fresh.

"Cyrus! I nearly stove the door in with my foot. I would have, except I was in stocking feet. Cyrus, I was actually swearing—"

"Okay, okay." Cyrus came around. His cool, bony hands cupped Saul's face, holding his chin between them. "Try apologizing to her. But let it go tonight, so you can preach." His hands dropped away.

Bennie pushed through the door from the auditorium, his face glowing. "It's full! Thank You, Jesus! To the walls. They're standing shoulder to shoulder down the outside aisles and around the back."

"Wonderful!" Cyrus said.

"All those rumors brought 'em in. Just like chumming for trout, huh? Did you hear?" Bennie turned to Cyrus. "KMC campus been buzzing all week, the janitor says. 'They punched holes in the ceiling so the demons can escape.' 'Someone spoke Russian in angel language, and he was actually cussing God, unbeknownst.' 'Saul MacNamara's received a top secret report from the FBI on the Russians, the date they'll A-bomb Washington, D.C. and—'"

"Bennie, get a grip."

Bennie's head sagged into his chest. It was fortunate timing, as Bishop Krehbiel was treading up the wooden stairway from the church basement. A moment later he filled the doorway with his rotund presence. His round cheeks rose pink and continuously out of his white collar, which circled precisely one-half inch above his black, top-buttoned, notch-collared coat. Saul noted the likeness between the Bishop's protruding cheeks and the rosy flesh of the mussel that thrust out between its curved, sooty bivalve shell that afternoon of the Creek Walk some years ago with Anna Mary.

"Sorry, men." The Bishop reached for their hands, one by one. "We got halfway up the hill and hit black ice and had to turn back and take the long way. Anyway, it's time, I think." He pulled his watch fob and peered at it. "Saul?"

"I'm ready."

They exited into the auditorium.

Paradise Valley was the flagship church of Bishop Krehbiel's own district, the largest and oldest church and the one he and his family personally attended. Consequently, the Bishop had chosen it when he initiated monthly Sunday night youth gatherings for the district. It was his innovative way of dealing with the post-War surge in extra-curriculars, like songfests, baseball leagues, car rallies, and literary societies, which threatened to splinter the spiritual consensus. He was liberal in what he permitted there—for example, couples might sit together, unlike Sunday mornings when they separated to sit on their respective sides of the church. Even so, the usual attendance for these meetings was only in the 150 range.

It was as Bennie reported. Every bench and seat appeared full, including the front two benches on each side, which usually stayed empty. The long, dark row of coats and hats that stretched across the rear of the auditorium was mostly obscured by standing couples, a line of white shirts and pastel dresses. There had to be at least 350 in attendance . . .

". . . and we're very happy to have him give his report on what the Lord's been up to at this year's Snow Camp," the Bishop said.

Saul hadn't seen her when they came out of the anteroom. Had she come? She certainly wasn't where he most needed her—front row, right *here*, next to his own seat. Her absence was as palpable as a missing molar.

"Brother Saul MacNamara." The Bishop extended his right hand and invited him up.

Saul knew, of course, why he was welcomed to the lectern on the floor below the pulpit, why he wasn't being welcomed up the steps behind the Bishop to the wooden pulpit. He wasn't ordained, he wasn't "official," and the physical symbols of power and God's blessing were not going to be his tonight. *I know it, but tonight,* he thought, *I don't care. If the Spirit shows up, it won't matter.*

He didn't notice the hushing of the auditorium, because he'd found her. She sat five rows back on the church left (the women's side on Sunday mornings), beside her mother, Mom Krehbiel. She'd brought her coat to the seat—the one he'd bought her with the dark, long-haired rabbit collar over black wool—and she slipped it off her shoulders now, pushing it down onto the bench back. Then she turned forward again without making eye contact with him. She seemed far away, perhaps in another decade of his life. Her mother, on the other hand, transfixed him with a steady stare, her withered cheeks and mouth pursed like a persimmon, the navy-blue sleeves with small, pink flowerets crossed over the spot where her long-fallen breasts rested on the bulged stomach that matched the Bishop's own round outline.

Not the time to grieve my own problems, though. I have a story to tell.

"We had this deep sense, all of us on the leadership team," Saul began. "We wanted God to move at Snow Camp. But it was Dan Yoder who suggested we fast until every single soul committed his heart to the Lord. Looked to me like we were all going to lose some weight at this camp."

The titter swept across the back rows, where the youth were most heavily congregated, like a skipping stone rippled a pond.

130

"Sixty-four kids and we had twelve unsaved, and I'm going to show you what happened by inviting up right now our new brother, one of those who made the commitment just ten days ago. Rolly Kurtz! Let's welcome Rolly Kurtz."

Maybe it was all those senior officer presentations he'd applauded in the Army, or maybe it was his training in Toastmasters, but he could never get used to the fact that no one ever clapped in this community. But he did hear the whispers—Rolly had a reputation.

Rolly came from the front right, where the Snow Campers occupied three full benches. They'd been quite noticeable before the meeting opened, enthusiastically hailing incoming Snow Campers as they arrived and exchanging hugs, which had this week become their greeting in a community where a reserved handshake or holy kiss were standard.

Rolly was simply unrecognizable. He'd been to a barber since camp and had his nape hair shingled. In place of the leather jacket and upturned James Dean shirt collar, he wore a plain, white dress shirt, his bulged muscles playing underneath, but buttoned at the wrists and neck. He looked completely housebroken.

Saul welcomed him with an arm over the shoulders. "Speak into the microphone."

"We . . . the whole Snow Camp . . . we did a hymn sing at Pomeroy's. And some gave out tracts. Back at campfire, everyone wanted to tell a story." Rolly usually wore an aura of street cool, but he seemed intimidated in this building, with this audience. "And then things just happened."

Saul waited for more, but it looked like that was all the boy had. He pulled Rolly against his shoulder and leaned into the microphone.

"He's being modest. Yes, everyone wanted to tell a story back at campfire. But what happened instead . . . the Holy Spirit visited us. One young man prayed for his father." He winked at Felipe, who was sitting with the other Snow Campers. "One prayed for a friend—that the Lord would find him. The Lord gave one a testimony in angel language. He gave another a vision of Himself, like Isaiah's vision, high and lifted

131

up, with seraphim crying as they flew: 'Holy, holy, holy!' And He gave one a scripture."

Saul began hunting the passage down in his Bible, looking for the underlining he'd done, so he didn't see the event start, but he did hear the audible gasp and the sharp crack of the wooden benches as numbers of people simultaneously shifted their bodies forward to gawk. He looked and did see one of the camper's outstretched hands above the bench, the fingers wide apart, a pallid face beneath sinking slowly. The camper's head emerged from the side of the bench into open air and thumped down on the carpet runner.

He found the scripture. "Acts 2:17–18. I'll read it then. 'And it shall come to pass in the last days,' saith God . . ."

The Head Usher approached the camper, who by now sprawled on his back on the center aisle carpet runner. He knelt, and then called rather loudly from the boy's side. "Doctor Lehman. Is Doctor Lehman—?"

Saul paused. "It's fine, Brother. No doctors necessary. Listen to the verse. The verse explains what you're seeing: 'I will pour out of my Spirit upon all flesh, and your sons and your daughters shall prophesy.'"

Because he was so focused on the text and working to overcome the little hubbub in the aisle, he didn't see Gloria elevating slowly in the row of Snow Campers. Her hands lifted slowly, and the voice began: "*O Jesus anoramo allelu*—" Her voice modulated to song, a sort of chant, with the words running together. "*AnoramoAlleluAnoramo.*" Her voice rose a fifth on the last "mo" and trilled.

"'And your young men shall see visions,'" he read.

A woman screamed. He looked for the source, because he thought he knew. Yes, it was Anna Mary, both hands clutching a white handkerchief over her mouth now as she stared at her sister.

"We saw it in Snow Camp." He said it specifically to her. "Nothing to be afraid of. When God's Spirit fills us with praise . . ." *Hallelujah! It's happening again. The Holy Spirit is visiting us tonight and*—

This time, it wasn't a Snow Camper. One of the young women at the rear of the church, a KMC student he'd seen somewhere before, was standing with her girlfriends against the row of coats when her knees buckled and cracked on the floor.

"Let me explain what's happening," Saul said. He stepped from behind the lectern, to the left. "The Spirit's here!" He waved his arm across the width of the hall, unexpectedly crashing it into the Bishop's chest. "Oh!" The Bishop had come up swiftly, unannounced, and was now standing next to Saul, his one hand tearing the lectern away from him. For a moment their eyes intersected, 12 inches apart.

"Sit down," the Bishop whispered in a voice audible only to Saul, as his back turned to the audience. "I'll take it from here." Then he faced the crowd. "Let's all stand. Folks, the ushers will take care of anybody having trouble, and—Brother Lester, a song!"

The Bishop came down to Saul in the front row. "The anteroom," he said, whispering again as he motioned for Saul to follow. He led the way around the chorister's back, toward the men's anteroom, as the assembly hymned up:

> Come we that love the Lord,
> And let our joys be known . . .

The Bishop held the anteroom door open, followed through after him, and then closed it behind them. Venetian blinds had been drawn over the large picture window looking out into the auditorium, and once the door was shut, the sound-seal was almost complete. The singing was hardly louder than a murmur.

Saul strode to room-center, the same place where they'd prayed only 45 minutes before. He turned to see the Bishop, his face as unperturbed as always, with his hand still resting on the doorknob behind him.

"What is going on?"

"We've seen it all at Snow Camp, Jacob."

"What is it? I'm trying to figure it out."

"It's God's Spirit. It fills them up and they have to sing—or fall under it."

133

"There's a spirit, I agree. But I don't think His Spirit. God's Spirit doesn't make confusion. Doesn't interrupt. Doesn't force the proclaiming of His message to stop, as just happened out there."

"Can't He do whatever He wants?"

"Chaos? Isn't that what's going on? Satan loves to disrupt. No. I can't let the meeting end like this with no message. No clear takeaway." His bulging, blue eyes fixed on Saul. "What'll we do now?"

"Let me go explain to them."

The Bishop stared back inscrutably. Was he about to agree to that? Saul often wondered about this afterward. Suppose he had. Suppose he'd just accepted what had happened as an extraordinary moment in time when God wanted to say something to his people. Suppose *she* hadn't come in right then. Or suppose the Bishop had exercised his godly authority over his family after she did come in.

Saul never knew, because right then the door pushed wide and the out-thrust jaw and penetrating blue eyes of Mom Krehbiel came through, followed by her heavy, navy-blue body. She back-flung the anteroom door so hard that it rattled against the doorframe. Without moving further in, her left hand still thrust back and gripping the door knob, she held up her right finger and waggled it between the eyes of the Bishop, who had turned to face her as she came through. Her ankle-high-laced shoes were thrust wide, 18 inches apart, in a pugilist's stance.

"What are you waiting for? Do something! It's chaos out there."

"But Brother Lester—" the Bishop said.

"Has sat down. It's chaos. Bennie Fisher is yelling mumbo-jumbo at the ceiling, and people are terrified. *Terrified*!"

Saul approached her. "Mom, let me—"

She turned on him savagely, her jaw working before she spoke. "Don't 'mom' me. Your own wife, Mr. MacNamara, thinks you're a sham. Introducing this holy-roller stuff. Told me more than I ever wanted to know about your business—" She pivoted back into the Bishop's face. "But it's *your* responsibility, Jacob."

"Mom, I can handle this," the Bishop said. "I don't want to quench the Spirit, if He's in it."

"Are you forgetting?" Mom Krehbiel continued, steely-voiced and composed. "Your own sister, Althea, and what happened to her when she went holy-roller. Where's she today? Out of fellowship, out of the family, out of her marriage, in and out of the mental ward. You promised all of us 'never again', and now look. Your daughter's out there babbling. Runs in your family, looks like."

The Bishop stood stiffly, unmoving.

"You want to end up like Cyrus Brubaker? A man nobody respects? A man nobody listens to? I thought not." She released the door handle. "Then be a man, Jacob. Send them all home. Now."

She passed by them on her way to the door at the backside of the anteroom. She didn't look back but exited the anteroom, and they heard the high, dark shoes clopping downward on the wooden steps.

The Bishop looked at him, his face still unperturbed. "I'm going to send them home," he said. "Now."

Eleven

ISN'T THAT A robin?" Saul and Bennie were stepping out of Cyrus Brubaker's solemn Buick, nosed into its niche in the row of 10 identical-looking sedans. The bird hopped on the rotting snow bank under the pyrocanthus bushes that fronted the red-brick Conference executive offices, picking fallen red berries that had sunk into the snow, its feathers fluffed against the cold.

"First sign of spring! It's an omen!" Cyrus beamed cheerfully. Saul looked at him. How old he'd grown in the few months since they first met. His face had gradually turned gray, like plasterboard, and his hair as well, which had fallen away until there was just a tuft glued fast to the plasterboard face, with an indigo vein or two painted on the temples. And he had the trembling hands to match.

Saul did believe in signs. In fact, the threesome had come to the Conference offices today hoping to get one. But just now, as he stood next to the condiment tray in the boardroom and spooned cream and sugar into his coffee, he wasn't sure it was spring they were going to see.

The bishops had driven in that morning from a five-county area to attend their monthly board session. They circled the coffeepots now like a flock of crows before a rainstorm, each outfitted in a black, frock-tailed coat of the type popular 100 years ago, when men rode horse in their suit coats, the tails split up the back to the waist. (And replaced some 50 years ago among the Mennonite rank-and-file by sack coats, except for the ministers and bishops, who wore the frock as a sign of their office.) The afternoon session was set to begin when the threesome walked in, led by Cyrus, who'd been unable to attend the morning session.

"God bless," Cyrus said, kissing Mose Gochenauer, the bishop from the west county and Paxtangville. Mose lifted his unsmiling scowl to Saul.

"You've met, I think?" Cyrus rasped with his half a voicebox, screeching like a cupboard hinge. He swung his hand sideways to rest on Saul's shoulder.

"No." Mose shook Saul's glumly, but he leaned forward to exchange the obligatory holy kiss. "God bless."

Bloodless lips, Saul thought. *Like the man himself.*

Were the stories true that in his youth, at the turn of the century, Mose was wild? That he'd run away to the West to join the cattle drives out of Texas to Abilene, Kansas, riding horseback for days, shooting coyotes? These days, he preached "the Church pure and unspotted by the world." His churches, all 10 of them, waited in fear for communion time, when he took counsel. "Are you at peace with God and man?" "Are you living in accord with the standards of Conference?" Last fall, he'd held back from communion 26 men who had purchased TVs for themselves or for resale in business.

At 70, he was Cyrus Brubaker's peer. They had been ordained bishop the same year, Jake Krehbiel had said. Jake was Saul's source on Conference history. Cyrus, he said, was the Conference visionary. In the '20s and '30s, he'd taught public school while he devoted years of weekends to opening mission churches in Philadelphia. He'd launched the church college in 1936 and started the *Youth Herald,* the periodical for college and high school, publishing inspirational poetry and publicly delivering poems at youth gatherings.

All the while, Mose Gochenauer plodded, grew wealthy with the grocery store he and his brother ran, preached his sermons, and raised his seven children. But these days, it was Mose who was rising—Mose, the assistant moderator. The man hardly seemed 70; his face ruddy, like a rough, red vegetable with fleshy tubercles, maybe a beet. His wooly eyebrows twitched. He told jokes in his quarrelsome voice while studying the floor, and then came up all at once at the punch line, slapping his thigh while his friends chuckled.

Cyrus was frostbitten. How did it happen that *their* bishop, their link to this board, was a withered tomato plant, already blasted by the fall frosts, while the man who would most likely oppose them today, the arch-conservative, greened with energy?

Then there were Mose's friends.

Saul eyed the two bishops pouring coffee and bantering with Sister Hershey, the office manager. Travis Yost's Southern twist on words gave away his Virginia roots. He oversaw the six churches in Paxtang County. B.B. Krehbiel (no relation to the Bishop) was one of the bright lights in the Conference. At 48, he was the youngest member of the board, but both he and Yost had linked their careers to their mentor, Gochenauer. Gochenauer had conducted revival meetings in both of their districts, and B.B. had recently begun to call for the same rigorous application of church discipline that his mentor had so successfully modeled.

"Okay, Brothers!" Jake Krehbiel lowered himself into the armchair at the head of the boardroom table. He dumped several files on its surface, including his oversized and much-used leather Bible. "Can we all find seats? Our guests . . ." He gestured to the two folding chairs placed directly behind Cyrus' chair, indicating that they were in some way connected to Cyrus. The men found the chairs, and Sister Hershey dropped mimeographed agendas in front of each one.

He's included my letter. The Bishop had broadcast the letter last week to the board. Everyone seemed to have a copy, and Saul noted lots of red scribbles and underlinings on Gochenauer's copy.

"Welcome back." Bishop Krehbiel smiled. His smile seemed irrepressible, even in this group of sober captains.

"A special welcome to our guests. Hiding there behind Cyrus—Saul MacNamara! If you haven't heard his testimony at one of his many appearances, be sure to catch it one of these days. And Bennie Fisher, minister at Nazareth."

The Bishop was the equivalent of an Army Major General—after all, he commanded a division 15,000 members strong in this Conference—but he did it with none of the pomp and polish Saul remembered from his father and the U.S. Army. No big cigars. No riding whips. No chauffeur-driven car. No striding entries to standing-room-only applause and salutes. *Yet he commands, and no one doubts it.*

"My son-in-law, by the way. Married to our Anna Mary." Bishop Jake beamed easily. "Well . . ." He sobered. "You've all read Brother Saul's letter, I trust." He rifled through the three-page, typewritten letter. "And so our next agenda item is these meetings they've been holding. I'll quote from our brother's letter: 'The Board may be focused more on symptoms than the problem that caused the symptoms. Our deviation from Conference traditions seems to be viewed as a bigger problem than the reason for the deviation.'

"This is what he writes. So, with your agreement, I've invited Saul and his colleagues, Brother Fisher and Brother Brubaker, so you can directly question them. The 'symptoms,' as he says, are the special, unauthorized meetings they've been conducting every week since early February—about a month; the meetings being led sometimes by our unordained brother, and the meetings featuring activities unusual in the Mennonite Church: tongues speaking, prophecies about future wars, trances, and some healings, apparently." The Bishop was referring to his notes.

"And they have requested—again I'll quote from Brother Saul's letter—'We ask for your blessing to continue our weekly worship services and to do so in a Conference church. We invite all of you to attend, to experience for yourselves the wonderful gift of the Spirit that we are experiencing.' Brother Saul. Maybe you can just stand where you are so everyone sees you clearly."

"We didn't plan this revival," Saul said, rising. "That's an important place to start. None of the teachers—which included myself, Cyrus, and Bennie—none of us spoke in tongues or prophesied before Snow Camp. Correction." He held up his forefinger. "Brother Fisher did have this experience privately. But what happened at the Snow Camp just erupted on its own among the students. We hadn't taught or even discussed such Spirit activities with them—all these signs that we've been talking about. And the signs have continued since we've returned to our own churches and, I understand, in some of your churches.

"We've been meeting weekly at Nazareth during the regularly scheduled prayer meeting time since late January. And truthfully, the experience of worship has been fantastic. In the past, this Conference has tried to evangelize outsiders and keep its youth and, as I hear from Bishop Krehbiel, many of these efforts have gone fruitless. But now the youth flock to our worship meetings." He turned to Bennie. "We had what, how many this week?"

"A hundred and fifteen."

"One hundred fifteen youth at the last meeting, as well as a number of folks from town. Folks not affiliated with any church. The town barbers! Could it be . . ." Saul paused. *Catch their eyes now,* he thought. *Transmit my conviction to them.* "Could it be possible that God is moving today, even as He moved in Acts? Could it be we've entered a new era in which God is personally taking control? Using yielded vessels—ordinary folks like me and you—to make His kingdom a real thing on earth? You've read my letter. Brothers, I didn't share this letter with anyone before I sent it to Bishop Jake last week—not even Brothers Fisher and Brubaker here. I wanted it just to be my heart to your hearts."

Saul stopped and handed the floor back to Bishop Jake. The Bishop's hand covered his mouth, and it was impossible to read him.

"Okay." The Bishop dropped his hand to the tabletop as he studied the faces around the room. "Open forum. Stay standing, if you would."

Saul stood erect, his hands folded behind his back. Oddly, it felt to him like that moment in front of the Commanding Officer at the Pentagon when the Officer read aloud his letter of resignation.

"I was quite struck by *this* in your letter." Bishop Weaver Hess held a copy of the letter in the air, his fingertip on the sentence he intended to pull out, and hawkeyed Saul over the top of the pages. "'The professing church, made up of hundreds of groupings, which includes all denominations, is undergoing a tremendous shaking at the present. What God is doing among Mennonites, He is also doing among Lutherans, Episcopalians, Baptists, Pentecostals. This is Harvest Time!'

"Brothers!" Hess surveyed the table. "This jells with my experience last year as I traveled cross-country and met folks from other denominations on the planes and in large meetings and read their denominational periodicals."

Hess had a quiet way. Bishop Jake had said he interpreted it as his Old Order Mennonite upbringing in a Dutch-language world. Others said it was his tenth grade education. But none of his bishop colleagues had higher education, except for Cyrus and Malcolm Wressler, the KMC principal. So it couldn't be that kind of intimidation.

He was nicknamed "peace warrior" by his friends, as he served on the church's Peace Problems Committee locally and also on the church's umbrella organization, the General Conference, whose committee met biannually in Indiana. In 1940, the year after he became bishop, he'd journeyed by train with a delegation of church leaders to the Capitol and FDR's White House and pled the church's case with the President. "If War comes," he had said, "we're willing to do civilian service. We love the nation, but our conscience before God won't permit us to fight." And the President had thanked them. During the middle of the War, Hess had drafted *The Non-resistant Highway of Life*, a little handbook that was distributed to every draft-age Mennonite boy. His churches in the Tauferville district were in line with Conference discipline, but Jake had said that it was remarkable how easily he moved between the strict Kittochtinny Mennonites and the liberal-dressing Mennonites who ran the broader Church's program for conscientious objectors.

"There's a lot of stirring in the land," Hess said. "People dissatisfied with post-War affluence and materialism and hungry for a real experience with God. You're right, Saul. Not just Mennonites."

So he is a friend. But strong enough to balance three archconservatives?

"Is it the work of God or some other Spirit?" B.B. said, pushing out with his arms and tipping back his chair. "My experience was the Congo, you know. Susan and I were posted there for three years during my civilian public service, Building houses and such for our Mission. We heard a lot about the spirit. There were spirits behind everything. The witch doctor regularly danced himself into a trance and *talked in tongues*—yes, he did! He spoke in tongues, just like we hear of in Acts. And from Saul's people. Then he twisted off a rooster's head and cast his spells with the blood drops. Tongues and trances—these things cut both ways." He slanted toward Gochenauer, who nodded steadily.

"But the results?" Saul countered. "Are the results love, joy, peace— the fruits of the real Spirit? We asked ourselves your question at Snow Camp. Could it be another spirit? Demonic? We'd never seen such stuff. But then we saw the love! A boy interceding with the Lord on behalf of his dad. Another one for his best friend. The joy of one girl who'd been under psychiatric care. The Holy Spirit is just using odd tactics to get our attention! And He's definitely got mine!" He grinned.

"Brother Cyrus?" Bishop Jake said. Saul sat down to yield the floor, knowing that Cyrus could shape the discussion in ways the board was used to hearing.

Cyrus spoke from his seat. "As Saul writes in his letter, 'Why don't we fall on our knees and weep over the evident spiritual decline and progress of apostasy?' This was my concern at KMC!" He shook his fist, and it seemed humorous. A frail man shaking his fist. "The lack of heart religion among the students. The need for Holy Spirit power."

The men all knew the KMC story, and Saul had heard the story from Jake. Cyrus Brubaker, the architect and founder of the church's college in the '30s, had defended the church standard of non-conformed dress in his bishop district and at the school throughout his years as principal. He had defended it through the War years and into the beginning of the prosperity. The 1950s had brought a crop of students who had one eye on American culture in the magazines, on the radio, and out on the streets, where their money was as good as the next guy's. Non-conformed to what? To their own generation flooding the schools, the markets, the radio waves? Boys showed up in school with GI haircuts, rolled-up short sleeves like James Dean, and two-tone coupes. Girls wore smaller and smaller prayer coverings, hummed Frank Sinatra tunes, and appeared at school outings in capeless dresses. Rumor had it there was bebop dancing and alcohol at some home parties.

Cyrus called the whole school together in the chapel one morning in the spring of '52 and announced a policy of zero-tolerance for rule-breaking. Expulsion for the violators. The scuttlebutt after the session among faculty and students was that he only cared about one thing: appearances and his own conservative beliefs. Cyrus retreated to his quiet garden in the county and spent two days in bed, weeping. Three weeks later, his daughter reported that he had suffered a nervous breakdown. He didn't return to school, turning over the precious principal role and school he'd created out of a dream to a man with a spine of iron, Malcolm Wressler.

To add more tears to his life, his district of six churches now began a similar journey of dissent. Fifty members of Hertzler's church had protested his strict discipline and asked the board to provide them with a new bishop. The board responded by putting that church under the oversight of Weaver Hess. But Cyrus's sorrows kept increasing. He developed thyroid cancer, and the doctors removed half of his voicebox. That same winter, his wife of 40 years collapsed with heart failure and died. A year later when he began to see the widow of Bishop Gingerich, a former colleague of his and Gochenauer's, his eldest daughter announced that she wouldn't bring her family to any occasion where the widow might appear. Rather than antagonize his daughter, he broke off the relationship. Brubaker was a beaten man. No one knew it better than Mose Gochenauer, his rival.

"I thank God for this outbreak of His Spirit," Cyrus croaked. He wrestled with the words, as if constructing each one in his throat before he offered it on his tongue. "And I pray that my bishop brothers will see the goodness of it—and give their blessing."

The room buttoned up. Several of the bishops were taking notes. Malcolm Wressler cleared his throat.

Why didn't I think of him? Saul thought. *Clearly, he's the swing vote.* If Hess and Brubaker were for them and Mose and his two lieutenants were against them, Malcolm might provide the balancing vote. And Bishop Jake? He would smell the tide and vote the way that kept unity. For the first time, Saul began to see an outcome of victory.

"Bishop Malcolm?" the Bishop said.

"You ask us to overlook 'the symptoms,' as you call tongues, trances, preaching by a non-ordained man, and unauthorized meetings," Malcolm propped his long, articulate arms and hands on the table in front of him, making a teepee with his fingertips, "and to focus on the problem instead. Now, Brother Cyrus and I, who have both worked closely with the KMC students, identify with that kind of language. Brother Cyrus and I both see the lack of spirituality among our students, and even in some of our teachers."

He winced. Was Malcolm targeting him with that comment?

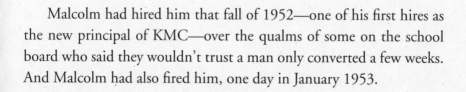

Malcolm had hired him that fall of 1952—one of his first hires as the new principal of KMC—over the qualms of some on the school board who said they wouldn't trust a man only converted a few weeks. And Malcolm had also fired him, one day in January 1953.

"You have a problem," he had said in his characteristically blunt manner. Saul stood before him in the principal's office in his new Mennonite suit, his tired leather satchel slouched against his knee. He'd found the note in the faculty mailbox. *See me immediately. Miss first period if necessary.* "Do you know what I'm speaking about?"

"Yes. Anna Mary is pregnant."

"So there was sinful activity—outside of wedlock. Do you admit it? Are you the father?"

How had he found out? He and Anna Mary had only told Bishop Jake the night before. Was there an early morning phone call?

"I am."

Malcolm stood and stretched out his open hand. "I'm sorry, Saul. You've been a fine teacher. Loved. Admired. But we can't have a faculty member caught in the very things we're trying to prevent among students."

"Yessir." He saluted Malcolm as he would have done his commanding officer, a knee-jerk reaction, and then whipped around and left to empty out his desk in his classroom.

It would have been better to go to him with the confession rather than have it dragged backwards out of the hole of his soul like a putrid rat in a trap. But . . . could there be no forgiveness? He knew the teaching on premarital sex, even as a five-month-old believer. But should he lose his job and all of his church responsibilities over an unfortunate error of judgment? After an abject public confession in the council room?

"Nevertheless." Malcolm raised one finger out of the teepee and shook it at Saul.

Nevertheless. He'd heard the logician's word repeatedly when they debated McCarthy and the House Un-American Activities Committee that fall in the faculty lounge. "Nevertheless, even if communism is widespread in this country, is it right to destroy a man's writing career by banning his books forever from publication? Just because he once attended a communist rally?" Malcolm would say. He'd seen the just side of the man. Would the just side fight for them today?

"Nevertheless, what is this 'second blessing'? Or just call it tongues, trances, prophecies. What's all the emotion for? Are we still Christians if we don't do that stuff?"

Saul stood again. "It's joy. Purely joy." A good answer, yes, but he felt the first droplets of sweat fall out of his armpit and trickle coldly, one by one, across his ribs.

"Joy?" Bishop Jake said.

"We didn't plan to do any of what you call 'emotional stuff.' But when the Holy Spirit fell, it just happened."

"'A gift,' you said earlier." Malcolm's eyes continued to drill him through the rimless glasses. "The 'gift of the Spirit.' Now, we believe—the Mennonite Church, I'm speaking of—that all believers get the Holy Spirit. But it seems you're talking about some special bonus deal. Kind of like gasoline." Malcolm smirked, savoring his analogy. "Some cars take the 87 octane, some get the 91. Two classes of Christians, if you will." Malcolm folded his arms and waited.

Bennie bounded to his feet, interrupting Saul's thoughts, and crowded against him in the chairs behind Cyrus. "It's a gift, all right. Acts 2:17–18: 'In the last days, I will pour out of my Spirit on all flesh; your sons and your daughters shall prophecy.' As Saul says in his letter," he hoisted the pages of the letter in one hand, rattling them in his shaking fist, and read, "'Harvest time in the professing church means threshing time. Threshing is a painful process, but necessary. The chaff must be removed in order for the pure kernels of grain to be revealed.'" He sat down and glowered at Malcolm.

Mose Gochenauer clambered arthritically to his feet. "Threshing? Is that what this is about? There's an uproar in our district. People telling other people they're not saved. They haven't been filled with the Spirit."

"That would be a misunderstanding," Saul said. "As Malcolm put it: 'All believers have the Spirit.' He used the example of gasoline. I prefer the image of your furnace. All have the pilot light of the Spirit burning, but pilot lights don't warm a house. It's when the thermostat calls for heat that gas flows down the tube and Hwooosh! The house gets toasty. We believe that thermostat is a Christian saying: 'God! I want all you got for me! I'm not content as a pilot light. Pour on the gas!'"

"A good answer," Malcolm said from his seat. "Helpful, really. Thought-provoking." He rolled his head side to side as if sloshing the answer in there to taste it, like a swallow of an old, rare wine. "Might be the best I've ever heard it explained."

Gochenauer stayed on his feet throughout the exchange. He'd been leaning his arms forward on his chair, but now he straightened. "Maybe it's an answer. Maybe not. But we had Sadie Miller get oil smeared on her forehead in the shape of a cross and announced 'HEALED' at one of your worships. Then she wouldn't take her diabetes pills anymore and had a fainting spell, till they got the insulin in her. Now, who put that oil on her and said 'HEALED'?"

Bennie lifted his hand.

"She's in my district. She's my sheep." Gochenauer's face grew even redder, his wooly eyebrows tilted like angry white caterpillars squaring off. "Who's your bishop?"

"I am." Cyrus said.

"Then you're responsible." Gochenauer glared. "'Sheep-stealing,' we always called it. And it's GOT TO BE STOPPED." He dropped into his chair.

"Wait," Malcolm said, holding up a hand decisively in Gochenauer's direction, like a traffic cop's. "Abuses happen in any ministry. People misunderstand things. I want to hear this brother out. In this letter, you said that God called you. Let me read it: 'True God-called servants will

instruct their people to fervently seek to know God intimately—to learn
to know His voice. He still speaks to us in a still small voice.'

"The Bible says as much about God's voice," Malcolm continued.
"But hearing His voice is one thing. 'True God-called servants' suggests
someone might see himself as called and arrogate to himself the role of
leader, preacher, pastor, outside of the route of the lot that our Conference
says is the only way leaders are called, in our Church. Will God bypass
the Church in this new era of the Spirit you're talking of?"

"Not necessarily," Saul said. He had stood throughout the interchange
with Malcolm and Mose. "But He will sift. He's sifting the professing
Church. Ours is an age of apostasy. Are you a true child of His, or are
you just going through the motions? Has He called you? Is the lot clear
proof of a call?" Saul knew he was on hazardous ground with this; the
cardinal doctrine of Kittochtinny leadership was at issue here. But one
could raise this question, surely. "Does God speak to you?"

"You're asking me, personally?" Malcolm struck his chest with his
open palm.

"I'm asking everyone. But, yes, you too."

Malcolm's ears and face flushed red. *I know the omen,* Saul thought.
Have seen it in faculty meetings. As if he's taken a hit.

Malcolm unfolded upward out of his chair and leaned forward, his
arms extended down to the table. He drilled Saul with his eyes, his voice
pitiless, "Would God bypass His Church to speak through a man who
should have repented publicly long ago of fornication?" He fell back.

The men stirred noisily, and Saul noted Gochenauer's leer before
he spoke. "I did!" he shouted, and then sank down into his chair. "I
told Bishop Hess in the counsel room! April 5, 1953." He was sweating
profusely. His underarms had developed large, dark ellipses.

"That's it!" Bishop Jake said, slapping the tabletop with both hands.
"That's enough."

"We should pray." Hess stood up, speaking in his low-key voice.

"Yes." Bishop Jake stood up.

Saul pinched his eyes shut against his nose with his fingertips and felt Cyrus' fragile hand on top of his free hand. The room went uncomfortably quiet.

When did I first recognize it? The sniffle of a cat? A small, sharp sucking of air, then a guttural "mmmph." Someone talking? No, more sharp sniffs, and now a large breath and moan. Weeping, for sure.

He kept his eyes closed.

Then he felt the hand on his shoulder, trembling. It fumbled across the top of his back as he sat there, and now it cradled his face and drew him back against its owner's chest. Even in his dress clothes and scrubbed down, it was impossible to scour out the sweet smell of fermented silage on the fingers that wrapped up around his cheek. *It's him, Bishop Jake, weeping for me.*

"I let it go on too long." The Bishop was whispering.

"No, you didn't."

"I did. Things were said that shouldn't—"

"He took it as a personal attack. I'm responsible."

The Bishop stopped whispering, though he still breathed in jerks. Saul saw Malcolm enter the space behind the next chair and go down into a crouch.

"Saul," he stage-whispered. His hand stretched out and grasped Saul's knee, and then Saul intertwined his fingers with the man's. They spoke simultaneously.

"I didn't mean the question as an attack. I'm sorry."

"Forgive me, Brother. I was absolutely inappropriate."

The Bishop stood paternally over both of them, one hand clutching Saul's face against his chest, the other hand on Malcolm's head. Then he began to sing out loudly, as jolting as the school buzzer going off in Saul's ear:

> Blest be the tie that binds,
> Our hearts in Christian love—

On cue, the men all joined in, and because they were skilled a capella singers—with 50 years average experience working their parts—it was as beautiful as a men's chorale. *Except this,* thought Saul, *the musical harmony completely clashes with the disharmony of our hearts.*

Afterward, outside in the March afternoon dank with the smell of rotting snow, Saul and Bennie walked to the diner next door to the Conference offices to wait for Cyrus, their ride home. Bennie spoke first. "You think we won?"

"No. They spent the whole time on the symptoms, not the problem. Some of the bishops feel threatened, Bennie, threatened by revival. So much for the good omen of our first robin."

Cyrus confirmed it 20 minutes later, when the voting was finished and the meeting adjourned. The three sat in their Sunday suits in the diner while the pony-tailed blonde in a poodle skirt, falsies, and thick, red lipstick smiled brightly and took their orders for coffee.

"*No* to our meeting in a Conference church house," Cyrus said. "*No* to the baptism of the Spirit. *No* to the gifts of the Spirit. *No* to you preaching."

"We're ruined." Bennie shook his head.

"We'll go back to meeting in homes," Saul said. "No human can stop the march of God's Spirit."

"How 'bout a tent?" Bennie lifted both hands, his callused fingers spread wide. "Like Billy Graham did in Los Angeles?"

Part Four

Riding on the Sun

August 14–20, 1956

Twelve

"*C*HI SON? CHI son? Son un poeta.*" (*Who am I? Who am I? I am a poet.*)

Wolfgang Landis sang it in magnificent baritone to the image of himself, waist up, in the three-by-five ornamental mirror that hung on the west wall. Evening sunshine filtered through the canopy of sycamores by the river that bisected the outlying areas of the KMC Campus. It mottled the inside of his mobile home with bright, moving shapes, shooting quick beams and stabs that lit up the room, the top of his hair, and his throat.

The nose prominent, he observed, beneath a forehead that the Julliard arts reporter had labeled a "noble brow." Deep-troughed waves the hue of the fall sumac leaves—more burnt orange than red. Languid eyes with the always-drooping lid on the left. He blazed a smile and missed the accent that the raking mustache had added during his Julliard days. He'd shaved it. Mustaches were *ganz verboten* in Menno-Land.

The mirror caught his image all the way to the belt, and he moved his shoulders easily in the "taverna" shirt, a present from Mother, incredibly. *She never let the Mennonite thing shut down her style.* Unlike shirts in the Sears catalogue, which cut to fit a man's shape, the taverna was Southern

Europe's answer to blistering, August afternoons in the sun—a loose-cut linen that belled at the shoulders, poofed in the sleeves, and bloused over the chest to let hot Mediterranean winds circulate through. He laced it up with dyed-black leather cords at the cuffs and the throat that were cut low over the breastbone to let a man's chest hair push through the crisscross lacing.

He'd memorized the pithy lines of the first review ever in his singing career, and he recited them now to the face in the mirror. "Landis bends all of his magnetic personality to the role of Marcello. That the whole cast is young and ravishing adds to the drama, for this is a tale of young lovers and a tragedy of untimely demise."

Ah, La Bohème*! Thank God for Giacomo Puccini!*

Reflected in the mirror, over the shoulder of that shirt, he saw the ranked photo frames hanging on the far wall of the trailer. He about-faced to study them. Chorale, 1953; senior chorus, 1954; junior chorus, 1954; chorale, 1954; and more of the same from 1955. Each framed picture was chock-a-block with fingernail-sized heads and regulation Mennonite dress, with he himself, the director in each picture, front and center in different Mennonite coats. The photos were all monochromatic, but he remembered the suit coats he'd worn: the navy blue of his first year on staff; the brown one of this last year.

Wolf pulled the heavy disk out of its cardboard cover with the monochromatic photo of the chorale. He dropped it over the spindle and lowered the needle. The player sent out the "live needle" sound as the disk whirled 78 revolutions a minute, and shortly the song began:

> And the glory
> The glory of the Lord . . .

Yes, we do sound good, and I owe the whole idea to Father, Wolf thought. His father had known his son was ready to fly this community when Mother passed. Wolf had already been accepted at Julliard, and Mother had squirreled away every penny of his tuition from 20 years of teaching piano and voice. However, Father controlled, the bank account—even when the son turned 21. "I want you to stay connected with the Church," he had said.

As the Conference missionary to the D.C. churches, it might be expected that the old man was fanatic about religious stuff. Dogmatic about the boy attending a church college. But they worked out a compromise. Wolf could attend a secular school like Julliard if he spent his summers doing church work. Specifically, he would put together a musical group to give purpose to restless young people after the recent war, which had become a major concern of the Bishop Board. Father released the money for him to attend Julliard.

Neither he nor Wolf was prepared for what followed. When Wolf ran auditions at KMC, almost 100 young people applied for the 20 available slots. The Landis family name and credentials, in addition to his Mennonite coat, pried open the minds of leader types who might otherwise have said no to public performances. When they watched their daughters and sons singing beautiful music—great hymns of the Church and the soaring classical oratorio choruses from *The Messiah*—they immediately accepted the chorale and Wolf.

The year Wolf graduated from Julliard, the KMC principal, Malcolm Wressler, hired him to open a music program at KMC in the Fall. In '54 and '55, in addition to keeping up the KMC chorale singers, he organized junior and senior choirs and taught music theory and music appreciation. During the winter of '54 they cut the first record, following it up with national tours in the summers of '55 and '56 and an early discussion of a tour to Europe in the summer of '57. Father was happy. And Wolf—could an artist thrive in the sober, circumscribed, and bourgeois community of Mennonites? It appeared so.

Then along came Musetta.

He scanned the set of photos for her. Yes, there she was, a tiny face in the rows of the junior chorus, 1954. But she didn't stand out. Chorale, 1955. There were fewer members in the photo, and now she was quite visible, especially in her assigned position as anchor on the riser.

Like the screech-owl,
She's a bird of prey.
Her favorite food
Is the heart . . . she devours them.
And so I have no heart.

He'd replaced the KMC chorale "Favorites of the Church" on the victrola with another disk, the second of the *La Bohème* set, the one introducing Musetta.

Quando men' vo soletta
per la via,
La gente sosta e mira
E la belleza mia . . .

As I walk high
Along the streets,
The people stop to look and
Inspect my beauty.

He admired Rodolfo and Mimi, but both on stage as Marcello and in real life he got Musetta, the vixen.

He shut down the victrola, closed the Venetians, and went to the sink, where the bouquet of long-stemmed roses had been watering all afternoon since he'd picked them up at the Red Steer. They were velvety and dimpled, like her red lips. He wrapped them in butcher paper and rubber-banded the bottoms to hold in the moisture.

The Volkswagen sat under the sycamore, the top still open from his earlier ride to the market. He drew the rose bouquet across the hood, the crimson blooms clashing wonderfully with the robin-egg blue, and dropped them through the open top onto the passenger's seat. He slid in, retrieved the Old Spice bottle from the glove box, and sprayed his palm, wiping his throat and the backs of his ears. He popped a peppermint Life-Saver.

The sun had been swallowed by an armada of nimbus clouds, and the building wind smelled of ozone and moisture. Sycamore leaves whirled ahead of the car in wind dervishes. *What do we do if it rains? Picnic in the car, I guess. Or in a covered bridge, if we can find one not much traveled. A memorable spot for a night to be remembered: August 14, 1956. The night she says "yes, I'll be your wife."*

He was driving down the highway now, pointing east toward the Bishop's farm. The VW acted like one of those airplane autopilots, remembering the route from daily trips, although most of them he had taken were for business as he performed his summer job at the Krehbiel farm.

The Mennonites' initial enthusiasm for public concerts had cooled. Father was certain he knew the source of the problem. "If you'd act with some Christian humility, instead of strutting—"

"Strutting? Whaddya mean? Who says I strut?"

"Wolfgang. When you come out on stage, it appears to me you're performing."

"We *are* performing. We're producing a concert."

"*You, I mean.* Marching to and fro on the stage, telling us the lives of the composers. People come to all-Conference get-togethers to worship, not to hear stories of adulterous men's lives. Lots of those composers weren't Christians. Mendelssohn, for example."

"If the man's music has a godly theme—"

"And the composer's a unrepentant sinner?"

"Then what?"

"Then we don't want to hear his music. He has nothing to say to God's people."

"Mother never made a litmus test like that—"

"Mother was wrong, frankly."

Wolf walked out of the house. He would not tolerate the man's criticism of Mother. His own wife, and dead, for God's sake. Where was the respect?

$$\Longrightarrow\Longleftarrow$$

He entered the gate at the Bishop's house and closed it behind him to keep the geese in the outer yard. He crossed the summer porch and opened the house door, just as Gloria had said he should. "We never knock."

Mrs. Krehbiel, however, looked as if she didn't have the same opinion about knocking and, as he'd noted recently, seemed to be one of those in the Conference who had cooled off toward him.

She turned from the stove. Her gray, ankle-length skirts and blue gingham apron swished as she crossed the room toward him. She didn't smile but stopped, heavily, and squared off with him, her feet apart like a wrestling opponent. She sneered at his chest; apparently she loathed the taverna shirt. She reviewed the roses and sniffed sharply.

Uh! The cologne, of course.

"Sit down. I'll tell her you're here." She passed by to the stairwell at the end of the kitchen, opened the door, and yelled, "Your friend is here!" There was no response. The door banged shut. "Make yourself at home." She gestured to the magazines that hung, upside down, over a wire stretched along the entire length of the kitchen table and flush to the wall. Mennonite newspapers, plus a couple issues of *Pennsylvania Game News,* and one of the *Farm Journal.* He retrieved the *Game News.* "She'll be right down," Mrs. Krehbiel said, moving into the next room. Her words floated back as she left, determinedly. "I'm shutting up some windows in the brooder house; 'pears we have a storm brewing." She disappeared through the house and exited by way of the front porch.

He heard steps. The staircase door opened outward, and there she stood. He drank her in. Even her feet seemed worthy of remarking. She wore tennis shoes—for the picnic, of course—but her feet seemed to be part of a package that included rounded and delicious calves, a flared periwinkle flowered skirt that surged forward even after she'd stopped, masses of dark hair unseen behind the white-bloused back but frisking at the beltline, and an immaculate, organdy prayer covering perched on top in the manner gaining popularity among Conference young women on outings (but certainly never permitted in school or church, when every lock had to be tucked into the knot behind). The flashing silver of her braces and the moving shape of her breasts all signaled to him, waving like friendly hands.

He leaped to his feet.

"My Musetta."

"They call me Musetta, I don't know why," she said, paraphrasing one of Mimi's *Bohème* lines. She'd been part of the group of students whom he'd driven to New York to see the new Julliard production of the opera. She descended the last two steps.

"Will it rain?" she asked, smiling cheerfully. That was it for greeting. He was used to it. His own father was the same. He suppressed his desire to seize her shoulders and ply her mouth with kisses.

"For me?" She touched the roses on the table behind him.

Wolf made a swooping pirouette with the flowers. He felt the "I love you" words rising but suppressed them for a better time. "Who but you, my best friend!"

"Let me put them in water."

She busied herself, placing the flowers in a milk pitcher since they didn't have a regular flower vase, and then found the picnic basket. She'd obviously worked on it earlier. A red gingham cloth covered the out-of-sight food. "It's heavy, Wolf. Can you carry it?"

"Of course."

They retraced his earlier trip, back out the stone path through the lawn. He held her hand with his right, the basket with his left.

"Where are we going?"

He squinted up through the catalpa at the moving thunderheads. "I'm recalculating. Maybe Stone Quarry Bridge."

"A covered bridge! How delightful! Oh . . . . I need to stop by the tent. I promised Saul—"

"Hmmphh!" He glared as he opened the car door.

"Only a couple minutes." She seemed not to notice his look.

He remembered his problem again. The Revivalists. They'd set up a tent in Bennie Fisher's field and had been holding meetings there every Wednesday evening and weekend since the beginning of June. And Gloria had been attending, to his chagrin. He bit off the satirical and angry words that surged up and demanded to be spoken. Only a couple minutes, she'd said.

They drove west to the 689 intersection in silence.

In the field next to the highway, teenagers wearing identical yellow "Noah Krehbiel Meats" caps and shirt breast ribbons directed cars into lines behind the brown canvas tent. Wolf pulled off the highway and drove into the harvested alfalfa field, the entry facilitated by several tons of gravel that had been dumped there and raked out to make the transition from macadam road to the field uneventful. The field was level, and by close packing them, the teenagers could bunch 500 vehicles (mostly black—the giveaway that it was a Mennonite gathering) into perfectly straight lines that had been marked off with the little lime spreaders used on athletic fields. Only a few cars were ahead in the queue looking to park, indicating they were very late for the meeting, which had started at 6:30.

Wolf parked the car. "Shall I come along?"

"Up to you. It's something personal, but you can stick your head in the tent. They're singing, I think."

He came around the front of the car to her door and caught her hand. He paused for a moment, and then on second thought, he scrambled back into the VW to crank the roof vent shut. A few large drops were splattering loudly on the windshield. She had run ahead to the tent, where the sides were rolled up all around to let the welcome breeze run through as it pleased. She motioned for him to follow. He dashed, even though the drops were still intermittent.

Inside the tent, he grabbed her hand again. The artificial darkness inside was lit by six large floodlights that hung like luminescent coconuts on each pole, just below the spot where the pole tip rammed the tent top upward. The lights and poles were moving slightly in the wind. Was it possible that the whole thing might collapse and smother them all? That would solve the Bishop Board's problem with the Revivalists!

His ears adjusted to the sound. It was like nothing he had ever heard before. Chirping in high monotones. *A woods full of small birds? An abbey full of monks, chanting Gregorian hymns? Once in college, we took a trip to a monastery . . .*

"On the third verse," the preacher said, interrupting the chirping. "Hold the note at the end and praise Him. Come before the Throne! Sing in whatever language the Spirit gives you." He in-breathed, and the sound was amplified. "And be conscious that you're standing with angels and archangels. You're with martyrs and the saints gone before. With Abraham, Isaac, and Jacob. You're with the four-and-twenty elders," the preacher's voice rose now, "written of in the Revelation, who toss their crowns before the Throne—" The preacher gulped to catch his breath and then threw his arms up in a large *V*. "Endlessly! And with the four praising beasts. One like a lion. One a calf's face. One the visage of a man. One a soaring eagle, the Revelator says, full of eyes about and within. They, too, are praising. Sing, people of God!"

Wolf saw someone stretching up. *What, a set of cymbals? In a Mennonite gathering, where only pitch pipes are permitted and all other music makers forbidden because they cause . . . what? Pride in the players' skills? Yes, cymbals! I love it!*

The preacher swept the group together, and the wave of punctuated climax over the sound boxes that hung on every pole seemed to lift the collective energy. Wolf noted how that served to send the pitch higher, against the natural downward gravity fall that all songs go through when untrained groupings of people sing. They resumed the song:

163

O that with yonder sacred throng,
We at His feet may fall . . . .

Wolf eyed her sideways. "Do you feel happy?" he asked.

Gloria's eyes were wide, blue pools of wonder, as if she'd just flown around the tent several times and landed on her feet right beside him. He patted her cheek. "You have belief all over your face, you know? I like it."

"You're making fun?"

"I'm not."

"I'll be back." She touched his arm. He watched her travel the length of the tent.

Why make fun? There was nothing new here. Trances, babbling in exotic syllables, visions, hypnosis. The lamas in Tibet did it. Some Indian tribes as well. The Delaware, wasn't it? Sent their boys into the mountains on their twelfth birthday. A rugged civilization, not like America's effete youth. And those boys starved in the snowy hilltops, stone piles, and unsympathetic woods and ate spiked mushrooms until they saw things. "*Minne-wawa!*" said the pine trees. "*Mudway-aushka!*" said the water. The Great Spirit himself, with a message. They went up the hill boys and came down men. Now some Mennonites believed they'd discovered spiritual fire, much like the first cave men in history.

Gloria skirted the rows of empty chairs, empty because people were standing, their hands and long, skinny bodies stretched out as if to grasp the ceiling of the tent and pull down for themselves handfuls of whatever holiness dwelt there. She disappeared behind the stage.

"Have a good seat about 10 rows up, outside section," the teenage usher whispered as he crouched, his eyes only a few inches away.

"I'm fine here." Wolf hunkered in the sawdust that covered the tent floor and smelled its freshness.

"*La Donna e mobile,*" he thought. *The Duke of Mantua had it right. Fickle woman, flighty as a feather.*

164

Thirteen

AM I GLOWING? Saul put his hands to his cheeks. *Heated, for sure.* Preaching always depleted him, but tonight the warmth spread upward from his gut, like the contented digestive process after hot scrapple and eggs on a very frosty morning. The warmth spread upward and filled his skull. The Old Testament lay open on the bench beside him, but that wasn't the focus. He watched the ceiling of the tent skipping up and down on the light pole with the coming thunderstorm.

Footsteps. I hear them again out there in the grass beyond the tent. Tent flaps shut off access on both sides of the stage and were sewn to the rear wall of the tent, which circled 15 feet beyond, to form a large "counseling room," as they called it. Usually, the outer wall flaps were tied up head-high to keep the air circulating on these hot August nights, but the ushers had just unrolled them to within a foot of the ground because of the coming rain, already pinging the canvas sides.

"Come in!" Saul called.

Can they—whomever it is—hear me? A summer thunderstorm for sure, and the singing from the main tent. . . . He crossed to the flap and lifted it. Against the darkening sky, the backlit face was barely readable. "Gloria!

Come in." She peered in but didn't enter. "Is everything okay?" He stepped out. "Something wrong?" She shook her head affirmatively.

"Come in." He urged her shoulder with his hand to indicate that she should go ahead. Finally, he went first, reaching for a folded chair and glancing back as he unfolded it. She hadn't moved through the opening of the doorway.

"You're glowing." She stepped in now and dropped the flap behind her.

"I am?" His hands clapped his face. It was still warm. "So are you." Her face seemed wonderstruck, especially her eyes, he thought—the expression of some childless women seeing a baby in a new mother's arms. *The Remnant? Is it a sign of the Remnant?* He felt goosebumps. *Is it possible? That the true believers are already changing into the likeness of the resurrected Christ?* Images from the John the Revelator flashed in his mind—the resurrected Christ with a face like lightning, eyes like glowing lanterns. "This corruptible shall be made incorruptible." God's Spirit, like a medieval alchemist, transmogrifying their lead bodies and faces into gold. *Our faces already glowing . . .* "Praise God!"

"It's like you're holy . . . and the room is holy." She flung out her hands to indicate the entire counseling room. "Like God is here."

"He *is!* Of course He is." *Lovely!* He noted the uncut hair that hung to her waist, the pleated, white prayer cap on top, the light glinting off the silver braces on the teeth of wet pearl. Even the braces seemed lovely. "Sit down, Sister."

As he held her gaze, she crossed the room with her hands folded in front and sat down that way, all the time watching him like a small child. *Is something wrong?*

The flash jolted them both. It flared through the hole around the light pole in the peak of the tent, and immediately the thunderclap assaulted them like an out-of-control P.A. system. The bulbs overhead blinked once and then went back on. Bennie's voice over the amplifying box in the corner shouted to compensate for the thunder and crackling sound system.

"There's your rams' horns and trumpets! All God's children need to do is the marching and *POW* on Jericho. Let's march! I mean everybody. I want to see all the people—" His trampling boots began a rhythm across the stage.

The honky-tonk of the piano ramped, and Bennie's voice and clapping led out. Apparently, his shirt sleeves were brushing the microphone. It fuzzed.

> I feel like travellin' on,
> I feel like travellin' on,
> This world below is not my home—

"Did Wolf bring you?"

Gloria dropped her eyes, her mouth pinched as if she was about to cry. "It's Wolf!"

"Something's wrong?" She had a Madonna-like quality about her. The mystery of womanness—vulnerable and fertile. Seductive yet faraway. *I only dare to touch my hand to her shoulder because she's family.*

"He's going to ask me to marry him." Large eyes, Carolina blue, like her father's, fixed on him.

There was another brilliant flash and almost instantaneously a thunder clap directly overhead. *What is Anna Mary doing right now? Is Schnoogie already in bed? Removing the screens, probably, and dropping the windows because of the storm. Or has she gone to bed herself? Her bed? Is she locking herself in behind the guestroom door even now?* He removed his hand from Gloria's shoulder. The shoulder had been soft and blood-warm, and when he took his hand away, it lost heat and seemed much cooler than the other hand. "Go on."

"I can't, Saul. I'm so miserable." Even when she said "I'm miserable" she seemed attractive. "I tried to write it to him, but I couldn't. I tore it up. Three separate times. I tried phoning, but I couldn't."

"Why can't you marry him? If he proposes honorably . . ." *What's that now? Rain! Let there be rain. Everything so fresh and full of God's touch tonight!*

"My spiritual life has been downhill ever since—since I don't know when. There's so much we can't talk about. We—" She hesitated. "We do the things all couples do. Nothing impure. Maybe he wants to—I mean, he believes differently about certain things we were always taught. But that's got nothing to do with why I can't—. It sounds confusing and dumb, huh?"

He dissented, shaking his head.

"It doesn't?"

"No."

"Do you think we should get married?"

"Gloria, I don't really know Wolf."

"But at Snow Camp, I felt so near to God!" Her small hands and her perfectly oval, smooth—even creamy—face grew animated. "The morning after the all-night meeting was the most fantastic . . . but that's the morning I first thought he and I could never—it's funny, isn't it? That was the moment I knew, but here I am, six months down the road, and still going with him." She counted the months on her fingers. "Yes, six." She sucked a deep breath noisily and exhaled in silence, examining her fingernails.

Brightening again, she said, "Remember how it snowed for 12 hours and how the next morning it was all clear?" Her long hair frisked out on both sides of her waist when she threw her head back.

That pendant on her neck—I'll bet her pop doesn't approve of that, either. Or of her hair, free-falling.

"I was waiting on the trail at cabin five for him. And watching chickadees. Fattest chickadees . . . I don't know if they were really fat or just had their feathers fluffed out. About then, the sun came up through those big, green pines, *exactly* in line with the trail! A big hunk a' snow dropped off a tree and almost hit the chickadees, but they all flew up together, just in time, and I thought, *They're alive.* You know? Alive,

alive, alive." Her fists beat the air like wings. "And I'm alive. And the snow so white. The sky just cracking blue, like it gets in January. The sun perfectly lined up with the trail, and about then I saw Wolf just in his pants and bare feet. He was shivering. Like so." She wrapped her arms around herself to demonstrate, and then laughed. "I felt—I *knew* God was right overhead. Some place close. And He loved me!"

Saul only nodded from time to time, observing her words well up from some overflowing storage tank.

"That was the morning I knew about Wolf and me . . ." Her voice trailed off. "We went to the lake after he got his shoes and coat, and all the way we didn't say anything. But I was still feeling that warmness, the way I'd felt the night before, and then it happened—tongues, my heavenly language. I guess I did it right there at the lake. I just started, saying words I didn't know to God, and Wolf hollers, 'You often do that?' I said, 'Do what?' He acted like something horrible had just happened and said, 'Is that what you did last night? Anybody fly?' Seriously. I felt led to say right then what God told me the night before, which was, 'God loves you, Wolf.'

"Well, he started ranting. He said chemistry explained everything. It's the sugar level in your blood, not the Spirit, and that it's happened often in history. He had examples. The priests in Tibet, I think, was one. And some Indian chief in the 1800s. Because we fasted, he said, like the Indians, and when your blood sugar drops, you see things. The Indians, when they're twelve or so, had visions. Like Rolly Kurtz's, only a bear or something with meaning for them.

"He said some chief in South Dakota got a word. If he danced without stopping, the spirits would assemble and drive all the whites out of North America. So he danced all winter—He and his tribe. Unfortunately, we didn't leave. I said I didn't care, Saul, no matter how many examples he thought up. I know the Lord's behind our Revival, but Wolf goes on confusing and confusing me and finally I just: 'What about you? What about your faith?'

"Then he talked about Julliard; how he lost it." Gloria gushed the whole story non-stop, feasting on Saul's face as she propped her arm between her knee and her chin. First the right arm, then the left. Then her right again. "'Like candy jawbreakers,' he said. Wait, I'm getting ahead—it started with his Mother dying. He told his Heifer Project buddies that she went to heaven, but I guess he himself couldn't really believe it. The night of the funeral he went for a walk, and that's when he decided not to lie to himself about what he felt and to throw off everything that wasn't really him.

"Just like you suck a kid's jawbreaker, he said, layer by layer. First the red, then the green layer, then the blue, and so on down to the gumdrop in the middle. He chucked layers off himself: Belief in heaven and hell. Prayer. The Church. The Mennonites. And he got to the last one, which was God. And he sucked that one off too, and all that was left was himself. His body. His feelings and what have you, which he calls the gumdrop. He says he's himself now, a real man.

"I didn't know what to say. But it's not what it's like for me. I love the Lord." Two tears, like liquid wheat grains, formed in the blue eyes. "I do. And I can't tell Wolf. He says it's hallu—hallu—"

"-cinations?"

"That." The rain drummed on the canvas overhead without interruption for at least a minute.

"We can't possibly get married," she said in a small voice.

"I understand." Oh, did he. It was his own story, only in the reverse. For him, it wasn't the gumdrop at the bottom that he embraced when all the layers came off, but the Lord Himself, "high and lifted up and His train fills the Temple," as Isaiah the prophet had said. *I also am a new man!*

He covered her small hand with his. "Sure, it's happened in history—religious phenomena. Wolf's *wolftrap* is . . . well, faith." He squeezed the hand. "You're right. You can't possibly marry him."

"You think so?"

"Isn't that what God is saying in your spirit?"

"Yeeeeeessss," she exhaled loudly, sinking back into the chair. "Oh, I've thought about it so long." She abruptly sat up, her voice registering the new conviction, "It's what I must do. But yet, I look at Edie and Anna Mary and your children and I think—it'll never happen to me."

"Yes, it will."

"You'uns are so happy."

What if Anna Mary felt like this? He scrutinized his arms—bare arms, widowed arms, like the arms of Hosea the prophet. How long had it been since they circled—well, actually only about an hour or so ago. He'd been hugged more often and with more joy in the last six months than he had the rest of his life. Not counting little Schnoogie, of course. God bless the critter, probably asleep with his arm around Bear-Bear. Yet there was still something empty. Lonely? Why did pieces of him ache sometimes—physically ache—for affection hotter and closer and more whispered, confiding into his ear, than the love of the brothers and sisters?

"You don't know what it's really like for us."

"What what's like?"

"Anna Mary and I don't sleep together." Her face registered shock. "Since Snow Camp. The night of the prayer meeting at our house, to pinpoint it exactly."

"You don't?"

"No."

"I didn't know." Her fingertips touched his hand. Salve seemed to flow out of those fingertips, up the arm and into his heart.

"She doesn't want to." There, he'd said it. Some nights it crumpled him, enraged him. Even now it seemed he was, as it were, stripping in front of . . . Wasn't it a sign he'd failed as a man?

"Oh."

"She locks the bedroom. The night we got back from Snow Camp—that was the first night she locked it. Gloria! When I went upstairs after our meeting, I could have smashed that door. And what prevented me? The Spirit of God. If I'd smashed it, what would I have done next?" He shuddered. He wasn't sure he'd have done anything. On the other hand, just noting how the blood howled right now as he remembered it—"I disassembled the lock in the morning, but she just moved to the guest room. She's been there since. Barred in."

"That's awful."

"'Don't touch me' she says. When I just touch . . ." His fingertips caressed the knotty pine bench between them. *Her breast, I was thinking, but . . .* "Even if I brush against her, accidentally, she goes stiff. Just stiff." He froze his neck and forearm muscles to illustrate.

"I didn't know."

He stood. "The singing must be about done." He looked at the hole above the light pole to see if he could see raindrops streaking.

Gloria's words continued to fall, soothing his heart like the masseur's fingers smooth the burning and knotted muscles. "It always helps when I talk to you," she said. "You . . ." He had no intention of hugging her, but her continuing softening words triggered it. She hugged back. *Oh glory—the brothers and sisters! 'Thy two breasts are like two young roes that are twins.' Where did* that *come from? Absolutely, I won't think of them. A Christian sister. No desire to dream of her body, picturing it, the parts of it.* He dropped both arms as if she were an overheated coal stove he'd bumped into, and he stepped sharply away.

"Do you need an umbrella?" He fumbled for one under the stage. The rain had ramped up to a deluge. They walked together under the umbrella, out of the prayer room, and into the rain. *Don't even brush her. Don't touch her. Where did that rogue verse come from?* He stopped at the edge of the assembly and let her precede him. On every side there were people he knew well, milling and talking around now that the worship portion was over.

"Say hello to Wolf," he called, shaking and folding the umbrella.

A small line queued up when the people saw Saul. They reached out to shake his hand or held both arms up for an embrace. He chuckled. *I must have been tense back there. Wrong to get distracted like that. We have a job—God's job—to do here.*

"Hello." Wolf's shirt was laced shut loosely, revealing the burnt-orange curls under the shirt. His hand clutched Saul's. "Moses!"

"Who?"

"Moses!" Wolf grinned. "Make it stop raining."

Saul watched him without letting go of his hand, then threw back his head and focused beyond the spot where the canvas roof sides met and were stitched together. *Stop. Show the unbeliever ... and it's stopping. It's down to a drizzle. No, it's not even drizzling. It's stopping ...*

"Check it out!" Wolf turned in astonishment to the people in the line. "Look at this guy."

"Ain't he wonderful!" A diminutive elderly woman in dark, plain clothes reached up bony fingers to pat Saul's hand, unaware of the challenge Wolf had just thrown at him. "Thank you for the Word of God."

"It was Him." Saul pointed at the tent seam. "He makes it rain."

"So, these are the rebels?" Wolf's jaw pointed to the mingling crowd behind them.

"Hmm?"

"Hey, Saul. I don't care. It's Camelot to me." Wolf waved his arms good-naturedly. "I love it. The big tent. Good four-part Mennonite singing, 'Just As I Am, Without One Plea'. Even cymbals and a piano! All we need is George Brunk to swoon us with that Virginia drawl. It's what I came back to Kittochtinny for. Camelot!"

This man's undercurrent cynicism. . . . He noticed his hands making fists. "How was your summer tour?"

"Okay. I just want to hear from you. What's going to happen? Are you going to split?"

"Split what?"

"Don't the church call it 'politics'? You know, the mainline against the 'holy rollers'. Pardon the term—is it offensive? They'll be a split. Always ends that way. The Conference won't tolerate dissent. Doesn't matter if it's over coverings and plain clothes or how happy you should get in church."

"I don't want a split."

"Who does?"

"If it does come . . . if it does . . . it'll be the church rejecting revival." He was about to turn back to the queue when he decided to insert an afterthought he'd had lately. "What does it take for the deaf and blind church to hear?" he asked, his voice so low that only Wolf heard. "Sometimes I think it's fresh dirt in the graveyard."

Wolf's eyes popped. "You mean . . . God'll kill somebody you want him to?"

"We can't know his methods."

"You have them hypnotized. I never saw anything like it." Wolf spotted Gloria behind him and reached back to seize her hand.

"Where do you stand?" Saul winked, working to lighten the conversation. "With the 'holy rollers' or against them?"

"Doesn't matter to me. Matter to you?" Wolf's hand clutched Gloria's, reeling her in toward himself. The wind had stopped, and the usher was now pinning back the tent flap in front of them. Rainwater ran noisily off the sides of the tent into puddling, yellow streams that formed in the alfalfa roots just off the edge of the sawdust floor. "This is what matters. Love!"

"I'll pray for you," Gloria said, standing in the shuffle now directly in front of Saul. He nodded and patted her arm. She lifted it, then the other arm, then threw both arms around his waist and went tiptoe to kiss his neck. He didn't respond in kind.

Wolf was already ducking under the tent flap. When Gloria followed, he pulled her hand impatiently, holding up the tent flap with his other arm. "Gloria, let's move it!"

Fourteen

"HE'S NO DIFFERENT."

"No different than what?"

"Than any of the others. Stick it to the peons: 'Lap it up, folks, lap it up.'" Wolf spoke in an erratic tone and used language of a type she hadn't heard him use before. Rrrummmppherrrr! The back wheels splashed down into a channel that the fast-moving current of runoff had cut sideways across the driveway. They popped out again, squealing. "Crazy hayfields. Why didn't they build a half-decent road in?"

Shhhhhhwoooossshhhh . . . the wipers chopped up the view of the rain bounding off the macadam.

Look at them hit! Gloria thought, deliberately distracting herself. *Like a ballet troupe pirouetting in white, flouncy things under the lights. Maybe they're doing The Nutcracker Suite, like we saw at Christmas. If so, what's this part? The sugar plum fairies.* She'd always imagined them as big, red plums of the kind her Mom canned, with graceful arms and legs and in burgundy leotards. But maybe the fairies wore white instead—like the raindrops—to disguise the indisguisable fact that they were plums. Big, fat plums.

"Check out the raindrops! Nutcracker dancers, I keep imagining. When they bounce up." Wolf didn't respond.

Even if he's mad for whatever reason, I'm not afraid. I'm good with people. Pop always said so. I take after him in that. She saw no reason why they couldn't go on being friends. She'd always liked Wolf; always admired him. He was the chorale director, after all. But now that she'd made up her mind, she wondered why it had taken so long. They could never marry. She wasn't afraid to tell him. *But not yet. What's he in a bad mood for, anyway?*

"How's come you're turning in here?" They'd driven south for about 15 minutes, entering an area of the county she didn't know.

"Huh?"

"Where does this road go?" The road was dirt and definitely didn't lead to Stone Quarry Bridge. Twin, once-graveled tracks with grass between them ducked through large sycamores at the place the dirt road left the main. In the dusk, the headlights shone on low-bending branches and leaves of tree after tree. Glistening. Dripping.

"The creek."

"What's down there?"

"See if it's up at the covered bridge."

Not one of the covered bridges I know. The bridge thrust from its limestone abutment like an elongated, faded, red house to its opposite partner 80 feet away. The chocolate water tossed riffs 10 feet below. The VW rattled the floorboards of the bridge. It recalled another era, before steel girders, when heavy, wooden beamed bridges needed protection from the stress of winter thaws and freezes. The galvanized roof and red-boarded sides did just that. This particular bridge, she noted, seemed poorly cared for. Several sideboards were missing, allowing one to see the churning creek below.

"It's high," Gloria said. The swollen, brown waters boiled and beat themselves against trees that usually hung over the creek but were now underwater to their knees from the downpour.

"Nah. I'd hate to swim it, but it's not that high." They came out of the unlit bridge into the dusk, and the headlamps lit the stone breakaway walls. Wolf U-turned smartly and pulled back up onto the embankment that overlooked the creek they had just crossed. The motor died.

"So . . ." She turned in her seat to face him.

"How about putting down the top? It's done raining."

"Yeah."

He cranked back the top, and immediately the hot air inside blew off. The rain hadn't diminished the heat at all. Here the air was woodsy, soaked, and crowded with smells. Tree smells, water smells, certain pungent weeds, and perceptibly, a skunk. The air was almost giddy.

"You want to eat now?"

"Sure!" He grinned broadly, the first show of warmth she'd seen since they left the farm 45 minutes ago. "Can't wait to see what you got."

"It's kind of . . . wet." Pools of water stood on every conceivable picnic spot. The floor of the bridge was dry but dark and hardly comfortable for sitting.

"The back seat."

They got into the back, flapping the doors open for circulation. She spread the gingham cloth on the flipped-down front passenger's seat, laying out all of her carefully prepared items: ground ham and pickle relish sandwiches between thickly sliced pieces of her mother's sourdough, sweet gherkins from the garden, two large bunches of Concord grapes, a quart of orange Kool-Aid with an inch of ice cubes still unmelted under the lid, and chocolate cupcakes with vanilla icing and pink sprinkles.

"Wow!"

It suddenly seemed a glorious way to spend an evening. If only she didn't have a sense of what he was up to, she could have enjoyed it completely. He ate the first of two sandwich halves with gusto.

"You're terrific!" He corralled the ground ham chunks that had fallen onto his napkin and funneled them down his throat. "Did I tell you I got reviewed?"

"No!"

He leaned forward to the glove compartment and retrieved the newspaper clipping. "The Julliard paper." He passed it to her. She read the first paragraph to herself, and then read it again out loud.

"Landis bends all of his magnetic personality to the role of Marcello. That the whole cast is young and ravishing adds to the drama, for this is a tale of young lovers and a tragedy of untimely demise. " She read with a voice of approval and warmth. She folded the clipping and gave it back. "Neato."

"You have no idea what that means to me." Wolf tapped the curled review on her leg. "Those people will go on meeting to revive each other till Doomsday, but there are other things happening in the world. I'm getting in on a piece of it."

"I'm really glad."

"But *they'll* never see." He noisily slapped the back of the seat in front of him. "Dream on! Dream on! Except for a few like yourself who come up out of the pond for oxygen."

She knew it would be more of this after the honeymoon wore off. He would talk reviews, and she would talk of Jesus. No. It would never work.

"I'm thinking London, Haarlem, and Bienenberg School in Germany," Wolf said, *a propos* of nothing. "There's Mennonite centers in every one, and they'd host us. Not house us, but *host* us ."

"We're really going to do it?"

"Of course! We'll add a couple of numbers in German. 'Gott ist die Liebe,' 'Nun Danket Alle Gott.' Maybe a Ralph Vaughn Williams for the London crowd." Wolf was crunching gherkins between sentences, practically swallowing them whole. "There are choral competitions in Europe in the summertime. That might be an entry point. We sign up for the competition, maybe even place in the semifinals. Then we do the circuit of cities."

"Won't it cost a lot?"

"We'll do offerings at each concert . . . and fundraisers before we go. Whaddya think?" He held up a gherkin dramatically. "A bake sale! An auction!" He tossed it and caught it on his tongue.

It quieted again. By now it was so dark that they could no longer distinguish the food items on the gingham cloth, except for the cupcakes, whose frosted heads glowed by themselves. She leaned forward and arranged what was left into the bottom of the woven reed market basket.

"Had enough?"

"Mmmm."

"Another cupcake?"

"Hnnh uhh." He had fallen back in his seat, flinging one arm out of the open door, and was studying the vented top of the car. The sky had clarified into dark, unlit cloud shapes, and the earlier mists were completely gone. She finalized the basket.

This is it. He's never silent unless he's gathering for a new sally.

"That was really, really good." He played with the hair on her back, stroking it. The woods seemed alive. Large drops kept falling out of the trees and splashing in the woods behind them. Bullfrogs harrumphed in the newly flooded areas along the creek, which had almost no banks on the out-current side of the bridge. She felt his fingers close around hers. He pulled them up and kissed them, one at a time. "Do you know how I feel about you?"

"I think so."

"Marcello never forgot Musetta, even when things went badly and she ran off with Alcindoro, the old, rich guy." He was kissing her fingers again, one by one. He stopped. He slanted away, and suddenly the seat beside her was empty. She heard footsteps around the back, and just as suddenly, there was his face, leaning in at her door. Only now he was down at the level of her hands, one knee on the leaf-covered and soggy embankment, his face canted up.

His cheeks and forehead were lit as clearly as if a flood lamp had flipped on. The dark clouds had broken apart, and shafts from an almost full moon were now falling through the canopy of trees, painting his face like a mime's make-up, not quite human.

179

"I want to take you on that trip to Europe as Mrs. Landis. I want to marry you." He grasped her hands, pulled them to his lips, and inserted his face between them. Her hands turned chalky.

Once upon a time she'd dreamed up scenes like this. She imagined she might be so lucky as to meet a romantic who actually proposed—on one knee, on a deserted K-County road. But that was before Snow Camp, before the Revival, before she cared about pleasing God first. Sitting in the darkened backseat, she knew her face was completely in the shadows and unreadable. She contemplated the white upper face held cradled in her hands by his. His eyes moved, like the eyes in a mask.

"Will you?"

She breathed in slowly, knowing the answer but not sure of the timing for it.

"Say something."

She exhaled slowly between pursed lips and then pulled her hands back. His hand was still attached to one of hers, and she pulled it along. He got up slowly, several leaves clinging to the knee that had been down. He leaned into the back seat, his arms on both sides of her and his face coming down against her. The Old Spice was intoxicating.

"Hi, sexy."

What do I do? I promised myself we wouldn't get started. Three times she'd had the words all ready. Twice in a letter and once in notes by the phone, but she couldn't. Couldn't what? Hurt him? And how had she felt as she fell off to sleep each one of those nights after she'd closed the door and watched him go whistling out the gate? Dirty. Dishonest.

She put her finger between her mouth and his, a solitary guardrail, and stopped his hand at her waist where he was rubbing his way upward. "Wolf, we need to talk."

"How's come? Always halfway through the kiss." His mouth was against her ear.

She laughed at the ridiculousness of it, despite her guarded emotions.

"I love you—" His hot lips ran up the cheek to her ear and began to munch wetly, noisily, wheezing ticklish, hot air into it.

"Wolf!"

He pulled back. "Okay, let's talk." He came around the back of the car again. For the first time, she felt fear. *He won't like this. He won't like this at all. Suppose—*

> Met her on the mountain,
> Swore she'd be my wife,
> But the gal refused me,
> Stabbed her with my knife . . .

She'd often pictured him, Tom Dooley the hangman's choice, in a red-checkered lumberman's jacket, holding onto a barred window through which the sun threw yellow lozenges. There were lots of stories like that. Lovers killing lovers. What about the creek? What if he threw her in?

He had settled back into the rear seat of the car, and both of their faces were in the dark again, although the moonlight through the open rooftop spilled a general reflected light that made both of their features recognizable now.

"Say something, Gloria."

Pop always said, "Just say it." It doesn't need a necktie and hair gel. If it's the truth, it will do its own work. If it's the truth, the other guy already reads it in your body or from hints you've dropped.

"I think you're a wonderful man—" She inched one finger back and forth on the hand that still held hers.

"A wonderful man, but . . ."

"But I don't think so. I want to just be friends. I wanted to tell you before, but I couldn't. Several times I wrote a letter. Two times, in fact. I tore it in pieces both times. I was afraid, I guess . . ." The humidity made her hand sweat as it lay encircled in his. "I didn't want to hurt you, but . . ." If only he would speak. Interrupt with something, anything, so she knew. What was he thinking right now? Her trapped thumb rubbed the top of his hand.

181

"There's all kinds of stuff messing with my mind right now." His voice was flat, his eyes straight ahead.

"Yes."

"*Why?*"

"Don't you feel it, too? That it won't work? We're going two different roads. You're heading for a music career, and it's everything in the world to you. For me, it's Jesus . . ."

"You said in the past you love me." The words were inflectionless again, and sounded tired.

"I always will. As I love all brothers—"

"Not that—rot!" He kicked the open door next to him, and it bounced out and right back against his foot. He slashed around and his fingers tugged her chin in his direction. "Tell me you're joking."

"I'm not, Wolf."

"Huh, huh." He laughed, grabbing the seat in front of him and punching it with a wild haymaker swing, twice. "Is that a reason for not marrying me? Yeah, we have differences. Like every couple. I appreciate your faith. Not in me, but in you, yes. You appreciate my music. My reviews. Gives me," he swatted his chest, "a great feeling. You read my review. You say, 'O wow!' I never got that far with a Mennonite girl before, but you—you're *it* for me. Huh, huh." He laughed mirthlessly. "How about next month. We'll forget it for now, but can I ask again before Thanksgiving? Give it some time—"

"The marriage won't last, Wolf. It'll bust up."

"What makes you say that? Our odds are ten times the average American couple. Think about us. Same culture. Same community. We're even related, your brother says . . ."

"But the biggest thing—the very biggest. I'm a new person since Snow Camp, and you didn't notice. Lately, I've wondered . . . do you even—"

"Even what?" His voice roughened.

"Even know the Lord? Because I can't marry—I'm going to marry someone that—" *That what? Believes in the Revival? How should I end this sentence?*

182

"What's love? Huh? If God is love, what's love?" He spoke impatiently, tossing his hands to emphasize his words. "I'm scared of people who say they love God and *only* God. Life is *people*. Does God need any love from us? No. He's got the angels. The Rorschach for love is people. Which people? This farmer over here, that schoolteacher over there."

"I agree with some of that."

Wolf's mouth cracked open, and a look of discovery came over his eyes. "*He* put you onto this, didn't he?" When he began again, she knew he wouldn't stop—that he would plumb this to the depth of his angry thoughts, a pit she didn't know the bottom of. "That's why you were back there," he muttered, as if just realizing it. "What were you's doing after the meeting? That's what those hugs meant. You're in love with him, aren't you? The big preacher, Saul MacNamara."

"He's a man of God."

"Men of God need women. It's common knowledge he and Anna Mary don't sleep together. You're in love with him."

"Don't be ridiculous. He's my brother-in-law. As I love you, Wolf, that's how I love—"

"Only one kind for a young woman and young man. Go-to-bed love." He spoke almost inaudibly again, addressing the creek beyond the car. "I thought there was something odd about the two of you."

"If I've hurt you, I'm sorry." It was out now. Except for the misunderstanding about Saul, Wolf had heard her. What was left? She needed to close things out right. They could be friends, couldn't they? He'd take her home, and she'd say goodnight from the other side of the gate. No goodbye kisses.

Before she could protest, he snaked his arms around her waist, pulling her against him. "I love you, Gloria."

She put both hands against his chest, with pressure. Not her full strength, but enough to say, "No, I mean it." She used the same weighted tone and looked straight into his eyes. "It's not that way anymore."

He moved himself closer and studied her breasts, one hand hovering, the other caressing her leg lightly. "Gloria," he said, speaking in a tender, solicitous way. "Gloria."

I have to get out. She flung both legs over the side of the seat and threw herself through the open door. She felt the dress snag behind, and when she twisted to tear it free, she saw that it was his hand snagging the dress. "Let go!" Both of her feet were already in the wet grass.

"Come back, or I'll tear it off."

"Let me go!"

He threw both legs over the transmission hump and propelled himself off the seat toward her. In the move, he lost his grip. *Up into the covered bridge.* She ran. *Will he just let me go?* The car's throaty rattle answered the question, and the headlamp beams swung out over the creek as the car reversed and then roared forward up into the bridge. Before the beams could find her, she pulled herself up onto the heavy trusses, falling backward against the bridge sideboards. The old boards felt weak and ready to send her tumbling backwards into the cold current, but she didn't move, hoping he wouldn't see. The lights of the car probed the bridge, and the motor vibrated noisily off the walls. It stopped. She could see the door on the driver's side open, but she didn't wait.

Run! Where to? Back out of the bridge the way she'd come, up the horse and jeep trail leading into the woods, splashing through unseen mud puddles and soaking both shoes. The car motor whined, and this time the Volkswagen roared backward out of the bridge, skidding sideways. The lights came up from behind, transfixing her, and casting her long, bobbling shadow out ahead. *He'll hit me. He's going to hit me.* The light swerved as the car passed and stopped a length ahead. Wolf, clearly visible in the splotchy moonlight, ran around the front of the car and flung out his arms as she hotfooted by, twisting to dodge his hands. "Where you think you're going?" Her wrist was pincered and she corkscrewed it away, but he hung on.

"Home. Let go!"

"It's 10 miles. And that's the wrong direction."

"Let go." She hissed the words.

He flung her arm down, gestured to the car, and walked around to his own door. He waited, one foot on the running board, watching her over the top.

"Don't touch me." She realized her voice was trembling.

"You're just a pathetic little revival sucker. Let *him* touch you."

She walked slowly to the car, opened the front door, and scooped the scattered cupcakes off the floor and back into the picnic basket. The radio came on, next to her ear, blasting.

> Hot diggity, dog-ziggity . . .

She got in. *I lost control. What's wrong with me?* She sat with both arms clutching her body, her knees shaking uncontrollably. Her hair was pulling up and out on the windsuck through the open top vent, and when she fumbled up a hand, she found that the prayer covering was gone.

"I'll get him!" Wolf shouted over the radio and the louder roar of the wind. "He'll hurt like he hurt me."

Saul stabbed, like Dooley's lover. Or something dreadful like that. She saw Saul with mud and coal slivers all over his engineer boots from running. Now he was lying face down in a pool of muddy water on the coal banks along Chilly Creek, an ax handle poking up from the side of his backbone.

"I'll get his kid!"

She pulled the writhing locks down with her trembling hands and twisted them into a bun.

> Mmmm—it's so new to me,
> When you're holding me tight.

Fifteen

SAUL CONVENED A meeting of the "elder board," as he had named it, at 9:30 every evening after the revival meeting in the tent. They met standing up in order to curb the meeting from dragging beyond 15 minutes, as everyone needed to get home to face early morning cows. Or work schedules. Or just be with their families.

Sister Baumgartner's twin, blonde, pig-tailed daughters set Dixie cups on the table in the large hall of the empty tent by the already draped-for-the-night piano while Sister Baumgartner shot lemonade from a large thermos into the individual cups. One daughter held the cup to keep it from tipping and plucked ice cubes and lemon cross-sections from two Bell Mason jars, dropping them into the empty cups in preparation for the lemonade to land. The other daughter, barefoot and well-tanned like her sister (and both thrilled to be allowed up this late), kept an eye on Matthew, their three-year-old brother, who liked sucking lemons. Just now his face was contorted, and tears coursed down his face from the tartness. He didn't understand why he couldn't pull all the slices out of the cups.

"Thank you, Sister Baumgartner. And girls!" Saul raised his cup and sipped. "As always, homemade everything except the lemons. Just-right, tart and ice-cold to keep our peepers open another 15 minutes. In gratitude to your family, we'll let Brother Elmer go first tonight."

"We'll wait in the car," she said to Elmer. Towing Matthew by the hand, she lifted the tent flap and exited, with the girls running out ahead.

The five men ringed the table, all in cuffed, long-sleeved dress shirts that were buttoned at the neck despite the terrible humidity. Bennie's back was soaked through between his shoulder blades. A weak breeze was passing through, and although he'd dropped the flaps for the night around the entire assembly hall of the tent, he had left flaps open on opposite sides of the piano, as well as most of the flaps in the council room area.

"Collection totals 731 dollars." Elmer laid the fat manila folder on the tabletop.

"Exactly what we owe on the electric bill. Exactly!" Bennie said.

"God is good!"

"No, Guys! To the dollar. It's 731," Bennie repeated, and this time they all agreed it was a small miracle.

"Anything else, Brother Elmer?"

"The guard from Susquehannock Security is here. Checked in with me a couple minutes ago, and he's out there in his green pick-up. Got his headlights off and a thermos of coffee and a lunch to keep him awake all night."

"Well, we haven't had a repeat on the vandalism since he's come, and with the sound equipment, the piano, and all these chairs here—"

"Worth it. Worth it." Bennie said.

"I'll be banking in the morning," Elmer said.

"Good. Brother Noah?"

"Nothing special to report. I'm about finished duplicating." Noah lifted two fingers overhead to indicate the sound of music emanating from the reel-to-reel recorder. The massed assembly was singing the gospel invitation tune, "O, Why Not Tonight?"

"I'd like one of those caps," Saul said.

Noah fingered the yellow "Noah Krehbiel Meats" cap. "Really?" He pulled it off and observed it. "I'd give you this one, but it's sweaty. Got lots in the car! You want it now?"

"No, no. Just sometime soon. I also want to get one of those tapes to Russell Howe at WKTY. Says he'll broadcast one of our services if we can get it to him."

Before they could remark on this good fortune, the bloodless, aged, beaming face of Cyrus Brubaker poked through the tent flap. A muscular, plaid-shirted man followed him, his workday clothes conspicuous because they identified him as a non-Mennonite in this crowd that always wore dress clothes to gatherings.

"I want to introduce—" Cyrus encouraged the man along, his hand gripping the man's elbow, "Sean O'Hara. Sean—Brother Bennie." Cyrus croaked the names. "Brother Elmer. Brother Noah. And you know Brother Saul, of course." O'Hara reached for each hand in turn.

"I'm a fan of yours," O'Hara said to Saul. "Best talks I've ever heard, and swell stories too!" The men laughed together. Saul gripped O'Hara's hand and turned to Cyrus, expecting some report.

"Sean gave his heart to the Lord tonight!" Cyrus seemed like a new father, glowing with his news.

"May God bless you." Saul gripped O'Hara's shoulder. "Feel those triceps."

"I'm a welder. A union man!" He nodded and turned to leave.

"The Lord can use a strong man. Think about Samson."

"Nobody's called me 'Samson' before," O'Hara called from the door flap on his way out.

"Shoulda we told him Mennonites don't join unions?" Elmer asked.

"Glory!" Saul said. "The angels in heaven are whooping it up over him. So we'll whoop too. Then the Lord'll clean him up in His perfect timing."

Cyrus beamed as he returned from seeing O'Hara off, liking Saul's response. "He repented with big tears," he said, joining the circle of men again. "An alcoholic. He's beat his wife and little ones frequently, in a drunken stupor. Of course, this should all stay in this circle." He ran his eyes from face to face. "He was so sorry, so sure God can't forgive—as I guess his wife's driven off with the children to her mother's right now—but I told him, 'Yes, the Lord can forgive that.' I'm going over to his mobile home in Frauheim tomorrow for coffee, or Kool-Aid." He smiled amiably throughout his report. "Other than O'Hara, 10 folks made commitments tonight."

"What's that make it for the whole summer?"

"Two hundred nine. No, 210! How could I forget Sean!"

"We've seen 210 souls come to life," Saul said. "Shining their little lights like . . ." He regarded the darkness outside the tent, where fireflies hovering in the humid darkness over the alfalfa field signaled each other in little, unpredictable bursts of amber. "Like lighting bugs. Their lights now shining where before they could only curse the darkness. And how many more quickened, their hearts pumping the full Holy Ghost when once they were living defeated? Over a thousand, I believe."

He turned back to face the men. "I'm weighed down, guys. This burden's on me. We've never wanted to make a *new* church. Just bring God into the one we have."

"Amen!" Cyrus clenched his frail, bony fist and shook it.

"But what will happen? Sunday night's the final night. I did promise Bishop Krehbiel that. And then what? People go back to their churches.

"And strangle," Bennie said. "Still can't figure why you promised him that."

"He's my father-in-law, that's why. He has a right to ask anything of me, and he asked for an ending date and I gave him one. A moment of weakness, perhaps. But will that be the end of the revival? Direction going forward—I want all of you to pray for that. Especially for Sunday night. It's got to be a shout for the Lord. Could you pray in that direction, Cyrus? I mean, right now?"

Things would never go back to normal, would they? Revival had brought a blade into the community, as Jesus promised, and it was already slashing apart old, cozy relations in some places and blood ties in others. Gloria said she'd cut off Wolf and tell him no, they couldn't marry. Noah seemed like a new man, with new confidence. Anna Mary wouldn't hear of revival anymore and isolated herself in their guestroom each night. She seemed colorless and ill. Mom Krehbiel had taken a firm stand against him, and they hadn't talked since March. That was just the toll in one family. Each of the thousand people who came to the revival had a family. What was happening in each? Was there a sword in every one?

"Amen," Cyrus said.

They kissed each other all around, and Elmer left immediately to join his wife in the parking lot. Noah went back to his recorder, rewinding the tape and sending Saul's preaching voice in fast reverse, like a gibbering, angry squirrel. Cyrus left and Saul headed back to the counseling room to pick up his notes.

And now home. Weariness, like an injection of formaldehyde, coursed through his veins and seemed to turn his body into a stiff, immoveable lump. Then, through the raised flaps along the counseling room outer wall, he saw the auto headlights approaching. He back-stepped to watch.

Wolf aimed the car. *Strike him! Hit him!* That was it, right there, growing like a great, bleached, poisonous mushroom, glowing red around its three canvas tops. A deadly mushroom sprouting up out of this hayfield in the darkness. The shaman's tent. The place where Saul MacNamara performed his witchcraft on the community. Like the Duke of Mantua casting his spell over weak women and spineless courtiers;

casting his spell over Rigoletto's pure daughter. *My Gloria. Poisoned against me by him. Strike him! Hit him!*

$$=\!\!=\!\!=$$

Wolf strode toward the tent, bobbing his head to avoid hitting the shoulder-high, circular brace. He bobbed his head up again 18 inches from Saul's face on the other side. Both men recoiled, but Wolf recovered first. His extended forefinger jabbed at Saul's chest.

"*You* did it! *You're* responsible!"

Saul eyed him carefully, his white-sleeved arms folded. "Is this about Gloria?"

"You know what it's about." They were three feet apart. Wolf's formerly easy manner was gone. The taverna shirt appeared sweaty, and his usually carefully combed hair writhed out in all directions from his scalp, like the Medusa's mask of agonized snakes. Wet, brown stains marked the white trouser cuffs, and diminishing streaks of dirt trailed upward toward the calves, as if he'd been running through puddles.

"Yes," Saul said. "Something's happened to Gloria Krehbiel. She's experienced a rebirth of her faith. And I don't know what path you're on, Brother Landis, but seems to me it's a different road. When she came by at seven o'clock, she told me that she couldn't marry you—for that reason."

"That's a lie. She said you told her she couldn't marry me." Wolf circled, first to the left and then to the right of Saul.

"Here's how it was. Gloria never planned to marry you, and she told me so tonight. I said, 'If that's what the Lord is saying to you, then you can't.'"

Wolf stopped. He glared, contemplating his next move.

"Listen, Brother. Let's sit." Saul waved to two overstuffed armchairs across the room from them toward the back of the stage. "I have a couple minutes."

Wolf slashed both hands downward savagely, wordlessly.

"Here's what I see." Saul delivered the message straight, his arms crossed, locking eyes with Wolf's, like dogfighting biplanes of the First War. "You're in trouble, right? This isn't all about Gloria. Your music's in trouble in this Conference. You're wondering if you have a future here."

"You're a hoax, MacNamara. I'm gonna expose you. I'm asking the Bishop to shut you down. Do you have permission for this tent? Zoning, I'm talking about! I'm going to the zoning board tomorrow. You're preaching without an ordination. That's a killer in this Conference. *We will shut you down.*"

"Why would you do that?"

At that moment, the taped music beyond the curtained wall clicked off and the tent grew completely quiet, except for the angry man in the counseling room, his voice now strident and shrill.

"Because you've ruined me, that's why. You debauched Gloria Krehbiel." Wolf's eyes flared wide. They seemed to Saul like the eyes of a cornered rodent. "She's in love with Jesus, she says, and you're his body on Earth."

"You don't know what you're saying. Gloria's my wife's sister."

"She loves God and thinks you're his body on Earth. She's in love with you, MacNamara! Fall-in-bed love!"

Bennie and Cyrus materialized together out of the darkness, looking dismayed and alarmed. From the tent flap behind Wolf, Bennie gestured a headlock. Wolf turned to discover them.

"I'll call if I need you," Saul said, waving them away.

He wants a fight. He wants the world as upset as he is, and I'm not game. At 10 P.M. at night? Definitely not.

"Is there anything I can do for you?"

"Tell Gloria your affair is over. You used her." Wolf jammed his forefinger into his palm like a nail. "Apologize to her. For seducing her and debauching—" His voice choked. "Debauching this beautiful—"

He's berserk. Or delirious. Been drinking, likely.

"I'm going to ask you to leave, Wolf. My colleagues are shutting off the power, and we're all going home." The lights in the main assembly hall snapped off as he said that, leaving only the set over the counseling room still burning.

"My message to you—go to hell, MacNamara."

Saul dropped his arms and strode away beyond the counseling chair. "I asked you politely." He picked up his notes, struggling to overcome the fact that his blood was rising and that a significant part of him wanted to end this conversation with a violent fistfight. He turned around from 10 feet away. "We don't allow talk like that in God's house."

"If it's true, I'll say it."

"Get out."

Wolf, still standing by the door, bunched his fists and advanced several steps.

"Security guard!" Cyrus rushed up to the flap, yelling, and the guard came in from behind him, his nightstick extended, but otherwise seeming more like a pasty-faced, middle-aged laborer with a paunch than someone who might prevent the likely outburst of violence.

"I wouldn't." Saul had not moved from the counseling chairs, which were in front of him. "I'm military, you'll remember. Golden Gloves." He waited silently, unconsciously squeezing and unsqueezing his hands, popping the knuckles.

Wolf turned on his heels and went out.

Bennie charged in from one of the side panels. "I was ready. I'd 'a jumped him if he put one finger on you."

"The hatred!" Cyrus entered the room from behind the security guard.

The headlights and engine came on 10 feet beyond the side wall as the Volkswagen aimed at the tent. The bumper, hood, and windshield came in between the tent uprights, onto the sawdust floor of the counseling room. As he braked to a stop, Wolf fixed his eyes on Saul through the windshield and glared. The security guard fell sideways to avoid being hit, truncheon still in hand as he somersaulted. He came up, knocking off woodchips with one hand, and advanced toward the car with his billy club extended.

"I'm not done with you, MacNamara!" Wolf shouted over the roar of the engine. "Round one, you win." The engine bellowed and the headlights fled backward, out of reach of the guard's nightstick. Wolf's shoulders and head came up through the open roof vent into the darkness, the braking car rocking his body back and forth. "Round two, you lose! You ruined me. I ruin you!"

Sixteen

IS THIS THE day? How will I know? Sadie Ebersole. When God punished her with a cancer of the uterus that bulged her belly out as big as the baby the hired man stuck in her the year before . . . Sadie, she left no one to cry over her. The baby died when it came out.

Poor Jakie.

The stars winked out beyond the front door window, and in the gray mist the murky shapes of the apple trees became visible. Beneath the huddled and crouching tree shapes, the cows still lay unseen, asleep.

Even the cows get to sleep, unlike me.

At the head of the couch—on which she'd again tossed all night for the third night in a row—the faces were now discernible. They filled up the frame from one side to the other as it rested on the white doily covering the end table. She loved this photo, the best of all the family that had ever been taken.

They all were in their Fall Sunday clothes, gathered around Pop and Mom in the shade of the catalpa tree in the front yard. Pop was in his preaching suit, the frock one, and Mom—in her forties, and many pounds lighter—was in a collarless, caped summer outfit, navy-blue as always for Sunday. She was seated by him in the white Adirondack loveseat they'd picked up for almost nothing off the truckback of a traveling peddler.

Aaron, just five years old in 1940, was seated on her lap, her blue-sleeved arm crossing his stomach. Gloria, about six, rested one small hand on Pop's folded, gnarly ones. Behind the loveseat, the five older children stood arranged slanting downward, left to right. Step, step, step, like those Halloween paraffin whistles you could blow and then eat: Norman, Noah, Daniel, Edie and . . . *me, just 13. Developed some, but nothing like Edie, who always had a figure the boys whistled at. I'll miss them. Will they miss me?*

The alarm sounded overhead, and she could hear him thrash and roll in the dark. Then came the loud THWATT! THWATT! The alarm rolled on. Predictably, the bed slats had slid sideways, and one end of the box spring had fallen to the floor again. He'd punched the alarm, apparently, as the only sound now was the soft pad, pad of his bare feet on the wooden floor overhead as he repaired the bed.

The gray was thinning, and from the barn a rooster sounded. November. She'd named all the animals and, like November, most of them were obvious. She'd bought that batch of chicks right before Thanksgiving.

The first cow lowed under the apples. They were levering their big, squared-off bodies up into eyeshot, several at a time, because their udders were full and their stomachs were empty. Their body clocks ran regular.

Unlike mine.

Saul pushed through the drapes and into the living room, bare-chested and bare-legged in his jockey shorts, his mouth a large *O* as the yawn progressed through a series of groans. He abruptly stopped when he saw her.

"Anna Mary!"

She'd been down and up for the last seven hours—on the left side, on the right, on her back, sitting with both feet extended onto the hassock. But no position had triggered loss of consciousness. She'd sat up again when the alarm sounded, snuggling the old quilt around her naked shoulders and tucking up her feet. And there she sat, the dark locks strewn wildly about her face, gazing hollow-eyed at him.

He crossed the room and stopped several feet from her.

No, he won't touch me. He knows better.

"You look—" He hesitated.

"I didn't sleep."

"At all?"

She shook her head side to side, his body looking caged by the waist-length strands of hair that swung like wind-blown curtains around her.

"How long has it been? Since you slept?" His arms hugged his bare chest, concealing the lick of dark hair there.

"Seventy hours, 30 minutes."

The Lazy-Boy knocked against the davenport, and he sat down on the front edge of the cushion, leaning toward her.

"Anna Mary." He stretched out one hand, but she pulled hers away, back under the quilt. His hand fell back to his knee. "Anna Mary, I wanna get our prayer team here and anoint you with oil and ask Jesus—"

Her head shook again. *It will never happen. No. Not his prayer team. Not his wicked oil. Perhaps if Pop offered, but . . .*

"Then let me take you to the doctors after the milking." He thrust his arms into a green, long-sleeved work shirt. He wasn't going to give up. "What is it, Anna Mary?" His eyes and lips pursed. He was trying to read her.

The artifacts of her all-night session were scattered around on the floor and on the end table around the photo.

"You've been worried about *this*?" He lifted the blue ledger, the one with the milking statistics, and unfolded the two pieces of ledger paper on which she'd done income calculations.

"You have no idea." Her eyes narrowed, moving to protect herself. "This will be the last month, I have no doubt."

"What are you talking about?"

"Bankruptcy. We'll lose the farm. Our monthly production's at 14,000. Losing money every month."

"You're not factoring in the coal. I have 7,200 dollars outstanding."

"Yes." She marveled. He seemed like someone in one of her old grade school readers; a character who was talking to someone who resembled herself, only very disheveled and with great, purple pouches under the eyes. She pictured her body levitating above him, hanging horizontally 12 inches below the ceiling like the angels always did in Nativity paintings, watching the scene below to take a report back to the Almighty One. And now she was the angel.

"Yes," the disheveled woman said through the hair that fell like a black waterfall. "Seventy-two hundred dollars outstanding. You've said that for two months. We missed the mortgage payment again."

She was glad the disheveled woman didn't get emotional about it. She'd seen conversations like this one fail before in this house, in this very room, because the woman became hysterical and screamed at him.

The man, who resembled someone the disheveled woman had once loved, said, "And your family photo." He picked up the frame. "The one you always love—"

The woman stretched out one arm, took it away from him, and held the faces safely. "They won't miss me," the woman said. "They've given up on me. Just like God." Anna Mary felt pleased. The woman was saying things that had needed to be said for quite some time.

"Miss you? What do you mean?"

"When I'm gone."

She marveled how obtuse the man was—that he didn't realize it was his own predictions the woman believed. If the lukewarm were all going to be spit out, then God was undoubtedly swilling them around his mouth right now. The only question left was whether it would be today or some other.

Saul pulled on his trousers, then his socks. He stood. He seemed so puny below her. "I gotta get out there and help Aaron. I just want you to know—" Suddenly, his face scrunched. It thudded when his knees hit the floor before her. "Anna Mary!" Her hands were wrapped in his now.

She knew they were her own hands, and she considered letting him hold them.

"I've just missed you terribly. Last night—last night, you know, in the middle of the worship, I looked down for you in your place—"

She pulled the hands back under the quilt. She saw the look of rejection, and now out came his salesman look.

"Anna Mary. It was such a wonderful meeting. Like you and I used to talk about. The Holy Spirit just came down—"

She was immediately on the other side of the front picture window, peering in through the glass at this couple, knowing that the woman needed to deal straightforwardly with this man. He'd loved her once but led her into fornication, for which she would now be punished. There were a couple things the woman needed to unmask.

"Was Frances Yorty there last night?" Yes, that was a good, strong opener. Not accusatory. Just establishing some damning facts.

"I think."

"Did Bennie take her home?"

"Why?"

"Oh, you don't know? Everybody at Paradise Valley has heard but you, I suppose."

"Well, tell me."

"Jack Yorty says he'll never take her to those meetings, so she walked. Bennie wouldn't let her walk back last weekend—four miles, in the dark. He insisted—she begged him not to—on driving her the whole way home, *through town,* in his pickup. Just the two of them. You didn't know, did you, but they went steady for a year and a half before he started with Edie."

"I didn't know."

"And Millie Kurtz. Did you know she's bedridden now two weeks? Vomiting and can't stand up. Because, she says, 'I'm going to hell.'"

"Conviction's a good thing."

"She's a baptized Christian. And Bennie said she'll go to hell for not coming to your meetings with her man."

"Anna Mary, I understand. I understand." He stood and latched his belt.

The man was getting angry, she saw, and was going to leave. He jammed his cap on. But she hoped the woman would not relent. Not now. Not at the main point. She wondered if he heard her pounding heart—it seemed that loud as it hit against the quilt.

"What about hugging between married men and women?" The disheveled woman clutched the quilt tightly around her shoulders but spoke with controlled fury. "Is it true? And you? Saul MacNamara? I've heard you *give your blessing—*"

His back disappeared into the kitchen, and the door to the washhouse slammed shut as he went for his barn shoes.

She was proud of the disheveled woman.

In fact, Anna Mary felt much better today than she'd felt for several days. She got the stepstool and pulled down the colander, tree hooks, and large, enameled pails for cherry picking. Then she went upstairs, carrying the new, green, corduroy jumpsuit she'd cut and stitched for Schnoogie the first night she couldn't sleep.

She gazed down at his blonde head on the pillow, cautiously moved the blanket back, checked the length of the jumpsuit against his body, and poked a straight pin into the cuff to mark the correct length. *What a doll, with his long, blond hair, which I can't bring myself to cut. Little precious. What will happen to you, Jakie? Will you be spit out, too?* As soon as she reached vertical, she clutched her abdomen. *No! Not just now!* She fell forward against the bed frame, her eyes fixed on the cowboys on the wallpaper behind. It was the pain that had visited her every morning this week right about this time.

Her whole body felt worn out, too tired to even notice the straight pin in the pants that had jabbed her thumb. It bled now, forming brilliant red beads that she inadvertently brushed across her chest. She sank onto the other bed, the one they'd bought a long time ago for the second child, who'd never come. Her eyes burned with graininess.

An airplane droned somewhere overhead. *The Russians, perhaps? Dropping the bomb?* But she never heard the bomb hit, because after 71 hours, her eyelids finally sealed, and a heavy, milk fog rolled in across the tortured landscape of her mind.

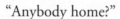

"Anybody home?"

She hadn't realized she'd been sleeping until the sound woke her. She rolled and gaped at the radio-clock. Nine-thirty. She'd promised Gloria she'd be there at nine. She ran to the guest room, where she kept all her things now, winding and bobby-pinning up her waist-length hair as she fumbled simultaneously in the chest of drawers below the mirror for a bandanna to hold her hair back.

"Anybody home?"

She became aware of the voice for the first time. A deep one. *Who would be calling at 9:30 in the morning?* Not Saul, already off to his coal beds. And where was Jakie? She dashed back across the hallway and saw his turned back, in his little white briefs, kneeling on the pine board floor as he drove a tractor up the pillow. She tiptoed backward noiselessly and descended the stairs, smoothing out the wrinkles on her denim skirt.

The man at the front screen door had already turned away, assuming no one was home, when she arrived. She cracked the door.

"Can I help—?"

He pivoted. They reviewed each other for a moment before she recognized him and pushed the door open wide. Wolfgang had slept somewhere in his clothes, his taverna shirt and white trousers by now completely rumpled and fatigued, his abundant hair flat on the left side and rising to a point. Dark semicircles of bad sleep and a red aura of stubble only added a level of interest to the normally handsome face. She was about to question his appearance, but he went first.

"What happened to your hand?"

She only now saw that a pin gouge had bled freely, smearing her palm. She didn't notice the stain on her breast, but he did.

"Oh, a pin. It didn't hurt at all. Where have you been? Did you want to come in?"

He'd never been to their house before. But as an expected brother-in-law in the near future . . . of course, he should come in. She backed in, holding the door open until he passed, and then let the taut spring pull back to bang it shut.

"Please." She gestured to the rocker opposite the velveteen couch. He took it while she sat on the couch, poised. "Something wrong?"

"Gloria."

"Gloria? An accident?" She unconsciously put three fingers across her open mouth.

"No. We broke up. She broke it up." He slid forward to the edge of the rocker, tilting it. She noticed mud on his shoes as several small, dried pieces fell off.

"No! You were such a neat couple. Why? If you don't mind my—?"

"Your husband. He told her to. I came to warn you, Anna Mary. That's why I'm here."

"Warn me what?" *Is it about the day? Is this the day things will happen?*

"I've seen them. Hugging and kissing."

"Them . . . you mean?" *Meaning what? Meaning who?*

She was floating near the ceiling again, looking down at this twosome in her living room. They were at the other end of a kaleidoscope, and the pieces turned and fell randomly this way then that.

"Gloria. And Saul."

"Hugging—?" the woman below her said, looking confused.

"And kissing. At least her kissing him. I was right there. If they do that with me standing right there—this is last night, by the way. In their counseling room, as they call it. In the big tent. She says she's dumping me for Jesus. Jesus, she says, and who's her Jesus here on Earth?"

"How long?" she said.

"Since Snow Camp."

"Snow Camp!" The woman's hand flew to her open mouth again, completely covering it this time.

"She cooled off after that, and I thought it was just a phase—just her testing me. Because she goes up and down like that. Musetta, the vixen."

"Do you think they're—?" The woman stopped. It wasn't a topic to be discussed in polite society around here. Not even mentioned. Certainly one didn't talk such stuff with a strange man. Even with someone you've known a long time. It was shameful . . .

He said the word, the common English vulgarity. "Of course they're doing that. Is he a man of passion? I guess you know what he's like when he gets aroused with someone, even if it's not appropriate . . ."

The pieces fell together like the diamond shapes shifting down at the far end of a child's kaleidoscope. Blue-green, torrid pink, then moving to red-black. Snowflakes now! Too painful. Too much like real memories. *Interrupt him*, she urged the woman below. *Interrupt him, about the snowflakes . . .*

"Snow Camp," the woman said. "We haven't had relations since Snow Camp." Anna Mary flushed, terribly embarrassed that the woman had come right out and talked about *that* to a third party. And yet she was glad the woman had the courage to say it.

"Now you know why. He's taking care of his needs with someone else."

She was no longer overhead. She was conscious that she was seated four feet from a man, a young, good-looking man. Just the two of them, participating in a fatal secret. She could feel his eyes traveling, coasting down her neck under the maroon collar and rolling and touching their way—wet and warm. Under the bra, and over each shape in the dark. Blood mounted in her cheeks. She stood up.

"I need to—"

"I only wanted to warn you." He stood up and laid a hand on her bare arm. "Anna Mary." The beige taverna shirt spun around, the screen door gaped and banged, and he was gone. She heard the Volkswagen engine and went to the window to watch, propping up her face with both arms on the sill. Like his once-white trousers, the blue Volkswagen carried the brown slop of mud puddles on every wheel and sprayed up over the back fenders. Motoring away, the engine sound diminished to a distant whistle. Now, the car was only a blue robin's egg that now-you–saw, now-you-didn't through the ebony locust tree trunks on the far hill.

Yes, it all makes sense now. He did it with me in the hay loft, didn't he? Does a man change his methods? "You know what he's like when he's aroused," Wolf said.

She scrubbed the blood from her hand and arm at the sink.

Yet the vulgar word he'd used to describe them. She was shocked that he talked like that. That he thought like that. A music teacher at KMC! Maybe it was a lie. Of course it was a lie. Who could know the truth, anyway? *Gloria, that's who! I need to tell her I know now. Then watch her eyes. She never could lie to me. One peep in the eyes and I know, every time.*

Inside her belly, the pain twisted slowly, a contorting copperhead sucking on her intestines. *Not another attack. Not yet. I have to know the truth. Not yet!*

"Jakie!" She called. "We're going to Pop-Pop's!"

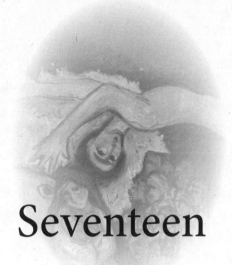

Seventeen

THERE HADN'T BEEN a pain in over an hour, and now one was due. What if she was driving when it came? What then? *If it's the end, we'll be together, Jakie and I. We'll go out together, and both of us will be spared.*

Schnoogie stood on the car seat, watching everything that passed outside. When they turned off the main road onto the Bishop's lane, he immediately spotted the tractor in the field.

"Hey, a fractor!" He pointed.

"Norman's Paulie." She smiled to herself. Normans let the little guy run the tractor, and he was only eight. The same age she'd been the first time.

It was a John Deere tractor and characteristically noisy. The window on Schnoogie's side was half-open, and he leaned against it. The door was locked. She'd done that before they started. "Putt! Putt! Putt! Putt!" Schnoogie shouted, his hands circling as if they held a steering wheel while he rocked his head back and forth with each shout. He goggled at her. "Putt, putt, putt, putt!" His long hair shook in rhythm again and he giggled, watching her every time he stopped.

"Not so loud." She brushed the hair out of his eyes.

"Putt! Putt! Putt! Putt! Putt! Putt! Putt! Putt! Putt!" He threw out the explosive sounds nonstop until he ran out of breath and could only soundlessly mouth the syllables.

"You want to be a farmer like Pop-Pop when you get big, don't you?"

"I'm going to drive a frac-tor!"

Maybe the pains were over for today. She'd just needed some fresh air. She cranked down her window. "Mmmm . . . I still smell the rain."

"Rain? I don't see rain."

"And the mint tea! Smell the mint!"

"Putt, putt, putt, putt," Schnoogie said in a small voice. With one hand his imaginary tractor drove outside the window, up and down in the wind current.

"Huh!" The pain struck without notice. She slashed the steering wheel right at the curb, fighting to keep the front wheel out of the ditch and away from the bridge abutment. They stopped six inches from the concrete wall of the bridge. Her head thudded against the steering wheel.

"Mommy . . . ?"

She fumbled in her purse for a handkerchief and stuffed it between her teeth to stifle the cry. Schnoogie slid down in his seat, watching.

"Are you crying?"

She blotted her tears, recovering. The attack was already gone. She turned her face. *I don't want him to go telling Pop I'm crying.* "See, there's another tractor." She smiled and identified a distant one.

"Where?" His body weighed against her shoulder as he craned to see. "It's just a little one, huh? It's just a little one." From a distance of just a few inches, his eyes were searching hers now, concentrating on a tear on her face. He tried to touch it with his forefinger.

She pulled his body against her with one arm. "You're going to be a big man like Pop-Pop, aren't you?" She sniffled. He returned to his window and started to play with the imaginary tractor again. She put the car in gear and drove slowly over the bridge and up to the fence in the Bishop's yard. *Thank goodness. No one saw that. I see no one. No one to see. But Pop must be here. He has to be here.* The engine died. She bit her fingertip. Schnoogie immediately pulled up the door lock and jumped out.

"Come here, Jakie."

"Huh?" He paused at the yard gate.

"Come here."

"Huh?"

"Come here." Obediently, he ran around to her open car door. She tucked the front and back of his shirt into his new pants, at the same time saying, "Now, don't get your new pants messy." She leaned forward. "Give Mommy a goodbye kiss."

"Are you going bye-bye?" His eyes flared.

"Give Mommy a kiss." He leaned around and kissed her lips directly, then leaped away. *So handsome; really handsome.* She got out of the car. *Home. The catalpa tree with swing scars on the low limb. Long green beans. The flagstone path on which we played jacks with marigolds and morning glories here, there the sun porch and Pop's bee equipment hanging up the kuhreeek kuhreeek kuhreeek of the iron water pump and cherries. And apricots. And the barn ooo so white and neat . . . Home!* She fumbled for the handkerchief again. *I'm so teary this morning—I must see Pop.* She hurried across the gravel driveway to the milkhouse. *Hope I didn't miss him. It's what? Thursday? What does he do on Thursdays?*

Everything was changing under Norman's administration of the farm. A new cinder block milkhouse had replaced the old one that she'd grown up with, and this one housed the stainless steel, thousand-gallon milk bulk tank, its motors purring steadily as she pushed open the door. Like the Bishop himself, the farm was a combination of the latest and the oldest innovations. Norman was ahead of his generation—one of the first in the valley to put in the bulk tank and pipeline milking. But he'd also left in place the concrete knee-high water trough that had been built in the early 1900s to chill the little turn-of-the-century milk cans with running water.

Cold water pulled up by the yard pump from underground limestone creeks flowed to the concrete trough here in the milkhouse and also to the reservoir on the summer porch. The trough still served a purpose, as it exited through a pipe beneath the barn floor into a large, iron watering half-tank in the beef-cow feeding shed below. A spigot controlled the intake pipe to the milkhouse trough, and just now it was cranked shut. The trough was cooling two fat, dark watermelons that floated hardly visible, like half-sunken heads of crocodiles.

She heard him behind the bulk tank, singing in his tuneless bass. "Doh . . . doh . . . sol . . . dohdoh."

"Pop! I thought you'd gone."

She came around the backside of the tank and there he was, his boots and barn clothes giving off the friendly fermented silage smell she associated with childhood on this farm. His once-red but now greenish-orange cap was jammed down over his forehead, and day-old whiskers decorated the face. He paused, an oil squirt-can in hand, and peered up over his bifocals at her.

"Well, well!" He peered around for a resting spot for the oil can and found a window ledge. "I was hoping—" His arms spread wide, and she rushed into them. "It's about time you came home to do some bookkeeping for me." Two gnarled fingers pinched her cheek.

Up close like this, she noticed his faded rose cheeks, the wart on his chin with the two hairs he needed to trim that refused to turn silver like his eyebrows, his magnified eyes through the bifocals, looking like large, blue cornflowers. *I am home. With the one man who understands everything.*

"I missed you, Pop."

"Well!" His embrace opened up and he turned for his can. "Are you okay? We haven't seen you around here for awhile. Schnoogie—"

"He went to see if Grandmom has a cookie."

Released from the security of his embrace, she wandered back to the cooling trough, its waters still and inky. It reflected her image back to her darkly, like a Puerto Rican version of herself, with long locks escaping from beneath the blue and white polka-dotted bandanna.

I don't look ill. Not like in the mirror at home, so pasty.

"I'm still washing up." The Bishop plunged the teat-cup assembly into the steaming, sudsy water. The splash drops also fell into the still water of the concrete trough. The reflected face rocked violently, mouth and nose distorting in opposite directions, stretching apart till they didn't resemble face parts. Then, slowly, the image sucked back together, rocking.

"You got something on your mind. Everything all right? How about Saul?"

"Let's don't talk about him."

"Things no better, huh?"

She was silent. If he knew they didn't have marital relations, would he say something? Would he make her go back to him?

He turned now, shaking the milker assembly to throw off the excess water, and then dropped it with a clang onto the rail shelf.

"Anna Mary!" His eyes narrowed.

She gazed back, hardly able to focus. What was it, anyway? Perhaps the cancer had sapped her energy. A tumor? Like Sadie Ebersole, whose belly had swelled as if she had a child in there while the rest of her had shrunk and dwindled until she was just the pushed-out stomach on a bony frame under a white taffeta dress she'd sewed herself, laid out in a maple wood box in her parent's parlor. Her face half-lit by table lamps and—

"Anna Mary, do your recall what you wanted to be? What you told us when you were little?" He was watching her and using the story as a gimmick to keep her focused on him. "You never played house and doll babies—you played with tractors. Remember that?"

She nodded.

"How about the little tractor I made you out of walnut wood with big, wood wheels and you used to take it to bed with you? I'll bet we still have that someplace." He'd forgotten he'd already repainted it and bequeathed it to Schnoogie. "I remember what you said you wanted to be. Do you? About three, Schnoogie's age . . . don't know if you'd remember. Huh?" He saw the beginnings of a smile. "You remember!"

"Was it something I said?" She felt woozy.

"'When I grow up I wanna be a tractor!'" His guffaw boomed off the cinder block milkhouse walls and seemed to clear the air of unwanted spirits. He looked at her curiously. "I wonder if you should see a doctor."

"It's nothing." She came out of the haze as easily as she'd fallen into it. The face in the water smiled brightly at her now. *I should let him know now, while he's listening carefully. But I will say it calmly, without panic.* "Something terrible's going to happen. You should know about that."

"Huh?"

"Something awful's going to happen."

"What's wrong, Anna Mary? What you talking about?"

"I don't know. Just that something terrible's getting ready to happen."

"To whom?"

"Us. You and me and Jakie and . . . ." *That's all I can think of right now.*

"Something's wrong, isn't it. You don't seem like yourself. So far away." The Bishop rested on the stepladder and retrieved a pocket watch on its chain. "We've got 10 minutes till the milkman. I want you to tell me everything."

How much to say? Her little sister and her husband, Wolf had said, doing *that* together. The destruction coming on like a tornado. And they would all be sucked up and spat down. Did he understand that?

"Is this about Saul?"

"Some."

"You think he's going to do something to you?"

"Hmm." She shook her head no. He didn't understand at all. "We're going to be spit out."

"That's a figure of speech. Is that what's bothering you? The church situation? Anna Mary, it's about over. I may be wrong, but I think so. They're going to break away—I haven't even told your mother what I feel about all this lately, but I'll tell you—they'll break away. He's made some big statements, and now he has to live up to them. He has to make a decisive move, or his role as a prophet is kaput. That's how he operates, on crises. Saul's a crisis man. He can't work with organizations and revisions and gradual growth. Or things that are planned. He has to . . ." His fingers snapped in the air between them. "Everything at once. That's the military way, I guess. They conquer foreign armies and do campaigns. Get themselves all riled up and then, charge!"

Things seemed so clear to her when he explained them.

"This 'spit out.' That's Saul's way of talking about 'apostasy,' in quotes, in the Church. Not that there isn't any, but I'd like to see us come to the place we say there can be latitude in interpreting the Scriptures. He wants handclapping and visions and tongues—that might be fine with me. Some of the bishops want to clamp down. I'll admit I fight the urge to say, 'Take your marbles and go. We don't need you.'"

Her eyes were glommed on his mouth, only some of his words reaching her. She mostly drank in the tone of his voice. *I like him. Even if he's big and powerful. He has things under control; he can stop bad things from happening.*

"Lately though, I decided we may as well tolerate them. If they don't overly disturb our members and worship, why can't we just include 'em in? I don't want any on the ministerial board if I can help it. I think we're safe on the Bishop Board for a few years, unless Cyrus Brubaker goes in over his head. Anyway, he's 70-something and won't live forever. So . . . what?" He thrust a hand downward into the washtubs, pulled up both plugs, and wiped his wet hands onto his trouser legs. "Does that help?"

She smiled faintly. It was time for another pain.

"Mollify as possible." The Bishop pulled out a stick of dried alfalfa that he kept in his breast pocket and began to chew it. He examined his pocket watch again. "Milkman's a little late, ain't he?"

She spoke in a small voice. "I don't know if I'm saved."

The Bishop swiped harshly at his pants. "Now I'm going to get mad. Did he say that?"

She shrugged weakly. "Didn't he say that?"

"You're saved. Don't let him do that to you. You made a decision when you were—how old were you?"

"Five."

"Five. That's old enough. You were baptized. You haven't missed communion."

The milk truck arrived, gearing down noisily and gunning the engine as it turned onto the dirt driveway. The milkman, whistling, pushed open the door. "Hello," the Bishop said, standing.

"Oh, I didn't know there was—"

"Just talking. You know Anna Mary? Anna Mary, our second daughter."

The milkman walked in with his big wrench and connection hose. Anna Mary watched. *I don't believe he understood a thing I said. He's too good. He's too optimistic. He only sees the good things. He doesn't see what I can see even now moving in, a terrible tragedy.* "Terrible tragedy. Terrible tragedy." She whispered the words again and again to herself. *As predicted, moving in.*

"Mom's baking cookies. She'll be glad for some help before you get at the cherries, I'm sure. Feel better?" Their eyes met. His voice sharpened. "Are you getting enough sleep?"

The milkman, she noted, was out of earshot, fiddling with the pump on his truck. "It would be terrible if he left me, wouldn't it." *Don't ask why. It'll kill you about Gloria. You don't know the half. I couldn't tell you, but it'll kill you.*

"Anna Mary, you pull yourself together. I'm going to talk to him first thing."

"I must, mustn't I?" She went to the door. "I'll go see Mom."

She was hardly out the door when it came. She toppled, her forehead colliding against the fence that enclosed the steer pen. She had just enough time to peer sideways and see that the milkman was still out of sight. Her mouth opened against the whitewashed board and moaned. Was it the cancer? *I'm gonna faint, gonna . . . what about Jakie? What will happen to him when the terrible things come? I'm afraid . . . .*

Eighteen

SHE PULLED OFF a handful of the maroon sweet cherries and watched them bleed where the stems had been attached.

It's hopeless. Hopeless. He's helped me every time, but he can't this time.

The moon-round face of the man with the orangish-green cap and aura of whiskers still stuck before her eyes. The sweet, intoxicating aroma of fermented corn silage and his arms wide open, chuckling, "Well, well!" Squeezing her today as he did that day when she was five, when they'd laid Mattie Mae in the ground, and they had sat on her bed together. She had seen tears running down his cheeks. She was on his lap and tasted saltwater in his whiskers when he pulled her face against his cheek. When she was 18, she couldn't make college because there was no money, but he'd said, "Work on the farm for me. You do the bookkeeping, and when things turn around, I'll pay your college." She was a good bookkeeper, too—they'd gone from two farms and 40 cows to three farms, 100 milkers, and 100 beef cows by the end of 1947. And he was good for his word, paying for two years at KMC and her A.A. in accounting and bookkeeping.

The third time he saved her . . . she was 25 and with no man in sight. No man the equal of Bishop Jacob Krehbiel, anyway. He brought

Saul from Washington, and she'd married him. Mom said, "No, you can't marry. He doesn't make any money." But after they found out the baby was coming, he'd come back again with a plan. He coaxed Saul with that plan for a whole weekend until Saul did the manly thing and agreed to work the new farm Pop had bought for them. It was always Pop saving the day.

But this time he couldn't save her. Things were way beyond his control. Terrible things were about to happen, and he had no idea they were coming, for he couldn't see what she saw. He said Saul was just talking and that nothing would happen at all. What about the tumor or malignancy or whatever it was? How many weeks—or even days—did she have left? With Sadie Ebersole it was five months, and already it had been seven months since the cramps and burning had first started in the winter.

He had no idea—"should you see a doctor?" he had said. And now the biggest thing of all—Saul's thing with Gloria. *Doing that,* Wolf had said. Leading to . . . would she sit with the old widow ladies upfront in church, like Sister Lutz, whose husband died last year when the tractor upset, leaving her with four little ones under six? Or like Sister Kleinfelter, whose man started sleeping with the blonde waitress at Bertha's Diner. Her family had kicked him out of the church, and today she also sat with the widow ladies and old maids—never to marry again, of course, as long as he was alive. Not in the Mennonite Church. All leading up to . . . *they'll take Jakie away so they can raise him as their own.*

The boy knelt at the bottom of the cherry tree, manipulating the homemade walnut tractor with the big wheels that his grandfather had made 25 years ago. He backed up the miniature wagon with high sides to pick up the cherry culls that had fallen in the windstorm last night.

"Rrrrrmmmm! Rrrrrmmmm!"

The day hung beautiful beyond belief. Everything felt more perfect, more peaceful than it had ever been, as if to mock her. The cherries were large and perfect and had hardly any splits or cracks, which you'd expect after a rainstorm like last night. The fertility of this farm was incredible.

The corn beyond the whitewashed fence on the west side of the yard had only just burst into tassel last week, sweetening the air with the smell of the cornsilk, snatching up the tassel sperms as they blew everywhere across the field. Bees streamed out of the five hives between the cornfield and the whitewashed fence, almost directly below her ladder. Winged messengers came and went with little packets of golden pollen latched to their hind legs, their stomachs bulging with nectar. Everything was organized and precise as if under some divine control.

Except the humans.

She continued to drop handfuls of the cherries into the enamel bucket she'd hooked onto the large branch to the left of her ladder, which was propped against the trunk of the tree. The limbs bent down as she tugged the cherries, and then flew back to their places. Through the leaves, she saw Gloria, her ladder propped on the opposite side of the tree. Now she saw a hand and long, bare arm closing on a bunch of cherries, now the top of her head, swaddled in a polka-dotted bandanna like her own, now a piece of face—an eye, her mouth. They hadn't spoken at all over the first bucket they'd each completed and already taken to the summer porch for Mom, who was busy preparing them for canning.

"Here, Jakie, you can have these." She pulled off a twigful that had half broken from the branch when she'd thrust the ladder through the branches to the trunk.

He crawled across the grass under the tree to retrieve the fallen twig and bent it to fit into the wagon, all the while making appropriate noises.

"Putt, putt, putt, putt! See!" He shouted, encouraged by her interest. "I put them in the silo, Mommy." His make-believe silo was a pile of 50 or so fallen cherries mounded in a crevice formed by two forking roots that humped several inches out of the lawn.

"He's so cute!" Gloria said. "I always dream I'll get a little guy as fine as you and Edie got."

Anna Mary heard it with disbelief.

"I don't know. It seems I won't. It seems I'll end up one of those—Pop always calls them 'Unclaimed Blessings.' I don't want to be an Unclaimed Blessing with the old maids and widows in the Amen Corner."

"You won't. You have a pretty face and a full figure, and Wolf—" She broke off, remembering the man in her front room this morning.

"I didn't tell you. And I don't know if Mom did or not—" Gloria lowered her voice. "I broke it off last night. He's here, you know. Up in the barn."

"Yes, I've heard everything."

"I feel so free. I should have broken it off at Snow Camp, but I just couldn't."

"Snow Camp?" The words seemed to keep popping up everywhere.

"I want to warn you and Saul." Gloria pushed a large branch down from her chin so she could see Anna Mary clearly. She stage-whispered again. "He's really upset about it and says he's going to hurt Saul. Or Schnoogie. I hate to say it, but he's not safe."

"Why are you telling me this, Gloria?" *Can she tell me with a straight face? Will she dodge me? Will she change the subject?*

"Because I care about you. I love you and Saul."

"You love Saul?"

"He's a sweetie. He agreed I should break it off with Wolf. And he cares. Everybody cares at the Revival, Anna Mary. I wish you'd come sometime."

Neither of them spoke for a minute, but they remained in their places, spying over the cherry buckets through the gap in the tree branches.

"So much love." Through the branches, Gloria's face appeared luminous and eager. "All share the Holy Spirit worship, and everyone's thrilled to see everyone. We hug all around at greeting time. Like heaven," she said, "no barriers between people. In the Resurrection there will be no marriages or getting married, just love between the sisters and brothers. That's how the Revival is. We're getting started with heaven, Saul says."

She could hardly believe her sister would say it right out like that, without a blush, without a cringe, smiling gleefully. "Saul says?"

"He leads the way. Last night we talked at the tent, and he just folded his big arms around me. You know how he does. So when I say I love him—"

Treachery openly confirmed. Gloria had told everything but their plans. She'd already broken with Wolf, and now Anna Mary realized what had happened after Snow Camp. He'd broken off with her then, too, even if they went on together in the same house like roommates. Thanks to the cancer, she'd fallen out of the picture now, leaving the two of them to fondle and caress on her future gravesite, while whatever the terrible thing coming ran over everything she treasured. Like a driverless Caterpillar, it would come smashing, crushing, obliterating the old, precious world she had known, leaving the two of *them* alone together in the new world.

"He's my husband, still." She said it and began the descent out of the tree, unhooking the nearly full cherry bucket and feeling it swing heavily alongside as she went down. "And I understand what you mean, Gloria." Her bare feet touched the grass. "I know you and Saul are doing things." She dropped the full bucket on the edge of the hill, where the hill descended to the peony bushes that lined the flagstone walk, and ran for the house.

"Anna Mary!" Gloria screamed, nearly falling off the ladder in a self-abandoned effort to catch her sister. "Anna Mary!"

Anna Mary ran through the summer porch and passed the open reservoir where Mom Krehbiel was cooling gallon jars of meadow tea. She turned into the washhouse that adjoined the house and ran down the small flight of steps toward the garden, yanking open the door to the toilet room. She latched the door behind her and, not trusting the latch, fell backward onto the toilet and squeezed the door handle between both hands, planting her bare feet against both door frames to brace herself in the opposite direction from which she was pulling the handle. The toilet smelled pungently. Unlike the rest of the home, this one next to the garden had no plumbing lines, only a drainage pipe to the septic tank outside and below ground.

She heard the screen door bang as Gloria entered the summer porch, and then heard her footsteps as she walked into the kitchen. "Mom! Mom!" She heard only a muffled conversation, but enough to tell that her sister was hysterical. More footsteps, and then the doorknob tested her hands. The door vibrated with Gloria's pounding.

"Anna Mary. You took it all wrong. There's nothing between us. Nothing! He's your husband. I know that!" The voice sobbed. "Not that kind of love, Anna Mary." Something banged against the door and bumped from side to side—was it her head?—while the hysterical voice diminished to a regular sniffle.

I would expect she'd deny when she sees how it hurts me. But it's much, much, much too late.

"Anna Mary. Hnh, hnh, hnh . . ." Gloria wailed. The shoes scuffled again and went away.

She released the door knob and fell back against the wall. *Hopeless. Hopeless. I just want to die.*

She got up slowly and retraced her steps toward the cherry tree in the front yard. Schnoogie was on his knees, his mouth full and oozing juice, holding up his tractor and wagon as he tipped the five-gallon bucket of cherries to fill his toy wagon. He snapped his head sideways when the screen door slapped and, knowing he was in the wrong, jumped to his feet with his toys. The bucket tipped on over, sending a plum-purple river of cherries down the embankment and into the peonies.

She ran as the bucket began to tip, but changed direction and went after Schnoogie instead. He was charging for the tree when she caught him by the bib straps and gave him two quick swats, not even remarking on the garish knees of his new trousers that were now permanently dyed with the blood of the cherries. He danced out of reach toward the gate, sobbing and giggling, "Mommy can't get me." She came back to the embankment and fell to her knees, facing uphill toward the cherry flood. Doubling over, her hands thrust down into the cherry bodies.

Her stomach muscles tightened like rubber bands, twisting and twisting. An attack was on the way. Gloria had confirmed, despite all efforts to elicit pity for herself, her disloyalty and eagerness to take advantage of the cancer. The terrible things were blowing in like a hurricane. They would engulf this valley and everything she loved: Pop, Jakie, the farm.

Hands fumbled on her shoulders. The body dropping next to her on the grass was Gloria's, one arm straddling her shoulder while the free hand trailed down the bare arm to grasp her left hand.

"Ann-a-Mary." She'd been crying and the voice broke and sucked sharply. "Ann-a-Marrrr-y!"

Anna Mary turned on her knees, staring directly into Gloria's face. "AHHHHHHHHHHHHH!" Her scream was horrific, a frantic squeal, like one of Noah's pigs on the butchering floor as it felt the knife slash across its throat. Gloria's hands dropped, and now her mouth opened, registering shock, a wrinkle rising between the eyes as if she was jointly suffering or wanting to suffer the unadulterated agony and distress of that scream. Anna Mary pulled her hands out of the cherries and beat the ground rhythmically with both fists, throwing back her face toward the sky. Cherry juice dripped from her clenched fingers. "AHHHHHHHHHHHHHH!" The second scream was identical to the first.

The beautiful day seemed impervious to the scream. Nothing changed. Instead, a hiss and soft cluck-clucking sounded just below the peonies. Gloria, angled toward the peony bushes, saw the geese behind the peonies throwing back their heads to swallow the spilled cherries. She scrambled. "The gate's open!" she wailed, not directly to anyone, but at the beautiful day.

Anna Mary instantly understood. She sprang to her feet and bolted through the open gate to the outer yard. "Jakie! Jakie!"

The robin-egg blue VW had parked next to her car. It guided her next decision. She ran up the stone and compact-earth ramp to the barn second floor, noting that the small swing door that notched into the giant double doors was also hanging open.

Darkness closed in as she dashed through the door, but thirty feet beyond she saw the boy. He was bent over the hole leading down from the second floor to the concrete floor of the steer pen, 15 feet below. Light from the hole silhouetted him, lighting his hands and his long hair as he bent forward on a bale that hung partly over the hay hole. She didn't call for fear he might startle and tip the bale downward through the hole. He faced her as she came, saying without any fear, as if the swats in the yard 10 minutes before hadn't counted, "I see the hommies!"

"Who is it?" The voice came from overhead in the mow, 40 feet up and almost at the inverted *V* of the pitched roof, as the mows were full from a summer of haying.

"Jakie!" She caught him by the bib straps and glimpsed, fearfully, five or more bales scattered on this level, around the hole. Schnoogie had been leaning on one of these as he squinted down through the three-foot square opening at the 10 or more steers that were horning and shouldering each other to get nearer to the dried, green alfalfa bales that had fallen through.

Still clutching Schnoogie, she lurched back 10 feet to the wheel of the corn planter and slanted up.

"It's us!"

"Anna Mary?" She could make out the figure of a half-dressed man now, stripped to the waist because of the terrible heat at the top of the mow. Wolfgang was doing his summer job of taking care of the beef cows.

"And Jakie! Schnoogie," she added, remembering he didn't know him by his other name.

"I'm throwing bales! That hole's dangerous." She didn't respond. She drooped still against the corn planter, gazing up. "He likes haymows, I've heard." The tiny figure silhouetted at the top of the mow waved its arms angrily. "Did he bring her up here?"

The attack tore her gut with ferocity. She sucked in sharply, bandaging her mouth shut with both hands. Schnoogie took the opportunity to wiggle loose and run back to the hole.

"He debauched her, Anna Mary! He ruined her! Or was it in the cornfield? Or both? Djaaaaaah! I can't stand it!"

His words were small and far away, as if over a long-distance telephone line, although each word cut through her pain like acid, etching. As *clearly as anything, I see it all. Just don't know how it will all come out. Do I collapse here and die? Hardly propping myself upright now. I could die. I could die. That solves all for me, but Jakie still suffers. Spit out with everyone else.*

The little figure at the top of the mow disappeared. Wolf was yelling something. "Okay? Okay?" Schnoogie was over the hole again, pointing excitedly.

She stared at the boy, down on all fours over the hay hole, where he was forbidden to be. Her eyes distended in shock at the unbelievable pain angrily lashing again and again. *We'll go together. Yes, okay! He'll be okay today! Safe in the arms of Jesus; safe on His gentle breast.*

Tarrum! Tarrummm! Tarrrrrummmm! One, two, three, the 80-pound bales came bounding off the immense wall of stacked hay, loose seeds and leaves flying. They almost blotted out the boy, but there he was again. His mouth gulped with an unutterable cry, his hands up flinging slowly out of sight and then down into the light, hayseeds blowing back up like chaff out of the combine. Thuddd. No louder than the sound of the refrigerator door shutting.

Silence returned. Wolfgang descended the long ladder fixed against the wall of the mow, rung by rung, still cursing. "The Jesus stallion! And his mare. Like a bunch of rutting animals!" He cursed him and stopped

10 feet up from the floor level, hanging by one arm to rubberneck. "Where's the boy?"

Gloria was shrieking from the steer pen below, and the Bishop's anxious shouts were coming closer. Anna Mary sank to her knees over the hole, and she felt the man drop down beside her and go to his knees. They gawked at the hysterical face 10 feet below and gaping back up at the two of them.

"What did you do?" Gloria's arms waved disjointedly, and she fell back so they could see where the boy had landed.

Like a Raggedy Andy doll, he was limp on the concrete below, laid out just like Mattie Mae when they'd pulled her up out of the grain chute. *He went first, and I'm left behind. What shall I do?* She grasped her face with hands over both ears, distending her cheeks and lips forward like a hideous gargoyle. The pitiful scream bounced back and forth in the tight shadowy opening between the two towering hay mows. "AHHHHHHHHHHHHH!"

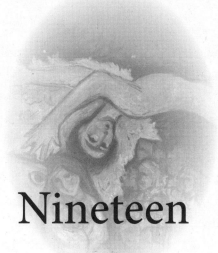

Nineteen

CHILLY CREEK SPILLED south like an eternally emptying cup of coffee at Harp-in-the-Willows, milky brown, and reduced again to its banks after last night's cloudburst and flooding. A new shoal of coal sand ran the entire length of the dig, 200 feet perhaps, and about two feet high, curving delicately like an ocean sandbar.

Ordinarily, Saul would have remarked on that: "Look at this! It keeps renewing itself as fast as we take it away! It's the golden egg the goose keeps laying! Ten thousand ton? Golly. By the time we get it hauled away, another 10,000 will have transported itself in, flake by shiny flake! A river full of them for as many years as the coal breakers and washeries in Suedburg and Pine Grove keep splitting coal into nut-size chunks and washing off the particles!"

Today, instead, he eased out of the old Ford and kicked viciously at the shoal. Flying coal bits landed in the pools left stranded by the high water, and a mist of mosquitoes rose to greet him. He slapped his hands and throat and went back to the pickup for the repellant, smearing the fragrant stuff over his cheeks, neck, and the backs of his hands left exposed beyond the cuffed sleeves. He kept his sleeves cuffed as long as he was here by the river, especially in the mornings before the sun dried out the dig.

He walked along the top of the shoal to the Caterpillar, leaned across the steel tracks, and upended the seat, the water spilling away.

No contract! He slapped himself again with this reality. Haul all you want, but they had legal ways to wiggle out of payment. He fetched the envelope from his breast pocket and, standing by the Caterpillar facing the creek, reviewed the figures he'd scrawled this morning. A thousand tons since the New Year, 561 loads at 90 bucks a trip. Fifty-one thousand, five hundred ninety dollars in earnings less the 10 percent land usage fee, equaled $45,360 divided by two, or $22,680 per man. For seven months work, a run-rate of $45,000 a year. A little less than he'd promised Anna Mary that night, but unbelievable wealth in the making and the possibility of really big money once they brought a second truck online. But along came this terrible reality: Susquehanna Electric hadn't paid for the last two months, of which his share was $7,200. He'd circled the figure three times in red on the envelope.

How could he have overlooked it so long? Let Bennie sweet-talk him? Blarney him along? They'd received the contract in October and signed it. Susquehanna Electric hadn't. Paid them anyway for what they got, but didn't sign the contract. In March he'd pressed Bennie, and he said they'd promised, but regardless, they were paying, weren't they? In June, he'd led Saul to believe they'd signed, that the delay in payment was just that: a delay.

And now here they were, eight weeks later without pay and, what's more, *no signature.*

The radio announced Bennie's arrival on the iron bridge before Saul could see him.

I LOADED SIXTEEN TONS OF NUMBER NINE COAL, AND THE STRAW BOSS SAID, "WELL, BLESS MY SOUL..."

The little, gray Ford pickup, its engine competing with Tennessee Ernie Ford, came bouncing over the corduroy that straddled the swampy entrance. It circled the lot, dropped into the Cat tracks, and stopped between the silent dump truck and the tin roof shack that stored the chainsaw, drag-chains, and diesel fuel behind a padlocked door.

"Hey, Gravy Train!" Bennie leaped from the cab, chewing gum vigorously. "It won't start?" He pointed the Caterpillar, walking toward Saul, sidestepping puddles and slapping at mosquitoes on his beefy arms all the while.

Saul fought a fierce urge to scorch him with dragon's breath. "I don't wanna start it."

"What's up? You don't wanna make money today?" Bennie moved to box his shoulder, but Saul caught the wrist and lowered it.

"Don't mess around."

"Hey! He get to you? That Wolfgang guy last night? He's no fighter. Anybody with pretty curls like that—"

"Bennie, shut up. You're the problem."

"I'm late, huh?" He pulled his pocket watch. "Eleven o'clock, huh? I have a reason! I was—"

"Where's the contract, Bennie?"

Bennie back-stepped. "In my glove compartment."

"I know. Without a signature. I checked this morning when I got here."

"Okay, okay."

"You deceived me, Bennie."

"I can explain." He swatted two mosquitoes that were drilling on the top of his bald head.

"Here." Saul tossed the bottle of repellant.

Bennie ran to the pickup, retrieved his cap, and came back, smearing the lotion on his throat as he jogged. "I was going to say where I was . . . why I'm late . . . when you . . . you interrupted." He was puffing from the run. "Susque . . . anhahnha . . . hanna Electric." Puffing again. "You know that Winerich guy I told you about?"

"The foreman."

"With two greasy side-kicks? Tattoos? Motorcycle jackets? Long hair? And every time it's this excuse or that. 'We'll sign that contract when the president gets back.' 'Nope, it's the Treasurer signs, and he's at our other plant in Altoona for a month.' Well, today, he's gone. Him and his sidekicks. Fired. And a new guy, Pookawskatty's there now. Potoskapy . . . these Italian names."

"Sounds Polish."

"Whatever. Old Country, anyway. Wears a—" He described a necktie with his hands, jerking it into a knot at the throat. "And fancy shirt. Nothing against bowties, just mean that this one's, you know . . ." His eyes narrowed, nodding with pregnant meaning.

"I *don't* know."

"A straight-shooter!" Bennie slammed a fist into his open palm. "Smokes a cigar, he does, and no cheap stogie like some Old Order Mennonite, but one of them Cuban ones . . ."

"Get to the point. Whadiddy say?"

"Susquehanna's figuring out if coal's best or not, and soon as they're done, 90 percent they'll sign. But if not . . ."

"Wait! This is news. '*If coal is best,*' you just said. What's that mean?"

"Best way to make electric. What? They been saying that all along. Winerich too. It's a whatchamacall 'experiment' for these guys. They'll sign for 10,000 tons, like they was talking last fall, but first—"

"Why didn't you say there were conditions before they'll sign?"

"I don't tell you everything. You're busy. You're an important guy. Small stuff like this—"

"Small stuff? *No contract* is small stuff?"

"We *have* a contract. Just not signed yet."

Saul clambered up on the Caterpillar and punched the ignition. "How can I trust you?" He yelled over the diesel roar. "Look out!" He shoved the Caterpillar in reverse and tracked back to line up the scoop with the new shoal. "Get your truck over here!"

How did I let myself get into this? He had $7,200 unpaid in back earnings. The dairy just covered the mortgage, the hired man, and the food, but the payment on his equipment and profit were all tied up in that $7,200. The Caterpillar began to devour the shoal, and the bucket lifted a load of dripping coal sand overhead. His wife was having a nervous breakdown, the Revival was ending Sunday night, and then it was back to whatever. And now he had a lieutenant he couldn't trust. *I should never have left D.C. to come here.* He hadn't thought of that, even once, before today. "Get your truck! What you waiting for?"

Bennie stood next to the torn ground where the Caterpillar had been parked. "If we don't get paid, why you hauling more?" Bennie yelled to outdo the roar of the engine.

"You're right." Saul let the bucket freefall to the ground, killed the engine, and sat, hands shaking on the steering levers, regarding the shoal ahead. "There's something else, Bennie."

"What?" His roly-poly body opposite the Cat waited, his hands open palm-up as he eyeballed Saul like a baby bird waiting for whatever grub or worm was going to be stuffed into its trusting maw.

"You have bad judgment. Driving Mrs. Yorty home when she was once your steady. Telling Millie Kurtz she's going to hell for not coming to our meetings. Ordering those ushers to give you 50 pushups in 90-something temperatures, because someone said something you didn't like."

"Called me a fat Amishman. It wasn't for nothing. Okay? Okay." Bennie dropped seat-first onto the ground like an off-balance toddler. "You don't trust me. You don't trust my judgment." He rolled forward onto his knees and grabbed tufts of grass. He pulled up the dripping clods of coal sand and, as he rose, threw one at the Cat. "You don't like me." He fired another one. It hit the dashboard of the Cat, splattering bits of wet coal onto Saul's face.

Bennie was heaving loose a sizeable rock, and Saul bailed over the far fender of the Caterpillar to protect himself. "So get someone else instead of me!" Bennie tossed the rock. It smashed into the headlight of the Caterpillar, and the glass tinkled as it fell.

Bennie fled toward the pickup.

"Stop!" Saul scrambled to intercept him. He jerked the door of the pickup and slid into the seat opposite his partner, who was attempting to jam keys into the ignition, in his fury using the wrong key. The jamming hand fell away and Bennie glared ahead, silent. The cab smelled like a high quality cigar. "Don't go."

"You don't trust me."

"You're all I have."

"And YOU-DON'T-TRUST-ME." Bennie pounded the steering wheel with both fists on each word.

"I just want you to tell me the truth." Saul lowered his voice, feeling remorse over the interchange. "The whole truth, even about the small stuff."

"Can you ever trust me?" Bennie's voice became a broken whisper.

He squeezed Bennie's hefty biceps. "I'll try."

Bennie reviewed the cab ceiling, and then looked back at Saul. "They've got a petition going around. The members of Paradise Valley, some of them." His voice crackled with emotion. "And members of other churches around the district. They have five or six sheets going. I just heard, didn't see any. Pappy Kurtz drove one sheet around yesterday, telling people they had to sign."

"Saying what?"

"For the Bishop Board to silence you and me and Brother Cyrus." He choked with fear. "And smash the Revival!"

"Can they smash the work of the Holy Spirit? You remember the apostles before the Sanhedrin in the book of Acts? 'If this isn't from God, it will die by itself. But if it's from God, keep your hands off.' Pray for Sunday. I don't know how to end our meetings in the tent, but it's got to be a blast on the ram's horn for revival."

"Yes." Bennie bobbed the top of his body. "You're right."

"I feel inadequate for Sunday."

"You always say that. Every time. You say: 'What will I say?' And then He gives you pretty words. Our hearts catch fire!"

Saul hadn't planned it. The thought stole in on its own. He crawled out of the cab and came around to Bennie's side. "Come out, Brother. I want to pray a blessing on you. Like you did me at Snow Camp."

"Right now?"

"Why not?"

Bennie dropped to his knees in the damp coal silt behind the pickup and closed his eyes. Saul's hands rested on the man's shoulders until Bennie's cap came off. Now he felt the smooth, round bowling ball under the warm and hairless skin.

"Bless this brother, O God . . ."

He wasn't prepared for the response. Slowly at first, and then in a rising tempo and crazy tumble of musical and nonsensical syllables, Bennie began: "*Mashdi ophala ump gara ga philala! Mashdi ophala ump gara ga . . .*"

The babble peaked and subsided, peaked again and trailed off into silence. Saul dropped his hands. Still on his knees, Bennie began in a stiff, ceremonial voice to speak in English, presumably a translation of what he had spoken: "The Spirit of God is well-pleased with this revival, and even now . . ." His eyelids twittered, although closed. "Even now at the house of Bishop Krehbiel, I'm doing a thing to bring many to their knees." The eyes snapped open. "Hallelujah!"

"Can we trust it?"

"Let's go see." Bennie swiped the dirt from his knees, leaving large, damp ovals. He opened the pickup driver's door. "Hurry up!"

"What's the hurry?"

"We're going to the Bishop's. Sumpin' . . . the Spirit said it. I believe it. You don't have to believe if you don't want to, but I do." The motor raced.

Saul shrugged his shoulders and slid in. The truck bounced over the lumpy lane.

"You ain't heard my little tale about the gift of tongues," Bennie said. "I was still in Amish Church. Still driving my team and all. A little beard." He tittered. "Wasn't married, but I was old enough, so I just started wearing one. Cute, little, red beard." He rubbed his chin and spoke in a squeaky, playful voice. "And Amish services are real serious. You never been to one, huh? They praise the Lord, but all serious. No smiles and such. Three hours long. The tunes are from *da Ausbund*—real old-timey, you know. Songs about the martyrs.

"Well, I just had to praise the Lord some other way. This was after the Spirit got holda me, and one day I just cried out, 'Lord, what You want me to do? I can't leave the Amish, but I gotta praise you or go wacko.' You know what I mean, Saul? And He give me the Gift. I was plowing in the evening. Ohh . . . the sun going down red and e-normous. Bloodshot eye. I was so dammed up inside. Pretty soon I'm rutching around and feeling I'm gonna go artesian, and then I'm shouting these things as I'm plowing along. And I just kept it up, by myself, like a secret all these years—'cept when Edie found out—till that day you spoke up at the Christmas party. ThankyouJesusHolyGhost!" A fist pounded Saul's leg. "The more you talked that day, the more I started plugging up again." One hand slapped his chest. "And pretty soon . . ." He retrieved the handkerchief from his back pocket and blew his nose with a powerful snort. They drove along in silence until they entered Paradise Valley.

"I'll pay for that headlight," Bennie said. "Sorry. Do you trust me, Saul? Can you trust me?"

With that, the unsigned contract came to mind. The bad judgment calls. And the man's penchant for incoherently babbled messages. *But it's true. He's all I've got. On the other hand—maybe I don't trust him.* Although it was against his better judgment, but feeling it was all he could do, he grabbed Bennie's shoulder and shook the handful of flesh and shirt. "Sure!" He chuckled.

They passed through town and out into the slanting wheat fields, glowing ripe.

"What's that?" Bennie asked.

"What?"

"*That.*"

He spied the Bishop's farm off the end of Bennie's finger. At first he saw nothing more, and then he saw the blinking red light—like the light on a state trooper's car, rotating.

"I knew sumpin' was happening!"

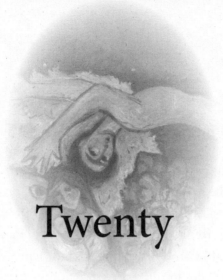

Twenty

IT'S A SAD occasion for our brother and sister," Bennie said. "But there's a bright crown, and the little ones all fall heirs to theirs. 'Suffer the little children to come to me and forbid them not, for of such is the Kingdom of Heaven.'" Bennie's roly-poly cheeks were burned red from spending long hours in the sun by the riverbed. His bald head shone like a Buddha's, and his burly frame was bursting through the plain coat.

"We don't want to forget any little one, but this little one . . . the Bible says 'olive plants,' the little ones. Not like fixed or stubborn in the ground the way of plants, but their little mouths open for water, so easy to snap off. That's what it means. This one would crawl up on my lap sometimes when I was visiting our brother and wanted a horsy ride, and I'd give it and what? 'Again, Uncle Bennie,' and after that, 'Again, Uncle Bennie.' Oft I thought, what if when he gets big, he be that eager beaver for Jesus? 'More, more, give me more.' Sadly, we don't see the grown-ups say that. And this one, he . . . he won't make a grown-up." Bennie's pitch rose. He blotted his nose with a handkerchief. "He won't . . ."

The death image assaulted him again as he gazed at the glossy oak casket four feet to his left on the wheeled, metal framework. He couldn't send the image away when it came, and it kept coming. In the middle of the night. In the middle of a conversation. The image was always the same: three hay bales lay on the concrete bay of the steer pen. He saw them as he swiftly rounded the corner of the steer barn. No tragic clues forewarned him. The ambulance that he and Bennie had seen was lost a mile away and wouldn't arrive until halfway through his desperate prayer. The steer pen gate was wide, the steers gone, and even that held no alarm. He saw their rusty noses pressed through the whitewashed corral boards, watching from the meadow side, and the sickly sweet aroma of silage and cow bodies and manure rose from the muck to the side of the concrete path.

The pale faces instantly turned to him as he came past the barn wall. Gloria addressed him. "I saw him . . ." Her head and shoulders shook. "Falling!"

"An accident!" Wolfgang pleaded with him. "O God! I know it's damning, after what I said last night. But—O God! It was an accident, Saul."

The Bishop also spoke. Saul heard all their voices before he saw the image, as they were standing between him and the bale.

"I'm sorry. So sorry, Saul—"

The image was always the same. The bale framed by their standing bodies, and right between them, laid out as if for viewing, the pale face, unrealistically white as if painted like a geisha's. Tiny red lines trailed from each nostril, and from the corners of the boy's mouth, four tiny trails that looked as if they had been painted there by a make-up artist. The stains on the belly of his new, green, corduroy jumpsuit matched the stains on his knees: cherry juice. His stocking feet didn't even reach to the end of the bale. But it was the odd angle of his head, as if he'd been lying on the bale twisting his face sideways and peering back at an airplane overhead. The boy's eyes were wide.

Anna Mary sat alongside on the neighboring bale, the boy's hand pressed in hers, watching Saul arrive. The others ceased speaking. Her voice was bell-like as she addressed him. "He's safe." She gazed up at him, her voice confiding and steady. "He's safe."

In the hours after that, whenever he saw the death image, he felt what seemed like water welling around his feet. It was either inside his feet, as if he were a hollow, plastic man, or rushing over them. The water deepened every second, rising to his waist, and causing his legs to feel unstable, then pressing under his arms and around his nipples, rising dangerously toward his throat. Would he be able to breathe much longer? He sucked large bites of air. But it wasn't water. It was a river of pain, flooding like water, staining all of his tissues, and raising the visceral questions: Will I finally succumb to its toxins? Will I die this time?

On that afternoon, he dropped to his knees on the concrete and bent over the boy's face, gazing into the wide, blue eyes and calling:

"Schnoogie! Schnoogie! It's Daddy!" One hand went for the boy's free hand, the other curled around the blonde head with olive straws of alfalfa thrust in here and there. He caressed the boy's forehead. It was cool to the fingers.

"Schnoogie! I'm here, son!"

He was certain he saw a twitch in the left eye, a movement of recognition.

"I'm afraid he's gone . . . ." It was the Bishop's voice, from above him somewhere.

"Bennie!"

"I'm here, Saul. Behind you."

"Everyone take hands." He reached across and squeezed Anna Mary's, which lay on the boy's right hand. "Take hands!" He didn't look up to see if they had followed his instruction. "Believe! 'I am the Resurrection and the Life!' Believe!" Words tumbled from his mouth, and he didn't recall later what he'd said, but he remembered the boy's face. "He's pinking!" he shouted. "Lord Jesus, we believe—" He didn't know how long he stayed there, saying the prayer over and over, his eyes squeezed so tightly that they ached afterward.

But he heard the unfamiliar male voice and felt the soft hand cover his. Opening his eyes, he saw the white-coated, middle-aged doctor with his hand on Schnoogie's pulse, then his carotid, then fiddling with the stethoscope.

Anna Mary was higher, seated on the bale, gazing down into Saul's eyes. "He's safe in the arms of Jesus," she said.

The doctor's large, puffy fingers stroked the boy's face, and when they came away, the boy's eyes were shut.

"I'm sorry, Mr. MacNamara."

He leaped up then, lashing out.

"No! No! You don't believe!" He remembered throwing things as he screamed. Stones, perhaps? The rusty noses pulled back through the fence boards and ran, bellowing.

Where were You when I needed you? I'm working for You. Why don't You work for me?

<hr />

"Why won't he be growing up?" Bennie said. "We can't be sad this morning, for he's in the brighter realm, where there's flowers and all tears shall be wiped." He pulled up the handkerchief and blew his nose. "Why not? Why couldn't he grow into that young man? I'll say why, brothers and sisters. Someone killed him, that's why." His aggressive eyes didn't drop. The small, ordinary noises of church ceased.

"Yes." Bennie leaned across the pulpit. "Because he was killed. 'Oh, don't say it, preacher. Don't say it. Death don't make sense.' But then they turn round and make up their own meaning for this little boy's too-quick passing. I'll say why he went before his time. The revenging hand of God. 'If you won't be obedient—if you rebel against My prophet, O Israel!' I'm burdened. Oh, I'm burdened!

"This petition to remove the Lord's own. Some here know whereof I speak, others not. Be thankful if not, but if you know—you know what you done? When the Lord raises up a man, do you and I decide we don't like his voice? Whose voice, anyway? A man's? Or Almighty God's? *What about Moses?*

"Moses, the Lord's anointed," Bennie repeated. "Was he appointed by the children of Israel? *Ordained,* we would say? Not by a church and a Bishop Board. No, sir. He was a shepherd out in the cactus desert and saw a burning something, and out of it a little voice nobody else could pick up says, 'You go speak to Pharaoh and the children of Israel for me.' That's who ordained Moses. The Lord did! How about the children of Israel? How'd they feel about the Lord's ordained? They griped. They murmured. You check it, Numbers 12—'Hath the Lord indeed spoke only through Moses? Hath he not spoke through us also?' O grumbling termites and cockroaches. They die, everyone. Every last one over the legal age. Yes . . . the Angel of Death!"

Bennie twisted open his top collar button. Even the top of his bald head burned red.

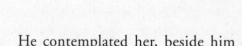

He contemplated her, beside him on the front bench, in her navy-blue cape and dress, very modest, matching her mother's, who sat just beyond. She was terribly young—and innocent. Not much more than a college girl, too young to carry a baby and now to be burying one. She didn't return his glance, nor turn towards the casket to his left, but focused upward on the preacher. Her eyes were dry. He held her hand, worn some from hard work. The hand didn't respond. It lay limp in his.

She'd undressed in front of him that night. Yes, after six months of secluding herself in the guest room behind the locked door, on that night when they got home from the hospital, she let him lead her up the stairs by the hand. And now she was pulling off the cherry-picking clothes—the blouse, the skirt—and stood with her back to the guest room bed, facing him, the flesh glowing around the cotton underwear. He pulled her against himself.

"I love you, Anna Mary."

She didn't resist his kiss on her mouth, but she didn't move in response.

"It hurts so much, doesn't it?" Her face was only a few inches below his, tilted upward by his hand under her chin. His tears dripped onto her cheeks, and he smoothed them away. "A bright light has gone out." He could feel her eyes watching his. "So glad he didn't suffer. Instantly. Instantly in Jesus' presence."

Her body was snug against his, and his bare arms crossed behind her, pressing in against her unclothed shoulder blades.

He sniffled loudly. "Don't want the tears to stop. A bright light has gone out."

Then he thought it was remarkable. "You haven't cried yet, Amz." He hadn't used the nickname, his own coined one, since sometime last summer, sometime before the trip, and just saying the name itself stirred feelings. "You haven't cried," he repeated. "How you doin', Amz?"

He wanted to ask much more—every detail of the afternoon leading up to the fall. He'd heard Gloria's version in the ambulance as they drove to the city hospital, Gloria's arm around her sister's shoulder. But Anna Mary hadn't volunteered anything, and he put it down as grief.

Her mouth whispered against his breast pocket. "He's safe in the arms of Jesus."

"Yes," he said. "He's safe."

"He was too good for Earth," she whispered.

He remembered the Creek Walk and Mattie Mae. It was what she'd said about her sister, and hearing it now, it disturbed him. *I don't know her. She's not the woman I married. Something's different. Something's come between us, even if our bodies are pressed skin-tight. She's a little lost child.*

"I know you loved Jakie." He deliberately used her nickname for the boy, although he never used the name (and, in fact, hated it).

"Jakie . . ." Her eyes drifted downward, but she made no attempt to escape his hug.

His hands descended, caressing the skin between his fingers to the waist. "We'll make another Jakie."

Her arms pushed out against his chest, pushing him back, his hands trailing backward along her retreating arms until she was at arms length, and then she collapsed out of reach onto the edge of the bed. Her eyes drilled the floor.

"I don't want another Jakie."

━━ ━━

"We ain't talking politics!" Bennie shouted. "People get voted in and you don't like 'em, out they go. Not in the church of Jesus—a popularity contest. No democracy. The Lord ordains, and He don't care if the church ordains him or not. Grumble against the Lord's anointed . . . Oh! It's slippy and unsafe!

"Dynamite!" He shook his Bible overhead with both hands. The pulpit top cracked with the sound that followed. He locked eyes with them, sniffled, and hoisted the Bible again. "I said *dynamite* . . ." He clobbered the pulpit with the Bible again. "To fiddle with God's anointed—" His finger jabbed. "The anointed of Almighty Gawd! Don't fool yourself. You . . . and you . . . and you. Don't think He'll wink. The Angel of Death is on the march again. That's right. That's why the little body's here, a scapegoat for this ornery, backbiting—" His usually calm round face was a Halloween mask. The eyebrows arched like black cats' backs, bright blood dyed his face and bald spot, and his eyeballs bulged out of the red mask, white and large. "Grumbling! People!"

"If my name were on that list—thank God, it's not—but if it were, I'd beg the Lord to forgive. Wasting no time, I'd tear up to Brother Saul soon as this service ends, funeral or no funeral: 'Forgive me, Brother Saul!' No, I wouldn't wait. I'd go right now!"

He paused. No one took the suggestion.

The service closed with the open casket again. It took 15 minutes for everyone to shuffle by. Saul had requested the family go at the end, so he could be the last one on Earth to see the boy and close the lid.

There was no emotion to it. The face really didn't look like Schnoogie's—something about the mouth and how it was set. The formaldehyde was also perceptible. Saul lifted one of the hands, and it felt like the ivory, marble hands of the Virgin he remembered from the cathedral in D.C., where his parents showed at Easter and Christmas.

"I miss the smile," he whispered. She stood alongside, her fingers trailing the white, long-sleeved shirt she'd sewn for the boy.

On the stand by the casket, he'd propped a four-by-five photo of the boy in his red cowboy hat, with neck strings to keep it from flying away, grinning mischievously at the cameraman. He took the photo and gave it to her, while he lowered the coffin lid, watching pieces of the boy disappear . . . the far shoulder, the face, the hands, the near shoulder.

Drizzle had been falling steadily since sometime before daybreak. He pitched her maroon umbrella over them and steered her across the short driveway, through the whitewashed board gate that led into the cemetery, and across the rather long, wet grass in need of a cutting.

He led her to the two open chairs under the army-green canvas tent, just on this side of the mounded-up, loamy earth. They were fortunate.

They got in the tent. The other 200 had to huddle under umbrellas or just stand in the rain, getting soaked.

Raindrops formed in perfect rows on the polished top of the casket. It seemed so small. The raindrops built as it drizzled until gravity pulled them one after another over the side. From his angle, Saul could see them ripple the puddle at the bottom of the hole. The piled earth was crumbly and loamy. Rich Kittochtinny soil that once brought these Swiss-German farmers here. Limestone soil with lots of earthworms and—earthworms, yes. He imagined them burrowing through the frost and water-damaged sides of this oak box as easily as if it were cardboard. Turning his son into more rich, black earth.

"Then I saw a new heaven and a new earth, for the first heaven and the first earth had passed away," the Bishop, in his best frock coat, read from a small pocket Testament. One of the deacons held an umbrella to keep the rain off his face and the pages of the Testament. "Now the dwelling of God is with men, and He will live with them . . . He will wipe every tear from their eyes."

You're there already, Schnoogie. You're there in the dwelling of God and—did you have any tears in your eyes? He's wiped them away. He hasn't wiped away mine.

The tears coursed easily and hung on the bottom of both sides of his jaw.

The tears were still coursing as they walked back across the parking lot, just the four of them together—her parents, Anna Mary, and himself.

The Bishop didn't have an umbrella and chose not to walk under his wife's. The drizzle pooled on his Homburg and occasionally shot off in a stream. He began weeping now for the first time.

"Schnoogie, Schnoogie. I'm remembering—" His voice choked and he fumbled for the folded hanky, then continued as they walked. "How much he loved the marble chute. . . . How he jumped on me with a big hug."

Saul had one arm flung around Anna Mary's waist and balanced the maroon umbrella over her with the other. Every memory like this one stirred his grief again and vented in tears.

Anna Mary began to hum. "Ooh, ooh, ooh, ooh, ooh, oohuhooh, ooh, ooh, ooh, ooh, oh." She gasped into the embroidered handkerchief that masked her mouth. "I'm glad I asked for it." Her voice cracked, and this time she sang the words. They walked steadily, and he listened. The voice was even and soprano, like her sister's. "Safe in the arms of Jeee-e-sus . . ."

"Just rest now," Mom Krehbiel said. She was plodding heavily between Anna Mary and the Bishop, her face pitched forward under the slate-colored bonnet that covered most of her head and tied in a bow under her chin. A crocheted, gray shawl draped her shoulders.

"She was too good for this earth, like people said," Anna Mary said, speaking for the first time that day. "But she's safe now in the arms of Jesus. It was my fault. If I'd just watched more carefully, she would'na fallen."

Mom Krehbiel turned sharply. "*He*," she said.

"I mean Mattie Mae," Anna Mary corrected.

"But it's Jakie we buried. Mattie Mae was twenty years ago—"

"Mom!" The Bishop's voice was harsh. "Let her say what she wants."

"There by His love o'er shadowed—" She resumed singing as they came down the concrete plaza in front of the Smyrna Church to the Bishop's Buick, its waxed ebony rooftop beaded with rain. "Sweetly my soul shall rest."

Saul opened the back door, folded the umbrella after she sat in, and shook off the excess rain. He leaned into the car. "I'll pick you up at Pop's tonight." He brushed his lips on her cheek. She clutched the photo of Schnoogie to her chest and looked unemotionally straight ahead through the rain-streaked windshield.

He moved around the back of the car. Mrs. Krehbiel, as always, took time to get seated because of her weight, which she manipulated awkwardly downward with the assistance of the Bishop's arm. He waited, the rain matting his hair and streaming a cold, wet path down the center of his back.

The Bishop closed the back door and spun around. "We need to talk," Saul said. They were both outside the car in the drizzle, and their voices were not audible to the congregants who passed now on the way to their own cars or to Anna Mary or Mrs. Krehbiel inside. "Something's wrong with Anna Mary. Her stomach pains. Her talk about Mattie."

The Bishop's eyes widened. "Stomach pains?"

"She tries to hide it, but she gets severe pains. It's not just about Schnoogie. She's been this way for some time."

"You're coming over, and we can talk," the Bishop said. "We'll have some of Susanna's apple pie and . . ."

"She needs a doctor. A doctor for mental problems."

"A doctor? Yes." The Bishop seemed distracted, maybe by the people passing. Some were wishing Saul well, calling to say that they'd pray for him. "Get in." The Bishop motioned the far side.

"That's just it. I can't. Tonight's the last night for the Revival, and I've had no chance to prepare a sermon."

The Bishop stared. His face abruptly chilled, almost as if a frost had blown in. "That was uncalled for," he said, his voice now rising. "Absolutely uncalled for, the way Bennie Fisher blamed—he practically accused us of murder. I'll have to repudiate him." He stopped. "Okay, then." He opened his door, threw the Homburg in, and then slid in himself. The door banged shut.

Saul turned away. He located his own car and began walking. The drizzle grew stronger and dripped off his nose.

I'm alone. Will I lose her, too? No! I can't. I can't live through another ripping of my heart. I have to save her.

247

He spun around and saw the disappearing taillights of the Buick.

The thought of a second loss brought on the same feelings as the first, the one they had just buried behind the church house . . . and the image of it.

The death image. He fell back against the Ford and felt the water soak right through his summer suit coat in a line below his shoulders. Three hay bales lay on the concrete, and laid out on the middle one, as if for viewing, the very pale face, unrealistically white . . .

Why didn't You answer me, Lord? Why are You out of hearing? The door into the Eternal Throne room seemed shut. Not only shut, but—it seemed he heard the bar on the other side fall into place. And then silence.

Twenty-One

I HAVE NOTHING to say to them. Precious souls, I've got nothing for you. I've been judged. King David, too, pled with the Lord. Ate nothing, spoke to no one, lay all night in the dirt pleading for his son, but the boy died. I pled, threw myself down on the little body in front of the policeman, the doctor, Anna Mary, the Bishop, and Wolfgang, and I pled. Resurrect him! And for one tiny second I felt. . . . I was wrong. I've been judged, they say. Illegitimate child; illegitimate preaching. I have nothing to say to these that have gathered, but I promised. So here I am.

Saul pulled up the tent flap of the counseling room and went in. Immediately, wet canvas and sawdust smells assaulted him. The singing grew louder as he got to the back stairway leading up to the stage. The back of Bennie's head appeared, silhouetted against the pole lights over the stage, his arm swinging in time with the music. He mounted the steps, and the people became visible, step by step.

Oh . . . see them. They stood shoulder to shoulder at the perimeter of the tent, even into the field. The rented wooden chairs were all filled to the back. Right down to the front. *It's never been this full!*

Bennie heard the volume of singing fall and saw the glances and the whispers. Without losing the timing of his beat, he smiled back through the words he was singing.

It was an important night—the most important, in fact, because it was the last. The remnant was gathering. Saul saw their empty, hungry faces, mouths gaping and shutting. Little robins, straining up for a worm, and he had nothing to give them. His neck went stiff, his palms and underarms were wet. *But it won't do to give them over to Bennie. He pressures. Emotions carry him away.*

=== ===

"You gonna lead us?" Bennie whispered off the back of his hand at the end of the verse. Saul walked to the edge of the stage, and Bennie led the applause, stepping sideways from the mic.

"This afternoon I didn't know if I'd be able to stand here," Saul began. Here, at the front of the stage, their faces swelled larger, more numerous than 10 feet back. They hushed. "But I asked Him for strength—and He's been supplying it these three days." Their eyes waited, watched. "Several times today this song ran through my mind. Which we used to sing at my mother's church in Vacation Bible School. 'Safe in the Arms of Jesus,' about the children who have gone to be with the Lord. Can you lead it?" He looked over at Bennie, who shook his head no. So he began himself, without a pitch pipe or beating time, conscious of his own monotone.

> Safe in the arms of Jesus,
> Safe on his gentle breast,
> There by his love o'er shaded,
> Sweetly my soul shall rest.

The song closed. *But they're not with me yet. So*—"We'll wait on the Lord," Saul said, the usual cue for the testimony period. He retreated to his wooden-slat chair, conscious of their watching, hushed eyes. *They're disappointed. What were they expecting? We could fall on our faces. The most important night. So many new ones, and we could fail. Doesn't anybody have anything to say?* Bennie leaned toward him. "Tell how the Lord got you through this, why don't you?"

He peered back. *What? Schnoogie's fall, Anna Mary's illness, your own harangue this morning and Jake Krehbiel's angry response? My feelings? Like I'm not inhabiting my body but someone else's? A body that the Lord above isn't speaking to. Is He even here tonight?*

"Oh." Bennie's chin jerked toward the aisle, where someone was coming. Ruth Ann's brilliant, analytical eyes hid behind her half-inch thick glasses as she ascended the stage. She wore her hair in the style popular among the college girls, with large, deep waves back from the forehead on both sides to the nape bun and the prayer covering straight-pinned fast to it.

"I never did this before." She smiled nervously over the mic stand. "Brother Saul always says that when the heart beats so you think people around can hear and your knees are knocking, that's when—" She swallowed and bumped the microphone twice, each time eliciting a painful squawk over the P.A. boxes. "I was healed, that's what I want to tell. My one leg grew miraculously to be as long as the other one." Her eyes roved across the audience. "I never believed in stuff like leg-lengthening. So when Brother Bennie invited me last Wednesday—" She rotated 45 degrees to see Bennie and then turned back to the lectern top, where she spread out her notes. "Well, I didn't think—I thought it was hocus-pocus." She smiled steadily.

Saul put his fingertips into his eyes and squeezed the tear ducts against his nose. *Is this what we will hear, because I have nothing? A little Christian magic? Genuine healing, yes, the Bible teaches that. But clubs of people going through rites of magic? Bennie has a weakness for it.*

"They measured with the tape, and my left leg was a half inch shorter than my right. I wore a built-up sole my entire school career. And the Doc said it would always be that way. I mean, the way it was up till Wednesday. Then Brother Bennie said, 'Do you want to be healed? You have to want it first.' It was just us two. Brother Saul and the others were praying for Rosie's tumor, which also got healed Wednesday night!" She beamed. "I said 'yes,' so the brother laid hands on my leg. I really started believing God to heal me until he said, 'I never did this before. I don't know if I can do it.' I mean, I . . ." She gasped a large sigh of desperation that elicited a ripple of chuckles. "I mean, already I didn't believe in leg-lengthening and stuff, and now he says he don't either. My faith went to zero."

Faith to zero, but still healed. A withered, thirsty, dehydrated soul, its tongue too stuck to the roof of the mouth to plead for water. Too dry to pray, too delirious to think "pray," too desperate to believe it might ever drink again. Does He know? Does He send water anyway?

"Yes!" He straightened in his chair.

"And this tingly something, like your leg's asleep and starts to come to, you know?" Her voice had been rising and falling during his testimony, each time cresting higher, and now it entered falsetto. "They measured, and it grew exactly a half inch."

"Yes!" He banged his hands together once, and that started audience clapping.

She beamed. "I brought my guitar. I wrote a praise song. If someone will bring it up for me . . ."

≡≡≡

He gives life where there's no hope, no faith. My motorcycle! He hadn't thought of it for years. He'd connected on the road from D.C. to the Skyline Drive and wound down along the tops of the Blue Ridge hills toward Charlottesville and the University. He was 19 and new at riding, but confident. So what if it was raining? The Goodyears were knobby and had special traction. Rain streaked across his bare helmetless face, and his overshirt flapped in back. *Oh boy!* Leaves covered the ground and the road—the October woods were turning. He leaned left for the curve. Leaned right for the curve. Pitched left . . . and hit gravel.

Little stones flew about like raindrops (he had to pick them out of his hair that night). The cycle came down on top of him, and he slid toward the drainage ditch, the motor roaring at his ear, blistering hot. (The hair above his ear was all singed back to the scalp.) The motor roared and roared. He felt wet beneath—the drainage ditch. But wet on top, too. And what was that, seeping toward his mouth? He tasted with his tongue. *Good Lord, gasoline!*

Gasoline dribbled down the engine. He pictured it as he slid along the ditch—tongues of fire first and then the explosion, his flaming body catapulted into the trees. He imagined them finding his body, charred like a fireplace log. But then the sudden click. Something was tearing away . . . and the dead weight slid off his trunk and legs. *Seize the air. Bend your finger; still works. Toes, fingers. Yes. Toes, hands, feet, arms, legs. Yes. Pop eyes—yes! Foggy green trees. Everything, yes!*

"I was back there with you, standing on the berm. Did you know that?" He heard that same small voice now. Perhaps it was not even a voice but an invisible message injected into the cells of the body like the encoded message of a molecule of DNA. *"You just had another crash, but I'm with you. I stood by the coffin today. Did you know that?"*

———≡≡———

"Praise God!" He sprang up and followed Ruth Ann as she walked offstage to the audience applause. "Sister." She pivoted at the head of the stairs and saw him, his arms open wide. She threw herself against his chest, the guitar awkward between them. He seized the mic stand. "The Spirit's in control of this meeting, people! He's supplying what we need. No message from me here—" His hands flapped helplessly. "But He's supplying what—did you hear her?—'God, if it happens, it's you because neither of us have faith.' That's super!"

Their faces lit up here and there like fireflies.

"Yes, Brother." He noted Noah Krehbiel coming, acknowledged him with a nod, and returned to the stage chair.

The motorcycle again. Wasn't it funny how real the memory smelled after all these years? He said right there he'd never ride again. The Colonel fetched him off the hill in a pickup and put the bike in the bed. It wasn't wrecked, just a headlight out and a large ding on the gas tank. He came out the following morning to have a look, and there she sat. He had bruises, big yellow and purple ones the size of dinner plates on his thighs and upper arms, and a few oozing red scrapes. He saddled the bike as they were talking, he and the Colonel.

Sell the thing before I kill myself. Just too dangerous, like people say.

"You gonna take it out or what?"

He twisted the key and inhaled the poorly combusting fumes in the Colonel's wood shanty where he kept it. Mmmphf. Mmmphf.

Turn the thing off before it explodes and throws me through the shanty door.

"What are you? Chicken? You don't ride her now, you'll never ride one again."

He pushed it out, just to show the Colonel he wasn't chicken, and clicked it into gear. Then he was off, with a jerk, weaving slowly uphill through the blue woods.

Always a little blue in the woods where the light can't get through. A cool feel—it's the fall of the year, but a lot of leaves are still hanging on. Check out my flickering, bluish hands and the dirt road, easily flowing beneath me like a blue brook. We go over the top and hit the macadam, me and the cycle. Sunlight splotching here in the green bushes. Fall, but still green in the ditches. Start down the other side. Out of the trees for open fields, and a straight mile to the bottom and out beyond.

Throttle, throttle. Yellow leaves streaking by, the air pushing naked eyes to make them do tricks, hands go yellow. Banana yellow car zipping this way and is gone. Still accelerating, the blurry road inches below, rushing now like an iron-gray current. Leaves, leaves, lemon and gold. Twist her all she'll go. Hands shake-a-shake-a-shaking. Air sucking at the eyes, drying up the tears till they burn. Blaze. Ruddy reddish hands, reddish leaves, reddish road. The blood cells hopping. Road red and hopping. Red, red. The sun hopping upward through the red sugar maples. Red, oh the merry red sun. Red, red, red, red. Alive, alive, alive, alive! I'm on wings. Straddling the red sun.

"They that wait upon the Lord . . . up with wings like eagles." *Yes!* He was on wings right now in this assembly, riding the feathered back of an archangel. He soared up from earth, free of trembling weakness, doubts, and death itself.

⇒⇐

Noah had hardly finished his story of youthful fears and the pressures on a preacher's kid when Saul literally leaped to the stage.

"He's a healer!" he said, one finger outstretched toward the lights. "He's resurrection, and the same power that propelled Him out of that Roman grave is here tonight. People will let their minds run on why my son died. In my own heart, I go to and fro—was it His judgment on me? My sins? I prayed God to heal him, even when it seemed too late. *He* was a healer; He raised the dead. He said if we have faith, we'll do greater than He. Then why didn't He raise my son? I just got this answer, fresh as a Western Union. God don't wanna give Schnoogie 66 more years on this terrestrial ball. He wants to start him on eternity. He wants to let him FLY!" He swiped the air upward with his fist and shouted.

Their hoots and wolf whistles launched him even more boldly. "Schnoogie isn't down here tonight, he's up here," he said, building an imaginary floor of heaven over his head. "If we could just see . . . this

tent has an upstairs. It's more of a Kitty Valley barn. We're below in
the stables, but up in the haymows are all the saints of heaven. They're
part of this service." He laughed, a spontaneous "huh, huh" out of his
chest, and spiraled his hands upward with the laugh. *Glory, glory.* "The
martyrs are with us, glued to our testimonies, praising with us. We're
rubbing elbows tonight with archangels and seraphim. Rahab. King
David. Jonah. Schnoogie MacNamara. They're all here!

"Huh, huh. If we just keep still, we'll hear them dancing before the
Throne. King David leading. And knocking hayseeds through the boards
down on us. Hweeeh! The preacher's gonna get excited." He jumped
several inches off the stage and clicked his heels together. *They laugh
because they're with me. They're being filled with the Spirit. Glory!* His hand
floated over the crowd, recruiting, like an auctioneer's. "Who's next?"

Smitty Smucker had been waiting for some time in a chair at the foot
of the stage. Now he stepped up, buttoning his vest with the colorful
quetzal birds of Honduras embroidered on the front panels and across
the back. He needed to lower the microphone, because he stood about
five-foot-two. "How do you do this?" he muttered under his breath.
Bennie adjusted it.

"Smitty Smucker." The voice came out flat. His eyes avoided the
audience and instead fixed on the lectern. "And I'm an alcoholic."
Where did this man come from? A Mennonite? "I know some of you'uns
knew me before. Just got back from Honduras, where we're doing the
Lord's work. Some don't know me, though. My folks are Mennonite,
and I have nothing against them. My folks wear the plain clothes, you
know—" He indicated the square-notched collar of a Mennonite coat
by drawing one at his throat. "Mom wears the prayer bonnet. Me, I
wasn't against them or for them." His voice neither rose nor fell, only
ran steady and flat.

"When I'm happy, I want everyone happy. I'm a people person." He
sucked air nervously over his teeth. "So I bought a round. I always got
snokkered. And I came home to my folks that way. I dozed off once in
the tub, and my Camel burned a hole in the towels. Yeah. Finally Pop

says, 'One more time and I call the police and have you locked up.' I can understand. He was scared. I coulda burnt the house down." Smitty finally acknowledged the audience with his eyes, and he continued to speak in the same unemotional tone, which was not at all in keeping with his flamboyant jacket or his self-designation of "people person" or his youth. Even with the prematurely aged face, he didn't seem over 30.

Alcoholic? I never went that far. Got drunk occasionally in the Army, but thank God. . . . it was a demon. Maybe that was the monster he used to hear hooting and taunting him there in the barracks. Predicting he'd never keep his vow to get out of the military.

". . . The wrists all bandaged when I woke," Smitty continued. He created an intravenous bottle in the air. "Bottles up here, with tubes. Pop was there, dressed in his coat and all. Looking outta place in a hospital. And he says—that's my Pop—'If it weren't for Mom locating you and the ambulance, you'd be in hell already.' I cut them deep. Still have the scars." He displayed his wrists and arms, purple with tattoos. "And he says, 'I have someone here wants to help you, Smitty.' And I say, 'Okay. Where?' 'Right here,' he says. I spy around and here's this—white hair, a little briefcase, looking 80-something, with a hearing thing, and all. Scotty, everybody called him. Says he wants to help. So I say, 'How?' 'Whatever you need,' he says. 'You can't help. I have to go to jail,' I say. Didn't mention I was driving without my license and under the influence as well.

"And he says, 'Praise the Lord!' I'm thinking, *Hunh? Praise the Lord?* A religious fool. I'm off to prison. What's this 'praise the Lord'?"

Oh, he has this meeting. He's tying it all together. Jesus, I'm on wings! I don't have to worry about this meeting.

". . . A circle." Smitty spoke more intensely now, his words tumbling over each other. "To pray for me. All these Keswick people, all strangers! And Scotty says, 'Your turn, Smitty.' I couldn't. I never did it out loud before. 'Reach to Jesus,' he says. I had my eyes open case anybody took a swipe at me, and I stretched my hand out. I remember feeling . . . this hand." His eyelids scrunched shut, and he rubbed his extended palm with a fingertip. "The nail holes and all . . . it was Him. Yeah, Smitty Smucker, too tough for crying. Not Smitty Smucker . . ." His head dropped onto his chest.

Saul returned to the edge of the platform and wrapped an arm around Smitty's shoulders, which were sagging together and shaking. Smitty's head only came to his chin. "Power over demons!" Saul shouted to the audience.

Smitty wrapped both arms around Saul's waist. "Jeeesus!"

"Over demons!" Saul grasped the mic pole and leaned with it toward the people. "Demon of Alcohol. Demon of Depression. The Unbelief Demon. He routed them at the Tree, and they're scared because they're castrated—*im-po-tent.* Unless you give them a chance. You see, this is a laboratory!" He dropped back to spread his arms in a *Y* to indicate the tent. "We're the Curies, Pierre and Madame. Experimenters, all of us, with life or death. You dabble with the demons or you dabble with Jesus. I've dabbled with life and seen Schnoogie resurrected . . . I want to go on. I never want to leave revival. I'm flying! Like the birds up on Hawk Mountain. I'm on hawk wings!"

Do they see the choice? Have I made it clear enough? Saul nodded to Bennie for more singing and left the stage.

Outside, the grass was wet. It had sprinkled heavily several times during the meeting. Overhead, the sky was strangely torn down the middle, one half full of dark rain clouds, the other full of stars. The moon hung directly overhead at the edge of the stars and struggled to light up the cloudy side. As he stepped out, it seemed as if the starry side were winning, but now the clouds pulled across the moon like a theater scrim, letting its reduced light flicker through. Drops fell. Abraham had seen those stars, and he believed. Isn't it the same stars he saw, the same God he believed? Yes. *He's here! It's Him! Talking to me as He did at the barracks. "I stood by the coffin today. Did you know it?" Yes, I know it now!*

Twenty-Two

"TOUCH ME HERE, *Anna Mary,*" *Edie says, guiding my hand. I open my hand and feel. She's like Mom; she has bumps too. And why don't I? "You'll have them soon," Edie says. "When you're 13."*

Smells like hay to me, alfalfa. We did 960 bales Wednesday, and Pop let me drive the John Deere. Lucky we got 'em in before the rain. Dadumdada! Dadumdada. It's clobbering the tin barn roof overhead. It's dark and cozy in the hay tunnel. Noah and Daniel did a good job of building it—even Pop says so.

"Anna Mary."

"Huh?"

"You think we're getting a boy or girl this time?"

"It's not a baby, Edie. Just a pain I get in my tummy."

"Not a baby? You mean not a boy. Mom's awful tubby and that's the way you get, Aunt Lena says."

"It's not a baby. I'm not having any more. One's enough. I don't ever want another one."

The door rattled, and the sound of footsteps came across the floor.

"I hear the door, Edie. He's here." No, he can't find me up here, because he doesn't know about the hay tunnel.

She tugged the crocheted afghan around her legs.

"Anna Mary, are you still up?"

It's him. My husband. It's his voice. Through the loops of the afghan across her face, she saw him spying for her. If she didn't talk, he'd never know. She rolled so she could see him full on. *Light! Oh, the harsh light!*

===

"If only you'd been there, Anna Mary. I know now where Schnoogie is. He's in God's Throne Room. The Spirit opened our eyes to see. Anna Mary!" He knelt by the summer sofa, his hands reaching under the afghan onto her arm. "Things are busting up, Anna Mary."

Busting up. A Caterpillar, it is crossing our cornfield, and Pop yells at it, but the man won't stop. He keeps coming. He'll drive over our Pop because he hates—I always knew he hated Pop, that's why he calls our Jacob "Schnoogie" instead of "Jakie," Pop's name. I halloo to Pop: "Pop! He won't stop!" Does he hear me? He don't move. The Caterpillar comes up over him and keeps coming. I see Pop flat in the tracks behind—a muddy track like a Venetian blind down his body—and he don't move. Our yard fence flies to pieces, and the geese are out. The silo goes down, the apple splinters and white-painted stones shake out of the house walls. A gray cloud of mortar rises. I halloo Mom and the girls: "Get out! It's gonna fall!" The precious walls tremble, pillars of dust rising. It's going down, and no one sees but me . . . I'm the only one.

"Anna Mary."

The teeth of the machine dug into her body, bulldozing her. She knew just this: *I'm only safe for now in Pop's house, even if the Caterpillar attacks it.*

"Are you sleeping or what?"

Sleeping, of course. She could see him now, his face and body inky. Why, he had two faces, side by side, with one shared eye in the middle.

"Remember I didn't think I could preach—" the mouths in both faces spoke. "Told your Dad after the funeral maybe never again. My heart so broken. But I got up, and the people ministered to me. I stood with angels and archangels. . . . I was flying!"

She felt herself falling into the three eyes. *Terrible things are happening. If I die, where will I go? Will I be spit out? I don't want to be spit out.* He cuddled her face between his hands.

"What's wrong with your eyes, Anna Mary?"

Close up, he scared her. She saw no eyes or mouth on him now. Was it him? Out in the kitchen, a bright light like welding and spikes jumped in and out behind his head, silhouetting his ears and neck. He wouldn't release her face, so she grabbed his wrists and pulled down.

"Anna Mary, your eyes are crossed."

"Let me go."

"What happened?"

He released her. She pulled the chocolate and orange afghan up and swaddled her face to protect her eyes. *I will not sleep. Watch him. See. He's dialing on Pop's telephone. I knew something—*

"Doctor Duttenhuffers? Ma'am, is your husband, the doctor, home?"

It's a trick. He wants to take me away. "I want to stay at Pop's." He turned around and flung his hand out to prevent her from grabbing the receiver. "Shhh!" he said. But it was now or it was too late. "I want to stay at Pop's."

"Shhh . . . we're going to the doctor to check on those eyes."

She lunged for the phone. He deflected her arm and tumbled her back onto the summer sofa.

"Yes, about 15 minutes," he said into the receiver.

Fifteen minutes. How can I stall him? Where were Pop and Mom? Why hadn't they rushed down when they heard him come in? Should she run upstairs and find them? His body blocked her from the stairway door. The spare room, of course, where her mother's quilt frames were set up. She could hide in the coats hanging on the wall, but she didn't dare turn on a light or he'd find her.

The phone dropped into its cradle. Click. "Anna Mary, are you ready to go?"

If she ducked under the coats, would he find her? She didn't answer. He was coming, though, searching for her. He exited into the lighted kitchen and hooked back into the spare room, looking right at the coats. Were her feet stuck out below the coats?

"Are you getting a coat? It's not cold, just wet. It's raining again." He came from behind, his hands feeling her ribs, moving around her waist. "What's wrong?"

She pushed aside the coats. "I need to stay at Pop's."

"You're going to see a doctor."

"I need to stay at Pop's."

"I made an appointment with Dr. Duttenhuffer. Now . . ." His hand loitered on her stomach, rubbing. She knocked it down and away. "Is it the pains again? You keep grabbing your belly."

"No."

"We got to see the doctor about those eyes. Here's one of Gloria's coats."

"I need to stay at Pop's."

"You can't stay here—they're all in bed. It's 9:30."

"I don't care. He'll get up if I ask him. I'm not going 'less we come back to Pop's after."

"We'll see. Here!" He held Gloria's dress coat up by the shoulders against her back. "Slip it on."

"Not that one. I want my gray sweater."

"Honey, it's at home. This'll keep the rain off."

"I want my sweater."

He lifted her arms and pushed them down the sleeves. They went through the doorway, his arm linked in hers. Like the sun, the naked light bulb over Pop's kitchen table assaulted her, its hot saw-points blazing, and she threw up the free arm to shield her eyes. The door opened up ahead with the void beyond. "What's wrong? Can't you see?" He said it tenderly, like she'd always heard him with the boy, but she knew. It was a gimmick to get her out of this house where she was protected. She couldn't think how to avoid it. It was raining and dark. *Where are we going, really? If I talk, I can give myself more time. Is TONIGHT the night? The night for something terrible? It's to be at his house, I'm sure. Just make sure we come back to this house, where I know I'm safe.*

"Guess what I'm making Pop tomorrow."

"Hmmm . . . what?"

"A peach pie. It's his favorite. With whipped cream."

"Oh."

"They're not hard to make." She felt better now that she was talking. Much better. "All you need is a crust, but it's tricky. Lots of women don't know how to make good crusts . . . *Mennonite Community Cookbook* is okay, but the best is the kind Mom makes. Your peaches must be Yellow Jubilees. I went by Brubaker's Stand last week, and the big, fat Jubilees are just coming in."

"Mmhmm."

"First time I ever made one, I accidentally dropped it. It was for Pop." She giggled, remembering. "Right on the floor at his feet, whipped cream and all. Some stuck on his pants—his new suit pants—and I had to get the dishcloth. I was only 13." *Why, so I was. It was my thirteenth birthday. That's why I made it for him.*

"Honey."

She stiffened her stomach to keep from snickering, which would make him cross. Why did his family use that dumb word? They wouldn't call each other "Milky" or "Radish" or "Molasses." Whenever he said it, she always pictured Pop out with his smoker, opening the hives and puffing in smoke while the groggy bees buzzed around his hands. He would lift out the comb, barehanded, brush them off, and never get stung. *He's really good at it. Honey.*

"Honey, did you hear?"

"What?"

"I miss Schnoogie so much it just hurts. I know you do too, even if you can't cry—"

That's what it was! He was taking her to the police, not the doctor. The police didn't think it was an accident—she could tell from the one without the uniform that day. He kept wanting to know *how, how, how,* but she couldn't remember. Was it this or that? Did Wolf say something, or did he just throw? She remembered seeing bales lined up on top. He was going to push them over, and Jakie hung by the hole. Then they started to come, and one hit his head and he fell through.

The town—already? Which way they turned at the light would tell. The lights blossomed and faded and blossomed again, pulsing at the end of their poles. What was it she had been thinking? Oh, yes, Wolf. They'd ask about him again. He started throwing, one bale after another, 80 pounds apiece, and she knew that they were going to hit. *I was hoping they'd hit me, but it wasn't my time, I guess.*

"Watch the steps, Honey." They'd stopped. It was the doctor's. The lighted letters on the sign wiggled, and she could hardly make them out. Saul came, hooked her arm with his, and slammed the car door.

The doctor smoked a cigar. His damp, cold fingers touched her here and there. He puffed, and then touched her again with chilly fingers. He asked questions. *He won't figure it out, I know. I'm the only one who can see the whole picture.* He fitted dark glasses on her and now, back in the reception room, the furniture and pictures on the wall seemed gloomy.

"Glaucoma? Or something bad like that? Tell me, I want to know." They were talking in low voices. *I can't hear, they think, as the door is shut. But it's so quiet, and he forgot the transom. I hear everything.*

"Nothing. Absolutely nothing."

"Has to be something, Doctor!"

"Any recent stress? Emotional crises?"

As she had predicted, the doctor figured nothing out, even after Saul told him what had happened. All he could say was, "She needs to wear dark glasses until we get a diagnosis on the underlying condition."

They left. "How much did it cost?" she asked. They were not going to the police station, she concluded. The car nosed out of town.

"Don't worry about it."

They were almost at the *Y* in the road, one leg snaking north over the mountain into Paxtang County, where they lived, while the other one went east. "I need to go back to Pop's," she reminded him.

"Anna Mary, don't be ridiculous."

"I need to go to Pop's." All of a sudden she saw it. A cloud hung dead ahead. It was little, but it was swelling up bigger and bigger. They drove for it, and it hung over the north fork of the *Y*, a boiling dark cloud. *I know what it is. The cloud of terrible things. Waiting for me. If I get into that cloud and can't see my way, anything could happen.*

He closed in on the *Y*. She held her breath. He turned north. "No! No! I needa go to Pop's! I needa go to Pop's!" The hanky couldn't stifle her cry. She didn't care if he saw tears, either, or if her voice was shrill. "I NEED TO GO TO POP'S!"

"We're going home."

"You don't see the cloud."

"What cloud?"

"There! Right up there!" It was right up through the windshield, as plain as any other cloud she'd ever seen. He wasn't looking where she was looking, because she couldn't show him. The cloud had seeped into the car and paralyzed her hands so that she couldn't lift them up to point.

"How can you see a cloud when it's dark and raining? We're in the clouds."

"I know. We're in the cloud."

We are moving in the cloud. It sits on us and squashes us. Oh, terror. Oh, things of terror. Falling, falling, falling to splash in hell. Thrust down to sizzle like an onion in bacon fat. White legs splayed like a frog on its back and kicking, but no use against the assailant with his twine and knife and pants down, tumbling. Uprooting juggernauting Caterpillar with its tracks running over the faces of the many who are hurled and soaked in the eddying saliva of Laodicea. Punctured and drilled and transfixed on the bayonets of soldiers—God knows whose—that prick like sticks of hay as cart-wheeling, spinning down, down, to the bottom the baby is created. Blood trickles slowly out of the Raggedy Ann doll lying there, her hair tousled, smashed, burnt, shot run over, raped, condemned, 40-stripes-save-one sentenced, suspected, scoffed at, and ridiculed by the two who gaily skip through the field, hand in hand, unlawfully made one flesh in the hay—the same hay I once lay in . . . .

"I NEED TO GO TO POP'S!"

The car jolted to a dead stop. She would not go into Saul's house, for she knew well what waited for her in there. The door banged and he appeared in her window glass, but she had locked the door. He knocked on the glass. She didn't open the door. He could do what he wanted, but she was not sleeping in that house. He headed back to the driver's side, but she'd already taken care of it. The glass vibrated fiercely with his blows.

Yes, yes! I thought I had one. I thought it was in my purse. She plugged the key into the ignition, but it wouldn't go in. *Aha, there!* The car motor rumbled. *I'm safe.* The car rumbled and rumbled and then died. She tried again. Nothing. And again. *What's wrong with it? It was just inspected.* He came up from under the hood, shouting through the rain streaming down the windshield. She saw his mouth open and close soundlessly, showing the dark hole of his throat. He pounded the glass in front of her. She shook her head. He went away. The rain began to drum rhythmically on the tin roof. Now what? He'd try something else, she knew. Maybe she could fix the car herself . . . but now he was coming back again and

266

knocking on the driver's side window—one, two, three—where she sat. She stifled her giggle. He looked like the ducks when they came up for air in the pond, his hair slicked down over his forehead and ears, with drops running off his nose like a duck's bill.

"Okay. Let's go to your Pop's."

He never lied, one virtue that she'd grant him. She pulled up the lock and moved over, and he got in, water streaming off onto the seat. The car motor rumbled again. She was saved for another night. She couldn't stop the tears, which had completely soaked the handkerchief.

Part Five

Melting Wings

August 29–October 13, 1956

Twenty-Three

THE MOOD INSIDE the tent was stiff and silent, like the viewing of a recently deceased body in a private home. As his eyes adjusted, he saw from the edge of the tent the four men of the elder board, plus one non-member, seated around a battered, wooden folding table. The silence and the bleakness inside the tent was an itchy, thick blanket that reached out and swaddled him.

Outside, a perfectly beautiful harvest day had unfolded early. A great crimson sun rose through the haze over the wheat field stubble, and by 2 P.M. its wonderful heat was baking the wheat heads in fields across the county to the 14 percent moisture content that was perfect for harvest. He had seen combines charging across fields all along Route 305 on his way south, while rabbits and ring-neck pheasants threw themselves out of the path of the combines and flew or ran alongside the road. Even now, a combine operator was revving his tractor motor as he started a new swath in the field next to Bennie's, the roar penetrating the tent.

His pupils dilated. Even with the tent sides rolled shoulder-high to access light and air—although there was no breeze—the contrast between the harvest day outside and the tent inside was enormous. The board acknowledged him wordlessly with nods. Bennie was chewing on a stem of dried alfalfa. He removed it and bobbed the stem in recognition of Saul.

The object of their grief—like the stiff, meticulously drained, injected, powdered, and painted body of a deceased—lay center table, in front of them all—a simple, mimeographed document. Saul ducked under the tent flap and, without the usual formality of greetings, went straight to the table and picked it up.

"You've all had a chance to read it?"

"They outsmarted us," Bennie said. "We're beat."

Someone had already unfolded one of the wooden chairs for him. He tromped around the back of their chairs in the now-emptied tent and through the much-walked-upon and ground-down sawdust that had converted this harvested alfalfa field in June into a holy meeting place for the last eight weeks.

What are they staring at me for? Probably the unshaven cheeks and the purple flesh sacs under my eyes. He hadn't been able to throw himself onto the bed until 3 A.M., when he finally got through the deluge of phone calls asking, "Now what do we do?" Some had said, "I quit. I quit the Revival." And others, such as Cyrus, had talked or argued with him for an hour or more about the responses in his home district since Bishop Malcolm, the Bishop Board secretary, had released the news at noon. Malcolm's drivers had stuffed mimeographed copies of the board's decision and ultimatum into the mailboxes of every ordained Kittochtinny man, as well as copies to each member of the Revival elder board. By suppertime, every Revival supporter had been phoned at least once with the news.

Nor could he sleep when he hit the bed. He tossed in the overheated, empty second-floor bed, absorbing this latest body blow, waking at 5:30 to help Aaron with the cows. Afterward, he spent an hour in the Scriptures, seeking light.

Bennie jumped to empty the pitcher of meadow tea into Saul's glass.

"Low-down!" Bennie set the glass before him, its sides sweating from the sudden collision of iced liquid with the warm and empty glass. "Their minds *shut*!" He hit his forehead with an open palm.

"Why don't you read it out loud for us, to get things started?" Saul said.

"Who, me?"

Saul nodded, tipping his chair back on its hind legs, draining the glass. "I appreciate all your time." He surveyed the five men. Cyrus, on his right, wore an open-collared, long-sleeved dress shirt, even on a day like this, under his forked dress suspenders. On Cyrus' right sat Noah Krehbiel, whose loyalty to him and connections with the Bishop's family had earned him a slot on the board. He wore the same plaid, short-sleeve workshirt that he normally wore under his butcher's apron. The mark where the cap usually rode dented his hair the whole way around, and the now-exposed forehead above the usual cap line was unhealthily pallid and unbrowned. Opposite him sat a somewhat scrawny man with thick, oversized glasses, his serge-blue, plain coat hanging on his shoulders even in this weather. Eby believed he should always be ready, while tending his Fuller-Brush customers between milking his small herd, for a pop-in with any of the families of his deaconate. Baumgartner was the non-Elder, a much-respected Sunday School leader and farmer, deep laughter cracks bisecting the leather cheeks and equally deep carat-marks carved back from the eyes.

Bennie stood off Saul's shoulder, gripping the mimeograph. He wiped the purple mimeo smudge from his thumb and index finger onto the red handkerchief he always carried, conveniently hanging two inches out of his back pocket.

"Dear Brothers . . ." he began.

"Just the points," Saul corrected.

"The points? Okay. 'One. The teaching of a second work of grace, the so-called "baptism of the Spirit." The extraordinary emphasis on the so-called "gifts" of the Holy Ghost. Byproducts of this teaching, including speaking in tongues, prophecies, "divine healing" in place of medical treatment, ex-'"

Bennie's face went vacuous, and he dipped the paper, pointing at the word.

"Exorcism."

"What's that?"

"Casting out demon spirits."

"Oh. 'Ex-ter-cisms. These violate our Conference practice.'"

The group sat silently. No surprises. They had all read it at least once.

"'Two. Preaching by persons not ordained in the Mennonite Church. Christ's apostles filled a vacuum among themselves by casting lots. And because the lot, with prayer and dependence on God, is also advocated elsewhere in Scripture for important matters, we believe it is a scriptural way of finding God's will (Acts 1:15–16). Conversely, non-ordained persons have no authority to use the sacred desk to instruct and teach the Body.'"

"A narrow interpretation of the Bible," Cyrus said. "I argued it yesterday with the Board. Isaiah's call in Isaiah 6—'Lord, send me.' Gideon's call. Paul's call. But—"

"They wouldn't hear of it." Saul finished the sentence, his body swaying forward and back to relieve the tension in his neck and upper back.

"Exactly."

Bennie glanced to be sure that their conversation was finished. "Go on? Okay. 'Three. Holding of Conference-wide meetings without approval of the Bishop Board. *Statement of Christian Doctrine and Rules and Discipline of Kittochtinny Conference, Article I, The Church, Section 10.* "Any movement or organization shall have the approval of the district involved or Bishop Board, when Conference-wide implications are evident. Non-approved meetings and non-approved protracted meetings are strictly forbidden.'" So we had it in a hayfield instead of a church house, and they still ain't happy."

274

"The conclusion," Saul said.

"'We, therefore, the assembled board of bishops, on this twenty-seventh day of August, 1956, hereby request the group known as "Revivalists" to cease and desist all activities, return to their home congregations, and submit respectfully to the authority of Conference-ordained leadership there. Your signature acknowledging compliance is requested below. All persons not signing will henceforth be considered outside the Body of Christ, and therefore Gentiles. Matthew 18.'"

Bennie trudged back to the one open seat at the far end of the table. Silence hung in cobwebs from the ceiling and looped from man to man.

Cyrus finally began, like a goose wheezing and quacking, the words straining over his painfully recovering voice box. "They've silenced me." He smiled incongruously, as he often did, in a manner not relevant to what he said. He propped both of his white-sleeved elbows on the table, balled his fists to support his head, and peered at Saul. "What if I don't sign? Excommunication. Cut off from my daughters and grandchildren. I'm 75. I can't start over making new friends and family—"

"You'd sign *that*!" Bennie's large eyes glowed hostile. "You'd go back to the old, dead Loodaseah?"

"I don't *want* to," Cyrus wheeled on his attacker. "I'm just telling you the price I've tabulated up—"

"My wife wants us to quit," Noah Krehbiel said. He was back to his old meek ways, his head lowered and looking at them cow-like. "She says there may be boycotting, like in 1893 when the Old Orders broke off. Do you have any idea—no Mennonites buying at my butcher stall? There goes half our sales."

"But it's your Pap's meat—Bishop Krehbiel!" Bennie said.

"So what if he stops supplying? They're his beef cows. Velma says he won't be able to help. Not after this." He pointed at the memorandum in the center of the table.

"What about your testimony Sunday night?"

"All true. But it's Wednesday, and—" He smacked his hand on the grievous papers.

"Got us by the throat either way," Eby said. With his thick lenses, it was impossible to know exactly where he was looking. He had the habit of staring one foot above his listeners' heads, cocking his head like a robin listening for worms after a rain while he spoke his mind. "We go back to the lifeless church. No prophecy. Questionable salvation. Or we hive off. Ignore this and get the boycott. Or worse. In 1893, people were locked out of church buildings. Permanently. And grandparents wouldn't eat with their children and grandchildren. I know; I heard it from my own Grandmom's mouth. For myself, I got a problem. Sylvester Stauffer calls last night to say he won't sell his second farm to me after all—and I been farming it nine years just to get first dibs next year—"

"How about you, Saul?" Bennie interrupted the dismal stream of news. "What you gonna do?"

Déjà vu. The chilly boys' locker room in February, 1945. Outside the locker room, the Washington and Lee fans whooped, cheering their victory over U of Virginia in the final seconds of the basketball season.

And there the five of us sat on the bench, staring at the object of our grief. Silent and lifeless after two hours of manic dodging, dribbling, lunging, back-flipping, and long-tossing—*a one-foot, orange ball with black lines curving across its stippled surface.*

Saul couldn't believe it. They couldn't lose. The Wahoos were better. Much better. He was better. After beating those guys in November, to lose on the very last toss, 49 to 47! He did know why. He and his friendly rival, Heffner, were both on their way to personal best records after three quarters (he had 16 points, Heffner 13) when the opposing coach of

Washington and Lee made a decision that sealed the game. Huddled with his guys during the timeout, he told them, "Double-team MacNamara. That big West Virginian—Armstrong—he's a dog. No threat." They pulled Armstrong's guard off him and put two guards on Saul.

Shut me down. I didn't even get the ball in my hands. Two enormous Washington and Lee guards jumped him every time they went up court. With the clock down to five seconds, the big, black metal numerals at 47–47, and the Wahoo fans screaming their heads off (*like the whole country would scream three months later on V-E Day*) . . . screaming like that and so sure Virginia was going to unleash the confetti and empty the ice bucket over Coach Tebell—with that as backdrop, Bjornquist got the toss from Heffner, who was stalled on the far left of the court. In the clear, Bjornquist trotted right under the basket, evading a single Washington guard, went out the other side, did a simple little hook of the arm, and released the ball. *The kind of shot I perfected eight years ago in junior high, for Pete's sake!* His shot hit the rim on the way up and deflected directly into that opposing guard's hands, who then power-fired it the length of the court. A Washington forward snagged it on the run and plop, plop, plop, plop, jump. He could just as well have stuffed it through the sagging mouth holes of the 500 stunned U of Virginia cheerleaders, parents (including Saul's), and news reporters.

Behind the closed locker room doors, Bjornquist spoke, miserable because he knew the morning sports rag would say, "BJORNQUIST BUNGLES AS WASHINGTON WHIPS THE HOOS." Or something similar.

"Whaddya thinking of, Mac?"

Right then, he knew the truth of the old sports bromide—*every team has got five types of guys.* There was the Dog—that was Armstrong—okay, but replaceable. There was the Unpredictable—their center, Gibbons, a star on the Wahoo football squad and a great rebounder, but no shooter. There was the Steady Reliable Guy, who would be the star, if there weren't one already—that was Heffner, who stood only six feet tall. He was deliberate and sometimes plodding, although a southpaw and a tremendous shooter. He wound up with 16 points that game, tying Saul. You had the Sparkplug—Bjornquist, his screen, the guy who made his shots possible. He blocked and bobbed and cleared a little safety zone around Saul, where the passed ball could hit on its fast passage from his skilled hands into the inevitable, absolutely predictable basket. That's what Stars did. They scored! Unless they were double-teamed.

They had the same team make-up here today. The Steady Reliable Guy, Bishop Cyrus, completely loyal, their credibility factor in Kittochtinny. If Bishop Cyrus, a former KMC principal, was for the Revival, then hey! Of course, the Bishop Board saw through that argument and silenced him. Noah Krehbiel was the Unpredictable. A loyal guy, but he had the eyes and tongue of a fox, not a lion. He shifted with uncertainty, giving the lie to his best statements and causing them all to wonder at the fear in his worst statements. Eby was the Dog, a good guy, but a harmless rat terrier who trailed behind, barking appropriately, defending appropriately.

"Whaddya think?" Bennie repeated.

Bennie, was the Spark Plug. But he'd muffed it, just like Bjornquist, and he knew it. Their fans were all repeating his words: "Bennie said Conference people are pretty much guilty of the murder of Saul's little boy." The bishops, beginning with Jake Krehbiel, wanted his head and the rest of the Revivalists silenced. *Bennie wants assurance from me that he won't be singled out for punishment, no doubt. I can do that for him.*

"None of us is to blame for this," Saul said, "any more than any of the others." He was on his feet now, one hand stuffed in his trouser pocket as he rattled the mimeo ultimatum. "It was coming sooner or later. We just need to tell ourselves that." He sat down again, the next step unclear in the murky gloom of the hot, dark afternoon.

"Maybe you have a scripture or something to encourage us," Cyrus said.

"I can do *that*." He retrieved the Testament out of his breast pocket. "Revelation 3:15, to the church at Laodicea. 'I know your works; that you are neither cold nor hot! Would that you were cold or hot! So, because you are lukewarm, and neither cold nor hot, I will spew you out of my mouth.'"

"So, will you sign?" Noah broke the silence.

"I've thought about it." Saul's eyes and lips scrunched as if he'd bitten into an unripe persimmon. "I've also thought about not signing it. In fact, I've thought more about not."

There was no more tea to drink, and none of the men smoked or possessed even a stiff paper to fan the stagnant, muggy air. There was nothing to do with their hands except pick at calluses or drum their fingers, which Bennie was doing.

"We'll do better next time," Saul said to the Sparkplug, Bjornquist.

"How do you know? Didn't we do our best?"

"We'll do better. I'll do better. Listen, we're good. Game-wise, we're still 13 and 4. We'll do better. *I'll* do better." How glad he was that it was only his junior year! He got a chance and they did do better, whupping Washington and Lee twice in '46.

"We'll do better next time," Saul said.

Several of them, Baumgartner, Bennie and Eby, guffawed. "Next time?" Baumgartner shook his head, his mouth sagging open.

"How can there be a next time?" Eby asked.

"There is. The next time we act. I was reading my Testament this morning." He peeled the pages to Revelation again. "Revelation 3:20: 'Behold, I stand at the door and knock.' This is Jesus speaking. 'If anyone hears my voice and opens the door, I will come in to him and eat with him, and he with me.' And two verses down the road, 4:1: 'After this I looked and lo, in Heaven an open door. And the first voice which I had heard speaking to me like a trumpet, said: "Come up hither, and I will show you what must take place after this."' What is that door?" He uncorked upward again, leaning against the stage and clasping his hands behind his back as he reflected on the thoughts that had crashed his sleep this morning. "The Rapture? Going up to be with the Lord? We do meet him in the air, don't we?"

"'There is going to be a meeting in the air, in the sweet, sweet bye-and-bye . . .'" Bennie sang it sweetly, and then laughed at himself.

"But we take the initiative in this passage. He calls, and we come. What does that suggest?"

"What?" Cyrus said. "I always thought the Rapture, but we do nothing when the Rapture happens."

"Just sucked up like tacks to the Big Magnet!" Bennie said. "I don't know if I can say it. Just a thought." He immediately backpedaled, uncertain. Wasn't it an interpretation of the Scriptures? Had others interpreted it that way? Was this way of seeing it too aggressive or over the line?

Cyrus got up carefully and walked in his traipsing shuffle over to Saul. "You need to, Brother." His fragile hand rested on Saul's shoulder. "We're like the disciples on Pentecost Day, wondering like everyone else what this babble is, and then Peter—Peter gets a word."

"Okay." Saul leaned forward, propping his jaw on the uplifted fist. "Emigrate," he said. "Leave Kittochtinny. Go through the open door. Emigrate."

The shock of this one word dwarfed anything they'd felt during the last 48 hours.

"Permanently?" Eby asked.

"To Western U.S.A.? To another country?" Baumgardner said.

"And then what?" Noah said.

Bennie and Cyrus both gawked and said nothing. Cyrus leaned forward, twisting his head back to peer into Saul's eyes.

"It'll split the church," he said.

"What church?" Bennie said. "Why do you care? They've already kicked us out."

"What about my farm?" Baumgartner said. "I run a profitable dairy. What about my wife and three children? Would there be farming at the other end?"

"I've got nothing to lose," Eby said. "Not since last night."

"I don't know *where*," Saul said. He went back to the table. "When Noah and his family got into the Ark, did they know where?"

"Well . . ." Baumgartner was finally going to come down on one side or the other. He flashed one of the magnetic grins that so endeared him to the youth in the Conference. "The Anabaptists emigrated, didn't they? Left their gardens, their livestock, their homes. Got onto those big, Atlantic ships. They did, however, know it was America they were sailing for. If they hadn't come, where would we be? Still hiding from Anabaptist hunters up in the Alps, according to your stories, Saul."

Cyrus had wrapped himself like a caterpillar in a chrysalis of silence, his arms crossed and two fine, uncallused schoolteacher fingers covering his mouth.

"Are you sure?" Baumgartner said. "Are you sure it's the Lord saying it?"

Voices, voices, voices. He was still in the gloaming he'd stumbled into this morning as he read this passage when the word had first come to his mind. It had grown like a swollen lotus bloom and unfolded its intense, pink, and spotlessly pure lotus petals above the dense and filthy swamp of his grieving imagination. *Emigrate. That's what these verses mean. For us. For someone else, maybe they only mean the Rapture. But Emigrate and the Rapture for us. Haven't we been praying?*

"Let's pray!" he said. "Cyrus, could you—" He tugged the man's hand, which was still lying on his shoulder.

Cyrus nodded. "Most merciful Father . . ." If anyone could get attention before the Eternal Throne, it had to be Cyrus. He was the most selfless man on the planet, the most pure-hearted, the wisest. He spoke words that penetrated the dull funk that stuck like earwax in most people. His only flaw was his lack of decisiveness and his reputation as a soft-sell. *Maybe that's why we're linked, like the Siamese twins. He'll petition you, Merciful Father. I'll carry out the command.*

Out on that laminated floor, the Wahoos streaked toward the orange rim and oversized fishnet. The clock ticked down. Ten, nine, eight . . . two big guards cordoned and corralled him. They were double-teaming him again, that old son-of-a-gun Washington coach. At that moment, there came Bjornquist, the screen, with the ball. "Heffner's free!" Saul lied, shouting over the guard's shoulder.

The big Washington guard with his back to the basket, practically on top of him, snapped his head right and away. His body half-turned, long enough to see that it wasn't Heffner who was free. He was still bottled up in the other corner. *It's me. I can do this. It's what stars are trained to do. I was born for this! I am unstoppable!* In that millisecond, Saul broke to the guard's right, the Sparkplug's ball splatting into his chest as he drove up and stuffed the ball. Yes! Yes! Right into the flapping mouths of the Washington and Lee cheerleaders, parents, fans, and news reporters.

We can do this. This Emigration thing. "I will spew you out," the Lord says to Laodicea. Who knows how soon the Destruction is coming? But to the faithful Church He says, "I stand at the door and knock. I'm here at the door. Come up. Come out." Has anything ever been clearer? The little word: "emigrate."

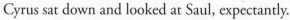

Cyrus sat down and looked at Saul, expectantly.

"Emigrate," Saul said. "We, the Remnant. Save ourselves from America's coming destruction. I've never heard the Lord clearer." Their faces were as stunned by his words as they had been the first time. "If I imagined it—" It was the first time he'd ever raised his occasional doubt to them. How did one know anything 100 percent? Had he imagined the voice of God in the barracks? How about his call to preach? He had the same feeling today that he did then: One of his own blood cells was whispering up the word that he would never in 10 decades of living have thought of on his own. *Emigrate.* Then what? Stake everything on what He says! *This ball goes in! This word . . . risk it all!*

"If it's just proceeding out of my brain and not from the mouth of the Spirit—" *What then?* "—may I be cursed. Struck from the Lamb's Book of Life!"

The men gazed startle-faced at the gamble. Saul himself felt a chill as the words fell off his tongue. But not Cyrus. He abruptly came alive, unwound his arms, and leaned back. Both of his hands clasped behind his head, his eyes closed.

"As I was praying just now, I got a picture," he said. "I never get prophetic words like you, Saul, but this was as clear as—maybe like an algebra student, befuddled, who suddenly gets the answer! Honduras! Just now when you were speaking, I saw a man's face—" His hand hovered before his closed eyes as if the hand were a mirror, remembering that man's face. "Conference sent us on a fact-finding mission a couple years ago. Where in Central America should we mission? We rejected Mexico and Guatemala, but then we got to Honduras and saw the poor little seacoast where the Caribs live—negroid and poor and harassed by the Spanish-lineage folks. And the land is large: banana plantations, coffee. But abandoned. No serious farmers. No infrastructure to get the goods to market."

Cyrus's eyes popped wide. "And in this restaurant in Belmopan, a fellow approached us with a photo and said he had a plantation—fifty-thousand acres—for sale."

"Where?" Baumgardner asked.

"British Honduras."

"Is that America?" Bennie asked.

"Central. South of Mexico, but technically, no, it's not part of North America. And it's more tropical."

"I can farm!" Baumgartner said.

"Now you're going?"

For the first time that afternoon, the funeral home mood cracked, and suddenly it was Cinco de Mayo. Great, broad smiles lit up the men's faces, and they slapped each other's backs, laughing without restraint. The men were all out of their seats, crowding around Cyrus.

"I have to ask my wife," Noah said. "But do they have cattle?"

"Beef cows. And markets too. With some refrigeration, you could transform that market place, where peddlers still sit on the ground with their wares and butchers shoo the flies off their meat with horsetails."

"Is there electric?"

"In Belmopan. In Orange Walk, where this farm is—"

"We've got an electrician," Eby said, his opaque and magnifying lenses turned in Saul's direction. "Stovie runs heavy duty electrical cables for your buddy, Susquehannock Electric."

Bennie read the new mood more clearly than anyone and, being the Sparkplug, knew what to do about it. He fished a felt marker out of the breast pocket of his bib overalls and stepped up onto his chair, his oversized body teetering until Eby and Noah wrapped an arm around each of his legs. He hoisted the loyalty statement overhead and struck a great, red *X* across it. Then he jumped off the table, embraced Cyrus, and kissed his pale, withered cheek.

Twenty-Four

WAS IT BERTHA or Calliope? He studied the lozenge-shaped, ivory and black face that ogled him, chewing noisily.

Anna Mary had named every one of them and claimed that each responded to its name. She affectionately scratched their ears as they stood in their stalls, asked them questions, and let them slaver in her hand as they licked up the handfuls of crushed grain.

He couldn't remember. "Okay, Calliope." He shouldered the animal's gut, forcing her to step sideways so he could swing the milker under her belly, onto the strap that held it in place so the machine could rhythmically suck the milk out of the udder.

The good thing was this: It only mattered for about another 30 days.

He'd put the farm, and all the cows as well, on the auction block. It would be good riddance. He'd auction off the farm equipment, such as it was, and sell the coal-dredging business, bundling the Caterpillar in with the electric company contract. That was the way to do it, like selling a restaurant bundled with the loyal customer base and liquor license. It would be worth a lot more than auctioning it off piece by piece. He had no doubt he'd clear all the debts and carry a good nest egg away for the trip.

He pictured 500 people, all doing the same thing. One hundred fifty or so farms or houses up for sale . . . it would make the evening news! This wouldn't just be a move but an Exodus. The American Dream in reverse. Give the TV newsmen something to send their cameras to cover. Let them analyze why these people are leaving.

He unhooked Calliope's milker and sent the steaming milk down into the steel bucket on the barn floor. The day was ending as it had begun: still and muggy. He did the routine that Aaron usually did, dumping the bucket into the strainer, lifting the empty strainer away, capping the lid onto the can with a hard smack of his fist, then heaving the 80 pounds of warm milk up and down into the icy waters of the cooler.

Every job had its routines. Who would plan this huge emigration effort? And what kind of land would it be on the other end? "A poor little seacoast where the Caribs live," Cyrus had described it. "Banana plantations—deserted."

Not unlike what the Pilgrims found. The east coast of Massachusetts was deserted because the Pawtuckets had died in a flu epidemic, leaving the land without tenants. What about the population they would find in Honduras? Would they be friendly or not? It took the Pilgrims a whole winter before they found some friendlies, and by that time, half the population was dead—seventy-five percent of the women, including the Governor's wife.

It's unclear, as I recall reading, why she died, Saul thought. *Drowned, they said, that December in Plymouth Harbor. A suicide some said, although others disputed that. Did she just give up and walk into the chilly harbor until the waves numbed and covered her?*

The sun slanted hard through the milkhouse window as he finished sudsing and rinsing the stainless steel milkers and racked them against the wall. His stomach signaled dinnertime. What good revivalist wife would drive up with it tonight?

Anna Mary could be ill for a long time. Mom Krehbiel's phone call the morning after the funeral had been tense and short. The Bishop must have heard him after all—they were taking her to Gerberville, Mom said, the hospital for the mentally ill. He would want to hear the results.

But meanwhile, he couldn't wait around for the recovery. *I'll go and come back. Will she want to come then, when she's gotten better?* He couldn't imagine it. He couldn't imagine her ever saying that she was ready for Honduras. So what did that mean? Would he leave her behind? If so, for how long? Forever? What would it be like to never see her again? *I'll never see Schnoogie again in this life. What about that? Who will trim the weeds around his stone, set out flowers, and put a little toy bear there on his birthday?*

"Let the dead bury the dead." That was Jesus.

I'm the leader. I set forth the vision for this group of people. I've got work to do.

Wheels sounded on the driveway outside, and he pulled the plug on the washtubs, sending the water down the drain. And what good sister had made supper this evening?

"Bennie!"

"Hee . . ." Bennie held up a picnic basket with its insides concealed under a linen tea towel. "Got your supper here."

"I was wondering who was bringing it tonight. But you drove all the way up here!" He slapped Bennie's shoulder as they entered the washhouse. Even though Anna Mary wasn't there to check on him, he routinely shucked his shoes by the washhouse door. He pointed at Bennie's in expectation that he'd do the same.

"Fresh from Mom Fisher's kitchen." Bennie positioned the basket on the tabletop and pulled off the tea towel. "Red eggs. You like red eggs?"

"Do I like red eggs?" He unscrewed the jar lid and grabbed one of the slippery pickled eggs between his fingers.

"Ice tea. Oh, Jesus—Some day, huh?" Bennie grinned, stretching forward the two-quart Mason jar of iced tea. "Aren't you just tickled?"

Saul bit the egg in half as he sat down, looking down at the beautiful maroon and yellow crescent. He sprinkled salt on the second half. "Mmm! Didn't know I was this hungry." He wolfed down the second half. "Sorry, Bennie. You asked something. I'm not acting like a decent host." He unscrewed the tea lid.

"Go ahead, drink up! It's meadow tea."

"Meadow tea." The joys of life in the country. He tilted the quart jar over his open mouth, directing a chartreuse stream, and then set it down and went for a glass. "Why don't you stay and talk?"

"I was gonna; you ain't busy."

"Me? No. Sit down."

"You still got some Mom Fisher to go." Bennie reached into the basket and brought out a small, covered, clay pot, which he opened. The sharp aroma of fermented cabbage was unmistakable.

"Sauerkraut? She really put herself out."

"Same thing we had."

"You ate already?"

"I did. They're fressin' theirs right now."

Saul forked out the sauerkraut.

"You miss Anna Mary?" Bennie asked.

"Did you notice how empty it is?" He hallooed. "There's an echo."

"Believe so." Bennie impulsively reached into the sauerkraut pot with the serving fork and speared a wiener. "Better eat another doggie. I don't know if they have 'em in Honduras." He rolled it onto Saul's plate. "What we gonna eat in Honduras, hmm?" Bennie chuckled. "Maybe we'll just pluck a grapefruit. Or no, it's bananas, not? How 'bout a couple bananas for supper? Send the boys to sickle off a bunch. Don't they grow up in trees? Won't that be something!" He chuckled again. "Love them fruits."

"I do miss her. Even though things were so bad this summer." He thought of Schnoogie. He said nothing, but fumbled in the basket and found a small jar. "What's this?"

"Potato salad. You like potato salad?"

"Didn't know I was so hungry. Starting to feel human again."

"What I wanted to talk about—"

"Yeah, I wondered why a busy guy like you brought the dinner. It's always someone from Smyrna. And it's usually the mom and kids." He jabbed another egg with his fork, tapped it on the edge of the jar to let the juice run back into the jar, and then bit it in half.

"About what we'll do with the Caterpillar now."

"Mmm." With emigration, what could be done? He still hadn't made up his mind about a lot of things. So many things remained to think over.

Bennie plunged ahead. "Everybody I talked to had no idea oil was going to come on this strong—"

"Oil?"

"And beat out coal."

"Oil?"

"Coal's kaput, Saul. Electric company don't want it anymore."

Saul dropped the speared second half of the egg and grabbed a large swallow of tea to keep from choking. "Coal kaput?"

"Give it another couple months of lean pickings. We was born 20 years late, Saul, we shoulda done this before the War."

"Who says coal's kaput?"

"You didn't hear?"

"Hear what?"

"About oil."

"What about it?"

"They're going oil. The Electric Company's gone oil. Didn't you read your paper?"

"They don't want our coal?"

"They're done with coal." Bennie stood up, back-stepped to the kitchen doorway, and paused, eyeballing Saul.

"They're never going to sign a contract?"

"No. And not pay for what they got the last two months, either, 'cuz they say it's no good. Been gumming up their furnaces. Surely someone shoulda told you. Last night they called the shot, and I was sure you saw it. It was all over the *Post-Dispatch* this morning—you get the paper, don't you? Someone musta clued you in."

Saul pushed the plate and basket away. "If they're going oil, they don't want any more coal, and no coal means we're out of a job." He stood clumsily and slipped against the refrigerator.

"Big deal. We're going to Honduras anyway."

"I owe $20,000—"

The sauerkraut, potato salad, and half-eaten red egg that remained on the table nauseated him. No one would buy their operation, nor the equipment. He'd sell the cows and still have debts. There wouldn't be a spare dollar left. "That's terrible. That's horrendous." He squeezed his eyes between his fingers and slumped into the chair again.

"It was a gamble," Bennie said as he came around behind him and pulled up Anna Mary's chair. "It was a gamble."

"That's right, *it was a gamble*!" He slammed a hand on the tabletop, rattling the dishes. He slapped Bennie's hand—crushed it. "It was a gamble, and we lost. I'm glad Anna Mary isn't here to—"

Bennie waved an index finger in front of Saul's eyes. "I'm filing for bankruptcy. I ain't leaving town in debt. They'll gobble up everything we get for the farm—15,000 something—and we'll bankrupt the rest."

"You can't do that."

"Says who?"

"The Church. Bankruptcy's a test of membership."

"The Mennonite Church?" Bennie scrambled away, heading for the kitchen window. He turned half around and continued backward, ending up facing him from across the kitchen. "I'm not a member of that church anymore. I don't live by their rules. Right?"

"I can't bankrupt," he said. *My debts are to the Bishop. Revival ends in a bankruptcy. BANKRUPT PREACHER FLEES TO HONDURAS. Not an exodus, a flight. On the other hand, what do I do? Pay the debts? How?* Coal was a gamble, and he'd lost. Revival was a gamble, too. Bennie's star would rise in the end, like Mose Gochenauer's. He hadn't lost anything. Bankruptcy would be the gangplank he'd use to cross to a new life in a new land.

"We don't have to do the same thing. I'm filing," Bennie said. "But you can't let past debts and an invalid woman stop you from doing God's command. You said it was God's word, Saul. Emigrate."

"I am coming. We'll get organized down there. Then I'll come back when I hear she's better and make her an offer."

"What if she won't come?"

Light was dying in the kitchen. Out the window and above the peaked gable of the barn, the clouds lit up like windrows of hay on fire. Saul studied the man silhouetted against the clouds.

"You'll come back to Honduras either way, right?" Bennie said. "You're the leader. You have to."

"Either way," Saul said, "I'll come back."

Bennie's voice dropped. "I got a prophecy, Saul. Right after I got home."

I don't feel close to him, not as I have at times in the past. As the sky darkened behind Bennie, he became a cutout figure. *I don't feel close at all.*

"I went to flip on the main switch to the milker motor this afternoon. A whopper spark this long—" he measured an inch-and-a-half between his forefinger and thumb "—jumped, and just that quick, I saw Jesus, talking."

Saul played with the fork, tapping the table top.

"And the Gift hit me. And Edie, right there chopping the cows, heard every word. She got an interpretation." Bennie tilted toward him. "'I'm coming very soon. *Coming* **before** *next year is out.*' Whew! Ain't it wonderful?"

"Next year?"

"Not this one but next. See how it all hooks together? Belly up for America. But we're all ready for Him. That's what we're to do in Honduras."

"I don't believe it's next year."

Bennie took a step toward him. "You don't?"

"We can't know for sure. No man knows the hour nor the day when Jesus will come. That contradicts Scripture."

"No it don't."

"Never spoken in tongues like you, Bennie. I believe in them. But I feel uneasy when—"

"Remember Schnoogie's accident—how it would bring many to their knees? How it was foretold us? Look what happened three days after at the last revival." Bennie's voice grew excited, his face animated. "Next year!"

"We don't know. Gotta be careful. Tongues are judged by Scripture."

"You don't accept the language of the Spirit? What's the difference between that and your prophecies?" The man's body swayed back and forth in the darkening window, his face indistinct. "I'll tell you right now: you're wrong. God's anointed you, okay. But He speaks to all of us. And He gave me this prophecy."

"I'm sorry you're upset. That doesn't change Scripture." He'd have to refute this thing of Bennie's, and he was very tired. Very tired of disagreeing with people. Very, very tired of preaching.

"You'll see!" Bennie said. "Even I could hardly believe it, but then . . ."

Twenty-Five

SAUL HEARD THE knock on the back door as he leaned over his kitchen table studying the red line hand-traced on the map. It was a long line that descended southwesterly to San Antonio, Texas, then south through Monterrey, Mexico, and past Mexico City before it swung east almost to the Gulf of Mexico, where a large, red asterisk marked the town of Orange Walk, British Honduras.

Curious, he pulled the kitchen door to the washhouse and saw a man's shoes at the bottom of the screen door.

He knew those shoes—old, black Oxfords, the creases now worn into cracks on the often-polished leather. The stout legs in a pair of Sunday black suit pants, good ones and undoubtedly hot in this heat, that modestly covered those loins that had fathered eight children. Saul noted the starched dress shirt with a row of buttons between two black lapels standing perfectly upright to the fleshy red jowls, firmly pressed mouth, and protruding eyes of the man known to most around here as "the Bishop."

"Is what I'm hearing true?"

Saul locked eyes with the man and then stepped forward to unhook the screen door. The Bishop stood, not moving, even when Saul pushed the screen door wide.

"Come in. Come in." Saul motioned.

"Emigrate?" The Bishop's mouth partly sagged open, as if in disbelief, his head cocked for the answer.

"Come in. So the flies don't." He led the way to the table, where the map was sprawled, its red line answering the question. He scooped up the map, halfway folding it, and tossed it behind him into the dry sink.

"Noah said you are moving. He called an auctioneer last night to sell his place." The Bishop crossed his stocky, white-shirted arms.

"Sit down." He gestured to the chair where he himself usually sat. "Do you want some iced tea?"

"No. I do not want iced tea." The Bishop's face flushed red. "I want answers."

"You forced our hand. We're out!"

"Okay, the loyalty statement. I personally cast my vote against it—"

"You're the moderator! The man in charge. You never get what you don't want."

The Bishop sat now. He studied his folded, beefy hands on the blue oilcloth daisies that covered the table and pursed and unpursed his lips. "There were better ways to do it. But the board had to act. For the sake of our unity." He glanced up on the word "unity." "The body of Christ, which you seem willing to tear apart. I'm here to ask you to reconsider."

The distance between them was only three feet, but Saul felt no desire to punch him, no desire to humiliate him. *If it hadn't been for this man picking up the phone that day four years ago when I called from the Library of Congress* . . . He poured two glasses of tea and set one tinkling with ice before the Bishop and one before himself.

"God is separating the wheat from the chaff, to use a farmer's metaphor," Saul said. "At one point, you agreed with me. We're in the middle of a liberalizing, compromising revolution. And what has Conference done to date? Shot the messenger that told them there's a revolution."

Saul took a large swig of the iced tea. It was the fourth day of this horribly humid upper-90s weather since the day they'd met in the tent to make the big decision, and moisture was coming out of the air, condensing on the pitcher, dribbling onto the table, and rolling down the Bishop's forehead. "What I've concluded is that the Conference system itself is to blame. We have a Bishop Board telling 200 preachers what to say and do, and 15,000 members trot along. What's the alternative? Each congregation, each minister and his people, discern the truth for themselves. If the head were sound, we might have a healthy body. I'm not speaking *ad hominem,* Jake—it's the whole leadership unable to take a stand for revival." Saul jumped to the conclusion he'd been steadily arriving at since his trip West. "Centralized conference government is not biblical, and it's not Anabaptist either!"

"I can bring up your concerns."

"Who represents our viewpoint at your meeting? Not me. None of us. We're not ministers. Not voting members, in your eyes. And Cyrus has been silenced already. The outcome is rigged before we even—"

"It's a valid concern. You come and address us."

"I did once. The bishops on that board haven't the foggiest. Not one knows what the Anabaptists believed, including you." He pictured the man pinned and wriggling on the historical tree limb on which he had been born—the larva, the pupa, and the full adult stage, knowing next to nothing of how he and his people had gotten onto that tree limb in the first place.

"All right, all right." The Bishop slapped both palms on the tabletop. "You call off this . . . *emigration.* I'll call a meeting, you and your people—Cyrus, Bennie, yourself—with the Bishop Board next week."

"You're backing off the loyalty statement? That's what is actually tearing this Conference in two."

The Bishop's mouth moved to say something and closed wordlessly.

The offer was tempting, hatching in his mind like a May Fly. It eliminated the need for the huge effort . . . 200 families uprooted, selling their homes, saying their goodbyes to loved ones under ripping circumstances. The long, dangerous caravan through Mexico and the Peten, where who knew what perils awaited, to a banana plantation where they might spend years of trial and error to connect with the local economy. But the thought died as fast and violently as the May Fly. *Against that, in my heart, the voice of God: "Come out."*

"Why didn't you come up with this two months ago? Not that it would work. Laodicea, the lukewarm church—our Savior Himself said, 'I will spew you out'. We're going to separate ourselves from this lukewarm church . . . and the coming destruction."

"But, emigration?"

"How do you think your ancestors got here? William Penn and his Quakers couldn't put up with the persecution of the Church of England, and they EM-UH-GRAY-TED—no less dangerous than the trip we're contemplating—to Penn's Woods. The Pilgrims! Reform that big, fat Church of England with its bishops and deacons and central government? Too much to hope for! They packed their belongings into a tiny ship and went across the North Atlantic. *Truth is that precious, Jake!*"

"You compare yourself to the Pilgrims?"

"Why not? They also read Revelation, chapter 4. The chapter after the one on Laodicea. 'I saw a door opening in heaven . . . the voice said: Come up here and I will show you what must happen after these things.' We're going through that open door, Jake, into Noah's big boat, before America's hour of destruction."

"That's millennialism!" The Bishop roared as Saul had never heard him raise his voice before. "Menno Simons didn't believe in it, and neither do I."

"Have you read anything else by Menno Simons? I doubt it. Let's go to the source. Matthew 24, the Great Tribulation."

The Bishop grated back his chair with agitation, crossed his arms, and gazed at the vases of expensive flowers on the kitchen counter. They were faded after two weeks, with little piles of curled and brown rose petals under one, the remains of irises under another. "So." He corralled the petals on the counter into his hand and then watched them fall between his fingers into the trashcan. "You'll stubbornly do what you and your people have settled on, against wisdom and common sense."

The Bishop was conceding, wasn't he? Those falling petals were his own failed arguments.

"I lent you a lot of money, Saul."

"That I have always appreciated, Jake, even if I hate the farm. *You have been generous* to me. I'm selling the cows, the farm equipment, the Caterpillar, and the truck. I'll repay the cow loans, the loan from the bank for the Cat and the truck, and you'll still have the farm."

"You'll get nothing for those cows. How many families are selling cows and farm equipment in this valley? Fifty-some in the next month, if you go through with this plan. You think the vultures won't gather for the easiest meat-picking they've had since the Great Depression?"

"I'll pay off your loan."

"Not with just that, you won't. And the bank demands before I get my part."

"What do you want me to say? I've thought of bankruptcy, like Bennie's doing." It was the wrong thing to say. The Bishop knew moral high ground on this one, and he came off the sink, both index fingers blazing at him like Jesse James in a shootout, feet wide-planted on the floor.

"Bankruptcy's a test of membership, and you know it! We don't believe in it. *Owe no man any thing.* And Bennie doing it just blows a hole the size of a corncob in my opinion of that man."

"Seeing as how we're no longer members of the Conference, anyway . . ."

"Okay, then. It's unethical. Wrong."

"And that's what I've concluded. How I'll pay off the delta between the sale proceeds and the loan amount . . . I'm not sure yet. I don't know what the economy's like in Honduras."

"Honduras!" the Bishop screamed. He dropped into the chair, his face florid and dripping perspiration. He propped his elbows on the tabletop, wrapping his hands in a united double fist, just off his nose, with his eyes riding over the top of the fist. "Honduras!" He hissed it, like a cuss word. "What's happened to my family, Saul? What have you done to it?" He popped a finger out of the fist, the index finger, and rapped it on the table. "*Edie and Bennie.*" His voice pitched up. "Edie's my right hand at the market, making . . . *the pies.* And preserves. And her two children, Joshie and Julie." He reassembled the double fist and popped up two fingers. "*Noah and Velma.*" He rapped the table sharply with those fingers. "I have a hundred beef cows in the lot I've got to think about, now that Noah says he's quit the butcher business and going to—" he spat out the word "—to *Honduras!*".

"I remind you that these people decided on their own," Saul said. "I didn't coerce, force, lure, cajole, didn't manipulate anyone. And Noah's always felt second-class in the family, he says. Not as good as Norman and Edie—"

"Not true!" the Bishop roared again. "And I thank you for not meddling in my family." He glowered. Saul shrugged his shoulders.

"*Gloria,*" The Bishop continued. He popped three fingers now, leaving them extended mid-air, not rapping the table this time. "Broke her engagement with that very fine, young music teacher, Wolfgang Landis, because you told her to."

"May I respond?"

"It's your house."

"Let's stick by the truth. I told her nothing of the sort. She came one evening to tell me she was going to break it off because he's a pagan under that nice plain coat. And I didn't disagree. Furthermore, 'very fine, young men' don't go to jail on manslaughter charges."

"Dismissed," the Bishop said, "for lack of real evidence. He was out the next day. Now!" The Bishop returned to his medley of anger, raising the fourth finger. "*Anna Mary.* The hardest blow of all, Saul, unless we count little Jakie."

"My family, too. Do I get blamed for all the heartaches in your family?"

"My little Anna Mary. Just a beat-up tulip bloom." The Bishop suddenly spread his sturdy farmer fingers and covered and gripped his lower face with them, bending towards Saul. "I regret—" He spoke in a choked whisper through his spread fingers. "I regret you married into my family."

In the awkward silence, Saul looked about the kitchen at the dirty plates and glasses; the bouquets needing to be tossed; the refrigerator jammed bottom to top with leftover portions of casseroles, spaghetti, remains of roasts, pies, a turkey, and too many uneaten desserts, all the presents of well-meaning people over the week and a half since Schnoogie's accident. Yes, the house itself mourned the loss of her presence.

He had to know. "How is she? I want to see her," he said.

Without moving his hands away from his head, which he now propped wearily on his elbows through the crevasse of his hands, the Bishop said, "She went for shock treatment. Mom took her to Gerberville."

"Shock treatment?"

"Going again tomorrow morning at nine. The doctor says it can break the depression." The Bishop rubbed his sleeves across his eyes and sat back slowly. "She says, 'I'm guilty, I'm guilty.'" Their eyes met over this terrible fact. "'I'm guilty, I'm guilty,'" he repeated, his voice teary. "In the middle of the night she wakes and goes outside in her white nightie, barefoot. The second time, Trigger wakes me, and I go after her. First time we didn't know she was gone, but there she was sitting in the sun porch at 5:30 A.M., with the nightie all dirty and wet and red clay between her toes like she'd been walking up Deer Lick Run, where you find such clay. Second time I went after her and caught up as she wandered through the pastures toward Deer Lick, with our collie at the fence just beside herself with barking. An hour before sunrise. Now I padlock the doors at night and got Aaron to pound a couple sixteen pennies into the upstairs window sill from the outside, so she can't take off the screen and shimmy down the porch pillars."

They studied each other's eyes throughout this conversation. When the Bishop stopped, Saul asked, "What does she mean, she's guilty?" The big vein on his temple thumped.

"God's judgment on her, is all I can think. You weren't married when Jakie—Schnoogie—was conceived. Didn't seem to bother her, I always thought, but now—she's under a wagonload of guilt, I think, imagining God punished that mistake by letting Jakie . . ."

His voice trailed off. They were united by this one common realization as they eyed each other: It had been a terrible loss. And it was unclear whether there would be more losses.

"She says, 'I just want to die and be with Jakie.' That's what makes me think."

"And the shock treatment?"

"They do that with people who have a death wish."

"I have to see her."

"She won't see you now."

"She said?"

The Bishop nodded.

"Then after the sale I'll go without her. I'll come back in a couple weeks."

"No, you won't!" The Bishop's voice was all iron now. "You won't come back, and don't deceive yourself. You'll get involved with a woman that don't have problems—"

"I'll come back."

"No. You won't go." The Bishop stood, his barrel body blocking the afternoon light from the window. "It would be desertion, and she's never been unfaithful, has she?"

"No, but—"

"You'll wait for her and stand by her, because I say so, and I'm her father. You have an obligation." Saul stood to face him. "Both to her, morally and legally, and to me, financially and legally. An obligation you sealed with your signature in both cases." His finger stabbed at Saul's chest. "On a loan guarantee and in vows you made before 300 some friends and family and God Himself." He motored toward the door but turned to deliver the *coup de grace*. "And I will not release you from your obligations. And neither will God."

The screen door crashed behind him.

≡≡≡

"I'm guilty," she said. The out-of-wedlock pregnancy, her father thinks. But he remembered Wolf's interview with the investigator the evening of the accident. They jailed *him*, didn't they? Saul had believed the investigator was onto something back then. Objectivity of the legal process and all that. But Gloria didn't think Wolf was one bit responsible for the death and, in the end, neither did the law. He'd run back to Julliard after they released him, people were saying.

What was it Gloria had said? "I suspect her," she said. "She wanted him to go to heaven," she said. "I called down and asked if it was clear and okay, and she said it was *okay*," Wolf said. "She sang 'Safe in the Arms of Jesus' after it happened," Gloria said. And now the Bishop's report: she wanders the meadow in the dark, saying, "I'm guilty. I'm guilty."

He collapsed onto the velveteen couch, playing and replaying the scene in slow-motion in his mind, just as they used to play and replay those atom bomb tapes, where the buildings would fly apart in slow motion when the bomb hit.

My Schnoogie, in the little, green trousers that she made for him, cherry-stained on the kneecaps, running from her. "You can't get me! You can't get me!" Up into the barn with its huge mounds of baled hay stacked up to the rafters, some 40 feet, he ran, and Anna Mary caught up to him, distraught, impatient as she got sometimes.

No. He reversed the tape and restarted. Anna Mary calmly leading him by the hand, into the darkness, through the little door that notched into the great swinging double doors that were closed, talking to him about the calves, which he loved to see, and leading him. Yes, leading him! For what purpose? The bales were falling out of the mow overhead. Wolf was doing his summer job and obsessed with the fiction that Saul was doing something with Gloria. Like what? Taking her in the haymow as he had taken Anna Mary once? *I would never. Never.* But Wolf was telling her that, yelling down at her from the mow, and she was listening and growing more certain in her soul. And then, impulsively, she led him right to the hole, between the cycle of falling bales, and said something to keep him there while she backed off. "Do you see the hommies eating hay, Jakie?"

Rewind. Anna Mary standing with the boy, wanting to go, as she said, "to heaven" together. But at the last second, looking up, she sees the murderous 80-pound bale on the lip of the mow and changes her mind, because she has to see the job get done. *Our little boy—*

Most likely. And thud! Hitting him on the head, breaking his neck. Wham! On his back, dropping him like a bomb out of a bay directly onto the concrete below.

Did he feel anything? At that last second, feeling his mommy release his hand and gyrating wildly, yelling "Mommy!"—did he catch her eyes when it hit? And what did she feel?

He recalled the image that he himself had seen when he got there. It would never be erased from the giant screen where it forever played in his mind—like the screen in the darkened instructional room at the Intelligence Center, playing over and over the cloud that rose slowly and magnificently, like a great, poisonous, and fantastic double mushroom, over blasted Hiroshima below.

The death image, and his heart break, break, breaking. His eyes gaze, gaze, gazing at this new reality that the gods had determined would trample and retrample his heart forever, like poor Sisyphus.

How could she? Her own son. Leaving her behind will not be difficult at all. A woman so sick she put her son in harm's way. I won't feel the smallest scrap of regret. I don't want to see her again. Ever.

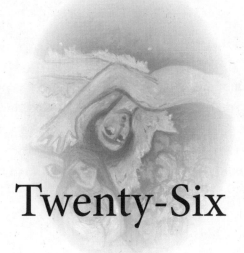

Twenty-Six

WHO'LL GIVE ME three now? We got 250 . . . 250 . . .
Burkholder—" The auctioneer banged the podium loudly and
pointed his crook cane at Burkholder, a massive, smooth-shaven Old
Order Mennonite who was dragging on his cigar. "You in or out?" The
auctioneer drifted his eyes over the little crowd, most of whom were
sitting on their wood-slat folding chairs. "He's in!" He announced
triumphantly to the crowd. "What is it?" His eyes moved back to
Burkholder.

"Seventy-five." The farmer's cigar wobbled in his mouth as he
said it.

"I got 275 for this . . . daughter of Winston Churchill! Eighty pounds
a day since she came fresh in September. Is that right?" The auctioneer
turned to Saul for confirmation. Saul stood by the white and black,
square-bodied cow's nose—not holding the rope around her neck, as
that was Butch, the auctioneer's son's job—with the records in hand.
The carefully penciled ledger Anna Mary had done on each cow.

"That's right."

"Two seventy-five for a Churchill! Eighty pounds of milk a day!"
The auctioneer shook his head. "What's wrong here, guys? I sold a

four-year-old just like her two months ago for 475." He slurped his drink before he pivoted back to the rival bidder, a lean farmer with hawk-eyes darkened by a feed company cap that was pulled down to the eyebrows, a small game hunting license pinned to the back of his blue denim coat. The man leaned against the barnyard fence, beyond which the 27 already-sold cows milled about, lowing.

"Boeshore? For 300? I got 275, 275 here now for a Churchill—"

Saul knew exactly what was wrong. Market glut. The Bishop had predicted the vultures would come in for bottom-of-the-barrel pickings, and they were here today.

"SOLD!" The auctioneer's Stetson-topped head dropped to convey the information to the clerk beside the podium. "Two hundred seventy-five dollars to Burkholder, who is number—?" His cane pointed again at Burkholder, who took the card from behind the crown ribbon of his fedora and held it up. "Twenty-three. That's it for the cows. Equipment's to the back of the barn." The crowd of men was already getting up, some folding their chairs to carry along. "Starting . . ." he studied his watch fob, "ten forty-five."

Butch led the cow through the corral fence to join the others. Saul found the auctioneer in the thinning crowd, a 50-50 mixture of Mennonite and non-Mennonite farmers, the former easily distinguishable because the locals generally looked less prosperous, cursed more, and talked louder.

"Shorty!" The Auctioneer downed the last drops of his cup. "Shorty, get me another cider." He scrunched the empty cup with his free hand and let it fall to the ground next to the men who were lined up to pay for their purchases. "Heads up!" His cane slashed toward the pickup that roared in reverse toward them, braking to a dust cloud stop among the farmers, who had managed to throw their chairs and bodies safely out of his way. "What's your hurry, cowboy?" the auctioneer said as he leaned into the window of the truck.

"Boeshore's always in a hurry," someone said.

"Getting me a wild turkey today!" Boeshore jumped out of the pickup. He circled to the rear and dropped the tailgate.

"What's up, Saul?" The auctioneer's puffy hand with the oversized turquoise stone ring dropped onto Saul's shoulder.

"I just want a total. How are we doing so far?"

"Golly, Moses." The auctioneer's Stetsoned head shook. "It's like serving up chicken and smashed potatoes to a bunch that's just had a pancake breakfast—with strawberries. These guys ain't hungry." He turned to his right. "Thanks, Shorty," he took the cup of cider. "I don't know totals, though. Hey, Ollie!" He hailed the man in the milkhouse at the head of the line of farmers. A cashbox and penciled list-up of the sales sat side on the table before him. "Saul wants a preliminary."

Ollie scratched something on the backside of a bidding card, folded it, and waved it overhead. "Just a rough, you understand."

Saul retreated, the folded bid-card in hand, to the little cider stand run by Sister Good, one of the Paradise Valley Church wives who'd been following the auctions around the tri-county for a month to sell her family's home-bottled apple cider. He sipped the cloudy stuff, already fermented to a sharp bite, and cracked open the card in his cupped hand.

Six thousand, one hundred dollars.

A heave of fear let loose in his stomach. Six thousand, one hundred dollars against a loan of $20,000 to buy these cows in the first place. Well, not quite. The 20 included the equipment as well, and they'd know in a little bit how that would sell. Maybe he got another $2,000 for the equipment, excluding the tractor. Eight thousand, one hundred. Still a delta of almost $12,000. "Morally and legally bound," the Bishop had said.

What could a man do? Yell at these farmers, these bloodsuckers? And there was Boeshore, loading his five little heifers right now. Sure, he'd been a good neighbor. But stripping a man's pants off, so to speak. Vulturing in for a piece of the good stuff because the market was glutted. Better just to file for bankruptcy, and whatever the creditors got, the creditors got.

The Colonel came to mind. Oh, pitiful to see. His own father, a proud Army officer, the light gone out of his bloodshot, deep-socketed eyes, teeth clenched on a cigarette holder, and mouth like a tight-wrinkled fruit as he gazed back across the lawn at that beautiful Georgetown brownstone that the Sheriff's men were locking up the day that it was sold.

"It wasn't so much the house as the sword collection and the library," he would say, referring to the three fine cavalry swords that MacNamara officers had carried in the Civil and Spanish-American Wars. They were antiquities now, and sold for a good sum to the Smithsonian. His library of first editions and leather-bound Greek and Roman classics had also been sold to a private collector. "All gone." They were watching his Mom, weeping, load what was left of her Wedgwood china collection into the station wagon. Two weeks later, a stroke would leave the old man, at 61, with a permanent limp and no movement in the left side of his face.

Financial boom-and-bust won't happen to me, I vowed. Adopted into this stable community. I'm safe, I thought. But now look. "Financially and legally obligated."

Behind the barn, the men loitered in groups, paying little attention to the equipment parked here and there on the ramping embankment that led up to the double doors of the barn's second-floor. Everyone knew already what he was or wasn't going to bid on, and they were exchanging community news right now.

Norman, the Bishop's son, stood jawing with a group of farmers from the Paradise Valley District. Only the back of his head showed as Saul rounded the tool shed.

". . . out of the creek, which is about as kooky as you get," he was saying. "It's junk black dirt."

"That's one thing about farming—" a high, nasal voice said.

"Like I said. Smart city wheeler-dealers don't make it around here—" Norman stopped, catching the expression of the farmer on his right, who had spotted Saul. Saul nodded to them as he passed, but Norman peered at the ground and itched his ankle with his free foot.

They were talking openly about him. They'd shown up to do the final skinning and nail his hide to the barn doors. "Look at him. I always knew Washington couldn't turn out anything but crooked politicians and gentlemen farmers." They were so smart in hindsight. *Go ahead, buy up our farms, skin us. "Fool! This night your soul is required of you." Require it of them, Lord! The fugitive king, David, said the same of his enemies. Require it of them!*

"We're gonna start with the disk and harrow. Yoh! Is this thing on?!" The auctioneer tapped the mic with his free hand, its wires leading back to a box under the giant maple, where the sound guy had just relocated and plugged in.

The giant maple stood topped with flaming red leaves above the still green and blood-spotted bottom leaves. Beyond the maple, Saul saw the clouds heading in. Flat, deflated clouds that surged across the sky above the rattling maple leaves. There'd been a weather change and should be a frost tonight.

Not like the clouds on departure day.

Bulged, towering, cumulonimbus clouds, like the straining, snowy canvas mainsails of the clipper ships, moved in packs across the sky. A metaphor for the cars and trucks now parked in Bennie's hayfield that were about to caravan the long road south and west to Honduras.

Saul pulled in late on that morning of the twenty-fifth of September. Bennie's hayfield was already one massive parking lot, with several teenagers directing cars into their assigned caravans. Six rows lined up behind the six leader cars, their noses already pointed toward the Pittsburgh Pike, the highway leading west to St. Louis. From there, they would head south to Mexico. It looked like photos he'd seen of the Okies moving ahead of the dust storms in their loaded Model T's bound for California.

Only the important stuff was loaded into these cars, and each piece left behind was to be cried over. Take the children, of course. A suitcase for each, all roped to the roof and covered with a tarp to protect them from the September thunderstorms. A couple of boxes of heirloom photographs and albums. The marriage license, birth certificates, passports, and vaccination and shot records. But no furniture. You could buy all that in Honduras. Lots of blankets and towels. Maybe a sewing machine. Axes, shovels, toolboxes, rope, medicine chests.

The truck fleet had been assembled from various farmers. Van-type bobtails were distributed to each of the six squads and loaded with potatoes, onions, bags of flour, disassembled tents, and camp stoves. A seventh slat-sided bobtail, attached to no particular squad, carried two cows and a mound of baled hay—milk supply for the expedition. An eighth carried chickens in cages, and a ninth, a flatbed, grumbled under a single John Deere tractor with a three-bottom plough, disk, bags of seed corn, and flats of vegetable seedlings. They would need to buy more, but this was enough to get a good truck garden going.

He marveled at the organizational genius of Bennie Fisher. He wasn't a preacher or business success, but the man knew how to organize three hundred people into an orderly cadre with an appointed place and role for each person, each vehicle.

The Revival tent stood beyond the rows of cars and trucks ready for departure. Since September, they'd converted it to a private school with classes Monday to Friday, 9:00 to 3:00, to accommodate the parents whose children were setting off on this great adventure. But today, it served as the assembly point and baby room while breakfast was cooking.

He smelled it as the Ford car nosed into the lot. Bennie's work, for sure! Pancakes and sausages, coffee and oatmeal cookies. Bennie's male crew griddled the pancakes over a long charcoal pit. The women had already started serving a line of cheerful folks at 7:30 A.M., while the people staying behind mixed freely with the emigrants. The two groups were distinguished mainly by their clothes—Saul had requested that those who were going dress up. "Wear your Sunday clothes," he'd said. "Look your best." It was easier to be nice if you were dressed smartly, and Lord knew they had 10 days of rubbing each other in cars, tents, and campgrounds before they got there.

He wore his signature, homemade, slate denim Mennonite coat, even though he wasn't traveling today. Denim for durability; homemade because he no longer tolerated the $70 the plain-clothes stores charged for the privilege of catering up a suit that fit Mennonite convictions.

Five hundred thirty souls, 106 families. As he looked up over the plate he was loading, it looked like that many had come. Two hundred ninety-seven were shipping out today, and the rest would follow when they got their homes sold—or when their encumbrances had been dealt with, in his case.

"Thank you, Edie." He caught the two incoming pancakes on the paper plate. "Where's Joshie?"

"Right there." Her spatula pointed out the boy. It was uncanny how much like Schnoogie he looked. He was seated by his sister in the early morning sunlight that was falling across the alfalfa field, wearing a short-sleeve, white shirt and suspenders and an enormous adult apron that tied around his neck to keep the pancake syrup off the shirt. Saul slipped in beside him.

"Hi Joshie!"

"Uncle Saul! Mom, Uncle Saul!" he said, eyeballing Saul without fear. "I'm going to 'duras!"

"I know, you lucky dog."

"We hadda give Rover away."

"I know. D'you say goodbye to him?"

They carried on in this way as they ate the syruped pancakes and sausages. Saul waved or shook hands with all those dear people until five to nine, when he started rounding up his team. The six members of the elder council were all in cheerful spirits, although Eby wasn't going because his house still hadn't sold.

"You guys ready? I want you all here around me when I introduce you—"

"Got it," Noah said. He was the most loyal of them all, perhaps, even if he was the Bishop's son.

He nuzzled the mike and squinted into the eastern sun towards them. "Some people are still eating—okay. Keep going—you need that energy for the trip ahead of you!" They laughed and jostled each other. "Good morning!" A few managed a "good morning" back. "Reach around, find someone you're happy to see, and give that person a big 'good morning and God bless you.'" He was embraced from behind by . . . Noah Krehbiel, as the general hubbub broke out. "God bless you, brother." He tweaked little Cecily's pink cheek under the homemade bonnet her mother had sewn for her.

"And you," Noah said. "I feel so fortunate. To go on this."

"I wish I was coming with."

"You'll come soon." (On that day, he'd believed Noah. Three weeks later, with Anna Mary still in the hospital and the price his herd had brought, Saul was no longer sure.)

The others on the elder board came to say their goodbyes, starting with Cyrus. He took Saul's hand carefully between his parchment-skinned claws. "We need you to come soon."

"You're the spiritual leader," Saul said. "You're the only ordained bishop, and people respect that. You do the Communion, lead them in prayers, watch to see who's flagging."

Finally Bennie came up, throwing his arms around him.

"Hallelujah! I just feel . . . Hwoooh!" Bennie looked around and caught the eyes of the other elders. "He's gonna bless us!"

He heard the growl in his spirit, a check, a caveat. He remembered the man's prophecy and certainty: *the Lord is coming next year.*

"You did a great job organizing things," Saul whispered. "I had no idea!" he said louder now, so that all the council could hear. "Six leader cars, six caravans, and a supply truck with each. It's like moving an army, and you just put it together."

"Someone had to do it," Bennie rubbed his chin modestly.

Saul signaled an end to the greeting time. After everyone was back in their places, he continued. "We've got a few things to cover this morning so you can be on your way by 10:00. Let's start with introductions. Our elders." That was one thing he loved about the remnant, as they'd been calling themselves since the decision—they applauded. In the Conference churches, applause was frowned upon as an opening for pride. But he took credit for changing a tradition. *When you're working with folks who don't get paid for what they do, at least clap for them.*

"And Bennie Fisher, who'll be our captain on the expedition south."

"Honduras, here we come!" Bennie's moon face radiated as they applauded.

His bowels growled again as he stood there under the maple, remembering the departure day. So far, there'd been two cables documenting their arrival at the Mexican border, and then one from Orange Walk a week ago, but no details of how things were going. *What is there to fear? Why this sense of dread, like something's going to strike?*

"And the Caterpillar, finally." The auctioneer led the way to the big, yellow Cat, lots of black silt and yellow clay still embedded in the tracks. "You want to show us it runs, Saul?"

Saul started the Cat engine and demonstrated the scoop action, then shut it down and jumped off.

"I want a ride!" someone said. A little towhead, not more than three, tore loose from an older brother and ran toward his father, who stood with the farmers by the Cat tracks. He knew the man—Burkholder, the Old Order man, who'd bought the Churchill daughter. Burkholder reached to shush the boy.

"You mind?" Saul asked. "I'd love to give him a ride."

The man shrugged and patted his son's behind to project him toward Saul. "Do what he says," the father called to the retreating boy.

"Let's start it off at four grand. Four thousand dollars. Do I hear four?"

Saul lifted the boy and set him on the Cat seat. As he did, it triggered a memory—lifting Joshie Fisher on his shoulders on departure day.

They formed two circles in the hayfield after breakfast, all of the emigrants in the center, while those staying behind made a larger circle around them. Some were already grieving the finality of this move. Edie Fisher clung to her sister, Gloria, not ready to release her and join the emigrants, while Gloria stayed in the outer circle. They wept copiously into each other's shoulders.

Little Joshie stood off to the side, confused by his mother's tears. Seeing him like that, looking so much like his cousin now in heaven, Saul scooped the boy up and onto his shoulders.

"Hold on!"

The song started, low and slow, then picked up strength and tempo and rising pitch. Meanwhile, the *New Cumbria Post Dispatch* photographer ran about, flashing photos with his big camera.

> God be with you till we meet again,
> By His council guide uphold you,
> In His arms securely fold you,
> God be with you till we meet again.

They sang with the unbelievable melodiousness of 600 experienced and blended human voices, unaccented and undiminished by an organ or guitar:

> Till we mee-eee-EET!
> Till we mee-eeet . . . .

His own eyes streamed, and he heard raspy gasps from his throat. He couldn't conceal them as the first caravans pulled onto the big highway. The procession was off for Johnstown, where a scout was even now finalizing camp arrangements for the night at the city fairgrounds.

Bennie's new station wagon, loaded to the point that the body hardly gapped off the ground, came alongside. Saul passed little Josh through the open window, head-first. "The mantle's passed to you till I get there." He swabbed his cheeks and eyes. Bennie, behind the wheel, grinned effusively. The children bent around their father to observe Saul swabbing his tears. Bennie should have been more frightened, more sobered by the responsibility of leading 297 precious souls to Honduras. *I'm frightened by it.*

And then little Joshie waved at him with both hands through the back window as the car pulled onto the highway.

⸺⸺

"Sold!" the auctioneer said. Saul climbed down and sent the little towhead to his father, who thanked him and walked off, the barefoot boy trotting to keep up and holding fast to his father's pant leg.

As he walked back through the thin crowd of farmers toward the clerk's desk in his milkhouse, the cars all around him in the driveway in a start-up roar, it hit him: *They're all leaving. Taking my cows and equipment with them, although God knows I didn't want them a long time ago. Taking away the tow-haired kid.*

⸺⸺

Everyone's leaving. The emigrants, their cars bumper to bumper as they bounced down and up, out of Bennie's hayfield onto the big highway, were going away. Their cars grew smaller and smaller and vanished. Joshie's face vanished, and the Fisher wagon window became a distant reflection of the overhead clouds, no bigger than a postage stamp. Schnoogie, too, had descended away in a box into a watery hole in the ground, and the next day the earth was already sealed over it, already obscuring his face forever.

I will lose more, no doubt. The certainty of it gripped his intestines, inch by inch. *Anna Mary. Her too? Have I already lost her?*

The song haunted on. They sang as the cars caravanned towards Honduras. It grew fainter and fainter as the cars shrank away, until those left behind only heard their own lonely voices. They still stood in a big circle, but without a center now, singing to themselves in the alfalfa field beneath the towering, puffy clouds that looked like clipper ships:

> Till we mee-eee-EET! Till we mee-eeet,
> Till we meet at Jesus' feet . . .

Part Six

The Plunge

October 20–21, 1956

Twenty-Seven

BABBLE, BABBLE, BABBLE *of the river wakes me. Girdle of pain that wraps my spine. Crown of my head like the pulsing town center redlight—off in a moment of calm, on with a fresh push of heat and pain. OFF. ON. OFF. ON. Sandwiched into this car, which doesn't accommodate a six-foot, sleeping body. Can't recline the Ford's bench-type seats, so I go sideways on the front seat, curled up and legs dangling to the floor offside. Leftover, masticated cardboard around my molars, it seems. Hamburger bun, actually, the remains still in the paper sack I picked up at the diner. Disgusting aroma of stale, sweet, old onions, so I pop the right front door of the Ford and push out with my arm.*

Chilly river-bottom air. He heard a pair of turtledoves calling back and forth in the tree, unseen. *Why am I here?*

He was sitting on the riverbank, huddled under the steering wheel of the blue Ford, and the river burbled out of sight over the embankment. The first hard frost had hit last night. The puddle below him, spanning the wheel tracks worn by numerous truckloads of coal dirt traveling out, sported a milky filigree of ice around its edges.

He kicked out the paper sack with the remains of the sandwich he'd bought last night (before he drove out here under the stars), and he used the elbow of his flannel shirt to wipe a porthole in the fogged window.

Coal silt washed here. Washed in. Washed away. Washed up. Like me. Worthless, like this coal dirt. We thought it was worth beaucoup bucks. Ten thousand loads times a hundred dollars a load. There's a million dollars. Maybe a million mosquitoes. That's the only million here.

He threw one leg out of the Ford and levered himself upward on the flapping door. Two blue paper butterflies fell away, fluttering toward the ground, and he kicked to prevent them from falling into the puddle. The previous night pounced like a summer thunderstorm.

The butterflies were aerogrammes, each triple-folded and bearing strange foreign stamps. There were tropical flowers on one and tropical fruits on the other, next to the pristine, regal face of Her Majesty Queen Elizabeth II, Head of the Commonwealth, including the tiny state of British Honduras.

The turtledoves again. How can they do that? Why do they do that? Go choke yourselves.

Horrific images from the letters ran through his mind like small, bright-eyed children tumbling across the green Kittochtinny lawns in the evening. Catching lightning bugs. Dropping them in jars with perforated lids. Poking their noses into the lilac flowers. Calling to their hidden chums, "Seven . . . eight . . . nine . . . TEN! Ready or not, here I come!" Then, like cut flowers, they wilted back onto their bedsheet hammocks, their faces feverish, their bellies and chests covered with deadly pink spots, their white bedsheets stained with feces and blood. Their screams of terror diminished as their perforated intestines drained their lifeblood away down the holes of makeshift toilets, thrown together by their enterprising Mennonite emigrant parents, and now collecting the draining souls of their children as they died of typhoid.

Finally, their demented, wild-eyed babble faded to only the buzz of flies.

GAWD! I'm responsible!!

Twenty-Eight

MIGHT THERE BE a letter?

The late October morning carried the smell of burning leaves, the ongoing sound of a chainsaw, and the flat, dark, moving clouds that signaled another weather change. Rain, maybe. He didn't consider how ridiculous a grown man cuddling a teddy bear might look as he crossed the road to the mailbox. *My first free Saturday since the sale. The cows are gone, the house is empty, and me living like a single man again, teaching world history until I'm in financial shape to join them in Honduras. It's the first day of the rest of my life!* He recognized it also as the first happy thought he'd had in weeks.

He pulled the mail from the roadside box and went down on his haunches, sorting. A seed catalog—getting to be that time of year again. Letters from Susquehanna Electric—no money in any of them, certainly. (The auctioneer's check already lay in the study, unopened, waiting for him to sign it all over to the Bishop.) And then he saw the envelope—a thin, floppy, blue aerogramme with an exotic stamp on the upper right corner and exotic flowers with the Queen of England off to the side. Who was it? He flipped it and saw the return address. "Benj. S. Fisher." He felt the shiver of dread again, dropped it in a pile by itself, and went on. More bills, and then—a second aerogramme. Different flowers, same Queen of England. Who was this one from? There was no return address.

$$==$$

He walked up the lane towards the barn, ripping open the first aerogramme with a finger and spreading it on top of Bear-Bear's head as he walked.

Dear Brother Saul,

Greetings in Jesus' name. We arrived Orange Walk night of the first and are now safe into temporary shelter—some banana wearhouses and some chickenhouses on stilts. For now, okay. I'm not much good at writing but just thought to let you hear all's well.

He exhaled noisily as he read this. "Hoh!" Safe! All well! Why so suspicious, anyway?

The land is better than Canaan. Grapefruits for breakfast, dinner, supper. Also mangos. Icekremaldo has settled us in. He is a nice man, although a hard look, like all down here. As per planned, we emptied trucks and took them all but one to Belize City and sold them. I could write books if I were a writer. How we spent a day in their capitol and a man just showed up who wanted all. But will save that until you get here. We are all praying it will be soon, there is so much to do. We paid Icekremaldo all for the property but now see we did one thing wrong. Left us with no money and only one tractor until fokes get their bank money veea the U S Ambussy, for you know we didn't carry our savings, going through that bandit territory. Land's not rich and black like up there, and there's plenty a bush to be cut. Also rain, rain every day.

How strange and far away it all seemed, like a story in a book or in a history text, not something happening to people he knew and loved. And they'd been gone what? Four weeks?

Ohh the people. Filth, stink, unsaniterry condishuns. How we should thank God for helthy bodies and Cleanliness next to Godliness as we were taught. Ohh the soles in darkness. Ohh the many who know not Jesus and his near return which we await. But of course, that is also true in the Layodisee (my spelling?) church up there. Ohh the joy of being in the family of God. If you could see our womenfokes. Glory! Our campstoves aren't enough, and plus we run out of propane by the time we got here, so we made out with charcoles in the oil drums Bombgardna rigged up. He's handy with his hands. Some even baked biskuts over them, and we had Comunyion last night. Onlevvned bis-kuts. It brought to mind Noah departing the ark and building an adler to prase God. About the stoves. Love. Love. 200 hungry families and everyone wants to use one, plus we're still pooped from the trip. Do you think there is impashents? No. As one gets done she calls to the next, "I'm done." And so sweet, no angry words, no impashents. Sweet, sweet. Love. Love. Love.

The text of the letter ran to the bottom of the page. Saul flopped the letter to find the ending.

So as we are short of money until it all comes through we can-not help with your debts nor have talked about it since we got here. Many feel like me—you should file for bankrubbsee (my spelling?).

Have I asked anyone to help with my debts? What business is it of Bennie's how I resolve the problem?

I must go. Someone is asking for me. Hurry and come.
Your brother in Christ,
Benj. S. Fisher

He was in the barn now. "Hwooh!" He made a high-pitched call. Several albino pigeons flapped rapidly toward the closed windows, veering off at the last moment and flying out over the open Dutch doors instead. The stables were still dirty. They had not been cleaned since the day of the sale, and cow manure filled the gutters.

He spread the second letter in the window well, to catch the light that fell through the cobwebbed set of 16 dusty, glass rectangles in the thick, stone wall that formed its casement. He leaned his elbows on the sill. There was the signature: "Your brother in Christ, Cyrus." The old man's overcareful and wriggly handwriting. Seventy-four, arthritic, weak-voiced, and fragile. But an unflagging revolutionary!

Dear Brother Saul . . .

The Revival was carrying on without him. They'd followed the prophecy into the brave new future, while here he rotted. Helpless hopelessness, as if his 29-year-old body, like Rip Van Winkle's, had aged during a long sleep. Where had his energy and youth gone to?

Dear Brother Saul,
    Greetings. How we miss you and wish you were here in the time of terrible testing. I am sending this letter via Manuel, our Spanish interpreter and liaison with "the outside world," one might call it. As you know, I taught Spanish during the school-teaching years, so the lot has fallen on this whitehead to be the

go-between. Manuel is on his way to Belmopan to contact the U.S. Embassy.

"In Rama there was a voice heard, lamentation, and weeping, and great mourning, Rachel weeping for her children, and would not be comforted, because they are not." Tragedy strikes the remnant for the folly of a few willing to tempt God. Today we buried our fifth child. Five in eight days. Oh, if you could hear the mothers!

OHHHhhhhhhh . . . a sensation like numbness entered the top of the skull and gravity pulled it down, chilling the body, as if freezing blood was draining right out the bottom veins on his feet. He plunged on.

All this could have been prevented by simple hygiene. When we arrived in Orange Walk, the authorities informed us that we by no means should drink the water in the lake on the plantation. This was told to us in broken English, partly in Spanish, with myself as interpreter, by virtue of my Spanish. All of us were, of course, surprised. Troubled, I should say. When we arrived at the plantation—Bennie has already written of the arrival, I believe—there were two policemen with guns. They took great pains to tell us not to drink the water. Again, I was translator, because they knew very little English. Absolutely dangerous, they said, maybe deadly. I spent considerable effort to convey this warning to our people. All well and good. People boiled water, which was flat-tasting but safe. A week ago . . .

When? When was this? He tossed the letter on its back and saw the October 13 postmark. *Why didn't Bennie tell me?* He pulled the first Honduran letter out of his breast pocket. October 6. *Why the difference? A whole week.*

323

A week ago, during Sunday worship, one man got a message by tongues that the water was safe, that God would protect us. Immediately I repudiated this, saying that I too speak in tongues, but even the devil can use tongues. When they go against the Bible or simple health rules, we must question them. We shall not tempt God. Someone—not saying who—rebuked me in front of everyone for lack of faith. My counsel was disregarded, and I don't know whether Bennie said how he stood, but at least he didn't support me. Almost everyone started drinking the water. The typhoid broke out, and since then, someone has died almost every day.

I should never have made him captain. Bennie—he's unbalanced and unsound. My God! Five children. Who? Who? And he doesn't say, but here's a name. The letter trembled so violently between his fingers that he couldn't read the jerking type. He seized it with his second hand and fought a powerful urge to vomit.

Tragedy on tragedy. Yesterday Rolly Kurtz . . .

Rolly Kurtz! Rolly Kurtz!

with two others was in the river swimming when it began to rain more than the usual—a cloudburst, they called it. Without warning, the river rose eight feet and washed him away. Presumed drowned. We have not recovered the body.

"Uhhhhh. Uhhhhh . . ." The groan squeezed from deep in his lungs. "Rolly . . ."

Rolly Kurtz, face full of light, singing "He Touched Me" while the lady in a turban with a Chihuahua in the aisle of Pomeroy's ogled. Rolly, rigid on the floor, stammering, "Turn in your Bibles to Acts." *Flash flood in Honduras. Presumed drowned.* Their faces began to tally, chattering like a grocer's cash register. *Rolly. Schnoogie. One, two, three, four, five. Children—!*

The worst is to tell.

How could there be worse? How could there possibly—

Naturally, Bennie, as captain, has been forced by the situation to speak out. To his credit, he forbid further drinking of any unboiled water. But he's lashing out. *Why* did it happen? He blames me for not emphasizing that the water contained deadly germs, for not translating correctly. Like the ancient Greeks, kill the messenger because you don't like his bad news. It's a warning from God, he says—that there's sin in the camp, unconfessed sin, he says, that brought on the judgment. Screaming at us, I might add. He's blaming you, Saul, for lack of commitment, for putting your debts and invalid wife "ahead of the Kingdom," he says. When our elder board challenged him, he announced you're no longer in charge. He's taken over. A one-man show. Lots of zeal and organizational ability, but *no* common sense.

I'm on his hit list. But all I care about is them—the ones who sincerely forsook all to follow Christ.

We're in chaos. It's not wise for you to come. Families are very angry, and some say they'll return as soon as they can buy a truck.

I am mailing a copy of this letter to Bishop Krehbiel . . .

I am now completely naked before the Bishop. All that we have accomplished with our revival is destroyed. He'll say, "I told you so."

Because he's always seemed to me a man of integrity, although perhaps stronger in diplomacy than preaching God's Word in its truthfulness. Perhaps he can use his power to intervene, even at this late hour.

≡≡≡

The letter fell onto the windowsill, and he bit a fingertip savagely until it bled.

I am ill. I'm going to vomit. The windows of the barn were revolving, turning on their sides. The juices in his mouth went sour. A hay bale caught him as his knees wobbled, and he clutched his knees to his chest in an effort to gain control of his body.

And then the thought, seemingly falling like a hailstone out of a clear summer day, clobbered him: *It wasn't God, was it? Those predictions about the coming destruction of Kittochtinny Valley. That voice saying, "Emigrate, go through the open door and get out." That voice in the barracks, saying, "I forgive you. Go and sin no more."*

He stumbled through the double-doors, carrying only Schnoogie's teddy bear tucked under his arm. He got as far as the Ford, where he bent over, retching.

And there he stood—one foot up on the chrome bumper, one hand seizing the hood ornament, the other outflung hand gripping Bear-Bear, and his stomach dry-heaving—as the car drove in the lane behind him and cut off, followed by "NRRRrrrrruhhhh," the sound of a motor needing a tune-up. Immediately Zwingli sounded from the dog kennel next to the milkhouse. He knew that motor sound. The Bishop had come for him, and there was no escape. It was an ambush, and this time he had no weapons left. The slow steps on the dirt driveway drew closer until they stopped directly behind him.

Nowhere to run. He, more than any other, cornered me, didn't he? Befriended me. Invited me to his community. Refused to share his power with us. Held onto it, dangling it over us, until we broke away. Now here to gaze at me, defeated, mortally wounded. He could also smell the man—the smell of cows, maybe the sweet, fermented smell of corn silage, but mostly the smell of a man who spends his time around cows and milk . . . an earthy smell. If seven generations of men and women tap-rooted into one spot on the earth like a unique species of tree could give off a smell . . . it was a smell of roots. Smells he still wanted to trust. But he couldn't lift his head.

"I'm sorry, Saul."

"I should go." His open mouth rubbed back and forth against his bare forearm.

"Go where?"

"D.C., where I came from. Leave you people alone."

"You can't. You're a part of us now—"

"I'm not a part!" He recoiled against the hood of the car and raised his head. He contemplated the man. "I came here and upset your family. You said it." The Bishop stood rooted, his feet apart, wearing another hat in his collection, an old fedora. "You regret I married into your family. Okay. I'll go away."

"Son, son."

"I take complete responsibility for everything that's gone on down there." Saul pointed at the blue aerogramme in the Bishop's right hand, with its tropical flower and Queen Elizabeth stamp on the upper corner.

"Stupid remarks I made," the Bishop said. "I'm sorry." For the first time, Saul noted how old he appeared. The man had lost weight. Raccoon rings circled his eyes, and the eyelids were swollen red. "So it didn't work out like you thought it would, huh?" The Bishop spoke without a trace of smirk or triumph. "What's unusual about that?"

"You never failed like this." Saul shoved his body off the front of the car with one leg. He wanted to go erect and address his adversary head-on, but again his stomach heaved. "Have to sit down . . ." He passed his hand down over his eyes and mouth in an effort to push away the nausea and dense mental fog. His mouth flushed sour. He fell against the hood, breathing heavily.

The Bishop lowered himself onto the chrome bumper, opposite him, his eyes fixed on the western sky, thick with cold weather clouds. "Think I did. Anna Mary's little sister, Mattie Mae. I had no idea she was in danger. I was just too busy. Unloading a load of hay and drinking tea. I never even kissed her goodbye."

"That's one. I've got seven. Seven lives I've—"

"Stop! As you said, they didn't have to go to Honduras. They chose to."

The man was backtracking on everything he'd said the Sunday after their big decision. What was he after?

"We could go down together and save as many as we can," the Bishop said.

"And what? Stand them up to confess their sins at council meeting?"

Their eyes crossed like infantry bayonets. The Bishop dropped his first. He reached across and squeezed Saul's hand.

"'Man of Sorrows, what a name.'" He quoted something Saul didn't know, but there seemed to be lots of poems unique to this region. Nor did he recognize it when the Bishop gave it a tune and sang the next line:

> For the Son of God who came . . .
> Ruined sinners to reclaim . . .

The Bishop's voice wobbled. Two large tears trickled over the rounded, leathered cheeks, and the nose streamed as well. He sucked air, choking perhaps.

"Hha! Hha! Hha!" The Bishop coughed each syllable. "'Hha! Hha! Hha!'" Then, in a near whisper, "Hhalelujah!" Still singing. The grip on Saul's hand was painful now. "What a Savior!" He swiped his nose with his sleeve and buried his face into the arm. When the arm fell away, he was back in control, taking off his glasses, wiping them clean with a pocket-handkerchief.

Saul found the song strangely comforting. It bridged their hatred, like the Olympic Games bridged the pitched hatred of the West and the Soviet Bloc for a few brief weeks every four years as the citizens of each nation applauded each other's athletes as they heard each other's national anthems. Like that, the nausea was gone. Saul stood up.

"Come to church tomorrow. It's Communion Sunday. We can talk about this stuff—" the Bishop shook the blue aerogramme in his hand, "—later."

"They'll lynch me. The news will come out. It'll be big."

"I didn't tell anyone."

"Nor I. Cyrus told the U.S. Embassy."

"Okay. Well. I guess I'll go."

"Was there anything else? You drove all the way up here—wait a minute." Saul jogged into the house and to his desk, which was piled high with the unopened mail from the last month. He returned with the auctioneer's check. "Made out to me, I suppose—so—" He ripped open the envelope and, without even checking the amount, signed the back. *Who cares if it's in pencil.*

"Thanks." The Bishop walked to his car, head down, and opened the car door.

"Listen." He peered back over the top of the car. "Anna Mary came home on Tuesday! She's with her mother, shopping today. *That strong!* She says she wants to see *you*." He jabbed forcefully at Saul with his finger.

"How is she?"

"Come and see. I think you'll be pleased."

Twenty-Nine

SAUL SUSPENDED HIS weight on the door of the Ford, his back against the chassis. The football-field-sized dredge that paralleled the curving riverbed, stripped of its trees and vines and coal, seemed a metaphor for his life. It was a wasteplace now, filled with small puddles and left-behind rubbish heaps of tree stumps and inverted root balls.

I've lost everything. Until the aerogrammes from Honduras, he'd been focused on when he'd have enough saved to join them, but now he could only think of what he'd lost.

This beautiful church he'd found in the pages of the Library of Congress' religions section under "Anabaptists," like sunbeams streaming into the dark cellar of his life. The pollution of his visions had fallen on them like the silent rain over Bikini Atoll—the hydrogen bomb rain that would implant in every cell a radioactive seed that killed. *Thanks to me, every Mennonite brain carries now the little radioactive seed of my toxic visions.*

He thought about Anna Mary and the farm. *Never cared about the farm, anyway, but what about Anna Mary? Isn't the woman crazy? Do I even know her? Do I want someone who couldn't safeguard the one child we had?*

He didn't have to conjure up the succeeding thought. The death image immediately sharpened, like a photographic image gaining clarity in the chemical pans of a darkroom. The unrealistically white face of a boy, sprawled downside up on a hay bale in the feeding lot of a cow pen. The dried-green sprigs of alfalfa from the bale that had broken his neck, still spiking his loosely-tossed, blond hair. The red blood like quick knife slashes beneath his nose and mouth.

My fault or Your fault? And where did that word "emigrate" come from as we prayed that day? What about the picture of Laodicea and the bombs falling on the lukewarm Mennonites and their troves of beautiful farms? "Someone to stand in the gap"—where did that idea come from, if not from You? And the voice in the Barracks saying, "I forgive you, now go become a peacemaker." If not You, then who? The other spirit in the universe, the lord of hell himself, dressed in light and deception?

"Go to hell!" Those were the Colonel's words, hearing I wanted to preach in a "peace church," betraying a hundred proud years of military commissions, bravery under fire, and chest medals. "You go to hell!" he snarled, flinging his cigar-clenching fist just under my nose, the smoke wreathing up to choke me.

Now Saul thought he could smell it. It wasn't mist off the river. It was hydrogen sulfide vapors, invisible but deadly when you stepped over a wide vent in the ground. He thought he could see the gleaming of the boiling rocks; red streams of moving rock. Thought he could taste that rotten egg gas that made the mouth sweet afterward. Thought he heard the hissing vents and the thundering of the lava, turning the eternal surf at the edge of the watery gulf between that place and heaven into great clouds of steam. Thought he heard the cries, too, of the damned, sautéing in puddles of molten fire, like raw doughnuts dropped into boiling grease.

"Aiiieee . . . Hwoooah . . . ! Aiiieeeeh!"

"I forgive you." Those aren't the things the dark lord says. He wants misery. "Go ahead, marinate in your sins." Not forgiveness. But if not God, and if not him, then who? Made up by me, the whole thing? The voice of

God? The prophecies? Didn't I say it the day we voted for Honduras? If it's me, if it's my imagination, if it's not from the mouth of the Spirit, then strike me from the Lamb's Book of Life. Have I been eternally crossed out? Finished? Is this how Anna Mary felt the day our Schnoogie died?

He pushed away from the car, feeling each defeated and fatigued muscle, the roaring in his brain switching ON, OFF, ON, OFF. He hobbled toward the creek, which would become visible in a moment. He expected he would see the rushing lava shortly, the currents of hell into which he could throw himself.

His foot broke loose a small rock and he stopped, curled his fingers and thumb around the black anthracite surface, and flung it toward the brown-backed river. Then he saw it, startled by the sound of the splash. An elegant, white-feathered creature indolently flapped its long, black-tipped wings and strained its yard-long neck forward to gain altitude.

"I want to be you!" he shouted at it. "Fly away! Away from here! Away! Away!" His voice echoed off the wall of trees across the river. *Away! Away!* He startled himself. The crane still flapped, 20 feet off the river, and disappeared upstream around the bend.

He flies, I stay. There was no relief here, which made the second thing he saw completely unexpected and completely set off from anything else on this dismal morning.

A face. And only a face, hanging about the right height in the air. Translucent, I still see the stream on the other side of it. Fading out, it seems, toward the edges, like rainbows do. The large, olive eyes open and moving, gazing on me. Not real, of course. Nothing scary at all about this face just seeming to appear there. Maybe only a thought, but there it is, as real as a toothache.

Anyone would know that face. The long, bloodied hair and the tiara of thorns on the forehead, squashed down by a blow so that dribbles of blood have escaped from each pierced hole and dried and the scraggly beard, but especially the bottomless Semitic eyes and eagle nose. The eyes surveying me, and the tears . . . yes, tears. One, now another, coming down into the beard. Large, rust-colored tears. He weeps for me.

I don't believe in visions and voices anymore. Don't trust them. I made them up. Where did this come from?

The face never said a word, but Saul experienced the message, deep in his stomach. *I forgive you.*

He had stopped walking the moment the face appeared, and now both knees morphed from bone and joints to pasta. They hinged and he went down, striking the coal bed, his hands flung out to prevent his body from pitching forward into the puddle. When he straightened, the face was gone. There was only the river ahead, moving easy and dark, stretching a hundred feet to the opposite shore.

Ezekiel fell on his face, overwhelmed for seven days, when he saw the vision on the River Chebar. His legs seemed like wooden constructs, unwilling to power him up. But he had to get up now. *Christ was weeping for us.* This was a message for Anna Mary, too. His legs seemed asleep. Rather than bending properly, they shot out robotically at each step, like the war vets he'd seen with prostheses.

When he finally made it back to the car, he let the motor rev as he waited to gain feeling back in his legs, for fear that he might mash the accelerator to the floor on this windy back road and hurl the car into the bridge abutment.

Anna Mary was riding the porch swing at the back of the Bishop's large, stone house, pushing with one bare toe each time the swing returned to horizontal, while she folded the other leg under the mid-calf dress that hid it. Swaying, spiraling strands of wool—one red, the other a Christmas green—seemed to tie her hands to two baskets of yarn on the porch boards, one to her right, the other to her left. All the while, the long needles between her fingertips made a small clack-clack as they went in and out, forming cables of finished knitwork on the emerging sleeve of a child's sweater. The spirals of wool strained forward, now back, as the swing creaked on its chains.

He'd intended to burst out onto the porch, but instead he stopped just inside the screen door, contemplating her through the screen. She was singing and didn't notice.

> Hush-a-bye, don't you cry,
> Go to sleepy, little baby.
> When you wake, you shall have . . .

The porch swing ceased, and she stared outward across the lawn that sloped away behind the house to the white, patterned, wire fence bounding the tractor path.

He followed her gaze.

Monarch butterflies, their Halloween wings folding and unfolding slowly above the snowy-headed milkweed flowers, were bobbing in the truck garden beyond the tractor path. The garden looked as if the frost had hit it good. Tomato vines sprawled about, the blackened tomatoes still fastened to them. Beyond was the truck garden, and beyond that the open meadow where the rust-backed steers lazed about, chewing, and beyond that, the weeping willows along Deer Creek Run. What was she seeing? A familiar, peaceful daguerreotype of her childhood, perhaps?

She collected the needles in one hand, pulled off her bandana with the other, and rubbed her temples. His mouth fell open in disbelief. Her hair was butched, not more than one inch long, like a military recruit's. The Bishop hadn't said anything about this.

"Lovely little what . . . ?" she said. The needles began to clack again. "'Pretty little . . . ?'"

Eeeeeeeeeekkkkk. The door swung out. Her eyes flew around, penetrating the screen, and abruptly the sweater dropped into her lap. *She's afraid.*

"Anna Mary." In one set of motions he crossed the porch, dropped on one knee, stopped the swinging porch swing with one hand, and picked up her fallen hand with the other. He grew suddenly aware that he was rumpled, unshaven, and uncombed. His hair flew all directions, and he had on yesterday's wrinkled and smelly tan work shirt. Her eyes now fixed downward on him, blue and poised. For what? Flight?

"Anna Mary!" His mouth dropped to her hand, rubbing it with his lips, lifting it. The hand had grown soft, he noticed, the muscles loose.

"I wanted to see you," she said. Her face lifted away, pointing toward the meadow.

"You wanted to see me?"

"You have no idea what I went through." Her hand pulled out of his, hurrying to unknot the bandana ends. She tied it on again, sliding it forward to conceal the entire top of her head. "I didn't know they'd cut off all my hair to do the shocks." Her head wobbled, still gazing above him toward the meadow. "The patients at the hospital. You have no idea. So many loonies. Suicidals. Alcoholics. A man said he was Josef Stalin. I felt so out of place. And since the shocks, I can't remember things."

"'All the pretty little horsies,'" he said. She'd sung it to Schnoogie, often to lullaby him to sleep.

"Yes!" Her eyes met his and locked. "'All the pretty little horsies.' And my favorite poem. I can't remember it . . . ."

> I like the fall, the mist and all
> I like—

She paused. "What do I like?"

He was speechless now that he saw her full-face. It was a face struck hard by an early frost. The rounded apple cheeks had collapsed and roughened. Harsh grooves rose between the eyes toward the bandana, and under the edge of it he saw several tufts of silver hair. The eyes had retreated into black pouches and watched him, moving languidly, like minnows ogling up out of dark pools.

"I saw Him by the river," he said, taking her hand again and caressing it with both of his. He hunkered down on the floorboards in front of the swing and blocked its movement with his body. He was going to add, "Christ—He was weeping for us," but he couldn't say it. It seemed irrelevant now. She was here in flesh-and-blood with him now, the only member of his family left.

"You saw who?" She pulled away her arms, letting the knitting fall to her lap, stretching both arms along the top of the porch swing. Her eyes, green again, gazed into his, probing them. Searching for the answer to something.

It's His face. Christ's face—and He looked down at me like that, too. His arms stretched horizontally like that. He hadn't seen arms at the riverbank, but he knew now there had been arms, stretched sideways like hers, like the arms of someone pinned to a crossbar.

"I'm here now, Anna Mary. I won't go away again."

"'I like the night owl's lonely call.'" She remembered the line of the poem triumphantly, and a smile broke, rounding up the cheeks, smoothing the groove between the eyebrows, and adding flecks of light to the eyes. "It's like that. I go in and out. I hardly remember anything from the last three months . . . even the funeral."

"Anna Mary, I don't care what happened. I'm here with you for good."

"He's gone," she said. Her face reverted to the mask of tragedy. She lifted the sweater, examining the needlework. "I don't know who I'll present it to . . . Schnoogie's gone." With her short hair and dark and peaked face, she looked smaller, very fragile and vulnerable.

"You miss him," he said.

"I miss him." Twin tears gathered in her eyes but hung there, after she said it, reddening the eyeballs.

"I'm sorry. I abandoned you." He didn't know how to take care of this central item of business, which he realized, all at once, was critical if he wasn't to lose her. He uncorked his body upward and slid onto the swing beside her, taking her hand into his lap. "Can you forgive me?"

Her face was a mask of suffering. "What about the farm and the cows? Pop said you sold them."

No answer he could think of seemed like one that might satisfy her. But suddenly, he thought of a way to dramatize his question, to show her how sincere he was.

Thirty

THE REPORTER THOUGHT he'd get to the church early. The cameraman with his big Hasselblad plus a 35-millimeter rode shotgun. A big story was coming to light, but all they had was the seven-line summary over the AP teletype they had received at the office close to midnight:

FIVE AMERICAN CHILDREN DEAD OF TYPHOID IN HONDURAS. PART OF EMIGRANT MENNONITE GROUP—THE REMNANT. ORIGIN: PARADISE VALLEY, PENNSYLVANIA. LEADER INSISTED CONTAMINATED LAKE WATER PURIFIED BY GOD. EMBASSY OFFICIALS CITE CONTRARY NATIVE REPORTS. EMBASSY REPORTS ADDITIONAL 15 HOSPITALIZED IN BELIZE CITY.

"Is this it?"

"Says so." The cameraman turned over the address slip in his hand.

The parking lot at the church was already partly full by the time they pulled in at 8:30 that morning—black cars, mostly. Several knots of people stood outside the church front, talking heatedly.

Up until this exodus-to-Honduras story in September, the reporter hadn't covered any Mennonite stories in the 10 years he had worked this beat, because there really weren't any to cover. These quiet, business-like people kept to themselves. And dressed different, of course—like the middle-aged women in the groups straight ahead, mostly in subtle flower print dresses below the kneecap, and their men in the notch-collared coats. On the other hand, he knew some of their kids. No different, he thought, under those "plain clothes." Like his friend Wolf Landis, a smart guy he'd sung with at the Civic Light Opera. He himself was Lutheran, like a lot of folks in this pocket of German America, and wore a good German name: Fahnestock.

He jumped out of the sea-green and white Nash convertible, pen and spiral notebook in hand, and his cameraman followed. He felt himself an intruder today. Obviously, they weren't there for the services.

People turned to look, but then rotated right back to their groups. The cameraman opened the Hasselblad to shoot the knots of people standing around, the large, gray limestone edifice backdropping them, but the reporter reached back with his hand to block the shot.

"Put it away until I tell you," he whispered. "We need the story, and *that* might kill it." He stepped into the first small circle and smiled apologetically.

"Morning. Anybody here know about the group in Honduras?"

There were four in the circle, all older couples. *These people all look alike. All the women with the same pattern dress. Wearing their hair middle-parted and balled up under those white, see-through caps with strings. What do the caps mean? Wonder if the camera guy knows? Men with the Nehru jackets and chunky, well-fed Kraut visage.*

"We do, but who are you?" The woman in the forest green, unornamented dress didn't appear unfriendly. On the other hand, he noticed the Kleenex, wadded in her hand, that she'd used to dab her eyes as he stepped in.

"Fahnestock." He stretched out a hand. "Eddie Fahnestock. *New Cumbria Post-Dispatch.*"

"A reporter," the balding man standing opposite said. He apparently was not her husband. That would be the man next to her.

"We know them," the woman said, "and our hearts are just breaking. I have a little grandson down there and—"

"He'll put it in his paper," the likely husband said as he gestured toward the reporter, who'd opened the little spiral notebook and uncapped his pen.

"I can't see it makes a difference anymore. It's a big tragedy . . ." She dabbed her eyes again.

"And our granddaughter with them," the balding man said. "My daughter, Yvette, and her husband."

"Why did they go?"

"Craziness!" The husband said.

"Church politics, you might say," the balding man said. "Come-outerism—it's a Mennonite trait going back three hundred and some years."

"Come-outerism. Is that come-out-er-ism?" He spelled it on his tablet.

"Yes. Splitting off if you don't agree."

"To purify the church, they say," the forest-green dress woman said. "But I just think, *Couldn't we have talked it out?*"

"Saul, maybe, but not Bennie Fisher," the balding man said.

"Saul? Bennie? Can I get their last names? Fisher, did I hear? Are they the leaders? Why'd they do this?"

He was scribbling furiously in his notebook. He noted that the group had grown, and now four or five eavesdroppers on the edges were adding details to the answers of the core four.

"Brother Krehbiel!" The balding man said as he broke off his description of the Revivalists. The group went silent. The reporter glanced around.

The balding man had pivoted to face a stout man in a black, unornamented Homburg and wire-framed glasses, his forehead and upper lip already dewy with perspiration. The two men grasped hands, leaned together, and, incredible to the reporter, kissed each other's lips. The rest of the group also reoriented themselves toward "Brother Krehbiel," who was stretching his hand to the reporter.

"He's from the *Post-Dispatch*," the balding man explained. "Hahnstock, was it?"

"Fahnestock."

"Jacob Krehbiel."

"Are you the reverend here?" The reporter gestured to the looming limestone structure, noting that by now even more black cars had arrived, and clearly, services were about to begin.

"He's the Bishop. Over the Paradise Valley district."

"We expected you folks to come." The Bishop turned face-on to Fahnestock. "Sure you must have a lot of questions, but we've got a service ready to start and . . . Brother Sensenig, if you'd encourage folks in and get the singing started." He opened his wallet, produced a business card, and gave it to the reporter. "You can call me this afternoon, but I'll just tell you . . ."

The rest of the group had turned their backs and walked away in a group. They were now massing with others at the church door to go in, which disappointed the cameraman, who'd hoped for a good shot of faces, with names, for the morning edition front page.

". . . we've never seen anything like this in the Mennonite Church before." The Bishop looked directly at the reporter, who noted how gaunt-eyed the man looked. "Two hundred and fifty people wandering around Honduras, led by a man who proof-texts the Bible. And now five children dead of the typhoid . . . we don't even know their names yet, so everyone with kinfolk there is in distress. Fifteen in the hospital. And they've expelled the one man who could bring some sense—"

"And that is?" The reporter sly-hand motioned the cameraman to line up a good shot with the Hasselblad.

"Saul MacNamara."

"How do I get hold of him?"

"Wish I knew. Nobody's seen him these past 24 hours. Gentlemen . . ." He nodded to both, shook the reporter's hand, and turned toward the church. The cameraman got a second good shot of the Bishop. His torso bulged in the viewfinder like an elongated barrel, topped with the black hat. He seemed very alone as he walked toward the church that beetled over him, the church front door now shut. Oddly, the cameraman thought of the wartime Winston Churchill—*without the cigar, of course.*

The men's side anteroom blinds were pulled down this morning as the fall council meeting got underway. Men stood in a continuous line around the perimeter, a line that could accommodate 25 easily. Elias Sensenig, the balding minister who'd spoken with the reporter, officiated the meeting, the Bishop on his right arm, two deacons off his left.

"Do you have peace with God and man?"

Sensenig's eyes circled the room, reviewing each man for the nod of assent or objection. He was accustomed to these council meetings going routinely, but this morning Pappy Kurtz, Rolly's father, had upset the routine recitation of responses. He refused to answer the question and stood uncomfortably, shifting from side to side, his eyes fixed on the ceiling light bulb.

"Do you want to talk privately, Brother Kurtz?"

"I can't help it." Kurtz's white head rocked side to side, his eyes still fixed on the ceiling. "I hate their guts. Not supposed to hate. Jesus said 'love.' But I despise, I detest, I wanna shoot 'em like groundhogs." He cracked all the knuckles on his right hand simultaneously. The men standing in the circle moved awkwardly and scuffled their shoes after Kurtz's outburst, but no one spoke.

Sensenig turned to the Bishop. Ordinarily, he might have whispered confidentially for advice. But given the situation of the last 24 hours and his own troubled heart over his grandson, he said it out loud.

"Should he stay back from the table?"

"We all might stay back in that case. Take the elements," the Bishop said to Kurtz. "You need them."

The council meeting did not hold back anyone from taking communion over the division related to the Revivalists. Unlike the spring communion in April, when the Revival was gaining strength, this time no one recused himself from communion over the second question: "Are you willing to work in harmony with the discipline of the church?" Those people were all gone.

Since the women had gone first, when the men were done the council meeting finished. Brother Sensenig gave the report from the pulpit: "Happy to report all members present answered affirmative on 'harmony with God and man' and 'in accordance with our church discipline.' On the other hand—" He cleared his throat. "On the other hand, since spring communion, 22 members from this congregation have refused to sign the loyalty statement which Conference requested." He read the names. Pappy Kurtz's face was buried between his rough carpenter's hands. His son had been named. "Removed because of death."

Sensenig read the familiar passage in Corinthians, and the congregation queued for the bread. The sisters had baked it yesterday; little squares without yeast, yielding a cracker-like wafer, only sweeter and moister.

"The body of Christ, broken for you . . ."

Then the cup. They queued up again—a men's line, a women's line—and drank. Sensenig turned with the cup each time so his deacon could squeegee the lip of the cup with a paper napkin before he turned to the next in line and said, "The blood of Christ, shed for you."

The deacons brought out six galvanized tin pans brimming with warm water and distributed them along the front row, dropping a white towel on the bench above each one. These were not bath towels, but special towels with straps sewn to the upper corners so a person could tie one on like an apron. Then, kneeling, each man took a partner man's foot and splashed water from the left, then the right. Washing and drying, washing and drying, in accordance, they believed, with Christ's model to Peter and the disciples.

Christ hadn't said anything on what to do with the women. Leadership had addressed that with a taboo—men would only wash men, women only women.

The chorister began a song as they queued for foot-washing.

> Man of Sorrows, what a name
> For the Son of God who came,
> Ruined sinners to reclaim . . . .

Thirty-One

A TREMENDOUS IDEA! Saul went back into her father's house, leaving her alone on the porch with her knitting.

It didn't take long. He found Mom Krehbiel's bread bowl—the stainless steel one she used every Thursday for kneading sourdough—and filled it with warm tap water. He took a clean hand towel from the corner wash sink next to the Bishop's rolltop.

The bowl was brimming, and he needed to slide his feet along to keep from spilling any of the water. He rear-ended the screen door and stepped back into the sunlight.

"What—?" She stared.

Wordlessly, he steadied the bowl downward in front of her and pushed it between her bare feet.

"What are you—?"

He draped the towel over his right knee and knelt on his left. As he reached for her foot, she saw his meaning. The foot-washing ceremony.

"A man doesn't—" She sat bolt upright, her eyes glued on him. It was a taboo, of course—a man touching a woman in the ceremony. Not to mention the sacrilege of doing it on your own, at home, without the supervision of an ordained bishop.

He balanced her right foot in the palm of his hand, splashing water over the foot in the prescribed manner. The excess water spilled over the sides and made puddles around his knee. "Forgive me, Anna Mary. I can't bear to lose . . ."

When he said the word "lose," it triggered an avalanche of emotions that overwhelmed his voice. The frost-clobbered face. *Christ's face. Christ's feet.* He caressed her foot, unable to speak. *It's the nail-pierced foot I'm washing, and I put the nails there.* He caressed it and tilted forward, laying his cheek against the wet foot. *I wounded her.*

He didn't know how long he knelt like that with his face buried against her legs.

Her face filled with wonder. After some time, she patted his head, as if it were a small child's. Her fingers moved slowly, and then ran forth and back through the hair. She bent down and cradled the sorrowing head in her arms and against her legs. When she spoke, it was in a small, childlike voice: "You love me, don't you."

He couldn't speak. Glaciers were melting inside. Huge ice shelves were breaking apart.

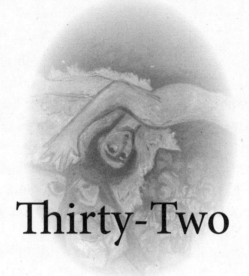

Thirty-Two

When he comes, our Glorious King
All his ransomed home to bring,
Then anew this song we'll sing,
Hallelujah, what a Savior.

THE MEN, QUEUING in two lines on their side of the house, sang from memory, each one meeting his partner at the front and going in turn to a wash pan. The washing, the drying—first one foot, then the other—and then the second man took his turn, washing and drying. They gripped hands solidly and exchanged the kiss of brotherhood on the lips before handing off the towel to the next pair.

On their side, the women filed into the anteroom to strip off hose and shoes. Then they padded back on the pine board floor in two singing lines, from which the head of each found her partner at the head of the other.

Pappy Kurtz was completely overcome by the horrific contrast between this scene, representing two thousand continuous years of order and ritualized love, and the overnight report of mayhem from Honduras. There was also the brief restored relationship he'd had with Rolly for eight months since Snow Camp, which had been so abruptly ended the night his son announced he was going to Honduras with the remnant. He'd never hear the boy's voice again this side of the Eternal City.

Kurtz began to sob. At first, only his shoulders bounced up and down noiselessly. Then he began to groan, "Mmmm . . . hmmm . . . mmm . . . hmmph," somewhat like the sound of a pig rooting for food. Then, louder and verbally, "Oh, my son! Oh . . . MmmmmHmmmmHmmmph!" His breath caught before he coughed out in the most grievous of all sounds, "MY SON!"

The congregation listened silently, their hearts bleeding and rigid like the stumps of fresh-cut pines. After a few long seconds, one of his older sons crept forward from several benches back, where he sat with his own small boys, into Kurtz's bench. He sat next to him and threw an arm around the curmudgeon's shoulder.

To see a video book trailer for *He Flew Too High* or learn more about the Mennonites, visit www.kyreed.com.

If you liked *He Flew Too High*, you'll like **Mennonite Soldier**, Ken Yoder Reed's first novel. The new paperback version from Masthof Press arrives March 2009, with a new foreword by Professor Joel Hartman. Order it from: www.masthof.com/bookstore

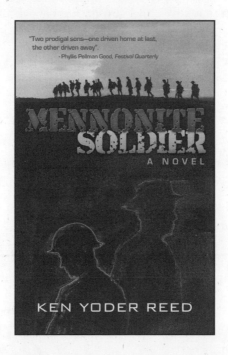

Mastie and Ira Stoltzfus, Mennonite brothers, face the draft in World War I, America's most popular war. Ira Stoltzfus chooses the traditional Mennonite position of conscientious objection to war. He refuses to cooperate with military officials at Ethan Allen Camp in Georgia, suffers repeated indignities, and is sentenced to twenty-five years in Ft. Leavenworth for refusing an officer's order to plant marigolds.

Excommunicated from church, Mastie joins the Army against the wishes of his parents and his intimate Mennonite girlfriend, Annie. Following basic training, he is shipped to the front lines in France and mans a machine gun in battles with the Kaiser's troops. Wounded,

Mastie finds himself in a make-shift hospital in a shattered cathedral, under the care of a Catholic sister. Through months of separation, Mastie continues to receive letters from Annie. She begs him to return to her and the Mennonite community, but Mastie believes his father has consigned him to hell for defying Mennonite belief.

As the story shifts back and forth between Ira and Mastie, you will be caught up in a powerful examination of love and war, duty and conscience, and the starkly different experiences of two boys from the same Mennonite home.

"Guaranteed, **Mennonite Soldier** *will dog you . . . It's the story of two prodigal sons, clothed in Mennonite tradition: one driven home at last; the other driven away at last, with the whys left up to you . . . The story is rhythmic, intense, suspenseful . . . Reed catches well the sometimes evasiveness of faith when one most intends to practice it, here in the lives of two young brothers, their worried parents, and lonely girlfriends."*

—Phyllis Pellman Good
Festival Quarterly